Dear Whistleblower

A Mystery Novel

Joan Rooney Riccitelli

iUniverse, Inc.
New York   Bloomington

iUniverse books may be ordered through booksellers or by contacting:

iUniverse
1663 Liberty Drive
Bloomington, IN 47403
www.iuniverse.com
1-800-Authors (1-800-288-4677)

ISBN: 978-1-4401-9282-1 (sc)
ISBN: 978-1-4401-9283-8 (ebook)
ISBN: 978-1-4401-9284-5 (hc)

Printed in the United States of America

iUniverse rev. date: 03/19/2010

Dedication - This book is dedicated to my husband Bob.

Chapter 1

He was thirteen years old and an eighth grade honor student when he killed for the first time. Afterwards, whenever he thought about that New Year's Day at Runnel's Pond, Gerry's death seemed kind of funny to him. Not exactly funny ha-ha, although he did laugh about it later, but mostly funny odd. He had certainly wished Gerry dead hundreds of times, but the strange thing was that he really hadn't made any plans to kill him that day. None at all. And when he thought about it, he had been more of a passive participant as the whole scenario had played out naturally and almost magically with one event following the other as though preordained. Not to say that he had any qualms about what had happened. And certainly no regrets. Actually, he felt quite satisfied with what had transpired on the first day of that New Year. Gerry had got what he deserved. Had paid the price that all bullies should pay. It had been perfect. Well, nearly perfect. He did have one question. Some might say an unusual question. But often when he thought about it afterwards, he would ask himself if this - the first of his murders - really counted.

Looking back with almost total recall, he remembered that morning so many years ago as white - white sky, white fields, the kind of winter white that swallowed up the faded colors of the bare chiseled oaks and snow-encrusted firs. He pictured himself on that cloudy day, a teenage boy cresting the hill and crunching through the unmarked open snow toward Runnel's Pond. Warmly dressed in fleece and wool with a plaid muffler scarfed around his neck, he carried the new hockey stick that he had just gotten for Christmas over his shoulder like a rifle, and his black skates were loosely laced around his neck. He slowed for a moment at the large wooden sign with the message *Private Property - No Skating - Trespassers Will be Prosecuted*

1

professionally painted on its surface. The sign was a joke. No trespassers were ever prosecuted by the wealthy Runnels who always spent the winter months at their Palm Beach home far from the Snow Belt. But the sign did keep most of the neighborhood children away and that made the pond almost always deserted and the skating all the better for those who dared to ignore the warning.

Powder kicking up ahead of him, the boy slogged on until he could see the pond through spreading firs at the far end of the Runnel estate. When he saw the lone figure in the distance, he quickened his pace. He had left within ten minutes of the phone call, but Buddy O'Hara was already there, skating on the cleared portion of the ice, putting one foot over and ahead of the other in practiced rhythm. There were calls of greeting, and the boy quickly changed into his skates and joined Buddy, easily falling into the pace.

They skated together for what seemed like a long time, the boy enjoying the cold air on his face and at the back of his throat - and enjoying the physical exertions of his maturing body. The pond was secluded, nestled in a vale, and the quiet was almost churchlike, noises from the Runnel mansion and the new residential streets muffled by the snow. The only sounds the boy could hear were the sharp scratching of their blades against the ice and the occasional cracking off of a branch deep in the woods.

"Glad you were home. Glad you could make it." Buddy, bareheaded, squinting, called over to him. Buddy was a short, fat-faced thirteen-year-old, but he was rich, very rich, a good athlete, and a class leader. The boy was glad too. Glad he had been home. Glad he could make it. He knew that Buddy had probably phoned him that morning because most of his popular friends were away for the Christmas break. Or maybe Buddy did have a foursome set up, and somebody had canceled out at the last minute. But the boy really didn't care why he had been called. It didn't matter. The important thing was that he had been invited. And this morning could change everything. Make a big difference in his life and advance his place in the pecking order at school. He had always felt different from the other boys. Somehow out of step and never really at ease with kids his own age. But this was the chance he needed, and he was thrilled to be asked to play pick-up hockey with Buddy and Jack Connelly, the two most popular boys in the eighth grade.

"It'll only be a couple of kids," Buddy had said on the phone. Well, that was fine with him too. More than fine. He'd stand out that way. The boy was a good athlete, and he was determined to show Buddy and Jack what an excellent skater he was. He was sure they would become his friends after today. This morning would be golden.

They finally skirted to a stop, ice chips flying.

"Jack is late. He should be here any minute," Buddy volunteered, looking toward the road above them.

"Who's the fourth?" the boy asked.

"Gerry Weshie." Buddy had turned back and was now looking him full in the face so the boy didn't have a chance to conceal his expression. He hated Gerry.

"What's wrong?" Buddy frowned. "Gerry's a good kid."

The boy bit his lip and lied. "No. Nothing. Nothing's wrong. Yeah. Gerry's a good kid. A real good kid."

The boy mentally kicked himself for the slip. Gerry was popular too. Mostly for his athletic prowess. Over six feet tall and husky at fourteen, he was by far the best football player in the eighth grade, and the only boy who could routinely park one over the fence when he came up to bat. Buddy could not know that Gerry was a bully, a sly bully who took pains to shield this part of his character from the students who mattered. Since school had started in September, the boy had been forced to check the halls before passing, and now he was even taking the long way home to avoid the torment. Gerry was a master at picking on smaller kids, and the boy who was a year or two away from his growth had become his chief victim. Punches that hurt disguised as horseplay. Noogies on the head. The names — sissy, fruit, pansy. The same names that his father called him.

The boy groped for an excuse to leave but it was already too late. Two boys, their arms full with hockey sticks and tall brown paper bags, had just appeared, churning the snow ahead of them as they hurried down the path from the road. It was Gerry with his grown man's body and ravaged complexion, wearing a straw sombrero for some reason that day, followed by Jack almost as tall, but boyishly slim with the Black Irish good looks that all the seventh and eighth grade girls found so appealing.

"Hey. Good to see you," Jack said with a smile and a friendly nod of his head as he sat on the rocks and put on his skates.

"How ya doing?" Gerry held out the sombrero, dramatically bowed in his direction, and gave the wide smile, which by now was so familiar to the boy that he even saw it in his nightmares. The boy could only manage a strangled "Hi," to Gerry before he turned and greeted Jack.

In a few minutes all four boys were on the ice. "You're with Gerry." There was unquestioned authority in Jack's young voice as he gestured at him. The boy could only nod his head up and down in acquiescence. What did it matter? Gerry would get to him. But within a few minutes, the boy was surprised to see that it would be all right. There was no bullying or teasing, and Gerry was more than cordial as they worked as a team for the next hour. They won repeatedly, humming over the hard surface, shooting the puck into the old frozen basket, which was locked into the ice. It was fun, more than fun, as they all whooped away at their efforts, and laughed good-naturedly when Gerry did a well-controlled pratfall and sprawled on his back. As the morning wore on, the boy began to think how wrong he had been. Gerry was quite a guy. Really funny. No wonder he was so popular. And the boy could imagine that now he would be popular too.

Years later whenever he looked back at that roller coaster day, he would remember the camaraderie of that morning — the skating, talking, smoking, and drinking the beer that Gerry had brought — as one of the best times of his life.

Around noon, they broke for lunch. "I've got food, guys. Tons of food," Jack said. Out of the two paper grocery bags came an assortment of sandwiches wrapped in waxed paper, crinkly bags of potato chips, Hershey bars, Hostess cupcakes, and bottles of orange soda and cola.

"And here's more brew, and our church key too — and I'm a poet and I don't know it," Gerry said with a smile as two more bottles and the bottle opener appeared. The four of them sat on the snow-dusted granite outcroppings near the woods, laughing and talking as they ate, hiding the beer from the only other skaters who had appeared after them — a young married couple swinging a red snow-suited child between them. Within a half-hour, the adults and their child were gone, and Gerry reached into one of his bags to produce a half-full fifth of Johnny Walker Black and smiled. "Here's something that should give us a charge. My old lady won't miss it. She was still sleeping off last night's party when I left. She'll think one of her friends walked off with it. Her hard luck. Our good luck." The bottle was passed around, and the boy swigged with the others, enjoying the harsh unfamiliar taste and the heat of the liquor on that cold morning.

Although when he looked around, he realized that the sun was struggling to come out, and it was considerably warmer.

After lunch Jack again asserted his authority as class president. He looked at the boy. "Sides aren't even. You take Buddy this time. I'll play with Gerry." Winning with Buddy as his partner, the boy was so intent on the game that he did not notice Gerry's face starting to turn red and ugly, unhappy at being shown up by the two smaller boys who seemed able to slip by and around him almost at will and score time after time. It was only a game, but it was a game where Gerry did not excel, and that was something that he could not tolerate. Soon he was back to being a bully, back to picking on the boy when Jack and Buddy were turned away. Pushing roughly using his superior weight, playing dirty.

Finally, just as the boy was going in for a goal that he could already taste, his legs scissoring, the puck in perfect position, he was blindsided from the left as Gerry stuck out his hockey stick and tripped him. The boy plunged forward, flailing to keep his balance as the gray ice rose up to meet him. Unable to break the fall, he landed heavily on his right knee, ripping his pants and tearing his flesh bloody. He tried to get up and slipped, falling back again. Now blinded with pain and anger, tears came to his eyes. Gerry was there first, apologizing in a loud voice, covering up in case Buddy and Jack had seen what he had just done. "Hey, I'm sorry. Sorry. I was just kidding. I didn't mean to catch you with my stick. My fault. I owe you one. Are you all right?"

And then in a lower voice that only the two of them could hear, "Little girlie OK? Little pansy crying? Little fruity gunna tattle on mean ole Gerry?"

As the boy sat on the ice, struggling to catch his breath, his heart pounding and his knee in pain, he saw how things were. How things would be. How foolish he had been to think that anything had changed because of today's hockey game. How crazy he had been to believe that Gerry would be his friend at school, and that the bullying would stop.

When he finally got up with a pull from Buddy's hand, the boy had to use every ounce of self-control he had to keep from hurling himself at Gerry. But reason prevailed. He knew that if he threw the first punch, it would be no contest. He'd be pulverized into the ground. The boy brushed the forearm of his jacket across his still-watery eyes, and turned away so that Jack and Buddy could not see his face. He forced himself to speak calmly and keep the tears from his voice. "I'm all right. It was just an accident. Let's take five. I need to see if my knee's OK. See if I can still skate."

Rage coursing through his body, he skated away from the other three boys toward the far end of the pond now gilded by winter sunlight. His mind was flipping through his options, and they were certainly few in number. Tell Buddy and Jack how Gerry had deliberately tripped him? How Gerry had been bullying him? It was unlikely that the two class leaders would take his side since he was the outsider, and Gerry was their friend. Go to his parents? He wished he could tell them how Gerry had been tormenting him for months now, but if he did, he knew that his father would just taunt him as a coward for running away from a fight. He felt cornered, all alone with nowhere to turn. No one to help him.

As he skimmed along the cleared section of the pond between white curved drifts, he thought of the one attempt he had made to settle the problem by seeking help from his eighth grade teacher, Miss Lane. Lois Lane just like Superman's girlfriend. He was a model student who went out of his way to butter her up and tell her what she wanted to hear, so he had been sure that she liked him and would intervene.

It had been during lunchtime in mid-November when Gerry had hurt and embarrassed him by bending his arm behind his back and frog marching him in the basement hallway to the hoots of some younger boys. That had been all he could take, and he had finally decided that he had to tell, even if it was tattling. He was disengaged from his studies all that afternoon as he planned his approach to Miss Lane. Lingering after the dismissal bell at three-thirty, he waited around in the playground until all the other eighth grade students had left. When he was sure that all the classmates were gone, he hurried back in to his room, and caught Miss Lane just as she was letting the Mercator map at the front of the room snap up into a roll. A slight, almost frail, woman, with a halo of over-permed hair, neither young nor old, Miss Lane had at first seemed very concerned when he began talking between gulps and sobs. Talking about the bullying. The name-calling. The hurt. But her concern had quickly turned to unease as he poured out the repetitious episodes of the bullying and his own humiliation. When he had finished, she had moved away to her desk and had nervously smoothed out the skirt of her shirtwaist dress.

Her first words were not encouraging. "I think you may be misunderstanding the situation," she had begun. "You're one of the brighter boys in class, and Gerry may just want to be your friend. He probably doesn't know how to approach you in the right way, and thinks that this horseplay will catch your attention."

"No, no," he had insisted, and gone over the recent incidents, this time much more vehemently. Finally, he was sure that he had gotten through to her, and that she believed him. But when she spoke, she was just mouthing empty words. "Bullies are all cowards," she had said. "You just have to learn to stand up for yourself."

She had seemed to be talking to a point just over his head as she recited the hackneyed words, which offered him no solace at all. Then she looked him directly in the eyes. "You've told me that you're thinking of becoming a teacher yourself someday. If you ever do become a teacher, you'll see that you can't get involved in petty quarrels between students. You can't take sides. It's better when students work out their problems themselves. It's good training for life."

He stared at her, mouth partially open, incredulous that she was not going to help him. Seeing the disbelief in his face, she went on, "When you're a little older, you'll come to realize that teasing is just a normal part of growing up. I know. I was teased a lot as a girl because I've always been as skinny as a rail. So my advice to you is just ignore Gerry and walk away. I think he may be teasing because he sees that he can get a rise out of you."

There was a pause. He gulped again, and she seemed to feel she had to say more. "I have an idea that you might want to think about." He waited. " Why don't you take one of those Charles Atlas courses and build yourself up?"

She looked away and was finished with him. Finished with a distasteful problem, which she did not want to take on. She reached for her coat, which was draped over the back of her desk chair, and started to shrug into it. "And now if you'll excuse me, I have to get some things together. I have a meeting at another school."

He stood there for a few moments, staring at her back as she packed her briefcase, waiting for some reprieve. Then, realizing that her dismissal was final, he turned and left the room. That had been six weeks ago, and since then she had never once asked him how the problem with Gerry had worked out, and he had never mentioned the bullying to her again.

The boy, now at the far point of the pond, was startled out of his thoughts by a crackling sound, and he looked down to see water on the ice and hairline cracks radiating out in the section near the feeder stream. With a surge of adrenaline he abruptly swung around, just saving himself from falling in. He skated back through hard winter sunlight with all intentions of warning the other boys to avoid that area. The ice there was unsafe.

But Gerry skated out to greet him. Sure that Jack and Buddy could not hear, he asked in a singsong voice, "Little girlie's tears all gone? Little girlie OK now? Little girlie put on a new skirt?"

The boy didn't mention the dangerous ice.

A half-hour later, it was warmer still, and all four boys had unbuttoned their jackets. The day was now bright and aglow under a striated blue sky. The fun gone out of hockey, the boy was standing with Jack and Buddy near the edge of the ice while Gerry, now wearing the high-crowned straw sombrero, was showing off, skating in wider and wider arcs as he circled the pond. Jack and Buddy were deep in conversation, talking about a physically precocious eighth grade girl while the boy watched Gerry over their shoulders, hoping, wishing, that he would move to the dangerous ice. Gerry suddenly came to a halt and the boy felt a frisson of disappointment, assuming that the bigger boy had looked ahead and realized for himself how treacherous that part of the pond was. But then, almost in wonder, the boy saw Gerry turn and push off again, now skating backwards, adjusting his sombrero low over his eyes, exaggerating his movements, waving his arms, skating nearer and nearer to the thin ice at the far end of the pond.

With all his being, the boy willed Gerry to go through the ice. And then as he watched, and this was the magic part for him, Gerry gave a loud cry of surprise and terror, and disappeared down into the pond. Ordinarily, Jack and Buddy would have heard the anguished shout, but with perfect timing, the boy laughed raucously to cover the cry for help. He talked quickly and in a loud voice to keep their attention away from the pond. "Have you heard this one? The Lone Ranger is captured by a band of lady outlaws." He told a series of bawdy jokes, using his hands for punctuation, feeling so expressive, so witty, so in control. As he talked, he smiled, picturing Gerry flailing in the cold water under the ice. Bumping the top of his head against his hard prison. Panicked. Desperate to get out. And the boy was letting it all happen. Relishing every minute of it.

Minutes passed and the jokes grew stale. Jack finally looked around and asked, "Where's Gerry?"

The boy turned away from the ice and gestured in the opposite direction toward the woods. "Probably springing a kidney."

The talk continued, yet the boy watched Jack and Buddy becoming restless, craning their heads from side to side, and scanning the white world around them. "I can't understand it. Where's Gerry?" Jack. called out, "Gerry, Gerry."

Buddy joined in, "Gerry. Gerry."

The boy shouted with them, "Gerry, Gerry." He let a few minutes pass, and then said, "Maybe he went home."

"No, he wouldn't just take off like that. He'd say something. And look. All his things are still by the rocks." Buddy pointed and then scratched the back of his head.

The boy wondered how long it would be before Jack and Buddy found the hole in the ice, and for fun, decided to time it on his watch, surreptitiously following the red second-hand go round and round as the other boys became increasingly agitated.

"Something's not right here. What happened to Gerry?" asked Jack. His wrinkled frown marred his good looks.

"Gerry, Gerry." Buddy's shouts were louder, repeated in echoes.

The boy joined in again. "Gerry. Gerry."

"Come out. Come out. Wherever you are," called Jack, his voice high and nervous.

The boy checked his watch. Exactly four minutes had passed before Jack started to move along the edge of the pond, skating slowly toward the far end of the ice, peering into the woods and scanning across snow-mantled fields to the mansion and the residential streets beyond. Exactly two minutes and four seconds later Jack spotted the straw sombrero floating in the hole in the ice.

"Gerry's gone in the water," he screamed in terror. "The ice is broken. There's a big hole. His hat's here. Gerry's gone in."

"I'll go for help," Buddy shouted out, panic in his voice as he turned toward the rocks, but the boy was already there, unlacing his skates. "I'll go. I'll bring help."

"Get some branches, Buddy. We can't get near the hole. The ice will crack under our weight. Get that big branch. Maybe he'll come up and can grab on to the branch." The boy listened as the other two shouted desperately to each other, laughing to himself as they concocted their foolish schemes to save the bully who had been in the water for over ten minutes and was probably already dead.

"I'll be right back. I'll call 911. See if you can pull him out," he yelled as he set off at a run up the path and toward the road. A few minutes later he looked back and saw that fir trees humped with snow sealed him off from the two boys at the pond. Knowing he couldn't be seen, he halted and took a satisfying breath. He was excited. No hurry, he thought. He zipped open his jacket pocket and fumbled for a package of cigarettes and matches. He lit a cigarette and enjoyed it slowly, drawing the smoke deep into his lungs, and then leisurely blowing it out through his nose and mouth. When he finished, he threw the butt down and pushed it into the snow with his boot. He started toward the road again, took a few steps, and stopped. He smiled to himself and thought again, no hurry. Gerry's not going anywhere. He can wait. He then took out the package again, shook out a second cigarette and smoked it slowly. Finally, he stomped the second burning nub into the snow and covered them both over.

It was nearly a half hour later before he was back at the pond. Buddy and Jack were lying on the ice, not far from the hole, sticking long, thick branches into the water. Jack stood up, his voice almost a falsetto. "Where have you been? What took you so long?"

The boy faked hard breathing, forcing his chest in and out, gasping for air, and playing his role for all it was worth. "It wasn't my fault. I went as fast as I could. No one home on Pond Street. I had to run all the way up the next block." His lips twitched and he had to dig his fingernails into the palms of his hands to keep from laughing at the way Jack's eyes were bulging out in desperation.

The flashing police cars and an ambulance with its siren wailing were there within minutes, but it was at least a half hour more before Gerry's lifeless body was pulled from the pond. Positioning himself near a clump of frozen weeds at the edge of the ice where he had the best view, the boy watched the rushed, frantic efforts of the emergency crew and the helpless gestures of the policemen across the way.

It was a spectacle, quite a spectacle, with the flashing red and blue lights of the vehicles whirling and bouncing off the snow banks and the stands of firs. A knot of curious onlookers from somewhere in the neighborhood had gathered at the sounds of the sirens, pointing and whispering together about the tragedy. The boy found himself among them, and then abruptly realized that he shouldn't be standing on the sidelines with mere bystanders. No, now was the time for him to be on center stage with the popular Jack and the popular Buddy. He hurried away from the small crowd and moved toward his new best friends. As he approached, he noticed that the two boys were still in their skates on the ice. Arms across their chests, hugging themselves for comfort, they were both openly crying.

The boy could hardly believe his fantastic luck. It was amazing. Gerry was dead. Gerry was really dead. And he hadn't even had to do that much. He had only looked on. And the best thing was that no one in the world would ever know the role he had played. No one could accuse him of anything. He was completely safe. Completely innocent. He could feel his body shaking, trembling with joy at the thought that Gerry was actually gone from his life. Gone for good. Gone for always. Manic, excited beyond reason, almost giddy with the power of life and death that he had so recently held in his hands, he turned to Jack and Buddy. "We're like heroes, you know. We'll be famous. We tried to save Gerry. It wasn't our fault we didn't. We'll probably get our names in tomorrow's paper. Maybe our pictures. I can't believe our luck."

The two other boys tore their attention away from the frenzied scene across the pond and turned to look at him, their eyes widening, their mouths opening in disbelief at his callous words and his flushed, triumphant face. He continued talking, so full of himself that he missed their reactions and compounded his mistake. "We should make the front page. Reporters will want to interview us. This will be a big story. I can't wait to hear what the kids will say on Monday. They'll want to know all about what happened." He stopped talking for a moment, and then corrected himself. "The kids probably won't even wait till Monday. They'll probably be calling us tonight to find out everything." He smiled in anticipation of his newfound celebrity.

Both Jack and Buddy now had looks of pure revulsion on their faces. Buddy's voice was a sharp hiss. "What's wrong with you? Gerry's dead. Do you hear me? Gerry's dead. Are you even on this planet? Are you some kind of weirdo? Gerry's dead, and you're talking about your picture in the paper. Being interviewed. Are you mental or something?"

Jack spat a vulgarity at him, and his bubble burst.

With his whole eighth grade class, he attended Gerry's funeral the following week. But when he went over to Jack and Buddy, and said, "I'm sorry," they turned their backs and walked away from him. They never invited him to play hockey with them again. They never even talked to him again. And they must have told all the other kids in the eighth grade what he had said because he found himself more isolated than ever for the rest of that school year. He remembered how glad he had been when Jack and Buddy both left public school and went to a private high school that next September.

Chapter 2

Patty Bass woke up early on the day of the interview. Instantly awake, she took a deep satisfying breath and marveled at her good fortune. An opportunity almost too good to be true. An interview at the best elementary school in Hastings. Probably the best elementary school in all of Connecticut. A wonderful chance at a wonderful job. She was so happy. Patty was twenty-nine years old and in the best of health, so her own death was the farthest thing from her mind as she yawned and stretched her arms out in the semidarkness.

Still in bed, she lay back and watched idly as shards of lights from behind closed blinds brought the forms and colors of day to her bedroom. She then kicked the light cover back, turned to lie on her stomach and without looking, reached across her marriage bed and felt the empty sheets beside her. She smiled to herself as she plumped up Noah's pillow and thought of her new husband in his silver airplane flying somewhere over Long Island Sound. In her mind's eye, she followed him as he powered the massive 747 through the skies of southern Connecticut toward Hartford, circling before slowing to descend through the clouds for the landing at Bradley International Airport. She could just picture Noah, uniformed in blue-gray and in complete control in the cockpit, as the tires thudded down on the runway for the safe landing. She took a deep breath. She loved thinking about him. Loved picturing him when he was away from her. Loved saying his name. She loved everything about Noah.

The calls of crows, hungry and strident caws, broke into her daydreaming, and a glance at the moon-faced clock on her nightstand told her it was time to go. With one graceful springy motion, she rolled off the bed and slapped down the alarm that was just about to go off. She pulled her nightgown over her head as she crossed the room. Dressing quickly, she pulled on shorts, an oversized T-shirt and white Adidas running shoes, tied her curly blond hair back beneath one of Noah's old baseball caps and left the house before seven. She tried to run every day that Noah was flying. Sometimes she drove all the way across town to Hastings Beach to run by the water or ran at the well-maintained track at the high school, but today she had promised to meet her cousin Rick at Stadler Park, which was halfway between their homes.

A few knee bends and stretches in her driveway, and then she eased onto the blacktop of Iron Weed Road. Cutting diagonally across the residential street of upper middle-class houses and well-tended lawns, she slowed as she reached Tish's gray saltbox with the front door painted red for contrast, hoping her best friend had changed her mind and would join them. Although Tish was full of vim and vigor, and loved to walk two miles each day, she still did not like to run. Patty had worked hard to change her mind, but Tish was adamant that she was not a runner. Impatient, Patty jogged in place for a few minutes in front of the house and could see lights through the shades and hear rock music pounding. She didn't want to ring the bell, but hoped that her friend would see her and just come out. But there was no sign of Tish or her two teenage daughters, so she sprinted on. She turned at the corner, and worked her way by the campus of the huge brick technical high school and across two tree-lined side streets to Parkway Drive and the park.

Reflecting back on the unexpected phone call the previous afternoon, she felt a tingle of elation. It had been just before four o'clock, and at first when she heard the professional-sounding woman say, "This is the personnel office of Hastings Public Schools," she had thought that it might just be Tish disguising her voice and teasing her. But it had been a legitimate call, and she had jumped at the chance for an interview for a third grade position right here in town. She found herself looking forward to the unexpected opportunity with a mixture of anticipation and nervousness. Mostly anticipation she decided since she felt she was ready, more than ready, to enter her chosen profession. As she entered the park, she silently thanked her lucky stars and hoped that the interview with the principal and a committee of staff members would go well.

It was just seven, but Rick was late again so she made a circuit of the empty tennis courts and the playground, and then swung down the wooded road to the duck pond. Running on the short grass toward the pond, she threw out her arms and sang out full voice the catchy words of a popular fast food commercial. After frightening a brace of mallards into the air with her loud approach, she skirted some wetlands rife with silver weeds and jogged around some picnic benches and over to where a thick curved chain strung between two cement posts blocked cars from the interior of the park, a successful effort by the town fathers to close off a Lovers' Lane. She peered across the chain and down the deserted dirt road, which curved away into the woods. There was still no sign of Rick so she did a few more limbering up exercises and let herself revel in the glory of the day.

It was a rare, sweet morning in September with the promise of a hot day like many near the end of summer in Connecticut, but around her she could already see the signs of the coming season in the tall Queen Anne's lace and the tinges of yellow and red in the trees. The woods were clean and fresh with the strong smell of pine in the air, and the young morning stillness was serene, broken only by the thin trilling of unseen birds somewhere in the park. Patty again thought how happy she was, how happy she was with life, but then the unbidden thought came to her that there had been other happy moments in her life, but then happiness had been taken away. The picture of her mother singing snatches of French songs in the kitchen that morning as she packed the picnic lunch for the trip to the farm sprang to mind. Patty pushed the sad image away, and forced herself to concentrate on the present.

Deep in her thoughts of the interview, she barely heard the calls of a runner cutting across the fields from the opposite end of the park. She turned her head, and from where she stood on the grassy bank, she could see her cousin sprinting toward her at full stride. She watched him for a few moments, admiring his natural running ability and perfect form — head up, chin out, his blond hair flopping long in the English style, crooked arms swinging at his sides, legs pumping. Then giving herself a head start, she transferred to the course for joggers, cleared her mind and gave herself over to the freedom of running.

Within a minute, Rick also in running shoes, shorts and a T-shirt had caught up to her on the broad path, and with the barest of greetings, slowed his pace and matched her stride for stride. They fell into the rhythm of running for the next half hour, moving in companionable silence along the trail, the only sounds their own breathing and footfalls. Rick had encouraged her to take up running the previous summer after she had moved back to Hastings, and when she had been a novice, they had usually talked as they jogged, but now there was no conversation as they loped along the path that twisted and wound around the perimeter of the park. Finally, as the trail once more turned back to the duck pond, she, sweating and exhausted, waved herself off as Rick, the stronger runner, continued.

Breathing hard, she bent forward with her hands on her thighs, and then walked herself down near the bearded greenery. Time passed and she felt her pulse return to normal as she watched the bobbing mallards on the pond and waited for her cousin to have his fill. When he pounded up fifteen minutes later, his face was glistening with sweat, his blond hair was slicked back from his forehead, and his shirt was damp, sticking to his chest. Struggling to catch his breath, he spoke first. "Patty, I'm sorry for being late. One of my agents called just as I was leaving." He looked properly contrite at the excuse, which he so often used for his chronic tardiness.

Patty owed him a lot and was quick to accept his apology. Rick had been her shoulder to cry on during her difficult teenage years, the support for her ailing father while she was living in New York City, and let us not forget, she reminded herself, the man who had introduced her to Noah, and of course to Tish. In recent months, she had noticed that Rick was not nearly as available as he had been, but she felt that the bonds between them were as strong as ever.

"I'll forgive you as long as it was business instead of pleasure," she answered with a laugh in her voice. She was proud of her cousin and proud of his accomplishments. Rick Miller was almost forty, of average height and looks with the lean build of a long-distance runner, a self-made man who had taken over his mother's small real estate business and turned it into one of the most successful agencies on the East Shore. Patty knew that he got a lot of attention from women and was not sure if it was due to his friendly open personality, or perhaps more cynically and realistically, because of the trappings of wealth that he now carried.

A flock of starlings wheeled and swooped overhead, and both Patty and Rick studied their flight patterns as they made small talk. Patty then turned to Rick and asked, "Are you planning on running in the town marathon next week?" When he did not respond right away, she added, "I think you'd have a good chance of winning, and it would be great publicity for your office."

Although Patty knew Rick to be a man of even temper, she could that he was faintly irritated by the question, which she had asked him several times before. He had often told her that he was in a cutthroat businesses, and he wanted to keep is running separate from that. He bent and picked up handful of stones, which he skimmed across the thick grass, and shook his head in an emphatic manner. "No, Patty, and that means no." He then chucked her under the chin in a playful way, and asked the question that she had been waiting for. "Not to change the subject, but what was that mysterious message you left on my machine about an interview? An interview for what?"

She spread her arms in an elaborate flourish, and sang out a drum roll. "I got a telephone call late yesterday afternoon. I have an interview for a teaching position this morning at nine o'clock." She paused for effect. "Right here in Hastings. At Island Brooke School."

Rick whistled in appreciation as he absorbed the information. "Starting at the top, aren't you? Island Brooke is a famous school. Nationally known."

Patty raised her eyebrows. "How would you know about schools? You don't have kids."

"But I am in real estate, remember, so I make it my business to know about schools." Rick brushed his hair back. "Whenever a house comes on the market in the Island Brooke School district, I always put *Award Winning School* in my ads. The same house is easily worth five thousand dollars more because it's in that area of town. So you see, Little Miss Teacher, I know quite a bit about the famous Island Brooke School. I've sold quite a few houses in that school district."

"I'll bet you have," she countered, "and judging from that shopping center of yours, you've sold quite a few houses in all the school districts from New Haven to New London."

With a self-deprecating motion of the hand, he dismissed his success in real estate. "And I even know the principal of Island Brooke. Harold Trelawney." He smiled at Patty's start of surprise. "I sold him a house right here in the north end of town about — let's see — it must be three years ago."

"Oh, what's he like?" asked Patty, suddenly very interested. "A real tyrant?"

Rick shook his head from side to the side. "No, not at all. He runs a tight ship of course. Type-A personality. But by all accounts, he's fair. Fair to his teachers. Wonderful to the children. And he seems like a regular guy despite all the publicity he's had. Really dedicated. He's an ideal principal. Whenever I met with him, his chief topic was Island Brooke School, and, 'My kids this, my kids that.' He sounded like someone who's found his true calling." He paused. "Do you want me to give him a ring and put in a good word for you?"

Patty looked pensive for a moment at his question, and then shook her head. "No, I think this is something I have to do on my own."

Rick seemed to agree as he cautioned Patty not to worry. "Well, I think Harold Trelawney is a good judge of character so the interview should go well." He paused and then smiled as he asked the next question. "Does Noah know about your interview or is he off somewhere in the friendly skies?"

"Oh, Noah knows. He called me last night. He's as excited as I am. He should be at the airport by now, and he'll be home sometime this morning. I hope before I leave for Island Brooke. I'd like to kiss him for good luck."

Rick gave her a light, playful tap on the shoulder. "I'll say this. That flying schedule of his will certainly keep the spice in your marriage. What is it? Home for a few days and then off across the country. Now you see him. Now you don't. Every time that Noah walks in the door, you'll be wondering who he is." They both laughed.

Then Rick pushed his hair back from his face with both hands, and started to speak. He stopped, obviously hesitant, and as though making a decision. He finally took a deep breath and let it out. "I might as well tell you. I've wanted to tell you for a while, and I think it's time. I have some great news too. Wait till you hear this."

Patty smiled automatically. Did Rick really have good news. Or was he kidding her the way he used to when she was in her teens?

Rick stood up a little straighter, and his words were evenly spaced, spoken with pride. "I'm back with Jordana."

"Jordana? Your ex-fiancée? I thought she got married." Patty could hardly believe that Rick was telling her that he was back with the very pretty but self-involved Jordana who had practically left him at the altar.

He shrugged. "She did get married, but it didn't work out. She's been separated for a while, and her divorce is almost final. I've been seeing her for about six months, but I didn't want to say anything until our plans were more definite. I ran into her in New Haven last March, and we've been taking it slow ever since. At first it was only casual dates, and now it's the real thing. Things are different now. Jordana is different now, and she wants to be with me."

Patty could hear the suppressed excitement in Rick's voice as he talked about his second chance with the woman who had left him for a wealthy stockbroker. Then there was an uncomfortable silence, and Patty realized that Rick was expecting some words of congratulations. But she wasn't a hypocrite. She just couldn't mouth the words he wanted to hear.

Rick finally spoke. "Now this is just between you and me, Patty. And of course Noah. I'm just not ready to make any official announcement until the time is right. I don't need any complications or any last minute hitches with her divorce." Then, he added, "And do me a favor. Don't, and I emphasize the word don't, mention this to Tish. I know you two are wired together by Southern New England Telephone, but this is important to me. Even if Tish promises to keep it to herself, there's no way she could keep that promise. Within a day, she'd tell all my other agents. I don't need everybody in my office gossiping about my private life."

"Scouts honor. These lips are sealed." Patty squeezed her lips together with one hand and made a zipping motion with the other to emphasize her commitment.

"OK. I'll keep you posted on what happens. And let me know how the interview at Island Brooke goes. Good luck. I hope you get the job." He started to move away and then jogged back. "Let's run this Saturday. I'll see you here about seven." He looked around and seemed to consider the bucolic scene for the first time. "You know, it's kind of deserted here so early in the morning, and I do tend to be late. Why don't we make it at eight?"

"Great, see you then. Eight. Right here. Saturday morning."

Rick waved and began moving toward the interior of the park with a fast gait as though he were being timed. Still fatigued from the running, Patty plodded up the hill at a slow pace as she digested Rick's unwelcome news. She felt a knot of frustration expand and spread over her whole body, and shook her head at the poor choice that Rick seemed about to make. Jordana Sumner. Typical Greenwich debutante. Born on third base and sure that she had hit a triple. Remembering how devastated Rick had been when Jordana had broken their engagement, she could only think that he was a complete fool to take her back. Why couldn't he just open his eyes and see what was right in front of him? But Patty knew that she might as well resign herself. Although she and Rick had been very close since her teenage years, she knew that there was nothing she could say to him that would change his mind. If he wanted Jordana — and Jordana now wanted him — that would be that.

Waving to two runners who were coming down the hill, Patty stopped for a drink at the water fountain near the tennis courts now crowded with retirees and young mothers playing doubles. Then she jogged across Parkway Drive and retraced her steps to Iron Weed Road. As she turned the corner of her street, she saw Tish's white Saab just backing out of her driveway. Although she had only met Tish eight months ago at Rick's Open House, there was an instant rapport between them, and they were now best friends. Bright and forceful, even hyperactive, Tish was a natural comedienne. Patty liked the fact that Tish was quick to laugh and find the humor in almost any situation, despite the fact that her husband had walked out on her two years before.

At that moment Tish's car came forward and braked to a halt beside Patty. As the electric window came down, Tish's expressive, round face appeared, her hazel eyes squinting against the glare of the morning sun. Her hair, the color called chestnut, was carelessly pulled back into a ponytail secured with a green rubber band, and Patty could see that she was dressed for the gym. A colorfully floral summer dress still in the plastic wrapper from the dry cleaners was flung over the back of the front passenger seat.

Patty was the first to speak. "Did you get my message about the interview?"

With her usual impulsive manner, Tish talked over Patty's question and asked one of her own. "Did you run with my one and only this morning?"

"Your one and only?" Patty put a blank expression on her face and creased her forehead as though she had no idea what Tish was talking about. Then she answered deadpan, "Oh, you mean Rick. Sure did. I thought you might jump into your spandex suit and join us."

Tish's deep laugh bubbled out and turned into a snort. "No way. No way. I look like a porker in sweats. And I don't want him to see me looking hot and sweaty. At least not from running. I've got other plans for him."

Patty rolled her eyes at her friend.

Tish continued her light-hearted banter, and then looked at her watch to check the time. "Can't stay and chat. Have to run. I have an eight o'clock with my trainer, and Rick's called an agents' meeting for nine-thirty." She then said belatedly, "Yeah, I got your message about the interview. Good luck. Break a leg. I'll call you tonight and you can tell me all about it. Have a good one."

Without waiting for any response from Patty, Tish shut the window and sped off. At that moment, Patty looked at her own watch and realized that she had lost track of time and was due at Island Brooke School in a little more than an hour. She broke into a sprint and ran the rest of the way home to the Nantucket-shingled house near the end of the cul de sac of Iron Weed Road.

Chapter 3

Although Noah had purchased the house a month before Patty had met him, it was exactly the kind of home that she had always dreamed of when she was a little girl. A standard cape with four rooms downstairs opening into each other and two large bedrooms on the second floor, it was simply but colorfully decorated, the dining room and spare bedroom almost empty of furniture. Patty took the house key from her fanny pack, unlocked the front door, and ran immediately up the stairs to the master bedroom. It took less than a minute for her to peel off her sweaty clothes and throw them into a soft heap on a chair. Then remembering that Noah, who was so obsessively neat that she called him Mr. Neat Gene to his face, would soon be home from the airport, she picked the clothes up and tossed them into a wicker hamper near one of the slatted windows. She then hurriedly tidied up the room and made up the bed, hoping that Noah would not do his "dime bounce on the bed" trick to amuse her.

She then padded onto the tiled floor of the bathroom, flicked on the light and the fan, and reached over to turn on the shower full force. Stepping into the tub and pulling the plastic curtain tight, she soaped herself all over, adjusted the spray, and for the next ten minutes, gave herself up to the twin pleasures of singing in the shower and a long, hot cleansing. Finally, she let the water sluice her body, and without thinking took some shampoo from the recessed slot at the side of the tub and washed her hair. Then she was out of the tub, towel drying herself vigorously before turning her face sideways to scrutinize it from all angles in the triple-sectioned bathroom mirror. After blow-drying and fighting with her curly hair, which had become slightly frizzy, she regretted washing it. Finally, in frustration, she gathered the unruly strains back away from her face, plaited them and pinned them at the nape of her neck with an amber clip. Examining herself in the mirror, she decided that it would do. It would have to do.

Back in her bedroom, Patty reached into the closet for her only summer garment that was dressy enough for the interview. It was a new outfit, a crisply cut navy suit with military piping and small brass buttons which had cost what seemed like a small fortune when she had bought it in Westport this summer. After applying minimal makeup, she dressed quickly but carefully wanting to look her teacher-best. In the mahogany-framed mirror, her reflection looked fine. She considered each aspect of her image and tried to imagine the impression she would make at the interview. She regarded the navy suit, the matching pumps and the rope of good pearls, which had belonged to her mother, and decided that her attire complemented her Scandinavian blond looks in just the right conservative way. She then carefully put on her prized possessions, the expensive gold earrings with fragile hoops that Noah had first spied in a shop window on Bermuda's main street. With her Coach bag hitched on her shoulder, she was as ready as she'd ever be for this very important appointment.

At that moment the sound of the automatic garage door rolling up and then closing announced that Noah was home. Within a minute Patty heard him downstairs in the kitchen and the living room and then coming up the stairs. "I'm home, Hon," he called.

Noah came into the bedroom, and without turning she posed prettily in the mirror for him. "Hey," he said in greeting. With her back still to him, she watched his reflection, and felt the familiar heady rush that she got when she hadn't seen him for a few days. She then felt such joy as he kissed the nape of her neck, that she turned toward him and found his mouth. Finally, he released her, and after taking a breath, she stepped away and with her arms high up in the air and her skirt swirling, did an exaggerated pirouette so that he could see her complete outfit and her new hairdo.

His face lit up as he looked her over. "Wow, Patty. Just like a schoolteacher. That suit. All that power there. And your hair. So proper and subdued."

"I washed it by mistake so I had to trap it in a braid. I don't want Harold Trelawney to see me looking like Medusa. At least not until I get the job." Her eyes met his and she smiled for him.

Noah reached out to brush back some of her escaping curly blond tendrils, and Patty went into his arms again, snuggling against his chest, and feeling so proud that she was loved by this passionate, caring man. When she looked up at his face, she saw him through the eyes of love and thought that she was the luckiest girl in the world. Her Noah. Her Noah from Idaho. Noah was thirty-four years old, and had grown up in a small Idaho town that was built around a potash plant. From his childhood years, airplanes and helicopters had fascinated him, and from his childhood years, he had known that he would be a pilot one day, and would not be living his life in that small town which did not even have an airport. He had learned to fly while at college, and had worked all his adult life as a pilot, first in airfreight transport in Boise, then in the United States Air Force during the Gulf War, and now for a commercial airline out of Bradley International Airport north of Hartford.

Long and lanky, a real long drink of water she had called him, Noah had an energetic manner and an abundance of confidence which could be mistaken for arrogance by those who did not know him well. The first time Patty had laid eyes on him, she had been drawn to his good looks, and with his dark hair, straight thick dark brows, and pointed chin, she thought his face resembled a celebrated picture of Don Quixote that had hung in her parents' living room throughout her childhood. Then she had immediately corrected herself. No, he looks like a good-looking version of that Don Quixote in the lithograph.

Five minutes after Rick had introduced them, she had dared to hope that this handsome man would become an important part of her life. They had been married for less than three weeks, and she could not imagine that her passion for him could ever be sated.

Before his admiring eyes, she again stepped back away from him, and swirled around again with girlish grace. In her nervousness, she fired a rapid question at him. "Do you think I'll get the job?"

"Patty, if that principal's a man, no way, he can say no to you. He'll be eating out of your hand." He took her gently in his arms, and they kissed again.

"Why an opening this time of year?" he asked. "Shouldn't all the teaching positions be filled by now?"

"The position was filled. My father got the scoop from his friend Jim Politano. He's the assistant principal at the high school in case you don't remember. Someone was hired in June for the third grade job, but the person called the day before new teacher orientation in late August and reneged. Jim said that Harold Trelawney went ballistic. He has a sub in the room now, but wants a regular teacher. That's good luck for me since the middle of September is a hard time to find a new teacher. It increases my chances of getting the job."

"You'll overwhelm this guy with your brains and beauty."

"I think it's a committee actually," Patty cautioned, not wanting to get Noah's hopes up too high and have them come crashing down if she did not get the job. "I was told that I'd be meeting with the principal and some staff members. I hope it's not a cast of thousands."

Noah looked at his new wife with a smile on his face. "You'll do well. You always do." He paused before asking, "Did you run with Rick this morning?"

"Sure did."

"How is he?"

"Fine," she answered automatically. "No, what am I saying? Not fine at all." She frowned. "I'm sure I told you he had been engaged once. To a girl named Jordana?"

Noah nodded.

"It was about seven years ago. I was a senior in college at the time. I remember coming back from Syracuse for their engagement party. It was one of those high society affairs in Greenwich in a huge tent right in their own little gated community. There were acres of flowers, a famous string quartet flown in from somewhere, and food to die for. But you could tell that Jordana's parents were not too pleased with her choice. I'm sure they wanted more than just a regular nice guy for their princess, and they got their wish when Jordana broke the engagement a month before the wedding. Need I say that Rick was heartbroken? He had just taken over my Aunt Vera's agency and was working day and night, and was doing quite well, but he still wasn't making the kind of money that Jordana was looking for. I guess she thought she could do better."

Patty took a breath. "Rick found out later that she was involved with some stock broker with deep pockets before she met him. As soon as she ditched Rick, she went back to this guy, and they got married. I read about it in the New York Times society section. But now it turns out that for whatever the reason, the marriage didn't work out, and wouldn't you know that Rick would have the incredibly bad luck to run into her last spring. She must have smelled the money on him because this morning he talked as though they were a twosome."

"Well, Rick can't be serious. He should be able to see Jordana for what she is if she's as mercenary as you say."

Patty shook her head. "I wish. I can read Rick like a book, and from the way he sounded this morning, I'd say he has all intentions of marrying her if she'll have him."

Noah shrugged.

"Oh, one more thing. Very important. We have to keep this whole thing about Rick and Jordana quiet. Rick doesn't want it to get around. Maybe he's afraid that Jordana will dump him again, and he'll look like a complete fool. He especially doesn't want Tish to know because he thinks she's the office gossip. And of course he has no idea how Tish feels about him." Patty glanced at her watch at that moment. "Here I am talking away, and I have the interview. I've got to run. I don't want to be late. It's not exactly the first impression I want to make on the famous Mr. Harold Trelawney. Walk me to the car?"

She fished in her bag for her car keys as she started down the stairs at double-time. He followed her down the stairs and into the front hall, and then they walked together out the front door toward Patty's red Mustang parked in the driveway. Noah took her hand for a moment, gave it a squeeze, and led her to the car. He then opened the driver's side door, and she slid in behind the steering wheel. They both said, "I love you," at the same time.

"Come right home," he then said. "I'll be waiting. Fingers crossed." Then he added, "This job would mean a lot to our finances." He leaned over, kissed both sides of her mouth, then her forehead, and then her lips. Then he stood back, his eyes on her.

Patty shut the door, belted herself in and immediately turned on the ignition. After throwing Noah a kiss, she checked the rear-view mirror before she backed out to the street. She looked over with love at her husband standing tall and lean in the driveway, bandbox neat, with his pilot's uniform with epaulettes, starched white shirt, dark tie, well-pressed trousers and dress shoes with a military spit-shine. She took a mental photograph, waved, put her car into drive and accelerated down Iron Weed Road into the heat of the late summer morning.

Chapter 4

Like the model for every child's crayon drawing of a school, Island Brooke sat squarely on the corner of Emerson and School Streets just one block from the business section of the affluent shoreline town of Hastings. The building was a traditional older three-story structure made of rosy red brick and concrete and topped by a cupola-dominated hip roof. Set back from the street by an apron of well-landscaped lawn with its American flag, that day hanging limply above the blue banner of Connecticut, the school was a local landmark both because of its classic architecture and its national reputation for academic excellence. Since Patty had grown up in Hastings, she had passed this building many times without giving it much thought, but on that day she slowed down to take stock as she drove by. She then steered her car into a large side parking lot walled from the street by a grove of Norway maples. She parked in the first free slot she found in the area farthest from the school, and unsure of how to enter the building, walked across the driveway leading to Emerson Street and around to the sidewalk at the front. Now really torn between excitement and nervousness, she stepped through a wide-open iron gate set in low hedges and moved toward the front door. She went up three broad cement steps leading to the door and looked up to read the inscription etched in stone above the doorway — *Island Brooke Elementary School — 1955.*

Catching a glimpse of herself in the plate-glass window, she made an effort to push some strands of her fair hair back from her face and neck. With the day growing hotter and muggier, she could feel herself sweating and wiped some beads of perspiration from her forehead with the back of her hand. The day is really turning into a scorcher, she thought. She then took

31

a few moments to anchor herself before entering the school through one of the dark-green double doors.

Inside it was cooler with high ceilings and wide shiny halls, and colorful with bulletin boards decorated with children's artwork, framed color photographs of class activities, and some bright mosaic murals in primary colors, red, yellow, blue, showing children at play. There was a hum of activity in the school, and Patty could hear the sounds of some high-pitched voices, laughter, and choral music somewhere deep in the building, but saw only a few fresh faced children in the hall. She walked down the corridor past dozens of steel-gray lockers, dutifully following the signs and arrows, which indicated that all visitors should report to the main office.

Reaching the office, she opened a wooden door, felt the welcome chill of air conditioning, and walked up to a rectangular central counter. A young, sprightly brunette left off some furious typing before a computer screen, got up with a smile, and came to the other side of the counter to greet her. Patty composed her features into her best schoolteacher expression and said, "Good morning. I'm Patty Bass. I have an interview with Mr. Trelawney at nine. I guess I'm a few minutes early."

The secretary nodded, and said, "Sure. Mr. Trelawney is expecting you. He's handling a situation upstairs, but he'll be with you in a few minutes. Won't you sign in here?" She pushed an open loose-leaf notebook across the counter to Patty who reached to take it. There was a pen attached, and Patty signed her name and wrote in the time — *8:45*. She handed the notebook and pen back and noticed that the dark-haired secretary wore a nametag that read *Mrs. Reilly.*

"You can have a seat right there," the secretary said, pointing to a bench set against the wall between a line of mailboxes and a well-lit display case filled with plaques, trophies, medals, and photographs. Patty walked over, sat down, and primly arranged her skirt. Some time went by and she grew accustomed to the bustle in the office — the door opening and closing — children and teachers in pairs and singles coming in and going out — and the frequent ringing of the telephone. She tried to focus on the coming interview, rehearsing probably questions and answers in her mind, reviewing some of the ideas she had written out the previous evening. *Emphasize what you can contribute. Tell why you're right for the job. Make eye contact. Smile. But don't smile too much. Don't be too interested in the salary. Ask questions at the end. Definitely, ask questions at the end.*

Time passed and then more time, and she began to feel impatient with the wait, frequently looking at her watch as though that would make Harold Trelawney appear. It was quarter after nine. This guy is rude, she thought. Or maybe he doesn't own a watch. By nine-twenty, she was feeling antsy, and needing a break from sitting in one place, stood up and looked over some of the awards and framed, matted photographs within the display case and was soon able to identify the husky man in the pictures, as Harold Trelawney since he appeared repeatedly, posing with groups of smiling children, the first selectman of Hastings, and one of Connecticut's senators. Patty also skimmed a framed article from a recent issue of *Connecticut Schools,* which extolled Island Brooke for *"its wonderful environment for learning and standardized test scores in the stratosphere."* The article ended by stating that Harold Trelawney had been principal at Island Brooke School for twelve years and had no interest in promotion or plans to give up his job, and in fact had recently turned down a prestigious job in the State Department of Education because *"he has no interest in a desk job in Hartford, but enjoys working with children."* As Patty mused on the fame of the school and its principal, the door swung open once more and the man in all the photographs entered the office as if he owned the place, which in fact, Patty guessed, he just about did. Then he was standing in front of her, extending his hand.

"Mrs. Bass. I'm Harold Trelawney. Sorry to keep you waiting so long. The problem upstairs was a whole lot more complicated than I thought, and I didn't want to send the boys back to class before they were completely settled down." His gaze, through designer glasses, was direct, and his handshake was firm, but not too firm, and Patty was pleased with his apology and explanation. Facing him, Patty decided that Harold Trelawney certainly wasn't a handsome man, but she noticed that he did his best to minimize his large, bulbous nose by wearing his silver hair fanned out high and just long enough in back to scrape his shirt collar. She also noted that he was not as tall as she had expected. She found him to be about her height in heels, and she was not a tall woman, but he quite definitely carried himself like an important man, with arrow-straight posture and his large head held high. So this is the famous principal of the famous school, she thought. About fifty, she estimated, but a young fifty. After they shook hands, he beckoned to Patty and led the way around the counter and toward his office. Harold turned as he opened the door to his office, and she noted that he was wearing a beautifully cut suit in a strong shade of gray with a rust-red power tie.

Patty entered the principal's office, a corner room, wood-paneled and bright with tall windows, which looked out onto Emerson Street and the side parking lot. The office was not large, or so Patty at first thought, but then realized it just seemed small because there was so much clutter, and the floor was crowded and crammed with too much furniture for its size. Her eyes took in the walls that were almost completely covered with student papers overlapping each other, an old, oak roll-top desk which looked too good to throw away, a leather-covered desk chair, piles of textbooks and magazines in one corner, a row of green file cabinets, and near the doorway a highly-polished round table partially covered with stacks of file folders and papers. Five comfortable-looking leather-covered chairs on casters were placed around the table, and one of them was occupied by another man who looked up from a stack of folders in front of him as Patty entered the room. The man half rose from his seat, stretched out his hand, and greeted Patty in an affable manner with a smile.

"Dewey Willis." he introduced himself. "Reading specialist."

Patty noted that Dewey Willis was balding, his brown hair receding from his temples, yet his boyish features and smooth skin made him seem young. She also noticed that he had the good shoulders of an athlete, yet wore the round glasses of a scholar. Although Patty could not know it at that time, a scholar he was, someone who had always delighted in an academic challenge. The superintendent of schools was well aware that Dewey Willis had been near the top of his class in college and grad school. Now in his early thirties, Dewey was highly thought of in the school system and was on the fast track for administrative promotion. Drawn to his friendly expression, Patty studied his face for a few moments before turning away.

Patty and Harold sat down and settled themselves. Harold then said, "Now as soon as Eunice gets here, we can begin." The insistent clicking of heels in the outer office announced the arrival of the third interviewer. The woman paused in the doorway although there was no apparent need to do so. She stood there as the seconds went by, preening herself and tossing her hair as Patty and both men turned to watch. Patty's first impression was that the woman was striking — trim and fine-boned with a small high-bridged nose, and a fall of honey-fair hair to her shoulders. Dressed like a model, her straw-colored heels were high, and she was wearing a form fitting strawberry-colored dress, which complemented her generous chest and small waist. Her nails gleamed pink with polish the same color as her dress. Patty smiled a greeting and gave the newcomer another automatic head-to-toe inspection, thinking that they were about the same age and might well become friends if she got the job. As she did so, she immediately realized that the woman's gaze was in turn sliding over her, but the look was given with unfriendly eyes, and the appraisal was critical. The woman moved from the doorway, and seemed to glide into the office as the scent of a light, expensive perfume came with her. All eyes and all attention were on her as she eased herself into a chair.

"Thought you had forgotten about us, Eunice," said Harold, his face lit by a half smile. Then he turned to Patty. "Mrs. Bass, this is Eunice MacKay. Mrs. MacKay is one of our crackerjack third grade teachers. I asked her to sit in on the interview so that she can answer any questions that you might have about how we do things in the third grade here at Island Brooke." He shuffled through a pile of manila folders on the table, and handed some materials to Eunice as she sat back with the hauteur of a royal princess, crossed her long tanned legs and flicked her hair in what now seemed to Patty like a practiced gesture. Patty smiled, said, "Hello," and started to stretch out her hand but quickly withdrew it when Eunice made no move to reciprocate but merely gave her a measuring look before murmuring a lock-jawed, "Hello." Eunice then immediately turned away and opened one of the folders, which Harold had given her. Patty felt a slap of disappointment. This woman would not be her friend.

Harold oblivious to the snub went right on talking and for the first time, Patty heard the consonants and vowels of Boston in his authoritative voice. "There's one more person who may sit in. That's Marielle Rossamondo, our math specialist. She had hoped to be here, but there was a math meeting this morning at Central Office so she will be coming late." Harold stopped talking and looked at Eunice and Dewey in turn.

"As I'm sure you've noticed, the resume and all the papers are in the name of Patricia Nelson. I guess you got married recently, Mrs. Bass."

Patty nodded, and her big smile held memories of days on pastel beaches and romance in the night.

"Yes, I got married at the end of August, and just got back from my honeymoon a week ago."

"Congratulations," Harold said. Dewey across the table also said, "Congratulations." Patty turned toward Eunice, hoping for some kind of positive response at this mention of a marriage, but the other woman was looking down, seemingly intent on studying the papers in front of her. Harold went on, "So that's why we had so much trouble running you down. We thought our interviewing was over, but yesterday afternoon I got a call from our personnel department about you."

Harold then began asking questions, sifting through the details of her resume, asking her about her early life in Hastings, her experiences in college, and her time in New York City. He then leaned his chair back, clasped his hands behind his neck, and in almost a casual manner asked the question that she had been expecting. "Tell us, Mrs. Bass. Why do you want to teach here at Island Brooke School?"

Prepared, Patty supplied the standard answers, which in her case were true, and discussed how she loved children, and had the educational background and work experience to make a real contribution to the school. She talked at length and ended by saying, "I graduated from college with a double major in theater and English, and then lived in New York City for six years hoping for my big break in show business. After coming back to Hastings last summer, I earned my master's degree in elementary education at Southern Connecticut State University in New Haven, and I completed my student teaching and internship in the third grade at Soderholm Elementary School right here in town. Island Brooke has an outstanding reputation. A national reputation for excellence. And I'd love to teach here."

Harold nodded approvingly when she had finished talking and said, "I've read through your references and they're all excellent. I especially like the letter from the principal of Soderholm. I know Peg Bucci well, and she usually doesn't write in such superlatives."

His voice then took on a pompous tone. "I'm sure that you are aware of all the awards won by our school and the fact that our standardized test scores are among the strongest in the nation. You also should know that teaching positions at Island Brooke are usually highly sought after. This is certainly a rare circumstance where we have to actively seek out applicants. We did interview a large number of candidates in June for the third grade position, and selected a young lady from my hometown of Boston. She was planning to move to New Haven with her husband who had been accepted at the Yale Law School. As it turned out, they had marital problems over the summer, and she decided at the last minute not to make the move with her husband. Hence the unexpected vacancy."

The wall phone rang at that moment and Harold reached behind him to answer it. He spoke impatiently. "Get his number, Grace. I'll have to get back to him."

Dewey then took over the interview. "What did you think of the reading program at Soderholm?"

Patty's face brightened as she answered his question. "I thought it was excellent. They use a wonderful eclectic approach that works very well. It's a combination of phonics, whole language, and multi-sensory. It seems tailored to the individual needs and abilities of the children." She went on to recount some of her experiences teaching reading as Dewey nodded enthusiastically. When she had finished with additional praise for the program, he modestly, said, "Actually, the reading program at Soderholm is modeled after the program we've developed here at Island Brooke."

There was a knock at that moment and without waiting for a reply of any kind, a brunette of about forty wearing a tailored dress and orthopedic shoes swung open the door and came into the office. She was small, tiny at barely five feet tall, with skin as pale as porcelain with no hint of the sun's rays or makeup on her thin face. Her dark eyes were magnified and protuberant behind thick bifocals. Her hair was even darker and sleek to her head in a gamine cut.

"Marielle, I'm so happy you could break away. Come right in and join us," Harold said as he smiled broadly and rose from his seat. He gestured at the woman and then Patty as he made the introductions. "Mrs. Bass, I'd like you to meet our math specialist, Marielle Rossamondo. Mrs. Rossamondo is also our part-time social worker and serves as our acting principal whenever I'm out of the building. A lady who wears many hats. And my good right hand." He gestured. "And my left hand." He gestured again, and went on. "Marielle, this is Mrs. Patricia Bass, a candidate for the third grade teaching position."

Marielle walked over and shook hands with Patty. There was a formality about her manner, yet she seemed kind-faced, and Patty caught a glimpse of keen intelligence behind her glasses. Patty noticed the name *Patricia Nelson* on a manila folder that Marielle was carrying in her left hand and hoped that Marielle had been reading good things about her. When Marielle spoke, she had a slow, thoughtful speech pattern.

"I'm sorry I'm late, Mrs. Bass, but it is good to meet you. I read through your resume last night and I'm happy to put a face with the name. I also talked with the math specialist at Soderholm, and he speaks very highly of you. I can see from your record that you did well in math."

"I've always liked math," Patty responded with a smile. "I guess math goes with music, and I love music."

Marielle sat down in the empty chair and opened her mouth to continue, when Eunice who had been quiet up to that point finally looked over at Patty and interrupted. Speaking in her gravely voice, she said, "Getting back to what Harold was saying, Patricia, these circumstances are very unusual, but they do open up a unique opportunity for some lucky teacher. I think I should also emphasize that our high standardized test scores and wonderful reputation come from a great deal of hard work by our teachers, our innovative reading and math programs, our emphasis on self-esteem throughout the building, and of course," she turned and gave Harold a fawning smile, "the leadership at the school."

Patty again noticed that Eunice always seemed to be on stage. As she spoke, she occasionally tossed her head, quite aware Patty was sure, of how the light coming in the front windows caught the nuances and gradations, which shot through her golden hair. Patty looked more closely at Eunice as the woman went on enumerating the many blessings of teaching at Island Brooke, and had time to consider that Eunice's colorful detailed dress looked expensive, and that some fine lines around her eyes and mouth indicated that she was somewhat older than Patty had originally thought.

Eunice's next question brought Patty back to the interview with a jolt. "Is teaching second choice for you, Patricia?" Eunice's tone was deceptively pleasant, her blue eyes innocently wide. "I ask that question because I do have some concerns about your priorities. You say that you lived in New York City for six years after you graduated from college and apparently tried to break into show business. And now at this late date, perhaps as a consolation prize, you've decided that you want to become a teacher. Would you run off and leave us if you were offered some kind of acting job in New York, or as you phrased it — offered your big break in show business?"

A chill settled over the room with the inquiry, and Harold's face creased into a frown as he contemplated the possibility of hiring and then losing a second teacher. On the defensive, Patty knew that she should break the strained silence. She raised her chin and looked at the four interviewers in turn as she answered. "I am not looking for jobs in the theater. I'm married now, and at this point of my life, teaching is my first priority, and if I'm offered the position here at Island Brooke, I would make a commitment for the entire school year." Then she added, "And beyond that if things worked out. My husband is a pilot flying out of Bradley International Airport, and we own a house right here in town so I, we, have no plans to go anywhere."

Dewey made eye contact with Patty and jumped in at that moment before Eunice could speak again. "Well, that answers that question. You're now made your commitment to teaching. Not to change the subject, but I see that many of your jobs in New York City were involved with children in one way or other. Can you tell us about some of them?"

Realizing that Dewey was trying to put her at ease, Patty sent him a smile of gratitude, and the atmosphere warmed as she recounted some of her work experiences. "For four years I worked part-time for a children's entertainment company in the city which involved dressing up as various nursery rhyme or cartoon characters. We traveled around to children's birthday parties and fairs. I also worked as a clown at special events and did simple magic tricks and face painting. In addition, I did some acting and directing of children's theater in New York schools, and as a result was hired as a substitute teacher. My experiences as a substitute convinced me that teaching was right for me."

"And were you paid for all your acting and directing?" asked Eunice.

"Sometimes, not always," Patty admitted. "I did have a few walk-ons on *All My Children.*"

"And why were you always changing jobs, Patricia? You were only working for six years in New York and you seem to have had hundreds of jobs." Eunice tittered at her own exaggeration.

The comment and Eunice's patronizing tone annoyed Patty, but she answered calmly. "When you're trying to break into show business, you have to be available for casting calls and interviews, so you tend to take subsistence jobs and just can't settle down in one profession. That's why I did work in a lot of places. But now that I've made a commitment to teaching, it will be a whole different story."

Harold nodded his head in a favorable way, but Eunice went on, apparently trying to unnerve Patty. "I see that you did some modeling." She seemed to be enjoying herself as she asked, "And why didn't that work out for you?"

"Yes, I did do some modeling at department stores and wedding shows, and I was told that I had all the qualifications but one."

She paused, and Eunice took the bait. "And what was that?"

Emboldened by the positive responses she had been getting from three of the four interviewers, Patty did her best Groucho Marx imitation, with waggling eyebrows and invisible cigar. "I was told that I was about half a foot too short." The two men laughed, and Marielle smiled, but Eunice kept her stone face and went back to turning pages.

Dewey cocked his head. "You left New York City and came back to Hastings last summer?"

"Yes, I did. I realized that I really wasn't doing what I wanted to be doing. I was working on and off in the theater, doing some substitute teaching, not making very much, and mainly supporting myself by working as a waitress. I was up for the lead in an off-Broadway musical, but it didn't work out. The lease was up at the apartment that I shared with two other women, so I had to make a decision, and I decided to come home and go back to school."

Up for the lead in an off-Broadway musical, Patty thought as her mind veered back to that very exceptional day. Well, I did get the lead. At least I had it for a few hours. She remembered how excited she had been when the director, a married man, middle-aged but trying to appear younger with his bleached pony-tailed hair, reddened face from a suntan parlor, and multiple earrings, had told her that she had the role. And it was a perfect role for her, one that might well have been the first important step to acting and singing career. Then in practically the same breath, the director had asked her to come back that evening to go over one of the songs, which he said needed some fine tuning. He had then told her that unfortunately, he wasn't available till eleven. Promptly at eleven she had entered the theater and found him sitting on a chair by the curtain waiting for her. After she stood on the stage and sang her heart out to a darkened theater, he had come up behind her, and with his hands and profane whispers in her ear had let her know what she would have to do to keep the lead.

She had left the theater in tears, and stumbled down the nearest stairs to the subway. Huddled in a seat on a dirty, noisy subway train, and breathing the stale air that thousands of New Yorkers had breathed that day, she had ridden for over an hour. Confused and overwhelmed, she had gone over the events of the day, wondering if she had given the director some signal that she was easy and available to him. She ended up reliving every triumph and every trial of her life, seeking some answer, trying to understand why the director thought of her as a piece of meat, why the director thought of her as nothing.

Eunice's comment interrupted her train of thought. "There is one other discrepancy I'd like cleared up, Patricia." Patty came back to the interview, wondering what objection Eunice would be making this time.

"You've told us that you made the decision to become a teacher over a year ago. And yet your application to teach here in Hastings wasn't received by our personnel office until June 30 of this year according to the date stamped on your papers. Why did you wait so long to apply if you were seriously interested in a teaching job?"

Patty took a breath, smarting over Eunice's needling, because needling it was. "Yes, there's really no discrepancy. You see I met my husband-to-be in January of this year. Before I met him, I was planning to return to New York and had taken the test for New York City and had applied to several communities on Long Island. Within months of meeting Noah, I knew that I would be staying in Connecticut, in Hastings, so at that point

I began applying to the East Shore towns. I realized that I was applying late and never dreamed I would be considered for a permanent job so I was in no hurry to get my applications in. Actually, I had planned to substitute."

Marielle smiled her approval at Patty. "That makes sense. You weren't planning to stay in the area. I don't see any discrepancy at all."

There was a shuffling of papers as Harold looked through Patty's resume again. Then he unexpectedly asked, "How would you describe yourself in one word, Mrs. Bass?"

Patty took a few moments to think how Noah might describe her, and then answered, "Fun."

There were three smiles in response, and then Harold went on. "What are some of your outside interests?"

"Acting and singing," answered Patty. "And movies. I love movies. Also, I'm learning to cook. My best friend used to be a caterer and she's teaching me. And of course running. I love to run. I run almost every day."

"Do you run along Hastings Beach?" asked Dewey with interest, leaning toward Patty.

"Occasionally," responded Patty. "Do you run?"

Dewey blinked before answering. "Well, actually, no. I've always been into sports, but I've never tried running." He quickly added, "But I've often thought of taking it up. I own a condo not far from the beach, and I often see all the joggers going up and down the boardwalk. It seems like such a great activity."

"It is. It's wonderful for physical fitness and mental clarity. I highly recommend it," Patty remarked.

"I've always wondered, Mrs. Bass," said Marielle. "What is the difference between running and jogging?"

"There's really no difference. You kind of self-identify. If you say you run, you run. If you say you jog, you jog. That's my understanding of it."

"This young woman certainly has all the right answers," Harold remarked. His voice had become vibrant, and he was smiling. He looked at Patty and said, "Do you have any questions for us, Mrs. Bass?"

Four pairs of eyes turned to her, and Patty knew that she should ask at least one question. "You've already covered just about everything, and I do know a lot about the third grade curriculum in Hastings from my experiences at Soderholm, but every school is unique. Could you tell me something about the third grades here at Island Brooke?"

Harold gestured at Eunice with his chin. She took the question and answered in some detail, and ended with, "All the third grade classrooms are located right here on the first floor near the office. We have four third grades. There's the vacancy, and I teach one, and we have a wonderful teacher Ellen Cherry in one of the others. We have weekly third grade meetings, and we all work together as a team."

"Isn't there another third grade teacher?" asked Patty, after silently counting.

"Yes," answered Eunice. "Sue Strauss. She's older, near retirement. She may not be with us much longer." There was an undertone of hostility in her voice, and Patty wondered what the older Sue Strauss had done to offend Eunice. There was an uncomfortable silence, which seemed to go on and on until Marielle broke it. She looked over at Patty, the glare from the lights reflecting in her glasses. She gave an encouraging nod as she spoke. "Sue Strauss is an extremely bright woman and a fine teacher. The children love her. She's been here for years and years. In fact, she's the only person at the school who has been here longer than Mr. Trelawney."

Marielle shifted her body toward Harold. "Mr. Trelawney started his career at this very school twenty-eight years ago. He came to teach in the fifth grade at Island Brooke right out of college, and he's never worked at any other school. And he's turned down some pretty big jobs to stay here. You probably know that Island Brooke has a national reputation for excellence, and educators from all over New England come here to observe our programs and methods. These educators don't always know what we on the inside know. That the amazing success that we've had at Island Brooke is due in large part to Harold." There was pride in Marielle's voice and her cheeks had become flushed.

Harold nodded along as Marielle spoke and took the praise as his due. He then settled back in his chair and looked at the others. "Any more questions for Mrs. Bass?" He went on when there was no response. "All right. There's just one more thing." Patty looked at him, put a polite expression on her face and waited, expecting more egotistical words about how great the school was and how honored anyone would be to teach at Island Brooke, but what Harold said surprised her. "We can look at your background, Mrs. Bass, and your fine academic record, but the most important thing for me is something that we can't teach you. And that is," he paused as she hung on his words, "a love of children. If you like kids, you're the kind of teacher we want at Island Brooke. All your references indicate that you do care about kids. As a matter of fact, I've rarely seen such fine references." He paused one more time. "Also, we provide a full program of after-school activities here. If you are hired, I would expect you to run a drama club."

Patty nodded in agreement, beginning to relax, her internal barometer telling her that she had done well. Bringing the interview to a close, Harold got to his feet and extended his hand. Patty got up too and tried to read his face, noting that his smile seemed sincere. "Thank you for coming in today, Mrs. Bass. You'll be hearing from us one way or the other the other within the next couple of days, so stay by your telephone and your mailbox. I want a regular teacher in that classroom as soon as possible."

Dewey also stood up, removed his glasses, and shook Patty's hand warmly. His blue eyes were alight with interest.

"Thank you for coming in today." One down, thought Patty as she looked at his face.

Patty gazed over at the two women. Marielle was sitting and nodding pleasantly in her direction, while Eunice also remained seated and gave a curt acknowledgment with the barest of nods. Patty gave thanks to the committee, and turned to leave, optimistic that she had impressed Harold, Marielle and Dewey, and might well be offered the teaching job. She was in a happy daze as she left the office and closed the door behind her.

Chapter 5

Eunice went on the offensive immediately. "I don't think we should hire another inexperienced person. We already have two brand new teachers at the school so Patricia would be one too many. I'd like to consider some of the more seasoned candidates." She pushed Patty's folder aside as though it held little interest.

"I don't know about that," Harold said lazily, loosening his necktie and then peering over his glasses. "I think Ellen Cherry would be happy to mentor Mrs. Bass if we hired her."

Dewey broke in. "I think Mrs. Bass would make an excellent addition to our staff."

Eunice dismissed Dewey's comment with an impatient hand. "No, I don't agree. I'd like to review Kim Stahl's resume again. She's taught here at Island Brooke, so it would be a much easier adjustment for everyone."

"No." Harold's voice was loud and firm. "Kim walked away from the job, so I won't consider her."

Eunice's face worked as she tried to hide her anger, realizing at that moment that she should have made the case for her friend Kim when she and Harold were alone.

Marielle took another folder from a pile and slid it toward the center of the table. "I certainly do like Mrs. Bass, but I like this candidate too. Marcetta Osborne. She lives right in the neighborhood, and she was a wonderful PTA president a few years ago. She's also something of a math scholar."

Ready to argue, Eunice immediately countered. "I thought we all agreed that we weren't going to hire any more parents from our school district. It creates a conflict of interest. And I hear that Mrs. Osborne is up for PTA president again this year."

Dewey nodded in assent. "Eunice is right. We did say that. Mrs. Osborne has tons of friends in the school, and it would be hard for her to be an objective teacher. We don't want to create any extra problems for ourselves. I don't think we should consider her."

Harold also nodded, and put Marcetta Osborn's folder on the bottom of the pile. He then tapped Patty's folder with his forefinger. "I guess that leaves Mrs. Bass."

The grim set of Eunice's face made it clear that she did not agree.

Dewey spoke up. "I was sitting here before the interview going through all the resumes again. Mrs. Bass has the best references and a strong academic record, and she's young and enthusiastic. I think she'll make a great teacher. She has my vote."

Marielle nodded her head. "I agree. They liked her very much at Soderholm and would have hired her if there had been an opening."

Eunice decided to make one last plea for her friend Kim. She leaned across the table and put one hand on Dewey's wrist. Turning her head sideways, she looked up at him in a coquettish manner. "Do you remember what a good teacher Kim was?"

But Dewey shook his head, and held up Patty's resume in his hand. Eunice looked over at Marielle whose face was set. Then Eunice shrugged, realizing that this was one battle that she would not be winning despite her special standing in the school. "OK, I guess I'm outvoted. I think you're all making a mistake on this one, but Mrs. Patricia Bass it is." She pushed herself up and gave a throaty laugh, masking her feelings. "I don't know about anyone else here, but I have a class to teach. See you all later." She turned and left the room.

Grace Reilly stopped pushing the keys on her computer and looked up when Harold's office door abruptly opened and was slammed shut. Eunice stood in front of the door with a pained expression on her face.

"How did it go?" Grace asked in a stage whisper.

"They decided on Patricia Bass."

"The cute blonde?"

"Right. The one who looks like an overage cheerleader."

Grace's hands remained poised over her keyboard as she watched Eunice walk toward the desk and then hover over the phone as she turned to complain. "I don't understand it. I really thought they'd hire Kim Stahl back. She was such a good teacher when she worked here. I don't believe Harold. He's usually so amenable, but on this he was like iron. Really pulled rank. I guess there's another side to his personality that we don't know about." She pushed in Kim's number. "I might as well give her the bad news. I did all I could. Kim will just have to understand."

Chapter 6

Patty was up early the next morning, but she didn't go out for a run. Afraid to miss a call from Hastings Public Schools and have them try someone else, she waited around the house and diverted herself by doing housework. With one eye on the phone, she stripped and changed the bed, dusted, polished, scrubbed the kitchen floor until even Noah would think it was clean enough to eat on, and did a big load of laundry. When the phone rang just before nine-thirty, she was halfway down the basement steps carrying a second load of clothes in a yellow plastic basket, and she quickly rushed back up the stairs to the kitchen and lunged for the phone on its third ring. It was Hastings Public Schools calling, and she heard the efficient voice of the personnel secretary saying, "Subject to approval by the Hastings Board of Education, you are being offered the third grade position at Island Brooke School."

The voice went on, "Dr. Callahan, our director of personnel, would like to meet with you this morning at Central Office. She will have a contract ready for you to sign and some insurance and IRS forms for you to fill out. After that Mr. Trelawney would like you to go right over to the school to talk with the substitute, meet the class, and pick up books and supplies. He would like you to begin a full day tomorrow. Would ten-thirty this morning be convenient for you to meet with Dr. Callahan?"

Barely able to contain herself, Patty murmured, "Yes, that would be very convenient," and when she hung up, she gave a mighty whoop and threw the yellow basket of clothes up into the air in exhilaration. Bubbling with excitement, she went right for the phone to spread the good news.

Chapter 7

It was almost noon by the time Patty reached the main office at Island Brooke School where Dewey wearing an unfussy suit and a friendly smile was waiting to greet her. "Congratulations, Mrs. Bass," he said. "Welcome aboard." He reached out and pumped her hand.

"It's Patty."

"Patty it is." He went on. "It's been a really hectic morning, and Harold's tied up with some irate parents who are complaining about the TAG teacher. The teacher for the Talented and Gifted program in case you haven't learned all the acronyms yet. This guy is supposed to be bright enough to teach the highest scoring kids in the school, and can you believe that he got on the PA yesterday afternoon and called for 'all the talented and gifted students' to come to the library right away. You can imagine how the other kids felt as one or two 'talented and gifted' students in each class got up and walked out. How insensitive can someone be?"

Dewey smiled and shook his head, and Patty thought to herself that he had a nice smile. A really nice guy.

"Since Harold's not available, he's asked me to introduce you to your mentor, Ellen Cherry." Dewey checked the wall clock. "She should be finishing her lunch in the teachers' lounge just about now so we can go right upstairs and catch her. I've told her that you'd be coming in today."

As they ascended the stairs to the second floor, he continued, "You'll love Ellen. Everybody does. Very professional. Very friendly. And a very bright woman." They had just moved from the second floor landing to the corridor when an all-call came on for Dewey. Disappointed at the interruption, he stopped in his tracks and sighed. "This must be the important telephone call from Fairfield University that I've been waiting for all morning. I can't miss it. I'm going to need some quiet, so I have to run down to my office to take it. You can either come back down with me or go right to the teachers' lounge to introduce yourself to Ellen. She's the good looking black woman."

Patty opted to enter the crowded teachers' lounge herself, and she walked directly up to Ellen who was sitting on one of the sofas reading the newspaper, and said, "Hi, I'm Patty Bass." Ellen dressed in a pantsuit the color of pewter stood up and with a handshake and a smile replied, "Hello, Patty. I'm Ellen Cherry. I would ask how you picked me out, but I guess I kind of stand out in a crowd."

They had both laughed, and as they chatted, Patty soon saw that Dewey was right. Ellen was indeed very friendly, very professional, and very bright. And a good looking woman, as slight and graceful as a dancer, with high cheekbones, flawless dark skin, and a calm self-possessed air. Within a few minutes they were talking easily about the responsibilities at Island Brooke, and with Ellen acting as her guide, Patty was soon immersed in the nuts and bolts of beginning a new job — walking into the first floor classroom that would be her own, meeting her class for the first time, meeting so many people that she couldn't remember all their names, picking out supplies, and one of her proudest moments — opening a new, brown, soft-covered lesson plan book, and writing in her teacher's neat cursive — *Mrs. Bass, Room 105, Island Brooke School.*

Chapter 8

The boy was sitting in his high school psychology class, hunched forward, legs spread to the sides of his desk, and feet planted in the aisles. He was scrawling a few notes and doodling shaded rocket ships in the margin of his loose-leaf notebook, but most of his mind was fantasizing about the built brunette in the tight green sweater who was sitting diagonally across from him. The drone of the lecture was little more than background noise when something the teacher said caught his attention. Mr. Hesse was now talking about "the sociopath." The boy tore his gaze away from the brunette in the tight sweater to look up at the ancient, totally gray teacher with the comb over, who went on, and said, "Listen up people. Here's a story to illustrate my point about the sociopath."

Mr. Hesse abandoned his lectern and paced back and forth in the front of the classroom as he spoke. "These two men worked together in a business for twenty years. Each day at noon, they would cross the street to eat lunch at a diner. One day a car came out of nowhere and knocked one of the men to the ground. What did the second man do? He calmly continued across the street, went into the diner, sat down at the counter and ate his lunch the way he always did without any concern for his friend who lay bleeding in the street." Mr. Hesse paused. "What do you think about that?"

With an arch of her back and a thrust of her chest, the brunette object of the boy's affection seemed to mirror the reactions of the rest of the class when she called out, "Disgusting." The words "Sicko," and "Weirdo" could be heard from the other students in the room.

But at that moment, the boy had a revelation— a revelation because he saw that his reaction was completely different from the others. He was thinking, How cool. How cool of the guy to ignore all the fuss and just go to the diner and have his lunch. He wrote the word *sociopath* down in his notebook and underlined it.

The next day was a Saturday and he was waiting on the front steps of the public library before it opened. A few minutes after nine, with his loose-leaf notebook in his hand, he stood by the circular checkout desk, ogling the younger of the two librarians as she talked on the phone and waiting for her to hang up and notice him. An engraved plate on her desk read *Miss Paternoster.* He liked the unusual name, liked the way her shiny dark hair hung long and wavy to the small of her back, and he really liked the way the glasses dangling from a silver chain around her neck fell down over the front of her full blouse.

She finished the call and looked up. "Yes?"

"I have to do a report for school. Could you point me in the right direction?" He opened his notebook as if he wasn't completely sure about his topic. "My teacher assigned me a report on the sociopath."

The young librarian got up and led him over to the wooden card catalogue. She slid open one of the drawers, flipped through some cards, wrote a number on some scrap paper and directed him to the freestanding shelves. He turned and watched her body as she walked back to the main desk. Then with the call number in his hand, he found three books, all with the same title, *Psychopathology.*

He then sat down at a side table in an alcove and under the light of a gooseneck lamp, spent the next hour reading about the sociopath. Reading about himself. When he had finished, he sat back and reflected. So he was a sociopath. A sociopath. That answered a lot of questions that he had been asking himself. He now knew why he was different. He now knew why he didn't feel emotions the way other did. Why he had no empathy. But this discovery didn't make him feel bad. On the contrary, he felt a surge of delight when he thought about it. He was special. He was superior. A prince among peasants. He thought of his future, and envisioned himself a predator, and everyone else in the world his prey. He said the word 'sociopath' aloud. He liked the way it sounded, liked the way it tasted on his tongue.

He opened his loose-leaf notebook and started taking notes, copying key words and phrases from the books. *A personality disorder. Smart and charming. Pleasant but superficial*

manners. No feelings for others. Feelings only for the self.
Amoral. Corner cutting. Knows the difference between right
and wrong but doesn't care. Able to verbalize appropriate
emotions but doesn't feel them. A person without a conscience.
He thought back to the incident at Runnel's Pond. Yes, a person
without a conscience. He hadn't seen Buddy or Jack in a few
years. He wondered where they were these days. He knew
where Gerry was.

Then he wrote down the word *persona* — and its definition
— *a public impression, a façade, a false front.* He tapped the
fingers of his right hand on the table, and thought for a few
minutes, forming an image of the kind of person he would
become — the kind of persona he would adopt. He felt he
was above the rules, but he did not want to stand out. He now
knew that there were certain words the clods said, certain facial
expressions they used, certain actions that were expected. He
was a consummate actor and he decided he would master them
all. He thought again of the mistake he had made that day at
Runnel's Pond, and how he had alienated Jack and Buddy. He
understood everything now. There was no question. If he could
go back in time to the day of Gerry's death, he knew how he
should act. He could just picture himself standing there at the
edge of the ice, blubbering along with the best of them.

Then he said the word *persona* out loud — so loud that an
elderly woman at a nearby table looked up and over at him.
For a second he felt embarrassed, wondering if he had given
himself away, but of course he hadn't. She couldn't know what
he was thinking. She couldn't know that he was making a very
important plan for himself. She couldn't know that he was
creating a persona. He smiled at her. He had a nice smile, and
he knew it. She smiled back and turned to her reading. He sat
there for a while longer, absolutely motionless, seeing his future
before him, knowing that his smile would be one of his most
valuable assets.

He stood up and pushed his chair back in under the table. He was pleased that he had come. He had learned a lot about himself from his reading. Ready to return the three books to the shelf, he gazed around the room. None of the other patrons was looking his way, and the two librarians, the pretty one, and the other one, the wrinkled old witch, were both busy. His eyes on them, he slipped the slimmest book, the mustard-colored one, into his notebook. He returned the other two to the shelf. As he walked by the main desk, he caught the pretty librarian's eye, and practicing, he said, "Thanks for your help, Miss Paternoster. I appreciate it. It really got me started." He gave her his best smile, his contagious smile. She smiled back in approval at the conscientious student who had worked for over an hour on his school report. He saw that he had conned her completely, and wished he were a little older. At home, he reread the chapter on the sociopath a few times. When he had the information almost memorized, he tossed the book out.

Chapter 9

The second floor teachers' lounge at Island Brooke School had recently been painted a pale blue, and although the color did not quite coordinate with the chocolate-brown sofas and the coarse russet wall-to-wall carpeting, the room had a cozy and comfortable feel to it, and all the teachers considered it a place of refuge for eating lunch, reading newspapers, correcting papers, doing lesson plans and socializing.

Traditionally, the first teacher to arrive in the morning was responsible for starting coffee and since Patty came to school early whenever Noah was flying, she often had that chore. On that morning in mid-October, she started two pots of coffee, orange handle for decaf, and then pulled back the drapes to reveal a wide bank of casement windows which looked out over the playground and beyond to several wooded acres which were owned by the town. It was a beautiful fall day. A few leaves were falling and kicking along the schoolyard, but much of the fall foliage was at its blazing peak, and the slant of the morning sunlight gave a surreal radiance to the sun yellows of lindens and the vivid reds of sugar maples across the way.

Patty had been looking out the window for several minutes admiring the splendor of the bright blue day when a tall, middle-aged woman entered the teachers' lounge. She was dressed in black ballet flats, a ruffled green peasant blouse and long flounced madras skirt which almost swept the floor. Numerous strings of red beads and chains of sterling and turquoise circled her neck and clacked and jangled as she walked. It was the other third grade teacher, Sue Strauss, the teacher whom Eunice had described at the interview as older and near retirement.

As a young woman, Sue's naturally red hair had been her greatest beauty, and it had been a personal tragedy for her when her glorious auburn mane had started to gray just as she edged over forty. She had immediately turned to beauticians to reclaim her color, but they had been unable to duplicate her natural shade, and by now ten years later, her hair was a rather artificial-looking orange red, which she wore, lacquered back into an elaborate curly cluster. In contrast to her overly formal hairdo, she always wore hippy-type clothes, which were vaguely reminiscent of the sixties.

Patty had heard on good authority that Sue had been a social activist as a young woman, involved in civil rights marches and anti-war sit-ins. She had also heard on good authority that Sue's finance had been killed in Vietnam. Whatever the truth to the rumors, Patty did know that Sue had never married, and had the reputation of being a prim and proper lady and a dedicated teacher who would always go the extra mile for her students.

Patty had liked Sue a lot at their first meeting. She still liked Sue, but with familiarity, the older woman had started expressing animosity toward Eunice and filling Patty's ears with personal grievances against many of Harold's policies. It wasn't in Patty's nature to be rude to anyone, but by now she was becoming uneasy about her unwelcome role as confidante to a teacher who always seemed to be criticizing the principal.

Sue's face lit up as she drew close to look out the window. "Good morning and it really is a beautiful New England morning." She stood at the window for a few minutes admiring the foliage, and then asked, "Coffee ready?" When Patty nodded yes, Sue headed over to the sink to take her mug from a wooden rack and pour herself some coffee. She then took a carton of milk from the refrigerator and added milk to her mug. "I must compliment you, Patty. You certainly seem to have hit the ground running here at Island Brooke. How do you feel about your first month?" She stood by the counter, stirring sugar in her cup with a plastic spoon.

Patty left the window and walked over in her direction. "My first few days were hard. There was so much to learn that I never thought I could get it all straight." Patty's voice took on a musical cadence and in high spirits she bobbed her head back and forth as she spoke. "Who's in which reading group — who's in which math group — who goes to speech therapy — who goes to resource room — who goes to Dewey for Reading Recovery — who gets occupational therapy — who gets physical therapy — who sees the school psychologist — who takes hot lunch — who takes cold lunch — who gets free lunch."

"But now you've got it all down pat?"

"I hope so, and thanks for all the materials. Everyone here at the school has been so welcoming and helpful." Patty made a mental reservation about Eunice who had been far from helpful, but she knew that if she mentioned Eunice's name, it would start Sue on one of her long-winded diatribes. Patty poured herself some coffee, and went over to Sue who was adjusting the beads and strings around her neck. They both sat down.

Patty went on. "I thought I'd be happy teaching, but I never thought I'd be this happy."

Sue frowned slightly, and leaned forward as her voice took on a conspiratorial tone. "I'm sure you'll have no problems. You're young, and Harold likes young teachers, so you won't come up against what I'd had to face. I've warned you about all the politics at this school, the favoritism, but you probably don't see it yet. I've had my administrative certification for years, but I don't have a friend at court, so I'll never get anywhere with it. Eunice, of course, is Harold's special favorite. She gets the best of everything. I think it's very unprofessional the way that she and Harold carry on."

Patty felt uncomfortable at the statement, which seemed to suggest that Harold and Eunice had more than a professional relationship. She sighed. It was bad enough that Sue was constantly criticizing Harold and Eunice professionally, but now she seemed to be hinting at something improper between the pair. Patty was considering what her response should be when the door opened, and Marielle and a sharply dressed Dewey came into the room. Patty was thankful for the interruption and noticed that Sue immediately dropped the subject of favoritism and started talking about the upcoming Activity Night, which was scheduled for November.

Dewey gave a general wave, tossed a copy of the *Hastings Morning Star* on the table, and continued his conversation with Marielle, "This whole thing is ridiculous. Why don't they set up a sugar free zone for kids who have diabetes? If they're going to ban peanut butter, they should ban all sugar products. Parents have to take some responsibility if their kids have allergies."

"And what about kids who are allergic to bee stings?" Marielle questioned. "Should we do away with outdoor recess for all the students?"

"There is another side to the issue," Sue ventured, turning in her seat, and joining their conversation. "Kids do die from allergies."

Not knowing much about the topic of student allergies, Patty picked up the newspaper and tuned out the talk. She had just finished reading a front-page story about a rash of burglaries on the East Shore when Ellen Cherry came through the door with a group of teachers. Patty watched as Ellen poured coffee and then sat down opposite her. "Anyone interested in going out for a sandwich after school today?" her mentor asked. "Al's investigating a hit-and-run and both my boys are on a field trip. It doesn't make sense for me to cook for one."

Most of the teachers were involved in the heated discussion on student allergies by that time and didn't respond, and Sue shook her head. "Sorry, I'm going to the hairdresser right after school today."

But Patty nodded agreeably. "That sounds good to me. My husband is working tonight too. He won't be home till very late." She considered. "And how about coming to my house for supper? It won't be much, but I made a dynamite clam chowder yesterday, and I can throw together some grilled cheese sandwiches."

Ellen gave a lovely smile. "Clam chowder. My favorite. I accept. I'll follow you home after school. I'll come to your room right before four."

Ten minutes later Patty was almost at the bottom of the stairs to the first floor when she heard the pneumatic hiss of the door behind her open with a swoosh. And then someone was clattering down the steps. "Hey, Patty. Wait up." It was Dewey. She stopped and waited for him to catch up with her, and he walked ahead to hold the first floor door open. The two started walking side by side down the corridor toward Patty's room.

"So, how goes it, Patty?" Dewey asked.

"Everything's fine," was her response. "Everything is just wonderful."

Dewey reached out his hand to touch her, caught himself, and pulled back. "I just wanted to tell you that Harold approved that personal day for you in December. So we can all go to the conference together." He pulled a flyer out of his pocket, unfolded it, and began reading about the upcoming conference. "It sounds really valuable. All teachers should know how to use the Internet. You just have to fill out the form in the office. It's the green one. Grace has them." He paused. "How are your computer skills?"

"Not bad," Patty answered. "I've taken a few courses. And one of my roommates in New York was a computer whiz so she gave me some lessons."

"Great. And it doesn't make sense for us to drive to Trumbull separately. We might as well all go together. So we can meet in the school parking lot at 7:00 and go in my car. It's a Pontiac. There's plenty of room for four."

Patty counted heads silently. "Four? How about five?"

"No, just four. You, me, Ellen, and Eunice."

"What about Sue? I know she's interested in going. She had her hand up at the faculty meeting when Harold talked about the conference. And I know she signed up with Grace. Her name was right ahead of mine on the sign-up sheet."

For a moment Dewey looked sheepish, and gave himself time by coughing into his hand. Then he shook his head. "No, Sue isn't going. Harold thinks that there should be at least one regular third grade teacher here in case any of the subs have a question. No, Sue won't be going to this one. But," he added, "we can get extra handouts for her, and I'm sure she'll be attending other conferences this year."

"Right," Patty responded, nodding her head up and down in agreement.

Patty stopped at her room, ready to walk in, but Dewey seemed to want to prolong their conversation. "Just so you know. Some of us get together for drinks and supper after school once in a while. Usually on a Friday afternoon. Wooster Street in New Haven. Pizza. Sallie's or Pepe's. So if your husband is away flying, and you need some friendly faces, just let me know."

"OK. I'll knock at your door."

"And I'll answer it."

"Got to run," she said, glancing at her classroom.

Touching her lightly on her arm, Dewey said, "OK, so it's a date for that Internet conference in Trumbull." Without waiting for an answer, he crossed the hall and went into the cafeteria.

As Patty sat down at her desk, she thought about the coming Internet conference. The conference that Sue would not be attending. It looked like Sue knew what she was talking about when she said there was a lot of favoritism at the school. As the children started coming into the room, Patty had time to wonder if anything else that Sue was hinting at was also true. She looked forward to the time after school with Ellen, and made a mental note to ask her if there was anything going on between Harold and Eunice.

Chapter 10

At four o'clock, the two women drove out of the school parking lot caravan style, and within ten minutes, Patty was leading Ellen through the downstairs rooms for a quick tour of her house. They ended up in the kitchen where Patty took Ellen's light jacket, and seated her in one of the brand-new wheat-back chairs.

"I don't have dining room furniture yet," Patty explained, "so we'll have to eat in here. Noah keeps a close eye on our finances, and he doesn't want to buy on credit. He's afraid we'll be sent to debtors prison or something, so we have to wait a year before we can dine formally."

Ellen nodded in an understanding way. "This is great. Your kitchen is cute. It was the same with Al and me. We had to wait a couple of years before our house was completely furnished." She looked around approvingly at the blueberry-colored walls, and the white lace curtains billowing at the window over the sink as Patty took the pot of chowder out of the refrigerator and put it on low simmer. Patty then reached up for two glasses from a glass-fronted cherry cabinet, and took an almost full bottle of white wine out of the refrigerator. She filled the glasses and started to put the bottle back. She stopped and laughed, "Let's do this right," and brought the bottle and the two full glasses to the table.

"Let's drink to Island Brooke," she said. They raised the wine glasses and clinked them together in salute and sang out in unison, "To Island Brooke." They drank deeply, again, and then again, draining the glasses.

"I needed that," said Ellen. Patty refilled their glasses, and quickly set the table for two. Then she said, "I have something to ask you."

Ellen looked up as Patty went on. "Exactly what is school policy about parent phone calls at home? Mrs. Hollister called me at home the other night. Noah was here and supper was just about ready. I wanted to get off the phone, but I didn't want to be rude to a parent."

"I don't think there really is a school policy, but I can tell you my policy." Ellen said, her tone light and amused. "When I first came to Island Brooke about eleven years ago, a parent called me at home just at supper time. Al was a patrolman then and had to leave right after we ate, and Matthew was crying in the background and Kyle was in his high chair throwing food. This parent started going on and on about how her son needed to earn all A's because he was on the fast track to Yale. After a few minutes, I just cut her off and said, 'Excuse me. You have reached Mrs. Cherry, the wife and mother. I think the person you are looking for is Mrs. Cherry, the third grade teacher. You can find her at Island Brooke School every day Monday through Friday from 8:30 to 4:00. Why don't you give her a ring there?' There was this long silence on the phone and then she said, 'Sorry,' and hung up. The word must have gotten around because I've never had a parent call me at home since then."

Patty laughed. "Oh I would never dare to do that. I just don't have the nerve."

"Then you'll just have to learn to enjoy all those calls at home," Ellen commented with her tongue firmly in her cheek.

They clinked their glasses together again, and saluted their principal. "To Harold Trelawney. Long may he rule," Ellen called out. Patty echoed her, "To Harold Trelawney."

They drank more slowly this time, savoring the last of the wine in their glasses, but when Patty went to refill Ellen's, she put her hand over it. "Whoa, I have to drive home remember, and it wouldn't do for a detective's wife to get arrested for a DWI."

Patty agreed. "You're right. After two glasses, I get really silly." She got up and put the wine back in the refrigerator and took out some cheese, bread and butter. She then stopped to stir the chowder on the stove, and started to make the sandwiches. She turned back to Ellen. "I really appreciate how you've gone out of your way for me. You've made my job so much easier."

"I enjoyed doing it," said Ellen. "I remember when I was a new teacher. I cried my eyes out when I went home the first day. And, Patty, someday when you're an experienced teacher, you can pay back the favor, pass it on, by mentoring a new kid on the block."

"When that day comes, I'll be happy to take on the role," Patty responded. She then said, "You know all the students in my room are so good. They're like a perfect class. It's almost as though they're handpicked."

"They are handpicked," said Ellen.

When Patty looked mystified, and said, "You're kidding?" Ellen went on. "No, I'm not. Harold knew that there would be a new teacher in Room 105. He didn't know it would be you, of course, but he knew that it would be somebody adjusting to the school, so he planned for that."

Patty raised her eyebrows. "So that's why I don't have any problem kids."

"Kids with problems," Ellen gently corrected. "Right. Harold knows everything about the kids, and he gave you a class that a first year teacher could easily manage. And I'm sure he's quite aware of everything you're doing. You'll soon find that he always knows everything that's going on. I don't know how he does it, but he does."

Feeling light-headed with the two glasses of wine on an empty stomach, Patty spoke without thinking, "Sue is sure that Harold knows everything because he goes through all the teachers' desks when he makes his rounds on the weekends."

Ellen shook her head and frowned. "Oh, no. That's just not true. Harold would never do anything like that. He does spend a lot of time at the school on the weekends, but he certainly isn't going through our desks. That sounds like something Sue might have made up. And when you stop to think about it, how could Sue possibly know something like that?"

There was a pause as Patty considered whether to go on. "Well, I'll tell you how Sue knows. Or at least suspects. You're probably not aware that Sue belongs to that high IQ society, Mensa."

Ellen shook her head.

"She told me that she doesn't like to mention her membership in Mensa because she doesn't want the other teachers to think that she's bragging about how smart she is. But she told me just to make the point about her story. Sue said that this all happened about a year ago. She brought in the monthly Mensa journal by mistake. It had somehow become mixed up with some papers she had taken home to correct. When she found it, she just stuck it in her desk and forgot about it. About two weeks later, she was at a meeting with Harold and happened to be looking right at him when Mensa was mentioned. He immediately turned to look at her. Then she told me it was like they were each reading each other's minds. Sue was thinking that Harold had been in her desk, and Harold was realizing that Sue knew it. He blushed and turned away. From that day on, she's been keeping her desk locked."

Ellen gave Patty a skeptical look. "That sounds like pretty slim evidence to build a case on. A look and a blush. I'm sure that Harold just happened to glance Sue's way, and she was reading a lot more into his look than there was."

Deciding not to prolong that particular discussion, Patty got up and served the chowder that was now simmering. When Ellen tasted it, she said, "Delicious. You're some cook, Mrs. Bass."

"I cannot tell a lie. I really didn't cook it all by myself. My friend Tish came over yesterday and helped me. She used to be a caterer and can do no wrong in the kitchen."

For a few minutes, they ate in silence, the comfortable silence of good friends sharing a meal.

Ellen broke that silence. "You know you have to be careful about Sue. You can't necessarily believe everything she tells you. Is she always running Harold down?"

"Well, not always," Patty reluctantly admitted. She went on, "What is her problem with Harold?"

"I really don't know. I guess we'll never know for sure. When I first came to the school they were the best of friends, but about say five, six years ago, they had a falling out for some mysterious reason. I've tried to find out what happened, but Sue is like a clam about it. I've even asked Sue why she doesn't just transfer to another school if she's so unhappy with the principal, but she says that she was at Island Brooke first, and if anyone should leave, it's Harold. I know she talks about favoritism at the school and from her point of view, I suppose she's right."

Ellen helped Patty clear the table. "How does Harold treat you?"

"Fine. Friendly. Always very professional."

"Professional," mused Ellen. "Al laughs at that word 'professional.' He says that teachers are always talking about 'professional' this and 'professional' that."

Patty laughed and then asked, "Do you think there's a lot of favoritism at the school? I know whenever I see Harold, he's either with Marielle, Dewey, or Eunice. They do seem like his three pets."

"They certainly are his favorites. I guess we have politics at Island Brooke just like at any other place. In fact, in case you haven't noticed, the three of them are like three assistant principals at the school. They have their administrative degrees, at least Dewey and Marielle do, so they do a lot of things a principal would ordinarily do, and that frees Harold up to spend more time with the kids. He knows all the kids by name."

"I've noticed that. He comes into my room about once a week and joins right in with the lesson. The kids seem to love him."

"They do. Say do I smell something burning?"

Patty jumped up and ran to the oven. She took out the cheese sandwiches on a rack. "Saved. I thought they were burned. They're fine as long as you like them on the well-done side."

She served the sandwiches on delft dishes and poured glasses of Newman's Own lemonade.

As they ate, Patty said, "I'm sure the parents would all go berserk if Harold ever thought of leaving. They all seem to adore him."

"And why not? He's really super with their kids, and a workaholic to boot. He's at Island Brooke by seven in the morning, and works till at least six. Then he goes home for supper and usually comes back at seven. He even works weekends and summers. I've gone by the school after nine at night in the middle of July and the light is on in his office. He really loves his work. His job is his whole life."

"Is he married?" Patty inquired.

"Yes. He has a lovely wife, Ann Marie. And a married daughter who's a lawyer out in Seattle."

"I've never seen his wife. Does she come to the school much?"

"Never. She's a teacher in Branford. But you will get to meet her at the faculty Christmas party. Harold has the party at his house the second Saturday in December, so save the date. We pitch in five dollars a head, and we all sign up to bring something — dessert, wine, chips and dip, hors d'oeuvres, whatever."

When the sandwiches were gone, Patty cleared the dishes and put out some fruit. She was ready to ask Ellen about any special relationship between Harold and Eunice, but decided that she would pave the way by first inquiring about a few others in the school.

"And what's Dewey's story?"

"Oh, Dewey kind of models himself after Harold. He's another one who never talks anything but school, school, and more school, and he's one of Island Brooke's biggest boosters. I know he socializes a lot with some of the unmarried teachers, and he's really well liked by just about everyone. He's originally from Vermont, and he taught English and reading on the high school level there. I guess he got tired of those cold, cold winters, so he decided to move to Connecticut. Once he got his sixth year in administration, he came to Hastings. You should know that he's considered the fair-haired boy in Hastings Public Schools. The word is out that the next big promotion in town is his. I find him really nice. One of the good guys."

"And Marielle?"

"She's an ex-nun, married with three kids. No question she's bright, but I find her a little standoffish at times."

"And how about Eunice?"

"Eunice and her husband live with her father in a big ramshackle house on the water in Guilford — at Sachem's Head. Her father owns the house. He's a well-known thoracic surgeon in New Haven. MacKay is her maiden name. She took it back after her first marriage failed."

"Does she have children?"

"A boy from her first marriage. He's away at prep school somewhere. I can't remember his name, but my Kyle knew him from soccer. He's a nice kid."

Patty was now ready to slip in the question she really wanted to ask. Were Harold and Eunice having an affair? It was on the tip of her tongue when they heard the sound of the automatic garage door rolling up.

Patty was surprised. "That must be Noah. He was supposed to work late. I didn't expect him till two a.m." Within a minute, the sound of the door closing was heard, and Noah looking handsome and neat in his uniform, was in the kitchen and meeting Ellen. He then crossed over to Patty and gave her a peck on the cheek and a quick squeeze before explaining why he was home early. "There was a bird strike in Boston on the plane I was supposed to fly. One of the engines was damaged so that's why I'm early."

Patty nodded in understanding. "Was anyone hurt?"

Noah shook his head.

Ellen looked puzzled. "What's a bird strike?"

"Gulls can't get out of the way of the plane and are pulled into the engine. They can cause some serious damage. No one was hurt in this case, but the plane couldn't be flown."

They exchanged pleasantries, and then Ellen rose to leave. "Well, it was nice to meet you, Noah," she said. "My boys should be getting home soon so I'll say goodbye."

"Don't run off," Patty protested. "Stay and talk with us."

"No, I don't think so. I think I'll leave you lovebirds alone. You two are still on your honeymoon."

Patty handed Ellen her jacket, walked her to the front door and turned on the porch light. Ellen stood at the door for a minute. "Noah seems really nice, and so good-looking. You're a lucky woman, Mrs. Bass. Have fun." As she walked out the door, she said, "See you tomorrow," and then looked over her shoulder and gave a big wink.

Chapter 11

Patty was getting married in the all-purpose room at Island Brooke School. Standing at the back of the room with her father, she could see that all the wooden folding chairs were crowded with friends and family, and she could feel all eyes on her as she started down the center aisle. Patty felt so happy and proud as she walked on her father's arm, and passed the people who were sharing her special day. With measured steps, she and her father headed toward the stage where Noah and the minister, Harold, were standing. Patty turned to her father, and was glad to see that he was strong and healthy again, the way he used to be before her mother's death. Then the bobbing faces of many of the important people in her life came into view — friends from school and her days in New York City. There was Linda Schwartz who had been her best friend in middle school, but strangely Linda was still only twelve. I wonder how she does that, Patty thought in her dream. There were relatives — her mother's three brothers from Quebec and their families filling several rows, and on her father's side, her Aunt Vera and her Uncle Ralph who were standing close together with their arms entwined although Patty knew they had fought like cats and dogs when they were married. And Tish was holding on to Rick's arm, and from New York City, her two ex-roommates Brooke and Ilona were there right next to Dewey who seemed somehow out of place wearing a caped Superman costume.

Then, Patty was on the stage and Harold was holding a brown soft-covered lesson plan book and asking her a question, "Do you take this man to be your lawfully wedded husband?" Patty was sure that she knew the answer to that question, but she just couldn't think of it. She was trying to remember what the right thing to say was when out of the corner of her eye, she saw a short, middle-aged woman with curly brown hair pulling herself up onto the stage. Patty didn't recognize her at first and wished that she would leave the stage and find a seat before she disrupted the ceremony. Noah took her hand in his, and Pastor Harold asked the question a second time, "Do you take this man to be your lawfully wedded husband?" As Patty was straining to think of the right answer, she looked at the short, middle-aged woman with curly brown hair again. Wrenching her hand away from Noah, Patty took to the air and glided toward her mother.

"Mom, I thought you were dead," Patty cried out. "They told me you were dead." Tears of happiness started sliding down Patty's cheeks as she reached out.

Abruptly, the dream shifted as dreams do, and they were in a different place. Patty and her mother were at the farm, a Dali landscape, as arid and treeless as a desert on the moon, and in front of her, Patty could see that wretched, weathered farmhouse with the broken-down porch. Before her eyes, the house began to stretch upward, until it was as tall as a silo, yet with a steep, slippery looking roof. Patty realized that the stairs inside would be steep, even steeper than they were that day when she was twelve. Her mother was walking toward the house.

Patty knew that she had to stop her mother before it was too late. "No, Mom," she yelled out. "Don't go in there. You're going to fall down the stairs." For some reason, Patty's words came out all garbled, and the harder she tried the worst they got. Her mother didn't seem to hear her or understand but kept walking toward the house. Patty started running, pumping her legs frantically to catch her mother before she entered the house, but she seemed to be moving in slow motion. "No, no," she yelled as her mother disappeared up the porch and through the front door of the house. "No, no."

"Patty, wake up, you're having a bad dream." Noah was shaking her gently. With a gasp, Patty woke up. Everything had seemed so real, and she could feel her heart beating wildly in her chest and her hands were wet with sweat.

"You're OK, you're OK." Noah snapped on the lamp beside the bed and the familiar furniture of her bedroom sprang into view. Patty sat up and clutched at his pajama top to keep the nightmare from returning.

"It was just a dream, a nightmare. It can't hurt you," Noah said. He put his arm around her, soothing her, stroking her hair. Gradually, Patty realized that it was only a dream, but she couldn't stop shaking. Finally, her heartbeat began to return to normal, but the fear of what had happened that day at the farm was still with her.

"Do you want to tell me about your nightmare?" asked Noah, gently. "Sometimes that helps."

Patty considered for a moment, and then said, "No. Not now."

Noah heard the fear in her voice, and knew that it was due to something more than a bad dream, but he decided not to press her. In her own time she would tell him. Wanting to comfort her, his words were gentle. "OK, that's all right. You're all right. I'll keep the light on for a while." He kissed her face as she put her head back on the pillow. Gradually she calmed down, and her eyes closed.

Noah said, "I'll hold you, Honey, until you fall asleep." And he did.

Chapter 12

"Do you know why Eunice doesn't like me?" Patty's question seemed to hover in the sharp November air for a moment as Ellen took her time about answering. They were out in the playground at Island Brooke School on recess duty. Streams of third graders moved by them in different directions while others around them played kickball or jump rope. Across the blacktop, Harold was refereeing a pickup basketball game, and shouting words of encouragement to both teams at the same time. Eunice, half a head taller than Harold, was standing right in back of him, a leather bomber jacket hanging from her narrow shoulders like a cape. Sue was at the opposite end of the yard with some boys who were kicking at leaves the color of tobacco that had collected against the Cyclone fence.

"Until you came here, Eunice was our resident glamour girl, so the fact that you're younger, prettier, and blonder might have something to do with it," said Ellen in a measured way.

Patty shook her head in disbelief. "I can't buy that. No really, what *is* her problem? I could tell from the very first moment at the interview that she disliked me. She usually just looks right through me when we pass in the hall, and she goes out of her way to be mean about supplies. And get this. Two weeks ago I reserved the stage for my drama club for Activity Night, and she came into my room this morning and asked me if she could have it for a panel discussion. I politely told her that I needed it for the play, and she told me that I was inflexible and unprofessional and stalked out."

"That sounds like our Eunice all right. But believe it or not, I do think your looks have a lot to do with her hostility. We used to have a very attractive kindergarten teacher here at the school. A former Miss Connecticut. Eunice gave her a hard time too. She finally just transferred out."

High voices cut the air, and they both turned to survey the playground. Four boys ran toward them chasing two girls who were shrieking in delight. Ellen and Patty both stepped forward and halted the running before turning to walk across the yard against the tide of children. A group of boys practicing karate and kicking at each other took their attention for the next few minutes. Then looking over at Harold and Eunice, Patty asked the question she had been holding back for weeks, "By the way, are Harold and Eunice having an affair?"

"An affair?" Ellen sounded horrified. "Absolutely not." She waved some children apart and continued, "Although Eunice would probably do anything to preserve her queen bee position at the school. I wouldn't put anything past her, but Harold's a complete innocent in matters like that. He's an honorable man who would never cheat on Ann Marie. I know there's nothing going on."

Patty and Ellen continued to drift across the playground toward Sue, making their way between eight-year old bodies at play.

A boy scampered by yelling, "Nyah Nyah, Nyah, Nyah," and they both called out, "Slow down." The bell ending lunch-recess rang at that moment, and the four teachers began separating the children and shepherding their classes together. Patty threaded her way among the knots of children and lined up her class. Standing at the head of her line, she let her eyes take in the scene before her, and caught her breath. The foliage was past its peak, the trees almost empty with only a few dry leaves still rustling down. The scene was right out of one of her favorite movies.

"Ellen, do you remember that scene in *The Godfather*. Where Diane Keaton is leading a line of school children, and Al Pacino is waiting for her in the back of his limousine. Look around. We're living that scene right now. I feel I have to decide if I want to marry the Don of one of the five families, or keep teaching right here in Hastings."

Ellen stood still and regarded the lines of children. "You're right. Everything but the theme music, but I can supply that." She started humming the familiar tune, and then said, "But as your mentor, I do have some advice for you."

"What's that?"

"Forget the Don. Noah's a keeper."

Patty's laugh was cut off by a sudden shriek of pain. She looked back and saw that one small boy from Eunice's class had fallen and was writhing on the pavement. Harold was quickly at his side, kneeling, ministering to him. In a few moments, the boy had stopped crying and was starting to get up.

Ellen smiled approvingly. "Harold certainly has a way with kids. I guess he's an ideal principal. Almost too good to be true."

Chapter 13

The young man stood on the sidewalk before the tall, narrow house with a bouquet of yellow flowers clutched in his hand. He could feel the perspiration on his forehead and under his arms, and knew he was sweating. But it wasn't the heat of the May afternoon. He was sweating because he was struggling to control himself and keep back his rising anger. He didn't want to be here. He wanted to be free of her. And he would be free of her, he thought defiantly. He had already made his plan, mapped everything out, but he was hoping that he wouldn't have to go through with it. He was hoping that she would listen to reason so that he wouldn't have to kill her. He had come today for one more time, for the last time, to convince her to let him go.

He studied the street for a few minutes. It had seen better days, had been residential at one time, but was now mostly commercial with only a few multifamily homes wedged in among machine shops and mom and pop stores. He took a deep breath and decided that there was no point in delaying any longer. He had to go in. He entered the tiny, shaded front yard, ran heavily up the railed steps of the porch, and pushed through the screened front door without ringing the bell. He moved toward the first flight of stairs, taking them quickly, and then crossed the landing and took the bare wooden steps up to the third floor.

He stood before her door for a moment, breathing hard, wanting so much to be somewhere else, wanting to be able to walk away from this conniving woman, and take the chance that she wouldn't carry through on her threats. He knocked once, and then again, heard some sounds from within the apartment, and then Debbie opened the door. She was wearing flower-sprinkled shorts and a faded T-shirt with a Disney motif running across her chest. Her bleached blond hair was pulled tight into a ponytail on top of her head. She was surprised to see him this early, and he saw pleasure come into her eyes as she greeted him, "Well, hello, stranger."

He handed her the flowers, and when she moved forward to kiss him on the mouth, he had to steel himself to keep from turning his head. She backed away and smiled her thin smile, the one he hated. He followed into her living room and took the nearest seat, the tweed armchair that always squeaked. She disappeared into the tiny kitchen for a few minutes to put the flowers in water while he looked around at her apartment. It was compact, just three small rooms. And it was spotless, but depressing to him with its odds and ends furniture from tag sales and second hand stores, cheap prints on the walls, and the bargain basement green braided rug over dull, mottled linoleum. Some half-finished knitting lay crumpled beneath stacks of folders. She made her living by typing, and her elaborate electric typewriter had the place of honor on a sturdy table between the windows. She loved to read romance magazines, and glossy issues from months back were fanned out on an open card table next to his chair.

When she came back into the room, he spoke to her in a neutral voice. "We have to talk. We've got to come to some kind of understanding on this. I don't want it to end this way."

"We're not endin'. We're just beginnin'." She set down the flowers very carefully, as though they were precious to her, centering the vase on the rattan and glass coffee table. Then she was gone to the kitchen again, and came back in a few minutes with potato chips and pretzels. She put the two wooden bowls on the coffee table and pushed them toward him.

"What can I get for you to drink? Would you like a beer?"

He thought back to the previous October when he had stopped by to pick up a report she had typed for him. He remembered how she had used the same words as she offered him a beer, and then without a beat, she had offered herself. "I'd like to sleep with you."

Momentarily taken aback, he had considered. Debbie Valenshak was a plain-faced young woman, certainly not good looking enough to be his girlfriend, but she had a quirky personality and made him laugh. Also, the tiny diamond on her left hand meant that she was engaged and safe. She would make no demands on him.

"It would be my pleasure," he had responded, and they had fallen into a casual affair. Once their relationship began, she did not want to take money for typing his reports, but not wanting to be in her debt, he wisely insisted and paid her by check. The clandestine nature of the relationship suited them both. Her fiancé was a long-distance trucker and was often away, so they had ample opportunity to meet in her apartment, or drive in her car to an out-of-town restaurant for an early supper. His senior year at college was an active one. He had a full schedule of classes, did well in sports, and dated several co-eds, so Debbie was merely a small part of his life. For him, she was a convenience, a sure thing, and nothing more. When he graduated from college, he had thought that he could just say goodbye to her and be on his way. But that was when things had started to go bad.

He shifted his position in the squeaky armchair and came back to the present. She had been blackmailing him ever since she had found the note that made his plagiarism clear. He refused the beer, and then said again, "We have to talk."

She sat down on the sofa opposite him and went on flatly, "We've already talked about this. Over and over. We've been talkin' about it for the last two weeks. I don't know what more there is to say. You know where I stand."

"I hate it when you do this. We're friends. Good friends. We've had a lot of fun together, but now it's over. I'm graduating in three days — on Tuesday — and then I'm going home. I've been honest with you right from the start. I told you that I have a girl back home, and she's coming to graduation. You can't be there too."

Her face tightened and her hazel eyes became slits. "I don't care about your girl back home. You weren't thinkin' about her all those afternoons here."

"Please —" he started.

"I won't budge on this," she interrupted. "I don't care. I'm not going to be used and then discarded like a Kleenex. I've already made some arrangements. I want to be with you."

He shook his head, discouraged, silence his only response as her mouth went into a pout that she had copied from something she had seen on a television soap opera.

She went on, "I don't know why we have to fight about this. It isn't as though I want you to marry me next week or anything. Why I haven't even bought the white gown yet." Although her attempt at humor fell flat, she continued to make her case. "It'll be great. We've had lots of good times this year. Why can't we just go on the way we've been? See how it works out between us."

"Debbie, let's not argue. Don't do this. Don't do this to me, and don't do this to yourself. Let's take a break. We both need some time to think about what we're going to do. I'm leaving in a few days, but it won't be the end of our friendship. I really like you. I'll come back to see you. We'll get together at the end of the summer."

There was no expression on her face, and her voice was toneless, as she said, "No. I will not go through the whole summer without you."

He decided to take another approach. He changed his voice, making himself talk to her in the gentle way that she had told him made her feel all warm inside. "I'm only going to say this once. You're special to me. You'll always be special. I won't forget you."

"Don't try to sweet talk me. I know what you're trying to do."

"But I'm only twenty-two. I'm not ready to make any life decisions at this point. I can't take you with me."

"Are you ashamed of me?"

"Of course not."

"Then I don't see why you object so much. What's the problem?"

He was starting to feel hopeless. He couldn't get through to her. He had actually threatened her with physical harm the last time they had met, but had backed off and pretended he had only been kidding when she said she would go to the police.

There was a silence and then Debbie played what she thought was her trump card. "I can't go on without you. I'm just feeling so depressed. If you leave me, I'll kill myself."

"Go ahead." His laugh wasn't pleasant.

For an instant, she saw him as he really was, and she recoiled. That was the instant when she could have let go. The instant when she still could have saved her life. But she was in too deep. She was obsessed with him. "You don't mean that." There was a quaver in her voice.

He realized that he had gone too far. He knew her well, and he was sure that she hadn't told anyone about the plagiarism. Not yet. Not while she still thought she had a chance with him. But if he alienated her, she would shout his secret to the rooftops. "No. No. Of course, I don't. I like you a lot. I don't want to hurt you. It's just that you're making me crazy with all these demands." He paused and then said. "I need some time to get my life on track. You know I'm starting a new job. I can't take this pressure you've been putting on me. I need some time." He was pleading now, and he hated the way he sounded. But he hated her more because she had brought him to this.

Her face twisted, and she spoke with anger. "A new job. I wonder how they'd feel if they knew that you've been plagiarizin' your way right through college."

His voice was loud in denial. "That is not true. I have not been plagiarizing. I told you the note was just a joke. My friend has this strange sense of humor."

"I don't think so. I think Heath has been writin' all your papers for you. I always wondered why your reports were mostly copies of typed material when you brought them here. I think Heath enclosed that note because it was your last report, and he wanted you to remember all you owed him." She paused. "And because it was your last report, you didn't bother to check it the way you probably usually did. I bet you just took that report out of one manila envelope and put it into another." She laid on a soft drawl. "And brought that note here for little ole me to find."

He thought quickly. "This is all just a misunderstanding. A misunderstanding. Heath and I sometimes work on papers together. We're in some of the same classes."

"Not very likely." Her thin smile returned. "Since Mr. Heath Raino goes to college in Michigan."

He gave a start at what she knew.

"Surprised?" She smiled. "Well, don't be. I just mentioned his name to a few of the guys in your dorm. I said you were planning to set up one of my girlfriends with some friend of yours named Heath, and I wanted to know what kind of guy he was. Lucky for me it's kind of an unusual first name. I know quite a bit about Heath Raino. You should be proud of what a good detective I am."

He clutched the arms of the chair so hard that his knuckles turned white, enraged that she had invaded his private life and talked to his friends. It was all he could do to keep himself from getting up and punching her in the face. He monitored his breathing and told himself to let a few minutes go by so that he could speak without anger in his voice. Finally, he said, "I came over here this afternoon so we could discuss this like two reasonable adults. You can't possibly think that you can force me to continue a relationship that's over."

Her pale eyelashes fluttered, and her eyes filled with tears. She didn't turn away. She wanted him to see that he had made her cry. She wept almost silently for a few moments. When she got no reaction from him, she wiped her eyes with the back of her hand as her temper flared. "You know something, Mr. College Boy, I type papers for a lot of guys at the university. In a way I'm a part of the college community. I think maybe I have a civic responsibility here. An obligation to inform the dean. I can give him Heath's full name and the university he attends. Maybe the dean can look into it and decide whether the two of you have been handin' in the same papers. Let him sort it all out. And Maybe your family would like to know why your grades are so good. And how about that job you're gettin'? Maybe they wouldn't be so anxious to have you if they knew what a cheater you are. I would think that honesty would be important in that kind of position."

He said nothing for a while, taking the time to collect himself, and when he spoke, he was amazed at how calm his voice sounded. He could have been discussing something that was happening to two other people. "You know this is blackmail. Pure and simple blackmail."

"I'm not askin' you for money."

"No, you're asking me for myself."

Now defiant, she said, "I'm not so hard to take. You didn't seem to have any problem with me before I broke my engagement to Vincent. You didn't choose—" Her voice trailed off. Then she became soft and pleading. "Be fair to me. I don't want much. I want to go to your graduation, and I want to go back home with you. We'll get a little apartment. I'm a good secretary. I can get a job anywhere. With both our salaries we'll do fine. You'll see. We'll have a great time. Just like it's been. No strings."

"You know something. You're skating on thin ice." The image of Gerry Weshie at Runnel's Pond popped into his mind, and he almost smiled through his anger. He went on, "No. My answer is still no. I will not be blackmailed like this." There was a clear warning in his voice, but Debbie failed to heed it.

The silence stretched out, and then she said. "OK. I didn't want it this way, but I guess I'll just have to make some calls." There was a tick in her cheek, and she spoke in a monotone as she reeled off phone numbers — the dean's, his home phone, and the phone number of his prospective employer. He winced when he thought of the power she had over him, and silently cursed himself for giving her information about his family and telling her about his job offer.

Then he put his face in his hands and reviewed his options. The whirring of the fan in the kitchen seemed very loud as he considered his position. There was one good thing. She didn't have the note. He had quickly snatched it from her hand after she had pulled it from the last page of Heath's report and read it aloud. But she did have the information. The information that could sink him. He thought about what could happen if he called her bluff and she carried out her threats and made the phone calls. His diploma held up. His job going up in smoke.

His father's scorn. He could not take the chance. He would not take the chance.

Finally, he breathed a heavy sigh and stood up. "OK. You win. I'll be here tonight. We'll work something out."

She smiled her thin smile again, sure she had him. "Where are you goin' now? I can make something for you to eat. A sandwich." She glanced toward the door behind her. "Or."

"No," he quickly said. "I've got lots to do. Packing. I've got to say goodbye to some people. Pick up some things."

"But you're comin' tonight? You'll be here?"

"Right. I'll be here at nine. Don't worry." An unwilling smile came to his face, as he walked over to her. "Nine exactly."

He smiled again and kissed her goodbye.

He left quickly before she could put her hands on him, hastened down the stairs and was out on the busy street that had turned blinding in the sunlight. He now felt he had made every possible effort, and was no longer responsible for what he had to do. Debbie had made the decision for him.

From her house, he crossed the street and walked across the city to a 'New and Used' sporting goods store. Ambling through the aisles, he spotted just what he was looking for — a used gym bag, — nylon — dark green in color — and big enough for its single purpose.

He also bought a black baseball cap, and a dark colored windbreaker. He was heading toward the cash register when his darting eyes fell on racks of shoes and sneakers. With sudden insight, he turned down the aisle, and with care picked out a pair of black sneakers, four sizes too large. Then he stood in line and paid for his purchases with cash, keeping his mouth shut and all his movements small, doing nothing to call attention to himself, trying to blend in. The bored cashier hardly seemed to glance at him as he took the money and put his purchases into a large white shopping bag with the store's logo in purple and green on the side.

Then he walked back to the university, crossed the campus, and turned into one of the paved parking lots, scanning the area for security guards or familiar students who might come over and interrupt him at a time when he didn't need any interruptions. He only saw four students in the lot, coeds laughing and talking and paying absolutely no attention to him as they got into a car. In the distance, he could see a few couples sitting on the lawn under some trees, but they seemed intent on each other, and he didn't think that they would notice him. He bent down on the pavement and untied and tied his sneakers waiting for the coeds to drive from the lot. When they did, he started to stand up, but got down again when a boy with a backpack passed by the lot without looking in his direction.

When the boy with the backpack was gone, he started at the first line of cars against the wall, trying the doors. The third car, a blue Chevy, was unlocked. He reached in and popped the trunk. He looked around to check once more. There were voices echoing across the campus, but no one was coming, and the couples in the distance still didn't seem interested in him. He walked around to the trunk, and pulled it open all the way. There were books, notebooks and clothes in messy piles. He quickly reached in and stuffed everything into the dark-green gym bag. Then he found what he really wanted — a tire iron. That went into his gym bag too.

He called Debbie at nine exactly.

"Hi, it's me. I'm still at the dorm. I'm running a little late. Can you pick me on the corner by the library where you usually leave me off? In about twenty minutes?"

"Sure. I'll be there at nine-twenty." She sounded happy, the way she always did when she was getting her own way.

He hung up the pay phone, walked out of the phone booth, and looked down the block. He could barely make out the narrow outline of Debbie's house in the night. Wearing the dark cap and the dark windbreaker and with the gym bag in his hand, he stood back in the shadows waiting for the traffic light to turn green and a line of cars to pass. Then he was on the other side of the street, Debbie's side, checking the now closed commercial buildings, shuttered storefronts and the front porches of the few houses. The sidewalks were empty, and everything seemed clear, but he made sure to walk at a normal pace so that he would not draw attention to himself. He didn't need some nosy old lady sitting at her window to remembering someone hurrying down the street. He turned into the driveway of the vacant house next to Debbie's, crossed through to her backyard, zipped open the gym bag and took out the tire iron. Then he stood in a crevice by the corner of the garage near some trash barrels, feeling the adrenaline surging through his body as he thought about what he was about to do. The minutes crawled by as he gritted his teeth and waited, hidden by the dark shroud of night, his eyes fastened on Debbie's car parked in the driveway.

The sounds of the night seemed elevated, louder than unusual, and from somewhere near he could hear what sounded like a Red Sox game on the radio. He remembered the last time he had been in Fenway Park. Another heartbreaker. The curse of the Bambino. The rumbling of nearby traffic caught his attention, and then he heard muffled conversation from the firehouse on the next street. His stomach was churning from nervousness and the heavy stench of garbage, and he had to swallow rapidly several times to keep from vomiting.

And suddenly Debbie was there, coming from the house. She was all dressed up, walking in his direction with a spring in her step, and humming. She was still humming in the final seconds of her life as she turned to unlock the driver's side door, humming so loud that she didn't hear the sounds of his running up behind her that might have allowed her to let out a scream. She had the car door open and was turning to slide in when he swung the tire iron with all his might against her skull. His rage exploding, he hit her again and again and again as she started to crumble and once more as she fell against the front seat of the car, her legs splayed awkwardly half in, half out. Looking down, the car's interior light showed him her terrible wounds on her head, and for a moment, he felt sick at what she had made him do.

He could again feel the bile rising in his throat, but he knew he must not vomit on the ground, so he swallowed in revulsion. He turned away, but then he had to force himself to turn back and tear the gold chains from around her neck and her left ankle, and pry two rings off her fingers. He picked up her purse and hurried back to the garage where he had left the gym bag. His mind was racing, and his hands were shaking, and he had trouble putting everything in the bag. Then he was ready to go. No. It came to him then. He had almost forgotten a critical part of his plan, a crucial part. Returning to her car, he carefully pressed one of his sneakers — his too-large sneakers — into some loose dirt not far from her body.

Rushing back to the dorm, he quickly showered and changed, and by nine-thirty, was drinking beer with two of his buddies on another floor of the dorm, making sure to get into a heated argument about the Red Sox and the Yankees which almost came to blows so that they would remember through their drunken haze that he had been there. As he was ready to leave right after ten o'clock, he also made sure to plant the suggestion that he had been with them since nine, calling out, "It's been fun drinking with you guys for the last hour, but now it's time for some female companionship."

At quarter after ten, he picked up the pretty coed he had been seeing and took her out for dinner. By then he felt exhilarated, high on what he had done, and how he had gained control. The fact that the gym bag with all its incriminating evidence was casually tucked under his bunk at the dorm made him feel reckless and powerful. He knew that he had a special aura around him that night, and he knew that his date, one of the most desirable women on campus, could sense it too. For the first time, she invited him to spend the night with her.

When he returned to the dorm the next morning, his roommate was still asleep. He took the gym bag from under his bed and opened it up in the bathroom. Everything was there. The blood-covered tire iron, the too-large sneakers, the cap and windbreaker he had worn, Debbie's jewelry and purse, the books, notebooks, and clothes that he had stolen from the trunk. Then, he went for an early walk, looking like the college boy that he was on the way to the gym. Away from the college, he pushed all the clothes and the sneakers into a dumpster, and then dropped the gym bag with everything else in it off a bridge into water. He watched it sink, and went back to the dorm, loudly announcing his presence to his still-sleeping roommate. He spent the next half hour talking to him and reliving in detail his night with the pretty co-ed.

Then he waited in his room all that Sunday, and while he waited, he used the mirror over his dresser to practice his lines, and the surprise, shock and horror that he knew he must show. The knock he had been expecting came at 9:30 the next morning, a Monday. He was glad that his roommate had just gone out. The two detectives introduced themselves and flashed their identification when he opened the door. Gill and Silverstone. Fat and Skinny. Both with short brown hair, blank expressions, and nearly identical cheap brown jackets. Gill was the fat one with blotched skin and a bulging Adam's apple. Silverstone was the thin one with bushy eyebrows and probing eyes. He was ready. He stood in the doorway. Silently, he counted. One Mississippi. Two Mississippi. He told himself to speak normally. Just an innocent guy wondering why two cops had come to his door. "What is this about?"

"We have some questions about Debbie Valenshak."

One Mississippi. Two Mississippi. "Yeah, what about Debbie Valenshak?" He opened his eyes wide yet still barred their way. Let them ask to come in. That would seem natural.

"Haven't you seen this morning's paper?"

One Mississippi. Two Mississippi. "No, what's in the paper?"

"She's dead. She was murdered."

He could actually feel himself go white. He backed up slowly and sank down onto his bed. They came into his room and closed the door behind them.

"Murdered?" His voice thinned out with the word.

"I'm sorry to break it to you this way," Silverstone said, "I thought it would be all over the campus by now."

He shook his head. "No, I hadn't heard. I hadn't heard anything about it. My God. How did it happen?"

"She was mugged getting into her car. She must have resisted. We're not sure. The mugger beat her to death."

He swallowed noisily, and then put one hand over his eyes. Some time went by as he played at being shaken by the news. They were waiting. He told himself to let them wait. Finally, Gill asked, "Can you tell us where you were Saturday?"

One Mississippi. Two Mississippi. He took a deep breath. "Saturday. Saturday. Let's see now. Saturday. You know, I can't. I can't remember. My mind is a blank. I feel so terrible. Poor Debbie. I can't believe this could have happened to her."

Silverstone spoke, "It's important. We're trying to trace her movements on Saturday afternoon and evening."

He said nothing through a difficult silence until Silverstone spoke again. "We understand that she did some typing for you."

He nodded. And then, he saw that this was the time when he should be able to remember. "Saturday. Yes, oh my God. I did see Debbie. I saw her on Saturday. Saturday afternoon. I brought her some flowers. She was such a nice person. I wanted to thank her for all the typing she did for me. I was over at her place Saturday afternoon about two. She seemed so happy. Just like she always was. Maybe someone on the street. Someone on drugs. It's so hard to believe. I just saw her." He shook his head from side to side. "What time was she killed?"

The two detectives glanced at each other, some silent communication between them. They both seemed reluctant to give him any information. He gestured toward the sofa, and asked them if they wanted to sit down. They declined, and then Silverstone spoke. "Her landlord saw her coming down the stairs shortly after nine o'clock. We assume that she was killed right after that although her body wasn't found until about midnight when the second floor tenant came home from work."

A question would seem natural. "Can you tell me anything else?"

Detective Gill sat down on his roommate's bed. "Just that she was going out. Maybe she had a date. Like I said, some mugger caught her in the back yard just as she was getting into her car. After he killed her, he took her jewelry and her purse."

He grimaced. "Poor Debbie. Why do things like this always happen to good people? Crime is out of control in this country. Something should be done about it."

Gill went on, "We're wondering if you saw anything out of the ordinary when you were over there. Anyone hanging around?"

"I honestly didn't notice. I was there for maybe for ten minutes. I just wanted to say goodbye."

"So you're saying that you left about ten after two?" Silverstone questioned.

"I didn't look at my watch or anything, but I'd say so."

"And where did you go then?"

"Came back here to my room. I had some packing to do. Last minute things. I'm graduating tomorrow morning and then going home."

"And how did you spend Saturday evening? Say from eight o'clock on?"

"Well, I was here, and then about nine, I went upstairs to see some buddies. We drank some beer to celebrate our rite of passage. I left them about ten, and picked up a date, and went out to dinner."

"And what time did you drop off your date?"

He shifted defensively before answering. "Hey, she won't get in any trouble, will she? She sneaked me into her dorm. I spent the night, and I got back here about nine or so yesterday morning."

The two detectives said nothing. He said nothing. Then Gill said, "So from about nine o'clock Saturday night till nine Sunday morning, you were with someone every minute?"

"Just about." He paused, and grimaced. "Why are you asking me all these questions?"

They didn't answer him. Instead, Silverstone produced a slim spiral notebook and a black ballpoint pen. "Could you give me the names of the people you were with on Saturday night from say eight o'clock on?"

Gill added, "And the times you were with them. And where we can reach them."

He furrowed his forehead and then gave them the information they requested, hoping that his buddies had been too drunk to notice exactly what time he had arrived at their room, and would only report that he had been there about an hour. He watched Silverstone make notes.

Silverstone asked another question. "Can you tell us what kind of a relationship you had with Debbie?"

A careless shrug. "Just a business relationship. She typed my papers this year. The woman who used to do them got married and moved from the area."

"And you and Debbie were friends?"

"Well, kind of. It was more like a business relationship."

"Her girlfriends seemed to think that the two of you were more than friends. That the two of you might have been dating."

He shook his head. "No, Debbie was a nice person, but we weren't close that way. Her girlfriends must be confusing me with somebody else."

Silverstone gave him a long look. "So her girlfriends were wrong when they said that the two of you had plans to move in together?"

"They sure were." He silently congratulated himself for turning down her frequent requests to meet some of her friends.

"Did you pay her to type your papers?" asked Silverstone.

"Of course, I paid her. She didn't do the work for free."

"Did you pay her cash?"

"No. I always paid her with a check. Why are you asking this?"

"We just need to be sure about you relationship with Debbie," Silverstone said.

"Hey. Wait a minute." He crossed his arms, thinking that now was the time to be slightly more assertive. "Debbie was a lovely girl, a very nice person, but she was a few years older than me, and really not my type." He gestured toward a few standing photographs of pretty co-eds that he had just that morning propped up on his bureau. He let some time go by and then snapped his fingers as though he had just remembered something important. "I just thought of something. She was engaged." He put his hand on his forehead and feigned deep thinking. "What was his name? I can't think of it. I can't think of the guy's name. I only heard it once or twice, but I'm sure one of her girlfriends would know. That's right. She told me about it. She was engaged. Have you talked to her fiancé?"

"We did. Her ex-fiancé. Actually, he broke the engagement in March."

"Oh, I didn't know."

Silverstone's smile held no warmth. "Debbie told several of her girlfriends that the two of you were dating."

He made no response to the statement.

Gill asked, "Why do you think Debbie told her girlfriends that she was dating you?"

He shrugged. "I can't possibly know that." He paused and mimicked deep thinking, cautioning himself not to overact. "Although you just said her fiancé broke up with her. Maybe she wanted her girlfriends to think that she had somebody else. You know to save face."

Silverstone asked, "Did you ever see Debbie outside her apartment?"

He took a moment to answer. He had to be careful here. "Let me see. Yeah. Once I ran into her on the street and we walked together, and a couple of times she gave me a ride back to my dorm when she was going out anyway."

Gill abruptly changed the subject. "You said you paid her by check. Do you have any of the canceled checks?"

"Probably. Let me see." He got off the bed and walked over to his large wooden desk, the only item of furniture that he had brought from home. He opened one drawer after the other, shuffling through a jumble of papers and supplies. Pretending to search in vain, he swore under his breath. Finally, he pulled back the flaps of a large packing case, which sat beside the desk and reached in for a shoebox filled with papers. With an overt sigh of relief, he produced some canceled checks. Gill rose to his feet and reached out as he handed them over.

"I knew I had these somewhere. Here they are. I don't know why you want them, but here they are." The two detectives looked them over. Then he noticed that they were looking at his feet. He said nothing. Silverstone broke the silence. "Do you mind if we look at all your shoes?"

He put a puzzled expression on his face, and gestured toward the closet. "Be my guest."

They looked at the shoes in his closet, and then talked together in low voices. "You have a small foot for a man," Silverstone said.

He said nothing, but watched their eyes.

"Do you have anything else to tell us that might help us in our investigation?"

"Not really. Debbie was such a great person. It's so hard to believe. I wish I could help. I really do. But I was there in the afternoon, and didn't see anything that looked out of place on the street. You know there were some people on the street, but I really wasn't looking around. I was thinking about graduation and all. Going home. My new job." He told himself to stop talking.

"All right. Thanks for your time. Contact us if anything else comes to mind. Here's my number." Gill took a card from his wallet and handed it to him. Both detectives then started toward the door, and although he knew it was irrational, for a moment he had the strangest feeling that they knew everything and were just playing him, and were about to turn at the doorway and ask him one more question just like the detectives on TV did before they pounced. But they kept going and went out of his room in tandem. He walked to the doorway right after them and caught the door before they could close it, watched them go down the hall and disappear into the stairwell. He waited a few minutes, listening to them thumping down the stairs. When he was sure that they were really gone, he closed the door and rested his head against it and shook with fear.

That night his buddies and the pretty co-ed he had dated that Saturday night told him that the two detectives had come by and questioned them. His buddies laughed, and he laughed with them when they told him how the detectives wanted to know exactly when he had arrived and when he had left their room. They told the detectives that they hadn't noted the exact time that he had shown up, but they had picked up on his suggestion, and said that he had been drinking beer with them from about nine to about ten. And they really believed that. When he saw that they had given him an alibi, he drew a deep breath of satisfaction and started to feel safe. That evening was a time of celebration for him because he was sure that he had gotten away with murder.

But he woke up in the middle of the night, thinking of a loose end, a loose end he hadn't tied up. The out-of-town restaurants where he had occasionally taken Debbie. If someone from one of those restaurants came forward and told how he and Debbie had been there together, the detectives would know that he had lied to them, and everything would unravel.

It was then that he started to worry. He worried about the police the next day as he graduated with honors. He worried about them when he went home. He worried about them for a long time.

Chapter 14

Rick often said that the East Shore between New Haven and New London was Connecticut's best-kept secret, and Patty agreed. A chain of affluent suburban communities with a touch of Cape Cod — she thought —and without the hordes of tourists. To her each of the familiar towns sprawled on Long Island Sound — East Haven, Branford, Guilford, Hastings, Madison, Clinton, WestBrooke, Old SayBrooke, and Old Lyme — had its own special character and charm with picture perfect beaches, quaint antique shops and fine seafood and Italian restaurants. Each of the shoreline towns was also bisected by both Interstate 95 and the Post Road, Route 1, so there was quick access to the art galleries, museums and theaters of the nearby cities, and to the shopping outlets, aquariums and Indian gambling casinos of southeastern Connecticut — and only two and a half hours away from her friends in Manhattan.

"Guilford is for class, Madison is for money, and Clinton is for clams."

"What's that mean?" asked Noah as he turned his car into the paved parking lot alongside the boardwalk at Hastings Beach.

"Just an old saying about the towns on the East Shore," replied Patty.

They parked and started walking toward the beach. "And what about Hastings?" he asked. "It's not mentioned."

"Hastings is of course the best and the biggest town so it doesn't have to be mentioned." Patty stood on tiptoes and planted a kiss on his lips. "And of course Hastings has us."

Their fingers laced together, they passed slowly by roller-bladers in the parking lot and runners on the boardwalk, and then crossed over and scrambled down the path that led to the beach. Patty and Noah both loved walking by the water, and Hastings Beach, a half-mile stretch of sand and rocks located at the southern tip of town directly on Long Island Sound, had been a special place for them since the summer of their courtship when they had often come for long walks by the water, clam bakes, fireworks, and to hear rock bands playing in the warm evenings.

On that Friday, they had slept in, and after a leisurely lunch of Thanksgiving leftovers, had decided to spend the afternoon at the beach despite the overcast skies. Dressing for the raw dampness of the late November day, they had put on jeans and cream-colored Aran Island sweaters. Patty had also tied a colorful scarf around her head. The beach itself, they saw, was deserted except for two other lovers walking close together near the boarded-up concession stand.

The day might be dreary, but Patty was still basking in the glow of love in the morning, and was content in Noah's presence. She looked out over the sound and thought beautiful the way the cloudbanks merged almost seamlessly with the water. They walked the length of the beach chatting comfortably and inhaling the salty air.

"Do you miss living on the shore?" she asked, playfully. "Do you miss your bachelor days with all those wild parties at your beach house?"

"Not really," he answered, "And not quite as wild as you think."

Patty knew that Noah had shared a rental on the water with three other pilots during his single days, and she had heard that young women had always been lounging around — swimming, sunning, drinking and cooking. Tish had also told her that Noah had been something of a womanizer when he was single.

"I did share a rental on the water before I bought the house, but I don't want you to think that I was some kind of Casanova with blondes running in and out at all times. That's somewhat overstated. Tish did stop by the beach house one time, and there happened to be a few blondes there, but you forget that I lived with three other pilots, so I was only responsible for a quarter of the girls that she saw."

Patty took Noah's explanation to heart. She knew that he had been rather wild in his youth, but that wasn't important to her. It was a subject they usually avoided, and Patty was sure that he had never looked at another woman since they had met.

Noah reached over and playfully pushed back her scarf and ruffled her hair. "And how could I miss my bachelor days when I have you? I love you, Patty Cakes. You make me forget I ever knew any other women."

Patty took the compliment smugly, and shook her blond hair into the light wind. Then using the scarf as a prop, she began dancing on the rippled sand close to the water, singing in her light contralto and snapping her fingers over her head, strutting and prancing like a rock star. Noah watched her for a few minutes and then joining in the fun, made a motion as though to dive in. Her face full of laughter, she challenged him, "I dare you and double dare you to go into this water."

With that, they both rushed to take off their sneakers and socks and rolled up their jeans as high as they would go, and put their feet in the cold waves. Jumping back, Patty was the first to make circles in the water with her hand and to slap the cold water at Noah, and then they were both laughing uncontrollably, running away and coming back, and kicking at bits of brittle seaweed at their feet. Continuing down the beach, they were deep into love play, tagging and tussling with each other, silly, half bent over with laughter. Patty felt like a teenager in love for the first time.

With that thought, she suddenly stopped and said, "Suppose someone from school sees me acting like I'm fifteen. I'm supposed to be teacher, a professional."

Half embarrassed, she looked both ways up and down the beach and then at the boardwalk where a jogger started to slow down. Then in a move that spoke of athleticism, he jumped from the boardwalk to the sand and crossed the sand toward them.

"Hi, Patty. I didn't expect to find you here."

It was Dewey, dressed in a black nylon running suit and a jaunty Red Sox cap, his boyish features looking attractive and flushed from the running and the chilly day. He had recently traded in his round glasses for contacts, and his blue eyes seemed to light up as they settled on Patty. She quickly put her sneakers and socks behind her back and made the introductions. "Noah. This is Dewey Willis. I work with him at Island Brooke. Dewey, this is my husband Noah."

Dewey stretched to his full five-feet ten as he turned to shake hands with the much taller Noah, and Patty had a chance to observe him objectively for a moment. For the first time, she saw something streetwise in Dewey's stance, and he seemed more attractive, leaner, more muscular, away from the school environment.

Patty started, "I thought you weren't a jogger."

Dewey partially turned and pointed his thumb behind him. "I live in one of the condos over there, so I just recently started jogging on the boardwalk."

When Dewey turned back to look at Patty, there was a lopsided smile on his face. "And how are you enjoying the long weekend?"

"I can really say I needed the break." Still embarrassed at the unexpected interruption, and searching for something to keep the conversation going, she said, "I haven't exactly been a lady of leisure though. I cooked my first turkey yesterday with all the trimming. And we had a few people over — my father, my best friend and her two daughters, and my two ex-roommates from New York. It was pretty hectic. How about you?"

Dewey gave an engaging grin, and said wistfully, "I didn't really celebrate."

Patty raised her eyebrows. "No turkey?"

Dewey shook his head. "Afraid not. You know my family's up in Vermont, and I just didn't have the time to go home. And unfortunately I didn't get any invitations. But I did cook something, and settled in to do some writing. I wanted to finish up a grant proposal that I've been working on." Dewey paused and then suggested, "Maybe the three of us can go running on the boardwalk someday."

"I don't run," Noah answered. "Trick knee."

Dewey nodded in understanding and then looked over at Patty. "Guess I'd better get going. Let you two get back to whatever you were doing. See you Monday, Patty."

He turned to move away, looked back, and, belatedly, added, "Nice to meet you, Noah." He gave a wave, crossed the sand, and athletically jumped back up on the boardwalk. He jogged away at a good clip. Patty and Noah turned to watch him bob away until he has disappeared from their sight.

"Who is this Dewey Willis?" asked Noah.

"The reading specialist at school. He's given me all kinds of materials. He's helped me a lot. Second only to Ellen. He's a really nice guy. Very hardworking. Very ambitious."

"Seems like a likable guy."

Patty agreed. "Oh, he is. I know that everyone at school likes him."

Noah thought for a moment. "So he didn't celebrate Thanksgiving? How about setting him up with Tish? She'll cook him a good meal."

"Wait a minute," squealed Patty in mock frustration. "I thought I was the matchmaker in the family." She stopped to consider. "But you know. You may be right. Tish really has to get over her infatuation with Rick. She's just wasting her time. I never even thought of Tish and Dewey together since they're so different. Dewey is kind of mild-mannered. You know the Clark Kent type while Tish has the personality of a talk show hostess. But I suppose opposites do attract. OK, I'll do it. I'll call Tish tonight and if she's interested, I'll talk to Dewey at school next week."

Alone again, they tried to regain the playfulness of the previous moments, but the conversation with Dewey had broken their mood, so they soon put their sneakers and socks back on and continued back down the beach. Then Noah moved ahead of Patty, and she hung back so that she could follow him with her eyes, admiring his masculine assurance, his easy stride and the long, straight lines of his body which were now so familiar to her. With his intelligence and easy temperament, he was perfect. Perfect for her.

Finally, Noah stopped and stood statue-still with legs apart and hands in his back pockets watching the waves rolling in from Long Island Sound and the ocean beyond, and listening to their rhythmic lapping on the beach. Patty thought what a beautiful picture he made against the sound. She couldn't take her eyes off him.

Then he took a deep breath of the salty air.

"New England is so beautiful."

"But Idaho was beautiful too, you've told me."

He nodded. "Yes."

"I suppose it's just like a set for a cowboy movie."

"In some ways it is. Plains and forests, mountains — the whole cowboy scene that you get in the movies."

"Do you think we'll be able to visit your home town?"

"Probably next summer. I'd like you to spend some time with my mother and my sisters. Everything was so rushed last August that I'd bet you hardly had time to talk to them. You'll like them. They're regular people. No airs." He added, "And my mother's always in the kitchen. Whenever I go home, I always find her there." Noah went on, making small talk about his family, talking about people that Patty had briefly met in the hectic days before her wedding, but really hadn't gotten to know.

A pale sun struggled through the now-pearly clouds and turned brilliant in the sky. Patty shaded her eyes and walked over to a seawall and sat down. The stories of Noah's family had brought to mind her own mother's face and voice. Memories of laughing and singing with her mother surged up. At that moment, the couple that she had earlier seen near the boarded-up concession stand walked her way. They were still holding hands, and as they approached, she was surprised to see that they were not young as she had assumed, but were people in their seventies. About the age of her father. And of her mother had she lived. "Good afternoon," the elderly man said, and the woman smiled as she said, "It's warming up. Looks like we're having a good day after all."

"Good afternoon," Patty and Noah both responded.

The sight of these two older people, still in love, as her own parents might have been, caused a drastic change in Patty's mood as her good memories were overcome by other memories. Idly picking at her sweater, she kicked the toe of her sneaker into the chalky sand at her feet, and then stared out to where

Long island Sound and the sky met. She tried to remember the happy days when her father and mother were so in love, but all she could think of was that terrible day at the farm.

After a few minutes Noah came over to her. "Where are you?"

For a few minutes, Patty didn't trust herself to answer. When she finally did, her voice was barely audible. "I want to tell you about that nightmare I had a few weeks ago."

He sat down beside her and put his arm around her. She began in a disjointed way, her eyes distant. "I was dreaming about our wedding — not really our wedding — not the way it was — but a big wedding with lots of people — at Island Brooke in the all-purpose room — and Harold was the minister. There were lots of people I knew from when I was a little girl — I don't know — just so many people — crowds — and the whole room was full." She then leaned against him and recounted her dream.

When she had finished, Noah shook his head. "When you told me that your mother had died in an accident when you were twelve, I just assumed it was an auto accident."

"No, it was a freak thing. I never talk about it except to family."

There was a long silence, and then Noah asked, "What was your mother's name?"

"Celeste. Celeste Biscay Nelson. Mrs. Arthur Nelson." She paused and then went on. "We were such a happy threesome. My mother, my dad and me. The three musketeers. My mother used to call us that. She used to say it in French though, and she used to laugh and laugh when my father tried to pronounce it." There was a longer pause. "I can remember the day she died as though it were yesterday. It was the end of May, close to the end of the school year. My parents were both teachers, you know. Dad was a gym teacher in Guilford, and my mother was a special education teacher in New Haven. At some point, my father got the idea to start up a summer camp for disabled kids. You know, kids who wouldn't do well in a regular camp."

"Commendable," Noah commented.

"Oh, I think he wanted to help disabled kids, but he also thought of the camp as an investment, something that might provide financial security for the family, for the three of us. I guess he knew somebody who had done something similar and struck pay dirt. We were strictly a middle-class family, with a nice ranch house and two cars, but he thought this would be a way of helping kids and providing for our future."

Patty stretched out her legs in front of her and narrowed her eyes as she looked in the direction of the sun. "My mother was against it from the start. She didn't like the idea at all. She liked having her summers off, and didn't want to have a second job. She thought my father was taking on more than he could chew. But my father can be very stubborn about something when he sets his mind to it. He said that he wanted her to help out the first year or two, and then she wouldn't have to work there at all. I can remember how they argued about it. I should say they argued a lot about it, and finally she gave in. She agreed to the idea probably just to shut him up. I had my own preteen things going on in my life, so I wasn't too involved. But of course I was aware when they bought this farm upstate which my father thought was perfect for the camp. They withdrew all their savings, everything they had, even took out a loan, and bought it. I guess some old farmer had died in the house, and his heirs, living out of state, were in a hurry to sell it right away so my father at the time thought he was getting quite a bargain."

Patty seemed unsure how to continue and then just plunged in. "It was hot that day. I had just turned twelve, and I really didn't want to visit their old farm. But they insisted that I go with them one Saturday, so I brought my best friend Linda Schwartz with me and we sat in the back of the car and talked about boys and school. It seemed like we drove for hours and hours, but it couldn't have been because Connecticut isn't that big a state, but we were really out in the boonies. Living near the coast, I never realized Connecticut had areas like that, all farmland and woods, not too many people. We finally arrived and my mother set up a picnic lunch she had brought while my father showed us around. I remember how ugly the area was. An industrial waste. All pollution. It really smelled. And the farm was ugly too. No trees at all. It looked like the surface of the moon. A dingy old barn. The farmhouse was a dump. I don't know how my father thought he could ever fix it up. It was dirty and moldy with peeling wallpaper and ugly, uneven floors. There were three rooms downstairs and two bedrooms upstairs and the only bathroom was on the second floor. I remember my father saying, 'Be careful of the stairs. They're really steep.' Patty paused. "But my mother was outside and didn't hear him."

Patty blinked and put her head down so that Noah could not see the tears in her eyes.

"You don't have to," he began.

"No. Yes. I want to." Patty drew herself up and put her head against his chest, talking into his sweater. "We had a picnic in the yard on this plaid blanket that my mother had brought with her. Then my father said we would take a walk in the orchards, but my mother needed to use the bathroom, so she left and went into the house. Linda and I just kept talking and laughing. A long time seemed to go by and finally my father said, 'I'll see what's keeping your mother,' and he went into the house. It seemed like a long time went by again, and all of a sudden Linda and I stopped talking and we just looked at each other and everything was — like still. After a while, we heard my father shouting, and he was running from the house, and he told us to get in the car. We ran and got in the back seat, and I remember asking what was wrong and where was my mother."

Patty seemed to catch her breath. "And I told you this was out in the boonies, and my father drove and drove so fast. I held on and he raced into a gas station and told us to stay in the car. He ran to the door of the office, and through the plate glass window I could see that he was using the phone. Then he came back to the car and took us into the gas station office and told us to sit on these two chairs and wait there for him. The chairs were covered with that cheap imitation leather, and it was starting to crack, and this really ugly color — what do you call it, oxblood, and we sat down and we didn't say a word. And then we heard sirens and a police car went by and then an ambulance, and we still didn't say anything. And finally the man in the gas station asked if we wanted a soda, and he went to the machine and gave us free cokes. I spilled mine on my shorts, and I started to cry because I had spilled soda on my shorts, and I couldn't stop."

Patty paused and stared at a boat out on the sound for a few minutes as though that boat was the most important thing in the world to her. Then she went on, "Dad came back after a long time and he pulled me up from the seat and walked me outside around to the side of the gas station. And I could smell the gasoline really strong and he told me there had been an accident at the farm, and his face looked all funny and red and he said, 'She's gone. Your mother's gone. She fell down the stairs and she died,' and I guess I had known it from when he came out of the farmhouse and shouted for us to get in the car." Patty curled against Noah's chest. The sun had disappeared behind the clouds again and she felt a chill. Noah held her for a long time as her shoulders shook with sobs.

Patty put her head up and continued talking. "Everything in my life was different after that, but one of the saddest things was that my father and I were never as close as we had been. Funny, isn't it? You would think that my mother's death would have brought us even closer together, but when she died, he kind of isolated, had some kind of breakdown. I guess he was living with a lot of guilt. If he hadn't kept after her to buy the farm, she wouldn't have died."

Patty gulped to keep herself from crying so that she could finish the story that Noah had never heard before. "After my mother's death, I became depressed and just wanted to stay home. I didn't really want any friends. And Rick was wonderful. If he hadn't made time for me, I don't know what I would have done. Rick is ten years older than I am, so we were never really close when I was younger, but after my mother died, he was just there for me. Always there for me. And of course Aunt Vera too. I even lived with them for a while because my father was so distraught. I don't know what I would have done without them."

"Your Aunt Vera, Rick's mother?"

"Yes, she was really good to me. I can never thank her and Rick enough. And finally when I was a junior in high school, one of my teachers got me interested in acting and singing. She called my father and said I had a good singing voice and should have voice lessons. So I did." Patty paused. "And for a long time the only place I was happy, was on a stage singing and acting. And then after awhile, I taught myself not to think about what happened that day."

Noah squeezed Patty hard as she went on, "And I never went back to finish school that year, but I guess all my teachers felt sorry for me because when my report card came in the mail, I had all A's." Tears rolled down her cheeks but she made no sound. "It was one of the best report cards I ever got."

There was a long silence as Noah held her to his chest. "Do you think it would help if you went back and saw the farm?"

"No, I could never go back there. It's a bad luck place. There was another death when the farmhouse burned down that winter. Some homeless person had gotten in, and was spending the night. He was killed in the fire." She shook her head. "And my father can't sell it. No one will buy it. It's an ugly place and with three people dying there in such a short time, no one wants it. Some real estate agent up there in the boonies tried to sell it twice, and now even Rick can't move it."

"Is that the property that Rick is trying to sell for your father?"

"Yes, it's been on the market all summer, but people think it's haunted because of the three deaths there within one year. Rick said that next spring he's going to advertise it in the New York Times. He said the right person will come along. The right person. Sure. Maybe some serial killer could use it as his home base." She started to laugh hysterically, and her laughter quickly turned into sobs.

Noah held her for a long time, stroking her hair over and over, and saying, "Honey, it's all right. It's all right." When her crying finally stopped, Noah helped her up, and she blew her nose. Walking slowly back to the car arm in arm, she kept thinking about her mother's death. That day at the farm seventeen years ago had been so traumatic for her that talking about it now brought back the same horror. She hated thinking about the farm, but she was glad that she had finally told Noah the whole story. She felt safe with him. As long as he was there to protect her, no one would ever be able to hurt her again.

Chapter 15

Patty was awakened by the grind of the snowplow early on the morning of Harold's Christmas party. Shaking off sleep, she pushed herself up on one hand and studied Noah sleeping beside her in the darkened bedroom. She listened to the sounds of his regular breathing for a while and then impulsively reached out her hand to caress his face. She checked herself just in time. She knew that he had not gotten home till 2 a.m.

She had gone to bed the night before about 10:30, and had had a solid eight hours, and she did not want him to be sleep deprived. She withdrew her hand quickly before she touched him, and for a few moments listened to his regular breathing. Then she snuggled back down into a warm spot under the covers, and buried her face in the pillow. Her only thought before drifting back to sleep was to wonder if the Christmas party would be canceled. Patty woke again in the middle of the morning and padded over to the window. From her position on the second floor, she could look through the frosted stripes on the glass to see that Iron Weed Road had become a dazzling white world. She could also see that the snow had stopped, and the street had been plowed.

The house was very quiet, and she instinctively knew that Noah had gone out. She looked over at the bed and at his side, now a mass of tangled sheets. When she went down to the kitchen, she found a note tucked behind the frog magnet on the refrigerator, and read the brief message.

Shoveled the driveway. Gone for a haircut. Will pick up three bottles of wine for the party. Home about noon. I love you.

She switched on the weather channel for a few minutes and listened for the forecast: an Arctic front would be settling in over the area and there was a 50% chance of snow that evening. A quick shower and a call to Tish and she bundled herself up in a cable knit sweater, woolen slacks, a warm jacket, blunt-toed high boots, wool mittens and a scarf, and trudged the short distance down the block to her friend's house. As she walked in the middle of the road, she marveled at the subtly altered vistas that the heavy snowfall had brought to her neighborhood. Everything on her street seemed slightly unrecognizable, a foreign landscape. Snow-covered roofs on houses — snow-filled yards — snow-humped cars — snow-heavy trees with outlined trunks and branches as black as India ink.

When she rang Tish's bell, fourteen year-old Zoë answered the door with a smile and greeted her with, "Hello, Mrs. Bass. You look cold. Come right in. My mom's in the kitchen."

Zoë was an effortlessly pretty girl who had her mother's wonderful chestnut hair and outgoing personality. Between her low-slung cargo pants and cropped blue leather vest, Patty could see her bare midriff and involuntarily shivered. As soon as Zoë let her in, she immediately disappeared upstairs in the direction of loud music while Patty followed the smells of freshly brewed coffee, apples and spices to the kitchen. There Tish with traces of flour on her clothes was standing, dressed in new embroidered dark jeans which hugged her hips and a man's black and white chambray work shirt rolled up to the elbows with shirttail out. A black apron was tied around her waist.

"The apple pies are for tonight," Tish said, pointing to the oven. "Dewey is picking up a fruit platter at Stop and Shop, and I told him I'd bake something." She paused. "Watch this," she said, stepping to the middle of the room and tossing her head and swinging her hair, which had been cut into a boxy Dutch boy, look squared off just at her chin.

"Tish, you cut your hair. It looks great."

"I finally took your advice and got it cut and shaped. I went to that great place on Chapel Street in New Haven. I think I look ten years younger." She laughed. "Well, Maybe five."

Patty took off her scarf, hooded jacket, mittens and boots, sank into a chair, and looked around at the kitchen. She loved this bright, gleaming room. It was the heart of Tish's house, an oversized area ringed by custom cabinets and a selection of copper pots suspended on the terracotta walls. Plants and herbs in tin pots were clustered in the bay window, which overlooked the snow-drifted backyard.

"Coffee's on," Tish said as she poured two cups and added milk. She put the coffee on the table, and then added a platter of pastries, and some empty plates. She slid into the seat across from Patty, and broke off a piece of pastry and nibbled at it.

Noticing Patty's glances, she smiled. "We bought this house because of this kitchen you know. I was doing a lot of catering and making some good money, but I ate up all the profits." She laughed at herself. Then, looking as if she needed to do something with her hands, she began stacking and unshackling the plates. Her mood seemed to change as she took a swallow of coffee. She then looked at Patty over the rim of her cup with an unhappy look on her face. Changing the subject unexpectedly, she said, "I think you're right. I think Rick is taken. He's seeing someone. Someone serious."

"What makes you think so?" Patty asked as she sipped her coffee.

"You saw how he disappeared right before Thanksgiving and came back the next Tuesday with a dynamite tan? Well, yesterday he told us that he was going to Aruba over Christmas."

"If that's the case," said Patty choosing her words carefully, "Maybe it's time for you to forget about him and get on with your life. There has to be a guy out there for you, and I don't mean Rick." For the last three months, Patty had been dropping broad hints that Rick was seeing someone and was no longer available. She wished she could be completely candid with her friend and tell her the whole story about Jordana, but she still felt she owed her first loyalty to her cousin.

Tish stated to speak, but was interrupted by the sounds of both her teenage daughters coming down the stairs and bouncing into the kitchen.

Zoë came in first, followed by the taller Amy. The older girl, just fifteen, had on skinny gray hipster pants, and a red jersey, and her thick fair hair was plaited back into a herringbone braid and tied with a piece of red wool. The two teenage girls were laughing and playfully arguing, and seemed to literally fill up the whole room as large as it was.

"Well, I don't think the coach should have taken him back. Once you quit, you're out," Zoë was saying.

"He's our best player. Like why shouldn't he play?" her sister countered.

"He gets away with everything. He thinks he's the only one who can play. And I don't see why you're involved. Are you a cop?"

"Don't go there," Amy cautioned.

The two opened the refrigerator and reached in for lunchmeat, cheese, jars, bottles, and containers. Then Amy turned to Patty. "Hi, Mrs. Bass. Is it really cold out?"

"Yes, the sun is out but it's very cold. And the wind is chilly."

"He's really conceited," said Zoë, continuing their conversation.

"Only sometimes," responded Amy defiantly. "And he's not like that when he talks to me. He's really nice when you get to know him."

"Basketball players at the high school," Tish said, raising her eyebrows.

Patty nodded, enjoying the girls' adolescent energy.

Finally, paper plates piled with sandwiches, the two girls left the room. The last thing that Patty heard as they started up the stairs was Zoë saying, "Am I so not going to miss him when he graduates," and then Amy emphatically disagreeing, "Well, I will. I know he's abnormal, but I like him best."

Before Tish could get back to the topic of Rick, Patty went for the preemptive strike. "So how are you making out with Dewey?"

Tish cradled her coffee cup in her hands and thought before answering. "This is only my second date, so we really haven't gotten very far. I don't know. I'm really not sure yet, but here's hoping. Anyway I'm glad I'm going to the Island Brooke Christmas party with him tonight. It should be fun. I'm looking forward to it, and I'm looking forward to meeting that famous principal Harold Trelawney. Dewey really seems to hero-worship him."

Patty shook her head in agreement. "Oh, he does. He really does."

An hour later, Patty was back hurrying down the center of Iron Weed Road on her way home. Looking up at the sky, she saw that the sun was gone and it seemed colder, the clouds prominent with the promise of snow. She hoped the storm would hold off until much later that night. She was looking forward to the Christmas party too. As Tish had said, it should be fun. And she really did want to see for herself how Tish and Dewey got along.

Chapter 16

That evening Patty and Noah were a half-hour late for the party, and by the time they turned into Harold's street in north Hastings, cars filled his driveway and lined both sides of the street, and they found they had to drive a block past his house to find a place to park. Hurrying back with the bottles of wine in his arms, Noah remarked on the beauty of Harold's large timbered lot, which was lighted by floodlights. Patty agreeing said, "Looks like a lord's manor. And I guess in some ways he is a lord here in Hastings."

The house itself was a mid-size neo-Tudor, defined by prominent gables and outlined for the season by icicle lights. As they walked up the plowed driveway, they could look through the living room windows and see a tall Christmas tree decked with shiny ornaments and winking blue lights. They rang the bell once, and as they waited on the porch, Noah reached for her and whispered, "Merry Christmas, my bride." He then drew her to him and kissed her long and hard. Eyes closed, Patty lost herself in his presence and thought how perfectly they fit together.

They were just pulling apart when a short dumpling of a woman bursting with Christmas cheer opened the front door. She was overweight and round in face and body, with copper-colored curls peeking out from a Santa Claus hat. Her full red skirt swirled around her calves, and her hand-knitted sweater was studded with small Christmas ornaments. The woman quickly ushered them into the two-story flagstone entry hall, and thanked Noah for the wine. Inside it was crowded and warm, and festive with Christmas decorations. Christmas music played from somewhere deep within the house.

The woman greeted them with, "Merry Christmas. You must be Patty. Harold has told me so much about you. And this must be Noah," and then, "I'm Ann Marie Trelawney, or you can just call me Mrs. Claus." She gestured to them to follow her right up a dramatic winding staircase to one of the guestrooms on the second floor where all the coats were piled high in heaps on twin beds. She had a hearty laugh, and quickly put them at ease. "I'm so happy you could come, and I'm so happy to meet you. Come down when you're ready. There's a yummy buffet in the kitchen, and lots to drink."

After she made them feel at home, she bustled away, and Patty sat on the bed to pull her feet out of her heavy boots and slip on the leather, thin-strapped heels that she had brought with her. While Noah waited patiently, she walked over to the dresser and primped in the mirror, brushing her blond hair into springy curls. She then checked her makeup and her fragile gold earrings. Finally ready, her eyes dancing, and feeling very saucy and very pretty in her new red dress, she turned to Noah and said, "It's Showtime." Together they descended the stairs, smiling, hand in hand, all ready to party. The faces downstairs were mostly familiar, and within minutes she was mingling with the other celebrants and introducing Noah to her colleagues.

With her hand on the crook of Noah's elbow, Patty steered him through the crowd toward the kitchen. Then with their drinks in clear, plastic glasses etched with Christmas trees, they squeezed through the crowd again and found Tish and Dewey seated at the dining room table, with Tish holding court and delighting her audience, mostly men, with anecdotes about the real estate business. Patty slipped into a seat at the far end, facing her best friend and took stock. Tish was wearing a periwinkle knitted dress with a V-which showed cleavage. Her shiny chestnut hair was artfully tucked behind her ears, and her face was all dimples and dangling earrings. She looked happy and seductive, and just couldn't seem to sit still as she talked, bouncing along with her conversation.

Patty was pleased to see that her friend was doing so well and looked so good. Patty then looked over at Dewey who was sitting with his shoulder touching Tish's, a content look on his face, not saying much, but laughing along with the others. Success, she thought. Noah had been right. The match looked like a good one. Seeking Noah's opinion of the new couple, Patty turned to him but he was involved in a conversation with someone on his other side, and she herself was soon swept up in school talk. Later, when she did have a chance to mention that Tish and Dewey seemed to be getting along fine, Noah agreed and said, "They should pay us a finder's fee." He then stood up and gave her his hand. "I'm interested in the new couple, but I'm more interested in chowing down. That buffet sounds good. Let's go."

They threaded their way through the bright chatter to the kitchen but just as they got there, Harold, with a host's smile on his face, and well tailored in charcoal green pants, a red plaid vest and a green sport shirt, appeared in the crowd and greeted them. "Merry Christmas, Patty, and this big guy must be Noah." He gave Patty an avuncular hug and an air kiss along her cheek, and shook hands with Noah.

Then looking at Noah, Harold said, "We're very lucky to have Patty at the school. She's a wonderful addition to the Island Brooke staff. One of the best first year teachers I've ever seen. She has a wonderful way with children." Patty beamed at the praise from her principal as Harold went on, "And I understand you were in the Gulf War, Noah. I'd like to hear about it. Come on, you two. I'll show you the rest of the house, and we'll have a chance to talk away from all this noise."

Harold and Noah walked away together, talking, and just as Patty started to follow along, she felt someone tugging at her sleeve and looked around to see Sue gesticulating with a bottle of wine in her hand. Sue was wearing a colorful folkloric dress that covered her from neck to ankle, and her red hair was pinned back with girlish butterfly barrettes and looped forward over her shoulder in one thick braid. Her brown button-round eyes were shiny, and there were pink splotches on her cheeks and nose.

"Notice," said Sue speaking slowly and deliberately in an odd whisper, "that you will at no time find Harold and Eunice together at this party. They're always together at school, but when Ann Marie is around, they avoid each other like the plague." Patty was taken off guard by Nina's frank talk, and looked around to see if any of the other teachers might be listening. Fortunately, everyone else in the kitchen seemed involved in other conversations. Sue picked up a plastic glass and filled it. "They're not really fooling anybody. Well, maybe they are. Maybe they're fooling Ann Marie. They say that the wife is always the last to know."

As Sue turned to put the bottle of wine down on a counter, Patty tried to think of a response, which would allow her to extricate herself gracefully from the situation. She liked Sue, but she simply couldn't stand there in Harold's house, among all her colleagues, and gossip about him. She took a step backward, but at that moment, Sue reached across and took hold of her wrist. "I'm really getting tired of working under such unfair conditions at the school. I would complain to the union representative, but that happens to be Eunice, so I guess I just can't catch a break." She went on quickly. "And I suppose you've heard that Dewey is in line for a promotion. The rumor is that he'll be the next Director of Reading. Fred Ernst is retiring in April. Dewey will get the job on an acting basis then, and it will be finalized in June."

She lifted her plastic glass in a salute with one hand while still holding on to Patty with the other. "Well, Dewey deserves it. He works hard. Unlike Mrs. Eunice MacKay who does another kind of work to get ahead." Patty could only stare at Sue, finding her manner and speech entirely inappropriate, but not realizing what the problem was until she caught a strong whiff of alcohol as the older woman leaned forward. Sue stopped talking for a moment to gulp down her drink, and before she could resume the one-sided conversation, Patty removed Sue's hand from her own, and made a fast excuse. "Sorry. Can't talk now. Harold is taking us on a house tour. I don't want to miss it."

Patty quickly moved away from Sue, putting, as much distance as she could between them without actually leaving the kitchen, but when she scoured the room with her eyes, she saw that she was too late. Noah and Harold were gone. She checked the dining room and then walked to the back of the house. The dark paneled library, all bookshelves, glass-fronted cabinets, and family portraits, was filled with revelers, but again Noah and Harold were nowhere to be seen. Flowing through the crowd to the entry hall at the front of the house, Patty returned a few friendly greetings and then spotted Ellen in a forest green pantsuit, holding a cardboard plate of food and waving to her.

Patty headed over to her friend.

Ellen gave her a one-armed hug. "Merry Christmas. Where's Noah?"

"And a Merry Christmas to you. I don't know where Noah is. Harold was about to take us both on a tour of the house, but

Sue ambushed me at the pass, and I lost Noah. They must have gone upstairs, but I'm not going to prowl through the whole house to find them." Patty looked around again, scanning the crowd for Noah and then turned back, noticing that Ellen was alone.

"Where's Al? I thought he was coming tonight."

Ellen shook her head. "He had to work. I told him that we're going to Europe in June to celebrate our twentieth wedding anniversary, and he'd better not tell me at the last minute that he has to work, or he'll be investigating his own murder." She paused. "I'm not staying much longer. I only wanted to make an appearance. Why don't you get yourself a plate, and we'll sit over there and eat and catch up."

She pointed to a burnt-orange colored sofa set alongside a grand piano in the living room. Patty nodded, and followed some other teachers into the breakfast nook where a red-clothed table was heaped with hot dishes and cold platters. She served herself some pasta and salad from the buffet, and then went back to Ellen. They settled themselves on the sofa near a magnificent Christmas tree, which dominated the dimly lit living room. From their position, they were a way from the crowd yet had a good view of the festivities.

"There must be sixty people here," Patty commented as they ate.

"At least," Ellen agreed as she sipped her wine. "Just about everyone at the school will make an appearance."

For the first time that evening Patty was able to relax and really take a good look at the surroundings. The room they were in was well furnished and gave an impression of money and good taste with velvet floor length drapes, Oriental carpets cut in rectangles, murky oil paintings, and gracefully carved dark furniture. There was a fire crackling in the gray stone fireplace, and rows of Christmas cards, red candles and red-ribboned wreaths lined the mantel above.

Patty said. "Not quite a mansion or anything, but it's really nice. Kind of old-fashioned and stately. Some of this old furniture looks valuable. Really antique. I guess Harold does well for himself. I didn't think principals made that kind of money."

"Well, I can tell you that Harold's not hurting for cash," Ellen said. "He comes from one of those wealthy Old Guard families in Boston. A family of lawyers and judges. I think his father was a judge. Harold inherited some of these things when his father passed on a couple of years ago." She paused, "And of course, Ann Marie teaches. So they do have a nice income."

At that moment, Eunice wearing a beaded blue dress that exactly matched her eyes appeared in the room. She stood by the doorway for a moment, talking to two men who had walked in with her, and seemed to be waiting for everyone to notice her entrance, as was her custom. Her honey-fair hair hanging loose and heavy to her shoulders gleamed in the subdued light, and matched heavy gold glittering at her throat and wrists. Her long legs in stilettos, she then crossed the room like a model on a catwalk, and turned to wiggle her fingers in a wave at Ellen and Patty as she moved in their direction. For a moment, Patty thought that she might actually come over and join them, but instead she turned at the last minute and walked out, the two men following along like puppy dogs.

"Which is her husband?" asked Patty, secretly relieved that she wouldn't have to strain to make small talk with Eunice.

"Neither. I don't think he's here. He owns a steakhouse, and probably can't get away on a Saturday night."

They finished up their plates and stacked them on an antique pie table.

"Harold goes all out for this party every year," said Ellen. "And he also throws a big cook-out in June at the end of the school year. Wait till you see his back yard. It's huge. Goes all the way back to the next street. We all pitch in five bucks for that too, but that doesn't nearly cover the cost. I guess he does it to keep up school spirit."

Patty finished her drink. "I will admit that I'm totally impressed by Harold. He's living up to all the wonderful things I've heard about him. And despite all his fame, he's very down-to-earth. He's always so nice to me, and I've noticed that he always goes out of his way to be polite to you."

There was a twinkle in Ellen's eyes as she spoke. "That's because my husband's a cop."

"What do you mean?" asked Patty.

"Years ago, when I first started at the school, Al was on traffic duty and pulled Harold over for going through a red light. Harold got really flustered until he realized that Al was my husband and was letting him off with a warning. I think he's scared of cops. From that day on, I never had any trouble with Harold."

After Ellen left the party a few minutes later, Patty made her way through the crowd, stopping to talk to Marielle and her short, dark-haired husband, but with one eye out for Noah. Finally, she spotted him coming from the back of the house. She hurried over to meet him, and she let a hint of annoyance creep into her voice when she asked, "And where have you been all this time?"

Noah slipped his arm around her. "With Harold. First, he took me upstairs, and then he showed me the entire first floor including his den. I was surprised to see that he was a quite an athlete in college. Would you believe that he was a champion wrestler? I know about all the awards he's won at Island Brooke for academic excellence, but I was really surprised to see all the huge wrestling trophies he has lined up. And he collects guns. Some of his antique guns must be worth a pile of money."

Patty's full good humor came back to her, and she responded with a hand on her hip and a smile in her voice. "So you expect me to believe that my dedicated principal has had interests other than school? He's actually won trophies for what did you say? Wrestling?" She paused. "But I guess I can buy that. Harold does look like a wrestler now that you mention it. With those powerful arms, he could probably squeeze someone to death. And a collection of guns too? Now I see that Harold is really a man to be reckoned with. No way would I ever get on his bad side. I wouldn't want him coming after me." They laughed together at the absurdity of the idea.

They spent much of the rest of the evening in the dining room talking to teachers with Patty making successful efforts to include Noah in conversations, which often centered on school. After a community sing led by Patty and the Island Brooke music teacher, a few teachers started to leave, but then Tish and Dewey appeared and seemed anxious to settle in with them. The foursome made themselves comfortable on opposite sides of the dining room table and continued their conversation for another half hour.

Then as Christmas carols played softly in the background, someone called out through the happy din, "It's snowing." Patty and Noah went to the sliding glass doors and looked out in the back yard to see small flakes falling thick and fast through the floodlights to the ground. The party quickly broke up after that, and with coats retrieved from the bedroom and goodbyes hastily said to Tish and Dewey and others, Noah and Patty joined the stream of people leaving the house.

Outside, the wind was biting, and the snow was coming down fast and piling up in drifts. They ran with their heads down to avoid the gusts blowing in their faces, their hands tucked close to their bodies to keep out the cold. By the time they reached their car a block away, their head and shoulders were coated with snow, and they saw that the car was encrusted in snow and the windows were hidden. Noah walked around to the driver's side, unlocked the doors and leaned in to start up the car. Then he got the scraper and brush and started clearing the windows. Before she got in the car, Patty reached down to pack up a snowball and hit Noah in the chest with it.

"That's war," he called, laughter in his voice, "You're going to pay." He too reached down to scoop up some snow, but Patty had quickly jumped in the car and was out of his reach. Once inside, Patty shivered and hugged herself against the frigid air, silently urging the heater to hurry and warm up. Within minutes, Noah had jumped in and had leaned over to give her a hug that was all too brief for her. Then he was steering the car with one hand, and wiping the inside of the windshield with the other. He was struggling to see through the windshield wipers batting in rhythm against the snow, but the heat had come on and Patty felt cozy and cocooned and liked being cut off from the rest of the world.

She said, "Nobody knows where we are but us."

"Nobody cares where we are but us," was Noah's unromantic response, but then he looked over at Patty, and, his voice husky with emotion, whispered, "I love you, my sweet bride."

Patty snuggled in her seat, happy with Noah, as he cautiously made his way through the falling snow to the Post Road, and from there was able to drive almost all the way home to Iron Weed Road in the wake of a town snowplow.

Chapter 17

Noah was flying on New Years Eve, and Tish had a date with Dewey, so Patty picked up the phone and made plans to spend the evening with her father in the gray ranch house with white shutters where she had grown up as the semi-spoiled only child of doting older parents.

"I'll bring dinner. Everything soup to nuts," she promised her father. "Don't buy a thing."

Late in the afternoon of the last day of the year, she stood before the stove in her kitchen browning ground round, simmering tomato sauce, cooking noodles and inhaling the scent of garlic. While the lasagna was baking in the oven, she made her own coleslaw, and defrosted Minestrone left over from Christmas dinner. Fruit, nuts and fresh-baked bread from the Korean green grocer and her homemade brownies were already in a cardboard box. Shortly after seven o'clock that evening the phone rang. It was Tish.

"Happy New Year, Patty. I was just going to take my shower, and I didn't want to miss you."

"Happy New Year to you," Patty responded. "What time is Dewey picking you up?"

"Not till nine, so I'll have lots of time to pull myself together. And I do want to be here when the girls leave. I can't believe they're both going out on dates this year. Thank God it's a double date." She groaned out, "I'm starting to feel so old."

"Right, you're thirty-five. Almost ready for social security. I don't know how you'll be able to last through all the dining and gambling at Foxwoods."

"I think I'll manage. And don't forget the dancing and the show at midnight."

"How could I forget?" She then asked, "So you and Dewey are becoming quite an item."

Tish's laugh was loud. "I guess you could say that." She went on. "I suppose you've heard that he's up for a really big promotion in the school system. He met with the superintendent of schools right before the Christmas break, and he's the leading candidate. Of course, the job has to be posted, and other people have to be interviewed, but Dewey seems pretty confident that he'll get it."

"I hope he does, although I sure will miss him at Island Brooke. And I must admit that I'm a little jealous that Noah and I can't join the two of you tonight."

"Don't feel too bad. Hey, why don't we plan to celebrate the new millennium together next year?"

"It's a date. If we can. Noah will probably be working next year on New Year's Eve too." She paused. "Anyway, send my love and New Year's wishes to Dewey. And also to your girls."

"I will." She paused. "So what time are you due at your father's?"

"Eight. I was just thinking about packing everything up now."

"OK, I won't keep you. I'll call you tomorrow. Will Noah be home?"

"I expect him sometime in the late afternoon."

"So have a quiet, restful evening with your father while I party like it's 99." She laughed. "Maybe I'll breeze by tomorrow — in the early afternoon. That is, if I can get up."

Shortly after Tish's call, Patty packed everything up carefully, and slowly drove to the end of town where her father still lived. It was snowing lightly by the time she left her house, but she wasn't worried about the trip home later since the weatherman had talked at length about the dew point, wind and humidity, and then promised that the skies that night would clear.

Patty's father had been visiting her Aunt Vera in Florida for a month, so she hadn't seen him for a while. Although he hadn't been in good health in recent years, she was surprised to see how bad he looked after his vacation. His lined faced seemed to have an unhealthy pallor, and his sparse white hair seemed sparser than ever. He was wearing a long sleeved white dress shirt that was tucked into belt-less brown trousers with slippers on his feet. She scrutinized him across the kitchen table set with good china and crystal wine glasses, and saw that his eyes were watery and hooded with age, and he looked every one of his seventy-four years.

"Dad, you've been to Florida. Where's your tan?" she asked him in a kidding tone which belied her concern.

He just shook his head. "I went to dances and played bingo. I played lots of cards. I spent a lot of time just talking to Vera about the old days. I wasn't some kid on spring break. I didn't need to get a tan."

"How is Aunt Vera?"

"Doing great. She loves Florida. Rick called a couple of times while I was down there. Told Vera that he's seeing that ex-fiancée of his. That rich girl from Greenwich. They're pretty serious." He snorted. "What do you think of that after the way she left him high and dry the first time?"

Patty heaved a sigh of helplessness. "Rick's over twenty-one. I guess he's going to do what he thinks is best for him."

Her father frowned. "I got on the phone and tried to talk to him about it. I told him that a woman like that only wants him because he's got money now, but he just changed the subject. I hope he comes to his senses before it's too late."

Patty could do nothing but shrug. "Actually, I haven't seen much of Rick lately. With all the snow we've had the last few months, we haven't been able to run together, plus he always seems to be racing down to Greenwich in his spare time."

Patty heard her father mutter something about a fool under his breath.

After they had the soup, Patty started to serve the lasagna and coleslaw on dinner plates.

"I'll have to pass on the cole slaw, Patty. I can't chew it."

Patty lightly hit the palm of her hand on her forehead. "Hell-o?" she said aloud. "You know I know that." Then she asked her father. "Do you have anything in your refrigerator I can make for you to go along with the lasagna?"

"That's not necessary. The lasagna is a meal in itself."

Later as Patty plugged in the percolator, she made an announcement. "I want to tell you about my New Year's resolution. I'm becoming a vegetarian."

Her father grunted in derision. "So you're becoming a fool vegetarian like Rick. I knew he'd get to you eventually. He's always after me. He keeps telling me to stay away from red meat. He says that chicken's no good either. What can we eat nowadays, I'd like to know."

Patty went on without answering her father's question. "I'm becoming what they call a pesco-vegetarian. Just giving up meat and chicken. I'll still eat fish and cheese and eggs."

She stood at the counter pouring the coffee.

"Well, I'm making a resolution too." He stopped talking for a moment waiting for Patty to turn around and look at him.

When she did, he said, "I'm moving to Florida."

Patty was surprised. "When did you decide that?"

"Just since I got back this week. I'm in my seventy-fifth year now. My arthritis can't take this cold weather anymore. I want to spend my days in the sun with people my own age. I called Vera this morning and told her. I told her I'd like to live in the same area where she is."

"Did you talk to Rick about it?"

"Why talk to Rick? I can do whatever I want." He then added, "I'm going back to Florida in June."

"But Dad," Patty protested, "Nobody, but nobody goes to Florida in June."

Her father's face was now set in stubborn lines. "Well, I'm going. I'll stay with Vera for the whole month of June and maybe a few days in July, and then she'll come up here with me and stay for the rest of the summer. I want to see what the summer's like down there in the Sun Belt before I relocate. If I can stand the heat and humidity of June, I'm going to have Rick sell this house, and I'll move down there before winter sets in."

"Are you sure you want to sell the house?" Patty questioned. "You know some people live in Florida in the winter and spend the summer months here. You could think of doing that."

"There's no way I could afford that. The taxes are too high here in Connecticut. My whole pension goes for taxes. Rick said he'd help me out next year, but I don't want to take from him. It's not Connecticut anymore. It's Connectitax. It's even worse than Taxachusetts." His voice got louder. "What do you think of that? Worse than Taxachusetts. I couldn't believe what I read in the paper when I got back a few days ago. Our Connectitax politicians are planning to use taxpayer money to build a gigantic football stadium, and then they're going to give it away to a millionaire, a billionaire. Why don't they call their gigantic stadium the Circus Maximus and have chariot races there too? Those politicians in Hartford are out of control. It's corporate welfare plain and simple. And I'm tired of paying for it."

Patty cleared the dishes and washed them in the sink. "Noah says the same thing. He's very aware of where our household money goes, and he thinks that taxes are too high in this state. He's waiting for the politicians to keep their promises to do away with the state income tax."

"He'll have a long wait on that one. I used to get mad when I read about welfare in this state, but I'd rather see my tax dollars go to poor people rather than rich people. Our politicians are all going wild."

Patty could see various emotions running across her father's face. She could see that he was angry, but mostly she realized that he was scared about being left destitute in his old age.

"Dad, you know that Noah and I will always help you out."

"No, I don't want to be a burden on you too. You're just starting out yourselves." His color had become high.

When Patty spoke, it was in a quiet, soothing voice. "Dad, you're getting too upset. Let's forget about the taxes in Connecticut. Why don't we play cards for a while? Then we'll turn the TV on just before midnight and watch the ball drop."

Her father smiled in agreement, got up and came back with a pack of red-backed Bicycle cards. "Let's play some cards."

Chapter 18

The time went by quickly as they played two-handed bridge and talked, and then at some point, Patty became aware of the staccato beat of sleet against the windows, and the whistling of the wind.

"The weather is getting serious out there. I think I'd better get home. It sounds like a blizzard." She got up quickly. "Happy New Year, Dad."

Her father hoisted himself up. "Happy New Year, Patty. I'm proud of you. You've done well for yourself. Married to a fine man like Noah — and a school teacher at that famous school." His lined face seemed to lighten as he leaned forward to give her a hug.

Patty gave him a hug back and a kiss on the forehead. Her father had never been a tall man, but now with his bent posture Patty noticed that she was the taller of the two, and gave him an extra hug. She quickly put on her coat, wound her scarf tightly around her head, and slipped on her leather gloves. As she opened the front door, she could hear the wind howling and see the sheen of ice on the road under the streetlights. The snow was still falling through the lights, blowing and whirling high in the air. A car coming down the street started to fishtail and almost went into a telephone pole before righting itself and continuing down the street at a crawl. Her father came up behind her and looked out.

"Patty, it's an ice rink, you're not going out in this. You'll have to spend the night. Is there any way of reaching Noah to let him know? I wouldn't want him to worry if he calls the house and you're not there." His voice suddenly seemed younger and stronger.

"Not to worry. Noah told me he'd call about midnight. He knows to call here or at home. He'll call both places. Anyway, I think he might be grounded with this weather. But don't worry. He'll call." As promised, Noah did call just before midnight. They exchanged New Year greetings through static, and then he said, "There's a long line for this phone, so I can't talk. We're in the middle of a blizzard here. I'm stuck at the airport. Everything is closed up tight. Logan included."

"I can hardly hear you," she said. "There's too much noise on the line."

Noah then seemed to be shouting, but his words came and went. Patty did hear him say, "I'll be home tomorrow. I love you," before he hung up. Later, comfortable and warm in her old bedroom right at the head of the stairs, she listened to the sounds of the wind and the steady thrashing of ice pellets against the windows. Away from the cold, she snuggled in her yellow brass bed, the bed she'd slept in as a little girl, the bed she'd lain in as a teenager wondering if she would ever marry and trying to imagine what her husband would be like. She touched each of the old stuffed animals that lay in the bed with her, and then buried herself beneath the familiar Shaker quilt. Everything was as it should be. She was here safe at her father's house, and Noah was safe in snow-bound Boston.

It was after midnight, and the old year was gone. It had been a wonderful year for her — a year in which so much had changed in her life. She had finished up the work for her teaching certification and even secured a teaching job. More importantly, she had met and married Noah. Not really sleepy, she went over every detail of that day the previous January when she had met him, relishing each one, and thinking how if one small thing had been different, they might not have met. It had been a Friday, and when she came home from student teaching at Soderholm, her father was closeted in the den with Rick going over some legal matters. "I want to put my affairs in order," Patty had heard her father shout. Then, there was only the indistinct buzz of their voices, punctuated occasionally about a louder comment on what was obviously business of some kind.

But Patty really hadn't been interested in what her father and Rick were talking about. Her mind was elsewhere. She had plans to go to Manhattan on an early evening train and was rushing to get dressed when she got a call canceling the weekend that she had really been looking forward to. "Brooke has the measles. Must have caught them from her PC. Everything's off," Ilona had told her. "We'll call to reschedule. Maybe in two or three weeks."

Moping around the house and feeling sorry for Brooke and just as sorry for herself, Patty had almost missed Rick when he was leaving. But she hadn't missed him, and he had invited her to an Open House at his office that evening.

"What Open House?" she had asked.

"I can't believe you don't remember," he had teased her with a smile. "It's one year exactly since I opened my new office, so I'm having a little celebration."

"Oh, do you mean your new office in your new shopping center?"

"You got it in one," he laughed. "You're quick."

"And who's invited to this Open House?" she had asked.

"My customers and my agents," was his response.

"Well, I'm neither so I won't fit in," Patty had said, turning away, still in a sulk about the cancellation of her weekend plans.

"Oh, yes you are. At least your father is, so that includes you. I'm going to sell that farm that he's been trying to get rid of for years. He just signed a contract. So you are a customer, and you're invited."

Even then, Patty was not convinced. "No, I don't think so." She waved and started toward her bedroom.

Disappointed, Rick walked to the front door and then called to her, his index finger pointed up, "Wait a minute. Noah Bass. Noah Bass will probably be there. He's perfect for you."

"Who's Noah Bass?"

"One of my agents just sold him a house. He's a pilot. He's been living in a big beach house in Madison with a few other pilots, but now he's just about to move into his own place. A great guy. Mid thirties. All the women in my office really sit up and take notice whenever he comes in. He's perfect for you. I don't know why I didn't think of setting you up with him before this. And I bet you'll love Tish, the gal who sold him the house. She's got a great personality. Really funny. I will not take no for an answer on this. Patty, you have got to come tonight if only for a little while. You have got to meet Noah Bass."

Reluctantly, Patty had agreed. She would go to the Open House to please Rick, and not that she was expecting to meet the love of her life, but maybe she was a little curious to see this Noah Bass. So that evening she fussed a bit more than usual with her hair, and then put on an ankle-length denim skirt, a tight fitting red top, and her navy coat, and drove to Rick's office at his new shopping center right on Main Street in the heart of town. When she walked into the party, balloons and streamers were everywhere, the phones were ringing constantly, and people were talking and laughing around islands of desks and an elaborate buffet on a long table. She had met Tish right away. Accompanied by Rick and dressed in a vivid violet caftan, Tish walked over to her and gave her a friendly hug. When Rick left to greet some newcomers, she and Tish had talked easily, exchanged phone numbers and then stood together at the buffet picking at hors d'oeuvres. As the evening wore on, Tish had introduced her to a few other people, but then had moved away to take the phone.

Ready to call it a night, Patty had stood alone for a moment, and turned as the door opened and a tall, lanky man in jeans and a red windbreaker walked in. Here comes Don Quixote, she had thought as she noticed that their colors — red and denim — matched. She watched him for a few moments until she realized that he was watching her. Smiling before turning away, she then looked back to see him shouldering his way through the crowd in her general direction. As he drew closer, she had time to notice that he was very attractive, and that his close-cropped dark hair gave him a military look. Before he reached her, Rick cut him off, and took him by the arm. They talked briefly, and then they both walked toward her. By the time Rick made the introductions, she already felt an invisible link with Noah Bass

Patty spent the first hour of January 1, 1999, lost in her reverie, and finally fell asleep thinking of Noah.

Chapter 19

It was just after one o'clock on the afternoon of January 2, 1999. The snow had been cleared and he had gone out for groceries. When he saw the sign for Gallo's Pond he slowed his car. Then on a whim, he abruptly angled off the well-plowed state road in north Hastings and turned onto the narrow, snow-packed road that led to the pond. The road took him past some spruce-studded acreage and a few sprawling cedar-shingled ranch houses with big, snow-filled yards, and then to the pond itself. The cars were tightly parked in a single row on a ledge that overlooked the ice, and he squeezed in at the end. He put his car in park but didn't turn off the engine. He would only stay a few minutes.

The pond below him was a scene right off a Currier and Ives Christmas card with about three dozen colorfully garbed skaters in athletic motion, following their icy breath. He looked down with interest as he turned up his heater against the cold. There were entire families skating together, and teenagers showing off. He could see some newcomers wobbling along near the edge of the ice, and then three pretty young women in their twenties skating with agility caught his eye. For a moment he wished that he had brought some ice skates with him, and chuckled when he realized that he probably didn't even own a pair anymore. He followed the progress of the pretty young women for a while, and noticed that one of them was a lissome blonde who looked quite a lot like Patty. She was slim, had the same curly blond hair, and the same sweet open face with an up-tilted nose. But she wasn't as pretty as Patty, he decided.

Four teenage boys who had separated themselves from the crowd and started to play hockey suddenly caught his attention. He felt a frisson of recognition as he watched the boys shoot a puck into an old ripped basket, and he thought back to the hockey game with Buddy O'Hara, Jack Connelly and Gerry Weshie. That had been another pond. Another time. It had been years ago. But coincidentally that had been an early January day too.

He shifted in his seat as he thought about his past successes and the promise of the future. Early January was the time for looking back and looking ahead. He reached to turn off the radio, but stopped as Van Morrison began singing an oldie about a brown-eyed girl. He sang along with the music, but whenever the chorus came up, he changed the words to blue-eyed girl. He had always been partial to blue-eyed women. At the end of the song, he turned off the radio and for some reason thought about Debbie. After he killed her, he remembered how scared he had been when the two detectives questioned him, and he remembered the vow he had made to himself at his college graduation ceremony the next day as some long-winded speaker talked about seizing the future. The vow was simple. He would never kill again. And he had kept that promise to himself through the years. He was now a different person. He was now a good person. At least this was how others saw him.

He shook his head. It never ceased to amaze him how easy it was to fool people.

Although he had been tempted to break his vow several times, the thoughts of arrest and imprisonment had always stopped him. The closest he had come had been just a few years ago right here in Hastings. Marcetta Osborne. Mrs. Marcetta Osborne. A small brunette with a neat little body. Marcetta was pretty, maybe too pretty for her own good. She was married to a man who spent long periods of time at his car dealership, and she had way too much time on her hands. Active in the community, a professional volunteer, president of this, vice-president of that, she seemed ripe for a brief affair.

Occasionally, he would enter into a long-term relationship, but after the experience with Debbie, he liked to keep most of his affairs short. He did not want any woman to get too fond of him. He had it all down to a science. The excitement of the chase. Then twelve encounters. And then the breakup. The woman usually got the message when dates were broken, phone calls were not returned, and he was suddenly unavailable.

But Marcetta didn't seem to know how the game was played. Just because he had been seeing her over a three-month period, she had come to believe that she owned him. Thinking about it now, he doubted that she was even that much in love with him, but he must have hurt her pride. Maybe she wanted to be the one who did the breaking up. She had a husband and two young children, yet she refused to leave him alone. And this was the part that was hard to believe — she had started stalking him. Stalking him. It was almost comical. She had no idea how close she had come to being victim number three.

He thought about how she had kept calling and calling him, and when he began to refuse to take her calls, she had started sending him unsigned letters, which were vaguely threatening. He remembered how he got to hate going out to the mailbox to find the perfumed salmon-colored envelopes.

Finally he had agreed to see her one more time. They had gotten into his car after a PTA meeting, and he had driven her to a beach in Branford. He had purposefully parked on the paved parking lot near a lamppost, so that there was dim light in the car, and she could see his face. Then he had cupped her chin in one hand, held her two wrists with the other, and squeezed very hard. She had cried out in pain, but he hadn't let her go. Instead, he had very calmly said, "I want you to look at me and listen very carefully to what I'm going to say. Your life may depend on it. The affair is over. I want you to stop bothering me. No more phone calls. No more letters. If you don't stop, I won't be responsible for what happens to you."

Again, he had to give her credit for being smart. She must have seen something in his face, recognized the danger she was in. Something that Debbie hadn't been able to recognize. He could almost see the electric light bulb going on in her head. When he had released her chin, she had spoken very quickly, "One of my girlfriends knows I'm with you tonight."

And then, when he had let go of her wrists, she had rushed to pull away, opened the door, and backed out of his car. "You don't have to come after me," she had pleaded. "I'll never bother you again." He had then thrown her bag out onto the pavement, and pulled away without a backward glance, leaving her by the deserted beach to fend for herself. And that was the end of that. There were no more calls, no more unsigned letters in his mailbox, and no more stalking. On the occasions he had seen her since then, she was always formal and polite, giving absolutely no hint of their former relationship or the threat he had made to her.

At that moment, a tapping on his window startled him, causing him to jump. It was a man he knew, crowding with his wife and their four school children alongside his car. He smiled and returned their friendly waves as they continued by. Then he watched them make their way down to the pond and change into skates. The whole family turned and waved up at him once more just before they stepped onto the ice. He waved back, and again smiled his practiced smile.

He was now ready to go. He switched the radio back on, and turned to the 880 News. The announcer was talking about New Year's resolutions as he put his car in reverse and backed up. Turning back onto the narrow, snow packed road, it occurred to him that just for fun he ought to make a resolution. He decided he would, and spoke aloud to the announcer at the WCBS radio station in New York City who could not hear him.

"I have some a resolution that should get your attention. Listen carefully. I resolve not to kill anyone during the coming year." He laughed softly at the thought. This was a resolution that he did not intend to break. He had too much to lose now.

Millions of people all over the world were making New Year's resolutions that January. Some would keep them. He had no way of knowing it on that cold January day, but he would not.

Chapter 20

Harold was very strict about beginning his faculty meetings promptly at 3:45, no exceptions, and Patty always made it her business to get to the second floor library-media center early to get a good seat near the front. As a non-tenured first year teacher, she was very conscious of being observed, and went out of her way to be visible and to make a good impression. She loved her job, and she did not want to give any possible reason to make her lose it. And her mind was often on the written evaluation that she would be getting the first week of June.

The children had already been dismissed for the day, and she was preparing to leave her room and go upstairs for the January faculty meeting when a small girl with brown hair curling to her shoulders came back to the classroom, crying, tears streaming down her face. It was Janie Viglione, one of her third grade students. Patty rushed right over and stooped down to see eye to eye with the child. "Janie, what's wrong?"

"I missed the bus. I went to the lunch room for my lunch box, and I missed the bus." Her lower lip was stuck out, and her crying became louder as she put her head down.

"Oh, Janie, that's nothing. We all miss buses once in a while."

Janie picked her head up and looked right at Patty. "We do?"

"Sure. This is no big problem. We'll take care of it. Let's call your mom and see if she can come get you."

With Janie's hand in hers, Patty led the way to the office and found the telephone was free. She pushed nine for an outside line, and then let Janie call home. She listened while Janie explained the situation, and then the little girl handed her the phone.

"My mom wants to talk to you."

Patty took the phone with one eye on the clock. She didn't want to be late for the faculty meeting.

"I'll be there in five minutes, Mrs. Bass, but would you wait with Janie? She's nervous."

"I'd be happy to Mrs. Viglione. We'll be right inside the side door by the parking lot."

Patty walked Janie over to the side door and stood talking with her. It was ten minutes later, not five, when Mrs. Viglione pulled up in the driveway between the school and the large parking lot and honked, and when a now-smiling Janie spotted her mother's car, she ran right out the door, calling back, "Bye, Mrs. Bass. Thanks for waiting with me."

Time was short so Patty hurried through the door to the stairway and was about to ascend the stairs when Mrs. Cushman, a talkative, nervous woman, coming down from the second floor crossed in front of her and caged her in by putting both arms against the wall.

"Mrs. Bass. Just the person I was looking for. I wanted you to be the first to know that we'll be moving to Kentucky next month. My husband got a wonderful promotion. And I wanted you to know how much my Zachary will miss you. You are the best teacher he has ever had. I love those monthly phone calls that you make. Most teachers only call when one of my kids has done something wrong, but it's so good to hear from a teacher when everything is going fine. And Zachary just loves going to the drama club. It was so nice of you to give him that part in the holiday play and I—" Quite aware of the time, Patty made several attempts to break in, but each time Mrs. Cushman did not seem to notice, but just talked on, caught up in the telling of her family's good fortune.

"This is the opportunity of a lifetime for us. My husband just couldn't turn it down. Of course we'll miss this wonderful school. With all its awards. And Mr. Trelawney. Such a wonderful man. And you are such an outstanding teacher. Couldn't we pack you up in a suitcase and take you to Kentucky?"

At that point, Patty made an elaborate show of looking at her watch, and then ducked her head down and wiggled under Mrs. Cushman's arm.

"Oh, look at the time. Excuse me. I'm late for a meeting. I'll call you tomorrow Mrs. Cushman, and we can make plans for Zachary's transition. I've got to run now." Patty was already moving up the stairs double time, and then she looked over her shoulder and called, "Thanks for the compliments. Zachary is a terrific boy. I'll miss him."

Patty expected to be late when she reached the library-media center, but when she pushed through the door, she saw that the meeting hadn't even started, and that Harold was nowhere in sight. There was the hum of social conversation, and teachers were either sitting at one of the three long boardroom-like tables pushed toward the center of the room or clustered around the square table at the back filling paper plates with refreshments or pouring coffee into Styrofoam cups. Breathing a sigh of relief, Patty slipped into the chair that Ellen had saved for her and looked around. The irregularly shaped room was large and crowded with bookshelves stretching around the walls, racks of periodicals, and row after row of computer screens and keyboards. Patty picked up the written agenda, which Harold always prepared for faculty meetings, and noticed that the first item was starred and read *Third Grade Standardized Testing.* The library door opened at that moment, and Harold and Marielle came in pushing an overhead projector on a gray steel cart. The few teachers still standing straggled to their seats as Harold set up the machine and turned it on. Displayed on the screen was a chart filled with numbers comparing standardized test scores in reading and math for all the elementary schools in Hastings. Island Brooke was at the top with Ridgeway and Dexter next and the other seven schools following.

"Where are the writing scores?" whispered Patty to Ellen.

"They don't go up," Ellen whispered back. "We're usually only third or fourth in writing."

Patty gave Ellen a questioning look, and then Ellen said in a joking voice, "Dewey just has to work a little harder."

Harold, arms crossed, stood back for a moment, giving his staff the time to inspect the chart and note the differences among schools. Silver hair perfectly cut and blow-dried, he was dressed in a navy three-piece suit, white shirt and a carefully knotted paisley tie. Patty read through the scores, and then set her eyes on Harold.

He certainly has presence, she thought not for the first time. Not a handsome man. But there's something about him.

She leaned over toward Ellen and whispered to her friend, "You know for an old guy, Harold is kind of interesting looking. He even looks like he teases his hair. And works out."

Ellen gave a dismissive wave of her hand as Harold drew himself up importantly, and began. "We all know that standardized test scores give only part of the picture for a school but it certainly is gratifying to see Island Brooke at the top of the chart year after year. Third grade testing will begin next Monday, and I would like to go over the instructions today. The regular faculty meeting will end at four-thirty, but I'd like the third grade teachers and Marielle and Dewey to stay."

At four-thirty, most of the teachers filed out while Patty, Ellen and Sue moved up to the end of one table where Eunice, Dewey and Marielle were already sitting. Harold took out booklets of instructions and passed them out, and for the next thirty minutes, lectured about the procedure of the testing, going over the details with precision.

Harold's eyes scanned the room, and then seemed to settle on each teacher in turn. "It's important that you all follow the directions exactly," he intoned. "And the test booklets and answer sheets must be kept secure at all times. That means locked in your desk or closet. Whatever you do, don't leave them on your desk where anybody can look at them or walk away with them." He rambled on, reading aloud to them and repeatedly stressing how important the scores were to the school. After a while Patty just let his words wash over her, thinking ahead to supper and the whole evening with Noah who was off for three days. As five o'clock rolled around, Patty kept watching the clock, and her foot started to jiggle impatiently. "Come on, Harold, " she whispered under her breath, "It's five o'clock." A few minutes after the hour Harold finally did finish with, "Monday for reading. Tuesday for math. Wednesday for written expression. I will handle all the makeups myself on Thursday and Friday. I have confidence that all your children will do well. That's it for today."

He gestured a farewell, and the meeting was over.

On the way down the stairs Patty and Ellen talked about the tests. "Harold certainly takes them seriously," Patty commented. "I thought I would fall asleep when he read all those instructions which were right in front of us."

"He wants everything done exactly right. The high test scores are one of the reasons Island Brooke has won all those awards."

"OK. I'll study these directions religiously."

"You've never given standardized tests before. Are you feeling nervous?"

Patty thought for a moment. "Not really. Oh, maybe I have a few butterflies, but it's kind of exciting. Oh, I do have a question. What happens if my class doesn't do well?"

Ellen looked straight at her. "Don't worry. They all do."

Patty spent much of the next Sunday in bed, nursing a bad cold, and only got up at about three to eat the Chinese food that Noah had picked up on his way home from the airport. As they sat in the kitchen eating vegetable chow mein and rice out of cartons, Patty looked out to see sloppy snowflakes falling outside the window. All through that evening, she kept switching to the weather channel to check the bulletins. A snowstorm had been forecast for the next day, and she turned to Noah as she turned off the television set at eleven o'clock. "I hope we don't have a snow day or a delayed opening. That would throw the whole testing schedule off."

"Those tests are really a big deal at your school," he said.

"They sure are. I hope I get through this OK. I keep thinking how terrible it would be if my kids' scores aren't up to the school's high standards."

"Your scores will be fine," Noah assured her.

During the night the temperature went up unexpectedly, and Patty was happy to wake up to winter rain. When she got to school, she picked up the test materials in the main office and had them on her desk at nine o'clock when the children came in. She quickly went through the lunch count and opening exercises, and had the test booklets, answer sheets and a large pile of sharpened #2 pencils lined up on her desk ready to be passed out when the PA system squawked once and then Harold's voice came on.

"Good morning, boys and girls. This is Mr. Trelawney. I am going to ask you all to do something important for me today. I am going to ask you to be very quiet in the halls near the third grade classrooms. Today the children in grade three will be taking some tests. That means it has to be very quiet in the halls, much more quiet than usual. I'm also going to ask any children who come to the office to avoid, if possible, going by the third grade rooms. If you do have to pass by the third grade rooms, please tiptoe and do not talk. Mrs. Rossamondo, Mr. Willis and I will be outside these rooms to make sure that the third graders are not disturbed. Teachers, regular bells will not be ringing this morning because of the standardized testing, and I am requesting that each teacher keep track of her — or his — own schedule. I also have a special message for all the third graders. Boys and girls, do your best. That is all that anyone can ask of you. You do not have to be nervous because these scores do not count on your report cards. I repeat they do not go on your report cards. They only help tell us what you have learned so far and what you still need to learn. Good luck to all of you."

At 9:15, two children who were taking the reading tests with time extensions in the resource room left, and Patty started to pass out the test booklets, answer sheets and pencils to the rest of her class. She read the directions slowly and carefully, and could see that all of the children were unusually attentive and eager to start. During the course of the morning, Patty looked out in the hall a couple of times and saw Harold and Marielle hovering outside her door, and later saw Dewey patrolling back and forth. At the end of the testing for that day, she collected the answer sheets and booklets, locked them in her room closet, and after school took them to the main office. For the next two days, Patty followed the same procedure. Math on Tuesday and written expression on Wednesday. At the end of that school day, she delivered the materials, in a sealed envelope, to Dewey in the main office. She also gave him a list of the students who had been absent.

"So?" he asked.

"So great," she said with a bright smile. The testing hadn't been as taxing as she had expected, but she breathed a sign of relief now that it was over. She knew that the results were very important to the school's image and she hoped all the students, especially her own, had done well.

Patty started to move away, but Dewey seemed to want to continue the conversation.

"Where are you hurrying off to?"

"Got to meet my boyfriend," she kidded. "And he should be flying in right about now." She tapped her watch with an exaggerated gesture as Dewey just stared at her.

Patty hurried back to her room. Today was the day that she held the drama club in her classroom. She was feeling a little tired from the effects of her cold, but the high spirits of the children soon perked her up, and she found herself feeling better as they brain-stormed ideas for the spring play. Also, that day she had brought in a dozen plastic hats — fireman, policeman, cowboy and hard hats — that she had collected at a wedding that she and Noah had recently attended. With the hats serving as costumes, she and the children had improvised skits. The children laughed a lot and Patty found herself laughing along with them.

By 4:45, all the children had been picked up, and Patty took a few minutes to put away all the hats in a cardboard box in her closet. She then walked over and tried to draw the drapes, but some snowman cutouts were in the way, so she decided to leave the drapes open and redo the snowmen in the morning. As Patty walked into the main office to sign out at the end of the day, she saw Harold and Eunice, standing just outside his office, their heads bent close together, talking. She watched them pull apart and straighten up as Marielle walked over to join them. Patty gave the three of them a saluting wave as she signed out. Marielle waved back at her over Harold's shoulder, but neither Harold nor Eunice turned her way.

Chapter 21

Once Patty left the building, she was pleasantly surprised to see that the rain had stopped completely and that the weather had turned unusually warm for January. There was a hint of spring in the air — a false spring she knew — yet everything seemed softer and more relaxed. The mounds of snow seemed to be shrinking, and water was dripping from the school building and the trees. She leaned forward to sniff the sweet air, and then jogged over to her car in the parking lot. By the time she reached home, it was very dark, and the first thing she did was call Tish. The phone rang and rang, and then she found herself talking to Tish's machine.

"Hi, Tish. It's Patty. I know I sound crazy, but let's take advantage of the January thaw and go out walking tonight. It's been so cold and snowy for the last month that I haven't been able to run at all. I don't want to miss this opportunity for some exercise. We can take flashlights and head down toward Stadler Park. Call me as soon as you get in. I'll be waiting." After she hung up the phone, she made herself a tuna sandwich, and heated up some Campbell's tomato soup. Eating from a tray, plopped in front of the television, feet tucked under her, she found the remote control and clicked on the Channel 8 news.

As she relaxed on the sofa, she stared at the phone, willing Tish to call.

She then spent twenty-five minutes leafing through the *New Haven Register*, but most of her attention was still on the phone. When it didn't ring, she went upstairs to change, and a glance in her bedroom mirror made her quickly look again. Her right earring looked lopsided. She looked at the earring closely and saw that one of the fragile gold hoops was missing. She frowned, and spoke out loud, "Oh, no." She retraced her steps through the house, doing a quick check of the floor upstairs and down, the garage and her car, but there was no sign of the gold hoop. Then she looked at her watch. It was five after six. As she well knew, there was no official closing time for Island Book. Harold was frequently working there in the evening, and teachers and parents were always free to stop by. She picked up the phone and called Island Brooke School. No answer.

She then tried Tish a second time. Again the machine. "Tish, I've lost a hoop from my earring so I am definitely going out tonight, and I'm going back to school to look for it. I must have lost it during drama club or maybe in the parking lot. I hope Harold's at the school, and if he is, I'll go in. If he's not there, I'll just have to wait till tomorrow. Call as soon as you get in. We can walk together and gossip away. I'm not leaving till quarter of seven." She went back downstairs to watch more news till after six-thirty, and then turned off the TV. She tried Island Brooke again. The line was busy. That was a good sign that Harold was there and the school was open.

Still hoping that Tish would call, she went upstairs, lifted her hair from her shoulders and pinned it on top her head and changed into gray sweats, running shoes, and Noah's white fleece vest. She also put on a reflecting headband, tied a scarf around her neck and took her fanny pack and a flashlight. She made sure to leave the living room and hall lights on and switched on the outside lamppost as she left. Tish's house was in darkness as she jogged by with her flashlight bobbing. It was still mild outside and the running warmed her up, so within five minutes she felt comfortable enough to slip off the scarf and undo the vest.

She trotted along at a slow and careful pace on the well-lit streets, past leafless trees, wired telephone poles, bright houses, and wood frame condos linked together, avoiding slippery patches of ice here and there. Traffic was light on this damp and misty Wednesday evening, and she saw few people in the brick and asphalt business area of town. The sidewalks were clear in the downtown area, and she picked up speed as she ran by Rick's shopping center, a large supermarket which seemed to be doing little business, a row of mostly darkened and locked offices and storefronts, and a few open restaurants and dating bars in the two and three-story buildings. As she waited on the corner of Emerson for the light to blink to green, she looked back to see Main Street glistening with the reflected colors of the traffic lights and neon flashing signs. Her mind felt clear from the run, and she stretched her arms out to the side, arching herself, unfolding her muscles, and feeling every one. She felt lithe and airy, so relaxed, and so glad to be alive.

Chapter 22

Threading her way around piles of snow that were packed and soiled with half-frozen mud, Patty jogged onto Emerson Street and toward the dark bulk of the school dominating the street. She could see only a few lights on in the building and in the parking lot, but that meant that someone was there and the school was open. She was in luck. A car passed her and turned into the school driveway, and she put on speed to catch up, but by the time she reached the parking lot, she saw only the backs of two people entering the school by the side door. Harold's red Buick was parked in front of the *Reserved for Principal* sign, and an unfamiliar Chrysler was beside it. Patty turned and jogged the hundred yards over to where she had parked that day and added the light of her flashlight to the overhead lights as she searched the ground for the gold hoop from her earring. There was no sign of it. She retraced her steps to the side door, crisscrossing the beam of her flashlight on the ground, but found nothing. With a sigh of disappointment, she shut the flashlight off and decided to try the school.

The side door was unlocked so she let herself in, stamped some snow off her running shoes and walked by the main office. Some of the first floor lights were on, and as she passed the office she could see Harold huddled together by the central counter in conversation with Marcetta and Bill Osborne, third grade parents and co-presidents of the PTA. Patty waved to them, but apparently they didn't see her because she received no waves in response, so she just hurried down the long corridor past Eunice's room, then Sue's, then Ellen's, and then to her own, the last one on the left, fronting on Emerson Street.

The custodian always locked the doors to all the classrooms at the end of the day, so Patty had to take her room key out of her fanny pack to unlock the door and gain entry to her classroom. She had been in the school at night on several occasions for PTA meetings and Activity Night, but there had always been a lot of people milling around, and on this evening, everything seemed unnaturally quiet in the almost empty building. Even the fluorescent lights in her room came flickering to life with an over-bright glow that for a moment made everything seem harsh and unfamiliar. Patty took a second look and felt pride as she looked around at her own well-ordered classroom organized around the theme of Winter Wonderland. Samples of children's artwork and literary compositions about seasonal topics were displayed against blue construction paper on the walls, and snowflake mobiles were hanging in the air. The Science Table was full of children's experiments, and math books were neatly stacked beside full shelves. The wine-colored drapes were not drawn and cutouts of potbellied snowmen could be seen hugging the six large windows.

Giving a cursory glance around the room, she saw no sign of the gold hoop, so she went directly to the supply closet where she had stored the plastic hats and taking her time went carefully through the cardboard box. She did not find what she was looking for. Closing the closet, she walked up and down the room checking the twenty-four neat desktops, clustered together in groups of four, and then moved aside reams of paper in an open cabinet and searched under and around science projects on Long Island Sound in the back of the room. She even checked the folds of the American flag, which pointed up from the white board with the thought that she might have somehow rubbed against it.

Discouraged, she then went over to her desk and sank into the swivel chair, twirling around in the seat and scanning the colorful wall decorations and the well-organized bulletin boards on map skills, the water cycle, and penmanship models. After sitting for a few minutes, she abruptly jumped to her feet and toured the whole area once more, her eyes on the floor. Finally, she just stood in the middle of the room and let her shoulders droop as she admonished herself that the gold hoop was gone. The earrings had been a honeymoon present from Noah, purchased in Bermuda, and she wondered where she could get the hoop replaced. Catching sight of her transparent reflection in the window against the darkness outside, she straightened her shoulders and stared back at herself, and it was at that moment that she saw a glint of gold against the wine color of the drapes. Sagging in relief, she went over to the drapes, and carefully detached the piece from the curtain and stored it in her fanny pack. She took a deep breath of satisfaction as she walked toward the door and reached to snap off the lights. She glanced at the large wall clock and noted that it was just twelve minutes after seven. Feeling triumphant at the success of her search, she practically skipped up the hall to the main office.

She opened the office door, walked in and checked her mailbox first before walking back toward Harold's office where she could hear his voice. Planning to just stick her head in and say "Hello," to Harold and the Osbornes, she moved toward the inner office, nudging aside a large packing case filled with Island Brooke T-shirts which partially blocked the way.

Harold's door was slightly ajar, and Patty reached out to tap on it, but instead of knocking, she pushed against the door opening it fully halfway. She was surprised to see that Harold was alone with no sign of the Osbornes. He was sitting at his polished round table, his back close to the door, but partially turned away. He was talking on the telephone, the wire stretched out from the wall, with the receiver cradled against his chin and resting on his shoulder. He had a pencil in his hand, and as he talked, he was erasing and writing on a sheaf of materials in front of him. Because of the position of the table, Patty was standing right in back of Harold, so close that she could see the texture of his silver hair and his clean pink scalp. She stood for a moment, unsure of whether to stay or go, and then looked over his shoulder and did a mental double take as she recognized the answer sheets from the standardized tests that had just been administered to the third graders.

Her eyes were fixed on Harold's actions, her mind trying to interpret and at first refusing to accept what she was seeing. There was a beat in time as she tried to make some other kind of sense out of what Harold was doing. But there was no question. He was changing the scores. Abruptly, she noticed a yellow legal pad in front of him filled with letters and numbers, and at that moment realized that he was using it as a guide or key. Harold was systemically checking the legal pad and erasing and filling in answers on the test answer sheets. Patty was dumbfounded. All this happened in seconds. It struck her that

this was a moment suspended in time. Disbelief flooded her —
and then understanding.

The high scores at Island Brooke, she thought. So this was
the answer. No wonder Island Brooke was always way ahead of
the other schools in Hastings. After the students took the tests,
Harold altered the scores.

Patty stood there waiting for Harold to notice her, but he
continued his conversation as he methodically erased and
changed answers. The moments ticked past, and at some point,
she became aware of the gist of his conversation. He was talking
in a kidding, intimate fashion to someone, someone obviously
not his wife, and Patty realized that she shouldn't be standing
there eavesdropping. Not only was Harold changing test scores,
but also it was apparent from his intimate banter that he was
planning an assignation of some kind. The identity of the other
party became clear with his next words.

"I have to go, Eunice. I have some parents waiting for me
in the outer office," Patty heard him lie. "I'll be with them for
about an hour and then I have some calls to make." He glanced
at his watch. "Don't come before nine. I have the side door
locked, so you won't be able to get in before then." He swung
around in his chair a few degrees and for the first time, Patty
realized the precarious position that she was in, and stepped
back from the threshold. She could feel her scalp tighten, and
for some unknown reason actually felt herself to be in physical
danger.

"OK, Nine sharp. I'll be looking for your headlights in
the parking lot." He had stopped his erasing and writing and
seemed to be winding up the conversation. As Harold made
his final goodbyes to Eunice, Patty reflexively backed up and
pulled the office door shut to the ajar position it had originally
been in. Carefully, without making any noise, she tiptoed away,
scuttling crabwise away from his office to the outer office door,
just saving herself from falling over the box of T-shirts. She was
trembling. She had seen Harold cheating; changing answers on

standardized tests, and had overheard his intimate conversation with Eunice.

So Harold and Eunice were having an affair, she thought. But the test tampering was even more of a shock.

Patty quietly let herself out of the main office and sidled toward the side door. It was locked from the inside, and for a moment she struggled unsuccessfully with the latch, imagining herself trapped in the building with a furious Harold who would be aware of what she had discovered. Then she undid the lock, opened the door and stepped outside, and as soon as she hit the sidewalk, heart pounding, she started running as fast as she could.

Chapter 23

Patty raced all the way back to Iron Weed Road, slipping and sliding on patches of snow because of her speed and agitation. Turning into her street, she was almost overcome with confusion and indecision. As she ran in front of Tish's house, she became aware that the lights were now on, and Rick's Lexus was in the driveway. Pulling up, she skidded up the driveway, ran up the front stairs and pushed repeatedly on the bell as she banged on the door at the same time. "Hurry up. Hurry up," she called. Tish, surprise on her face, threw open the door and let her in. She took one look at Patty's face said, "What's wrong? Are you OK?"

Rick was sitting at the kitchen table propped up on his elbow as he studied some papers in front of him. As she rushed into the room, he looked up at her, surprised, and then concern came into his face at her obvious distress. He got up and quickly moved to her. " Did something happen to Noah?"

"No," she sputtered out. "I just saw Harold Trelawney changing test scores."

Both Tish and Rick looked uncomprehending. "What?" Rick asked.

"I had to go back to the school, and I saw Harold changing test scores — the standardized tests — the scores that are so high at Island Brooke."

Tish still seemed baffled by Patty's agitation, although Rick's eyebrows had gone up a notch, and he was shaking his head with understanding.

Patty's words came out quickly. It was like a bad dream trying to make Tish understand. "The test scores. The standardized tests. Every year, all the third graders take them. Island Brooke is always the highest in Hastings, one of the highest in the country. It's not because the kids are really doing better. Harold is erasing and changing them."

"Harold is cheating," Rick broke in. "How did you find out?"

Patty slipped into a chair. "I had to go back to the school. Harold was in his office, and he was on the phone. I could see over his shoulder and he was changing scores. I just —"

Tish jumped in, interrupting, "Well, those scores don't mean much anyway, do they?" She paused at Patty's look of distress. "I know it's wrong to change them, but he really isn't hurting anyone. I mean even if he's changing the scores, they don't go on the kids' report cards. He's just making the kids feel good that their scores are so high, so it's really not that bad. He's not hurting the kids."

Rick shook his head.

"Yes, it is hurting kids," Patty responded fiercely with balled fists. "It's hurting the kids who can't live up to their high scores. Their parents expect more from them than they can give. They can't possibly get the grades that match their supposed achievement."

"Oh, I didn't think of that," Tish replied weakly. Then she went on, still trying to defend the position that she had taken. "But nobody pays too much attention to the scores. I barely looked at them when the schools sent them for my girls."

"I can't agree with you. Kids who should be getting extra help may not be getting it because those false high scores tell the school that they're just lazy." Patty gripped the side of her chair tightly, still caught up in anger and confusion.

"What happens to those test scores when these kids go on to middle school?" Rick asked.

"They must go down," Patty answered, "And the kids must be criticized for slacking off or the middle school teachers are criticized."

"These scores seem to be very important to Harold," interjected Tish.

Rick agreed. "I think they're very important to the whole Island Brooke area. But what you're saying here, Patty is almost beyond belief. Harold Trelawney cheating. This is incredible. If anybody but you told me this had happened, I'd say they were nuts."

Tish went over to the sink and ran water over a washcloth. She broke in. "Don't take this the wrong way, Patty," she said, "but you look awful. You're sweating. You look as though you might faint. Here. Put this cloth on your face for a minute. And maybe you'd like something to drink."

Patty took the washcloth, and held it over her face. Then she said, "Yes, I'd like a glass of water. I ran all the way from the school. I can't seem to catch my breath."

Tish took a glass bottle from the refrigerator and poured water into a large tumbler that she gave to Patty. Patty drank deeply.

"Did you say anything to Harold about changing the scores?" asked Tish.

"Say anything to him? Are you kidding? I'm a first year teacher, and he's my principal. And more important that that, I was afraid that maybe he would attack me to keep me from telling anyone what I saw. I think I was all alone in the building with him."

"Does he know you saw him?" Tish went on.

Patty shook her head. "I just got out of there as quickly as I could. I'm sure he didn't see me, so he couldn't know."

"Are you going to report him?" asked Rick.

"I don't know what I'm going to do. He could just deny it. It would be my word against his." Patty ran her finger around the rim of the glass nervously and then set it down. At that moment, she noticed some maps of the East Shore on the table, and realized that she must have interrupted a business meeting. She looked up and became aware that Tish was wearing makeup, a dark cashmere sweater, and well-cut worsted trousers with a fine weave, her hair carefully waved. Rick looked casual in wide wale cords and a loose collarless shirt.

"I've broken up your meeting, " Patty shook her head. "I'm sorry. I think I have to go home now. I wish I could reach Noah. This has hit me like a ton of bricks, and I don't know what to do."

Rick rose to his feet. "The meeting doesn't matter. What you saw tonight does matter."

Patty stood up abruptly and headed for the front door, Rick following right behind her. He put his hand on her shoulder to slow her down and gently turned her around. "Patty, look at me and listen to what I have to say. Be careful with this. Think about it carefully before you take any steps. As you said, you're only a first year teacher, and Harold is — what can I say — Harold is a town treasure. You could be sitting on a powder keg." Tish came up behind them and nodded her head in agreement.

Then he asked, "Do you want me to drive you home? I could come in, and we could talk this out."

Patty was about to say, "Yes," until she saw Tish's face take on a stricken look at the thought of losing Rick's company.

"No, I don't think so. I need some time to decide what to do." She considered her predicament for a minute. "Look, please don't say anything to anyone about this. You guys have to promise." Rick and Tish both shook their heads in agreement, and Patty waved goodbye, turned and was quickly through the door and down the steps. Her mind still spinning, she broke into a jog toward her house. When she unlocked her front door and walked through the den into the kitchen, she threw off Noah's fleece vest and without giving it any thought automatically went to the phone and punched in her father's number. The phone rang and rang, and just as she was about to hang up, her father's voice sounding breathless, said, "Hello."

"Dad, it's Patty." She made herself speak as calmly as possible. "You know those high standardized test scores at Island Brooke School." Her voice took on a tinge of sarcasm. "Those impossibly high scores at our award-winning school. Well, I found out tonight how Harold Trelawney does it." She paused to catch her breath. "He cheats. Once the tests are done, he changes the scores." She narrated the startling events of the last hour.

In outrage, her father half-shouted, "Why that's unfair to the kids. He's not helping them. He's hurting them. And he's hurting the teachers at Island Brooke. And what about the teachers in the other schools here in Hastings? Those false scores make them look bad."

Patty could then hear her father talking to someone else and immediately regretted her call.

"No," she heard him say, "Patty just caught Harold Trelawney changing answers. On the standardized tests. Here, you talk to her, Jim."

In a moment Jim Politano was on the phone. "Am I hearing right? You caught Harold Trelawney changing standardized test scores?"

The first prickling of anxiety came over Patty as she repeated the story to Jim. Her trip back to the school. Standing in the doorway of Harold's office as he changed scores. Her frantic run home. She ended weakly with "It's still sinking in. I can hardly believe it myself."

Jim seemed even more upset by the story than her father had been. He groaned aloud and said, "You know at an administrators' meeting just the other day the high test scores at Island Brooke were discussed, and somebody jokingly suggested that maybe the Island Brooke teachers were giving the kids extra time."

"No, that's not the reason. It's all Harold."

"This is terrible news," said Jim, his voice shaking.

Patty nodded her head up and down although Jim could not see her. "I agree. And the worst thing is that I don't know if I should even do anything about it. Maybe I should just forget what I saw. Pretend that the whole thing never happened."

The silence on the line seemed to go on for a long time and just when Patty thought that they might have been disconnected, Jim spoke, his words clear and definite. "I'm afraid you don't have that option anymore, Patty."

"What do you mean?"

"I'm an administrator for Hastings Public Schools. Now that I have information about test tampering at Island Brooke, I can't possibly let that go. You'll have to report what you saw to the superintendent of schools." He paused, and somehow Patty knew what he was going to say next. "Or I'll have to report it for you."

Patty felt her stomach drop, and when she spoke, there was a quaver in her voice. "Is that really necessary? Can't we just forget the whole thing?"

"I'm afraid not." Jim went on, "I know the superintendent is out of town, away at a conference, and won't be back till Monday. I'll talk to him as soon as he returns and call you as soon as I can. I'm sure he'll want to meet with you and hear this for himself."

When Patty got off the phone a few minutes later, she slumped into one of her kitchen chairs and mentally kicked herself for making the phone call. If only she had hung up before that last ring. If only Jim Politano had not been at her father's house. If only.

Chapter 24

Patty's appointment with the superintendent of schools was set for four o'clock the following Tuesday afternoon.

"Lucky it's not Monday," Patty told Noah that morning, "or I'd have had to let Harold know I'm blowing off the faculty meeting because I'm blowing the whistle on him."

"How much are you planning to tell the superintendent?" asked Noah.

"I guess I'll have to tell him everything." Patty paused. "Everything except the fact that Harold and Eunice are having an affair. That has nothing to do with the test tampering, and it's really not his business."

Jim Politano said he would meet Patty at five of four in the parking lot of the administrative building and true to his word, the tall, graying man was getting out of his car as she drove up. They greeted each other with a few words and then silently walked to the building together. One of the first schools in Hastings, it was a small clapboard structure which a previous superintendent had thought to paint barn red some years back, leading to the affectionate title, "The Little Red Schoolhouse." The superintendent's office was right on the first floor, and as soon as Patty and Jim entered the outer office, a secretary rose from her seat, as though she has been expecting them.

"The superintendent will see you right away," she said as she motioned toward the inner office. She opened the door, and Patty could see John Larraway sitting at his desk. He got up as they entered his office, and walked around his desk with his thick hand outstretched. Patty has seen the superintendent from afar at several meetings but had never met him. He was big, a bear of a man with a thatch of russet-red hair and the milky skin that often goes with it. The superintendent gestured Patty and Jim toward two club chairs in a semi-circle before his desk and took a similar chair himself. The superintendent was well liked in the town of Hastings, and Patty had often heard that he was congenial and engaging. A different man sat before them that day. There was nothing friendly about his face. He looked dead serious. Cool and collected. A man who had grown used to the power and authority that he held for a number of years.

"Mrs. Bass," he said, literally sitting on the edge of his seat, "why don't you just tell me your story?" Patty began by recounting the events of the previous Wednesday evening, telling of her lost gold hoop and her unexpected trip back to Island Brooke. John Larraway let her talk; nodding his big head occasionally, and she went on without interruption for over ten minutes. When she was finished, the superintendent then asked the questions she had already heard and would be hearing again.

"Are you sure Harold was changing scores? Could he have been looking the tests over, and um, I don't know, maybe putting them in alphabetical order? Or just tapping with a pencil in an absent-minded way?"

Patty shook her head. "No. He was changing scores."

He raised his eyebrows, which were sparse and reddish. "I've heard that some teachers erase stray marks on the answer sheets although they shouldn't. Could he have been doing that? To clean them up? To present a neater package?"

"No, I stood there right in the doorway. He was on the phone at the same time or otherwise he might have heard me come in. He was having a conversation with someone — you know with the phone kind of tucked into his ear — he kept right on talking and at the same time he was using some kind of gyp sheet with the correct answers. He was deliberately erasing and changing scores as I watched."

John Larraway thought for a minute. There was skepticism in his eyes as the silence lengthened.

"This is a very serious accusation you are making, Patricia. May I call you Patricia?"

"It's Patty."

"All right Patty." He went on talking, and Patty was very aware that he did not suggest that she call him John.

"Are you 100 percent sure of this?" He paused, "Because if this is true, Harold will lose his job — and never work in a public school again. So I'm going to ask you one more time. Are you sure Harold was changing the answers? Could he have been doing anything else? Could you be mistaken?"

Patty thought back. She had no doubt at all, but felt that John Larraway was really putting her on the spot. She brought the picture of Harold sitting at his desk into her mind. She could see the scene in her mind and see exactly what he was doing. Finally, she answered mechanically, "Harold Trelawney was erasing and changing answers on the third grade standardized tests."

"How long were you observing him?" the superintendent asked.

"A few minutes. If I had to say exactly, my best guess would be about three minutes. I was just standing there. I couldn't believe what I was seeing at first so I couldn't move away. He was talking and at the same time making changes."

John Larraway seemed skeptical. "How could he do both things at the same time? If he were in fact making changes on the answer sheets, why would he be talking on the phone? I would think he would need to put his complete attention on what he was doing. Why talk on the phone?"

Patty screwed up her eyes for a few moments as she thought back. "Well, he was doing it in almost an automatic way — as though he had done it before. I'd say most of his attention was on the tests, and the phone conversation was secondary. Maybe the person had called him. Maybe he was working on the tests when the call came in. I don't know."

"Did you hear the phone ring?"

"No I didn't. When I came into the outer office, I heard his voice and assumed he was still with the Osbornes. His office door wasn't completely closed, and I just opened it wider to stick my head in and say, "Hello.""

"Do you know who he was talking to?"

Patty dissembled. "I couldn't say."

"How was he erasing? Were both his hands free?"

"Yes, he was holding the telephone, the wall telephone, with his neck. The cord was stretched over to the wall. He had several pencils that he was using."

"And the eraser?"

"The erasers were on the pencils. They weren't separate."

"And he didn't see you at all?"

"No, he was turned away from the door and he was working and talking on the phone at the same time. If he hadn't been on the phone, he probably would have heard me when I pushed the door open."

"Have you seen Harold since that night?"

"Sure, a lot. He came into my room Friday to co-teach, and I saw him at the faculty meeting yesterday. And just passing in the hall. Oh, and he came out to third grade recess today and played kick ball with the kids. He just waved to me and the other teachers."

"And no one at Island Brooke knows what you saw?" There was a pause. "Or what you thought you saw."

Patty felt herself growing rigid with anger, and silently asked herself why she was here. Her position was untenable. She felt that she was being forced to give information, and that the information was not being believed. "I know what I saw. And I haven't told anyone at school."

John Larraway then looked at Patty intently, and there was steel in his voice when he asked the next few questions. "How do you get along with Harold? I mean before this happened? Did the two of you get along?"

"Yes, he's always been a terrific principal."

"Do you like him?"

"Yes, I do." She thought for a moment about how Harold had always been unfailingly polite to her. Then she thought about him changing the third grade scores. "Or at least I did. Now with this, I really don't know how I feel about him."

"Did he ever bother you?"

Patty laughed. "No."

"Make a pass at you?"

"No, of course not."

John Larraway looked her squarely in the eyes, and his tone was gruff. "Harold is a lot older than you, but he is a man of some renown. Did you ever make a pass at him that he rebuffed?" The superintendent's eyes were bright and probing, and Patty felt herself growing red. She shifted in her seat, bridling with indignation at the suggestion that she had done anything improper. She felt foolish, foolish for coming forward. "No."

Then Jim, who has been sitting quietly through the whole discussion interjected, "Patty was unsure about coming forward with this. I think it was a very brave thing for her to do."

"Yes, murmured the superintendent. "It certainly was." He suddenly leaned back in his chair, causing it to creak so loudly that it made Patty jump. "All right Patty. I thank you for coming in, and I ask you not to repeat what you've told me today. How many people already know about this?"

Patty quickly counted out loud, "My husband, my cousin, my friend, my father, Jim here and now you. Six counting you. And of course, I'm the seventh."

The superintendent's eyebrows were drawn together, and his face was seamed with stress as he thought of the hurricane that was about to be unleashed. "All right. I think it's important to minimize the chances that this story will get out. Let's keep it at seven for the time being. I'd like you to go back to the people you've already told and ask them to keep this whole situation in confidence." He heaved a heavy sigh as he rose from the chair. Patty knew that the meeting was just about over.

The superintendent shook his head back and forth. "I have to think how I'm going to handle this. Probably contact the testing service. The tests came in from the elementary schools yesterday. Maybe there's some way of telling. I don't know. I have to decide what to do." Patty got up stiffly, turned and walked toward the door. Jim followed. She glanced back at the superintendent's face.. He looked worried — and he looked sad.

"One more thing, Patty. I must tell you that Harold Trelawney and I have been personal friends for many years. I like the man a great deal, but if you are telling the truth, I guarantee you that he will never work in a public school again." He walked by them and opened the door. "Thank you both for coming in today." Patty and Jim left the Little Red Schoolhouse side by side, but said not one word to each other as they walked to their cars and drove away.

Chapter 25

When over a week had gone by and Patty still hadn't heard from the superintendent of schools, she wondered if some decision about the test tampering had been made behind closed doors. She discussed various scenarios one night at the end of January with Noah, and he concluded, "It doesn't seem fair for Harold to get away with it, but who ever said that life was fair? Larraway probably gave Harold a warning, and told him that booklets from Island Brooke would be picked up on the day of testing. That will take care of the problem with the least amount of turmoil for everybody."

"I guess you're right," Patty agreed. "All those administrators stick together, so it looks like it's all being handled quietly. Well, it's probably for the best. That way nobody gets hurt."

Chapter 26

Patty's bubble was burst at the first faculty meeting in February. At the beginning of the meeting, Harold announced in a grave tone that the meeting would be short for most of the teachers, but that the third grade teachers, Dewey and Marielle were asked to stay. Patty noticed that Harold seemed ill at ease, not his usual confident self, as he went through his brief agenda. Patty wondered if his agitation had something to do with the test tampering she had reported. As soon as the rest of the teachers filed out, Patty's question was answered right away.

With Marielle at his side, Harold stood before them, his finger toying with the inside of his shirt collar. "There have some concerns about the third grade standardized testing which was completed in January," he began quietly. "Three schools in Hastings have been asked to retake parts of the math and reading sections. We'll be taking the retest this Wednesday morning. All third graders present that day will take selected subtests over."

There was an immediate puzzled reaction from the teachers, and even Eunice who was usually privy to all information in the school looked surprised. "Why are we doing this?" she asked with a frown on her face.

Harold answered simply, "It seems that there are some concerns about irregularities."

"Irregularities? What does that mean?" Eunice asked sharply.

"I'm telling you all I know," Harold answered. "Island Brooke, Soderholm, and Ridgeway Schools are involved in the retake." He then added, "Personnel from the other schools in town will supervise the administration of the retests and will take the tests away to the superintendent of schools as soon as they're finished."

"Is this some kind of quality control?" Dewey questioned.

Harold just shrugged his shoulders as if he didn't know and he didn't care.

In a quiet voice, Marielle asked, "Is this being done all over the country, or just here in Connecticut?"

Harold stepped to the side. "I believe this is just for three Hastings public schools. John Larraway stopped by this morning." Everyone looked surprised. Generally, when the superintendent of schools was in the building, the news spread like wildfire from teacher to teacher. Harold went on, "He said that three schools in Hastings would be having retakes. He was only here a few minutes so that's about all I know."

All the teachers exchanged looks again. All the teachers except for Patty, who looked down and wiggled uncomfortably in her chair.

"I can't make any sense of this," Dewey commented out loud, as Marielle questioned, "Irregularities?" under her breath. Patty raised her eyes and was relieved to see that no one was looking at her.

As they exited the library after the meeting, Ellen caught up with her and asked, "What do you think is going on?" Patty opened her mouth to speak, but nothing came out. Fortunately, Dewey joined them at that moment and took over the conversation, "What a waste of time this whole thing is. Does the superintendent really think that our kids have nothing better to do than take tests they've already taken?" He dominated the conversation as they descended the stairs to the first floor and walked out the side door together. Patty was happy when they reached the parking lot, and she could break away.

Two days later, the retests were held. Again, Harold's voice crackled over the PA system. Again, he asked the children to be especially quiet in the first floor hall because of third grade testing. Again, Harold, Marielle and Dewey patrolled the corridor. Again, Patty distributed test booklets and answer sheets, and read instructions aloud, but this time, a diminutive, blond woman, who was the math specialist from one of the other elementary schools in town, sat in the back of the classroom. When the testing was completed in the late morning, Patty put the test booklets and answer sheets into a large manila envelope. The math specialist said, "We both have to sign our names across the sealed flap to preserve security." Patty scrawled her name with a shaky hand. Then the math specialist shrugged her shoulders and said, "Don't ask me why. I know as much as you do."

"No." Patty said under breath as soon as the other woman had left the room. "You're wrong. You don't know as much as I do. You don't know that all of this is because of something I saw that I shouldn't have seen."

Another week passed and Patty found herself watching Harold's every move closely, and noticed that at first he seemed more outgoing than usual. He had always been interested in the children, but now he seemed to spend even more time in the classrooms and out on the playground. Also, he had always been polite to her, but now he seemed to be going out of his way to be friendly and make casual conversation with all the teachers. She was unpleasantly surprised to find Harold following her down the corridor to her classroom one morning before school, but he was in apparent good spirits as he caught up and handed her a thick black notebook. "I don't think you've ever seen this, Patty. I've written up some curriculum changes for the system, and I thought you might like to look them over, and give me some feedback." He went on before she could comment. "You young teachers have some good insights. I always like to get a different perspective on things."

Patty took the notebook, wary, looking for a hidden meaning in Harold's words and wishing that he would end the conversation and continue on his way. But he then extended an invitation. "Ann Marie and I have been thinking about having the new teachers and their husbands over to supper in couple of weeks. We'll have to get together. I'd like to get to know your husband better. Seems like an unusual man. A real leader. He had some interesting stories to tell about the Gulf War when we talked that night of the Christmas party. I'll have Ann Marie give you a ring in a week or so."

Patty forced a smile onto her face. "That sounds great," she said in a strained voice before Harold turned and hurried back to his office. She didn't quite know how to react. She felt very defensive about Harold's invitation, and wondered if he had any inkling that she had been the person who reported the test tampering. The conversation gnawed at her all morning, but then Lauren Siegel and Linda Hicks both mentioned that Harold had extended much the same invitation to them, so she realized that she hadn't been singled out.

By the next week, Harold's behavior was more erratic. At times, he was his usual charismatic self, but at other times, he seemed grim and distracted, abdicating his school responsibilities to others. This was most apparent to Patty at a Planning and Placement Team Meeting that was scheduled just before February vacation. The meeting was scheduled for ten on that Friday morning, but ten o'clock came and went. Finally, at ten minutes after the hour, Dewey turned to Karin Shugrue the school psychologist, and asked, "Did you think to call Mom and remind her?"

"I left a message on Mrs. Post's machine," Karin responded.

"So did I," Patty and the special education teacher Shannon Cook chimed in at the same time.

"That makes three reminders then, and I know the invitation letter went out. Let's give her five more minutes. Then, I'll ask Grace to give her a call." When the five minutes went by, Dewey left the office briefly, and Patty chatted casually with Karin and Shannon, both young, button nosed and pretty, both petite with iron straight dark hair to their shoulders, both all dressed up for the meeting. Harold was also sitting around the table in his office, but his head was turned away, and he was just staring into space, his body moving slightly, apparently in time with some silent rhythm that only he could hear.

When Dewey returned, he said, "No answer. Mrs. Post could be on the way," and began reviewing Owen Post's reading scores with the others. Abruptly, Mrs. Post appeared at the door and interrupted Dewey loudly, "I wish you could have waited for me." She was a big woman, not tall, but wide and big boned, and she seemed to fill the doorway. Her brown hair was teased and stiffly sprayed into a high dome.

Mrs. Post's tone was brittle as she went on. "Three calls on my machine. You people must think that I'm a little simple-minded." A strong smell of Listerine over an undercoating of something else came over the room as she entered. There seemed to be no answer to her comments, so there was an uncomfortable silence as she took the sixth chair around the table. Dewey immediately offered Mrs. Post a copy of her parental rights, explained them, and introduced everyone. He then went on, "As you know, Owen has been having some difficulty—"

Mrs. Post cut him off. "I really don't want to hear that. I only want to talk to Miss. Cook."

Dewey's forehead furrowed. "But surely, you've talked to Miss Cook about Owens's progress. She's been giving him reading support since September."

"Oh, really, and is that every day?"

Shannon Cook learned forward and answered. "Yes, I see Owen one half hour per day. He receives his reading instruction in the classroom, but then he comes to the resource room for support."

"But Owen hasn't been doing very well in reading. Has he, Miss Cook?"

Dewey tried to smooth the storm, which appeared to be building. "That's why we've come together today, Mrs. Post. Owen has been receiving help in the resource room, but we all feel that support is not enough for him. He would benefit from direct instruction of his reading in a small group setting with Miss Cook."

Mrs. Post again turned her attention to Shannon. She seemed to be glaring at the special education teacher. "And do you remember our meeting last October, Miss Cook? Do you remember how you told me that I should discontinue the private tutoring in reading that I was providing for Owen?"

Shannon seemed confused for a moment, but when she spoke, her voice was definite. "I remember the meeting in October, Mrs. Post, but I don't remember recommending that you discontinue the private tutoring. In fact I believe I said that if you continued the tutoring, I wanted to speak to the tutor to coordinate our efforts in reading."

"No, you didn't." Mrs. Post's tone was now sharp. "I remember distinctly. You said you would be helping Owen, and you also said that I should discontinue private tutoring outside of school."

Karin spoke for the first time. "I'm sorry, Mrs. Post. I was at that meeting, and I don't remember it that way. I remember you talked about the outside tutoring, and I believe both Miss Cook and I made it clear that it was your decision to continue or discontinue private help. We both did tell you that the school system would not pay for the tutoring, but I believe we both made it clear that the final decision was up to you."

Mrs. Post actually huffed, and now seemed to be directing her wrath at Karin. "Well, I would imagine that you would stick up for her. I guess it's a closed corporation at this school." A malicious glint came into her eyes. "I've just recently heard that there's something funny going on with the standardized testing. That's why the children had to do a retake. I guess there's something funny going on everywhere in this school."

Dewey started to protest, but Mrs. Post went back to her original subject. "But I don't care what anyone says. I distinctly remember, Miss Cook that you told me to discontinue private tutoring for my son. And now he's way behind, and I just wonder what you're planning to do about it?" Her voice had become louder, and some of her words were slurred.

Dewey was able to break in this time before Mrs. Post could continue "I can see you have some concerns, Mrs. Post, but I think the best thing might be to continue this discussion right after the PPT. Let's talk about Owens's program now and get that worked out. After that, we'll close the PPT, and send Mrs. Bass back to her classroom. Then we can discuss the meeting you had in October with Miss Cook and Mrs. Shugrue, and see if we find out how this communication problem occurred."

"No, I'm tired of being pushed around, and I won't wait. This woman," she pointed her finger across at Shannon, "has wasted months and months of my child's time." By this time, Mrs. Post's voice had become a shout, and Shannon's face had turned bright red.

"I don't know what kind of teachers you have working in this school. People like Miss Cook who lie about what they say to parents, and people like Mrs. Shugrue who back them up. Liars. That's what these two are."

"Just a minute, Mrs. Post." The voice was authoritative, and Patty expected it to be Harold's, but it was Dewey who had risen from his seat, and was holding his right hand out like a traffic cop. "Let's stop right there, Mrs. Post. We are here today to discuss Owen's educational program. If you have any issues with Miss Cook or Mrs. Shugrue, I'll be happy to set up a meeting for you to do just that. But I cannot tolerate this shouting. This tone of voice. I would like to continue with the PPT, but if that is not possible, I will call a halt right now, and we will have to reschedule. I will not have any teachers at this school spoken to in this manner."

Mrs. Post was still shouting. "I'll speak to these two any way I want."

"This meeting is over." It was still Dewey's voice with a note of authority that Patty had never heard before. There was a stunned silence before Mrs. Post lurched from the chair. "You'll be hearing from my attorney, Mr. Willis. And I assure you that I will report your rude behavior to Dr. Larraway, superintendent of schools. I'm a taxpayer in Hastings, and I don't have to put up with this." She left the office somewhat unsteadily.

Patty could see how shaken Shannon was as she watched Karin leaned over to comfort her.

"What just happened here? Why did she shout at me like that?" asked Shannon.

Karin had the answer. "I know she was arrested for a DWI last week. It was in the paper. I think she has a serious drinking problem. I could smell the liquor when she came in."

Dewey nodded as he stood up. "I could smell it too — under all the mouth wash." He paused. "OK. We'll have to reschedule this PPT. Everybody can go back now."

Patty rose to her feet and started to follow Karin and Shannon out of the office. She glanced back just once at Dewey who had so unexpectedly taken the lead, and gave him a thumbs up sign. It was at that moment that she looked at the still seated Harold, who seemed as preoccupied as ever and completely unaware of anything that had just occurred in the room. He was still staring into space moving in time to silent music. Patty wondered what was going on in his head.

She continued to wonder what was going on in his head as February wound down. On the last Thursday of the month, Noah came in with the mail and handed Patty a white business envelope with the printed address of Hastings Public Schools in the upper left hand corner. She ripped it open and read the brief printed message addressed to *Teachers of Island Brooke School:*

John Larraway, superintendent of schools will be meeting with the entire Island Brooke staff on March 1, at 3:45, in the school library. Attendance is mandatory.

"I wonder what's happening now," she said to Noah. "Will this ever end?"

Chapter 27

In the staff room that morning Dewey seemed agitated and kept repeating to anyone who would listen, "I hope everything's all right with those third grade tests. I hope everything's all right with the third grade tests." And all day teachers exchanged looks and comments, questioning the unusual meeting with the superintendent.

"I bet there's some trouble with the tests," Sue suggested to Patty and Shannon Cook as they ascended the stairs together right after school. Patty and Shannon exchanged glances since it was impossible to miss the note of glee in Sue's voice.

The air in the library was tense that afternoon, and the room was almost filled. Patty looked around and saw that Dewey was waving to her. He gestured toward a seat he has saved.

"Is there room for Ellen?" Patty asked, looking around.

"Sure," he called and squeezed in a chair from the side of the room. Ellen soon arrived, and then Harold and Marielle came in and headed toward the front of the room, talking together in low, worried voices. At exactly 3:45, John Larraway, carrying a thick stack of papers walked in the door and went to the front of the assemblage. For a moment he stood beside the much shorter Harold who looked diminished and seemed to shrink away from him.

The superintendent nodded a greeting to the teachers and then went right into his prepared message. "I have some very serious news. Some news that will not be welcome." He paused. "Last month, there were retakes of standardized tests which had originally been given in January of this year to third grade students. Statistical analysis of results from both January and February in the three target schools indicates that January test scores here at Island Brooke were tampered with."

There was a collective gasp, and Patty could feel the uneasiness around the library build. John Larraway continued, "Both of the other two schools, Soderholm and Ridgeway, saw a slight increase in their scores. But both math and reading scores here at Island Brooke plummeted beyond any logical explanation. Because of the statistical improbability of this happening, personnel at the testing company visually reviewed answer sheets from both January and February and determined that the January scores here at Island Brooke were erased and changed by someone at the school." There was a moment of dead silence and then everybody seemed to be talking at once. The superintendent held up his hand for order. "Let me finish. Statistical analysis has confirmed these findings. And there's more to report. Something you should all know."

Patty could feel the color rising in her face, sure that John Larraway was going to mention that a whistleblower had instigated the investigation into test tampering.

"Because of these findings, answer sheets from the standardized tests taken by third, fourth and fifth graders for the past three years were also reviewed. Unfortunately, the testing company found the same high erasure rate, and the same impossibly high percentage of answers changed from wrong to right. There is no doubt about it. There has obviously been tampering with third, fourth and fifth grade scores for a number of years at this school."

Eunice raised her hand and was called on. "Are you saying that the third, fourth and fifth grade teachers at this school are suspected of changing standardized test scores?"

The superintendent's response was emphatic. "No, I'm not saying that at all. What I'm saying is that analysis has proven that test answers here at Island Brooke were erased, and students' scores were changed from wrong to right. At this time, no charges against any one person are being made."

"At this time?" queried Dewey. "Does that mean charges will be brought at a later date?"

The superintendent shook his head back and forth. "I don't have that information."

There was whispering in the room, and his voice quickened. "I want to fill you in on something else."

The whispering stopped as all eyes turned back to him.

"Tonight at six o'clock, a representative of the testing company and I will be holding a news conference at the main office of Hastings Public School, the Little Red Schoolhouse, as we know it. At that time, this information on the test tampering will be released to the press."

He fielded a few more indignant questions from the teachers, and then Dewey, sounding defensive called out, "Why? Why release this information now? Why not wait till we know more about what actually happened?" Patty could see Eunice nodding emphatically in agreement with Dewey.

"The decision to release this information has been made jointly by the Hastings Board of Education and the testing company. I will have nothing further to say at this time." John Larraway passed some handouts to Dewey and Marielle. "Please distribute these to all the teachers. They show the statistical analysis of testing results." He then turned and left the room quickly, ignoring further questions called out by teachers.

It was bedlam. Teachers were grabbing at the handouts. Shouting. Calling across the room. Patty turned to see that Marielle looked paler than usual. Eunice and some of the other teachers were crying. Ellen was sitting with her face puckered and tears in her eyes. Harold looked devastated, his face blotchy. Dewey, white-faced, stood up and walked over to him, and clapped him on the shoulder. Patty quickly rose, and started toward the door. Ellen wiping away tears soon joined her on the stairs. "What do you make of all this?"

"Trouble," was the only answer that Patty could give.

Chapter 28

Noah was waiting for her at home. "How did it go?"

Patty went over what John Larraway had said at the meeting. She ended with, "The superintendent had already made up his mind that he was going to inform the press. I thought Harold was going to have a heart attack when he heard that. And I thought Dewey would have one right along with him. Half the teachers in the room were in tears. The only positive thing I can say is that John Larraway didn't mention a whistleblower.

I guess there's enough information from the retests — the discrepancy in scores and the high erasure rate. Now with the findings from the fourth and fifth grade tests, Harold can be stopped without my name being mentioned at all."

Patty and Noah were glued to the television that evening. The test tampering charges led the six o'clock news on the local channel as John Larraway and Dr. Polchowski from the testing service spoke in detail about the findings. Using charts, they showed the erasure rate among the three schools and the discrepancy in the scores from the January to February testing. Before going to bed, Noah and Patty watched the eleven o'clock news. Some archive films of two school buses pulling up in front of Island Brooke filled the screen, and then the familiar photogenic anchorman came on and reviewed the story. He ended with the comment, "Times have really changed, folks. In the old days, children would bring an apple for the teacher. Nowadays, it looks like teachers are more in need of erasers."

The last thing that Patty said to Noah that night was, "This whole thing is awful, but at least Harold knows he won't be able to change the scores again. This will be the end of it. And no one will ever know that I had anything to do with it."

Chapter 29

Patty ate breakfast with Noah the next morning so she was later than usual leaving home and was surprised to be caught up in a line of stalled traffic as she neared the school. There seemed to be some kind of disturbance ahead, and by the time she reached Emerson Street, she could see that the area in front of the school was seething with activity. Several TV trucks with satellite dishes and antennas were parked in the street and some reporters armed with microphones were interviewing a small crowd of Island Brooke parents who were milling around on the sidewalk. Two police cruisers were parked in front of the building, and a uniformed officer was directing traffic. When Patty put on her blinker to turn into the parking lot, the policeman came over to her and motioned for her to lower her window. He then asked, "Do you have business in the school?"

"I work here," she answered.

The policeman stepped back and waved her by. As she slowly drove through the commotion and turned into the lot, she heard a voice call out, "She works here."

Patty parked and eased out of her car, and started walking toward the side entrance of the building. Carrying school materials in her arms, she found that she had to step around knots of adults and children, and a jostling group of reporters. She heard someone say at that point, "She's a teacher," and within seconds a young woman wearing a bright scarlet coat, had dashed toward her and stuck a microphone in her face. "Do you think the teachers changed the scores?"

Patty did a quick sidestep and broke into a half walk-half half-run to beat the woman to the building. As she did, a policeman came running from the driveway and put himself between the reporter and the school. Patty heard him say, "Get back. I told you to stay off school grounds." She opened the door and let it quickly close behind her. Dewey was coming up the hall with a look of complete bewilderment on his face, and quickened his pace to come over to meet her.

"I can't understand what's going on here," he said as he held the office door open for her. "Isn't there any other news in the country today? Any murders? Any bank robberies?" He walked ahead of her around the counter, knocked once and then disappeared into Harold's office.

Behind the central counter, Grace Reilly was just hanging up the phone, looking worn out. The phone rang instantly. Grace shook her head. "It's been like this since I got here at eight o'clock. They're just going crazy." She picked up the phone, and after a few seconds, Patty could hear her say, "No, Mr. Trelawney is not available for an interview." A few seconds later, she said, "No, I am not available for an interview either. Thank you for calling." She hung up the phone and it rang again.

Marielle came into the office and looked blankly at Patty, her eyes troubled behind her thick glasses. They stood side-by-side and emptied out their mailboxes. They then both signed in and left the office together, walking in silence, each in her own thoughts. As Patty started to turn into her room, she looked at Marielle and asked, "Do those reporters really think we teachers changed the scores?"

Marielle nodded. "It looks that way." And then in a lower voice, more to herself than to Patty, said, "But those statistics show something else. I think they'll have to look higher than the teachers to find the person who did it."

Patty was flabbergasted. Could Marielle, Harold's oldest ally, be hinting that Harold was responsible for the tampering? She was about to make a response, but Marielle had hurried ahead and was already pushing through the cafeteria doors. Patty had little time to think about it because within a couple of minutes the children started coming down the hall and into the room. They were unusually noisy and uncontrolled, a few collapsing in giggles at all the attention their school was getting. Patty found that she had to be very stern to get them seated and to keep them from leaving their seats and staring out the front windows at the camera crews interviewing Island Brooke parents. Patty hoped the situation would get better once the school day with its routines began, but the children were charged with excitement because of the media attention and the uniformed policemen standing in front of the school, so maintaining order was a problem through the morning even after the TV trucks had left. Just before lunch, Dewey popped his head in and mouthed, "The kids are wired." Patty shook her head in agreement. In the teachers' lounge at lunch, the teachers were talking about the media coverage, clustering together to try to make sense out of what was happening.

During afternoon recess, Patty, Ellen and Sue huddled together at the center of the playground as the children scampered in all directions around them, calling out in high, clear voices, which sounded louder than usual. The schoolyard was clear of snow, but the wind was hard and cutting. Eunice, who had become noticeably friendlier since the retest, crossed the schoolyard to join them.

Sue folded her arms in front of her and hugged herself. "It's too cold for outdoor recess today. Harold should have called indoor recess."

Ellen immediately came to Harold's defense. "He's got more on his mind than recess today. The poor man probably can't think straight."

"I know I can't," Eunice added. "I barely slept a wink last night." She shivered despite her thick parka.

"I didn't sleep well either," agreed Ellen. "It's hard to believe this is really happening."

"This whole thing is preposterous," Eunice added, shivering again. "I feel so sorry for Harold. It's so unfair."

Sue interjected briskly, "And all those reporters. I understand the police had to throw a news van out of the parking lot this morning. A news van from a New York TV station." Sue seemed to be in a strange mood, her voice energized.

There was a brief silence, and Patty felt that she had to say something. "I was surprised to see all the reporters. I don't know why this is such a big story."

"I don't know why, either," Eunice agreed. "I wish they would just go."

The four chatted amicably for a few minutes longer, and then Ellen and Eunice drifted away to another part of the playground to quiet down some raucous laughter. Patty found herself left alone with Sue who immediately said, "Well, we've really had some big changes at the school since the retest. Have you noticed how different Eunice has become? She's a whole new person. Almost human. She's even speaking to me as an equal. And I see she's a lot more polite to you."

"Yes, she is a lot nicer recently."

"And how about Harold? Have you noticed how he's changed in the last month since the third grade retest? He spends a lot of time hiding in his office, but when he comes out, he's so friendly that I hardly recognize him. He even came into my room yesterday morning and asked me if I would like to represent the school at a conference next month."

Patty nodded in agreement as Sue went on. "And we don't see Harold and Eunice hanging around together much anymore, do we? I've been watching them, and they are actually going out of their way to avoid each other." She smiled. "No more standing together in the playground at recess. No more very private conferences in his office."

"I have noticed some changes," Patty admitted cautiously. And then, "I wonder why that is."

"That's a no-brainer. Harold is building support for himself. Once the superintendent picked up on the problems with the test scores, Harold knew he was in for it. And he's keeping away from Eunice because now he's under the spotlight and he doesn't want anyone to recognize their — how shall I say — special relationship."

Patty couldn't stop herself from asking the question. "What makes you think that Harold and Eunice have a special relationship?"

Sue answered quickly as though she had been waiting for Patty to ask that question. "Body language. I've done a lot of research on body language." When Patty gave a puzzled look,

Sue went on. "I've done work on my doctorate, and I planned to do my dissertation on body language in the schools. I'm ABD — all but dissertation. I've probably read everything written on the subject of body language, and for the last six years I've watched Harold and Eunice give themselves away. Those little touches. Those glances. At a child study last year, Eunice even threw — if you pardon the expression — an eraser — at Harold, and he picked it up and threw it right back. Just like two young lovers." She paused, "And I do have a clincher. Last August I came in early to decorate my room. I had just turned the corner by the cafeteria, and Harold and Eunice were right in front of me. They must have just come out of the cafeteria, and sure didn't realize that anyone was in back of them because Harold reached over and put his arm around Eunice's waist, and then slipped his hand lower. The walked like that for a couple of seconds. A man doesn't put his hand on that part of a woman's body unless something is going on."

Patty looked thoughtful, but said nothing, as Sue went on, her face coloring as she got into the subject. "I'm really fed up with it. And it may not be any of my business what they do in their private life, but they shouldn't carry it over into the school. The favoritism at this place stinks. And I do object to the way that Harold treats me. I'm a good teacher and a hardworking teacher. I've always volunteered to do extra things at the school — serve on committees, chaperone overnight field trips, run Homework Club and Odyssey of the Mind, and represent teachers on the PTA board. I'm everything here but chief cook. I've never married and I don't have a family of my own, and I love the kids at this school."

She was now speaking without censor, throwing caution to the winds. "But no matter what I do, he never gives me any credit. He always puts me down. I don't know why. Probably because I knew him when. We taught together when we were young. He came here a couple of years after I did. I remember that he was a good teacher. But I also remember how the standardized test scores in his classroom went up one year and stayed up. I also remember how I happened to pass his room one day while he was giving standardized tests. He was walking up and down the aisles and checking answers as the kids worked. I'm also sure I heard him say, 'This one is wrong. Do it again.' That's against the rules. Now we find that there's been test tampering. And I have no problem at all believing that Harold did change the scores." Sue's voice has gone up an octave as the bell ending recess rang. Patty waved, moved away, and started shepherding her students together.

Chapter 30

Sue stood back and chided herself for getting so emotional in front of Patty. She would have to be more careful in the future. She had kept the secret for years, and now was certainly not the time to let it out. She would not be able to bear it if the other teachers started to think of her as the woman scorned. No one must ever know of the relationship that she and Harold had once had. No one must ever know that Eunice had taken her place in Harold's affections — and she thought with an angry shake of her head — in Harold's bed. She waved her hand above her head and walked forward to lead her class into the building.

Chapter 31

By the afternoon the reporters had all gone away, and Patty was grateful that her students were able to focus on a hands-on math lesson. But around three o'clock when she glanced outside the front window, she saw the first camera crew pulling up. Fortunately, her students were deeply involved with colorful blocks and counters, and seemed unaware of the reporters until almost dismissal time. Once she led them up to the office to wait for the buses and they joined the other classes, there was minor turmoil. Harold, looking tired, was the only one who could calm the children down, and it was the first time that Patty had ever heard him raise his voice. Twenty minutes later all the school buses were gone, but the reporters and onlookers were still out in front of the school.

Patty was sitting at her desk just thinking about the day when like a jack-in-the-box, Harold appeared at her doorway. "I'm canceling all the clubs for the rest of the week, Patty, so no drama club tomorrow." Then he was gone down the hall. She looked out the front window and began getting her books and papers together to take home. Just then Ellen came in through the door. "Come on, we're having a meeting in Eunice's room. We all have to plan something to answer this attack on the school."

Patty did not want to go, but afraid to stand out, unwillingly followed Ellen to Eunice's room where half dozen teachers were squeezed into desks made for eight and nine year olds. Eunice stood at the front of the room, and gave Patty a smile, while Marielle who usually ran meetings in Harold's absence, was seated in one of the back seats. Patty slid into a seat next to Marielle. A few other teachers came in and then everyone's attention was directed toward Eunice as she banged on her desk for quiet and started to talk. "This is a nightmare that won't go away." She gestured toward the window. "I know all the teachers here support the school. This is really last minute so I could only pick up a small group of people, but I felt we needed to talk about what is happening to our school. I think it's really important to present a united front to fight this. Probably the best thing to do would be to discuss what's happening to each of you. Would anyone like to start?" She combed her hair nervously with the fingers of one hand as she looked around for a volunteer.

Julie LaVoie, one of the fifth grade teachers, her face contorted began to talk. "Today, just now, one of the fifth grade parents asked me if I thought that the other — and I emphasize other — teachers at the school had changed test scores. I knew what she meant. Did I change test scores? I've worked at this school for eight years and I've never had any kind of problem, and now people think I've cheated on standardized tests." Julie seemed about to cry. .

"Julie," Marielle called from the back of the room, "Nobody thinks that the teachers changed the scores. Right now we have twelve teachers among the third, fourth and fifth grades at this school. Nobody could possibly think that twelve teachers either individually or as a group decided to change scores. It's too preposterous."

Patty looked over at Marielle who had now taken off her glasses and was polishing them with a square white handkerchief. She could see confusion in Marielle's naked eyes.

"This whole thing definitely is preposterous, Marielle," Eunice chimed in. "Nobody at this school could have changed the scores."

Linda Hicks, the new first grade teacher asked, "So who changed them if not somebody at this school?"

Eunice seemed at a loss. "I don't know." She thought for a moment. "Maybe the superintendent himself did it."

There was a low murmur in the room.

"That's over the top. What possible reason could John Larraway have to change the scores?" asked Ellen in an incredulous tone.

"Maybe jealousy," Eunice quickly answered. "Maybe John Larraway was jealous of Harold so he set him up." Even Eunice looked disbelieving as she said the words.

"Weak," somebody whispered.

"Eunice, that is awfully farfetched." Again it was Marielle. Many of the other teachers were nodding in agreement.

"Well," Eunice went on, "we're not even sure that the scores were changed. Statistics can lie, you know."

"I want to say something." Lauren Siegel, the young redheaded second grade teacher, had risen from her seat. She also looked distressed. "At the end of the day, today, Bret Yaffee came up to me crying. You know Bret, the little blond boy with the big grin and no front teeth. Well, he came up to me crying and promised that he would never erase again, so I could tell the policemen that they could leave the school and the people in front could go away. I explained to him that second graders didn't even take the tests, and he had nothing to do with the tampering, so I hope I convinced him. But we can't let this go on. We can't let them affect our children this way."

Heads all over the room bobbed in agreement as Dewey came through the door. He stood next to Eunice at the front desk and looked over the room, counting the number of teachers present. He nodded at Patty when he noticed her. "Sorry I'm late. I was talking to Harold." Eunice quickly filled him in on Lauren Siegel's comments. Then he spoke to the group, swelling up with righteousness, "I'm not even sure that there was tampering. What was it that Mark Twain said? There are lies, damn lies and statistics. I think the whole thing is some horrible statistical fluke."

Patty saw that many of the teachers, including Ellen, were nodding in agreement with Dewey's comment. She heard someone at her side, and looked to see Marielle stand up and walk out at that moment, and remembered what Marielle had said in the hall that morning. A few other teachers spoke, many asking if somehow the reporters could be kept away from Emerson Street and the school. A fourth grade teacher reiterated, "It's hurting the kids. We can't let this go on. My students learned absolutely nothing today. They're all overexcited."

Eunice broke in. "I think that this will be a one-day wonder. There has to be some other news in the country. I think that everything will return to normal tomorrow."

"For some reason I don't think so," Dewey responded. "And if it does continue, it's important that we all stick together. Nobody at this school could have changed the scores," he emphasized vehemently, pounding one of his hands into the other, "and it's important that we let our friends, family, the Island Brooke parents, everybody in town, know that. We must be advocates for the school." He pounded one of his hands again. Patty had never seen him so worked up before. He seemed to be a new person.

"And what about the press?" someone cried out. "I don't think any of our teachers should give interviews to the press. Let's make that a rule."

A murmur of agreement went around the room, and as several teachers started talking all at once, Patty found her chance to slip out. As she left the building, she was hoping for once that Eunice was right. This story had, just had to be a one-day wonder.

But as Dewey had predicted, the next day was a unwelcome repeat of the previous one — news vans, crowds milling around on the sidewalk in front of the school, parents with placards, police officers, and inattentive students. The rest of the week was the same. That weekend on the local television station a message from the Hastings Board of Education and the Island Brooke PTA was read. It was a joint plea to the media to stay away from the school since the excessive attention was interfering with the children's education. Reporters were asked not to congregate on school grounds or in front of the school. The appeal was broadcast over and over and also appeared in the weekend newspapers. It seemed to work since on the next Monday morning, there was only one newsman, a reporter from the *Hastings Morning Star*, in front of the building. The story seemed to die out in the New Haven and New London newspapers, but the local paper kept the test tampering scandal on its front page day after day.

One day the next week Dewey stopped by Patty's room at the end of the day, and said, "How low can those reporters get? Harold just told me that a guy from the *Morning Star* sneaked into the school today posing as a parent. He lied to Grace and told her that he had just moved into the district and had two kids who would be registering at the school. He began by asking a lot of questions about the curriculum and the bus schedule, and then started pumping her for information on the test tampering. Finally, Grace caught on, and called the policeman to escort the guy out. That local rag should start paying us. They have Island Brooke on their front page day after day, and they have pages and pages of letters to the editor on nothing but the test tampering. I'm getting so sick of all of this." He turned to leave, and then threw back just one comment. "Oh, and by the way, Harold told me to tell you. He really appreciates your support."

Chapter 32

On the third Saturday in March, Patty and Tish had plans to go walking. The two left Iron Weed Road about eight in the morning and headed in the direction of Stadler Park. Tish was clearly intrigued by the test tampering scandal and, excitement in her voice, she immediately brought it up. "Are you aware that this situation at Island Brooke is the biggest story in town? Every client who comes in the office wants to hear the latest about the test tampering. That's all anybody wants to talk about anymore. Did the principal do it? Did the teachers do it? I went food shopping yesterday and when I walked into the store, I ran into a friend who has kids at Island Brooke, and she told me that she has it on the best authority that the custodian did it."

"Oh, poor Mr. Tupper." Patty smiled, and then her smile became a laugh. "Well, at least the butler didn't do it."

"But listen to this. By the time I got to the checkout line I heard that all the teachers at Island Brooke routinely get together and change the scores."

"Right," said Patty, sarcasm in her voice. "We have a club, the cheaters club. It meets on alternate Thursdays right after school."

"You know what gets me," Tish went on, "is that the Island Brooke parents seem to think that everybody but Harold is guilty. Have you seen those pages and pages of letters to the editor in the *Morning Star*? You would think that Harold is a combination of Gandhi and Mother Teresa. Most of the parents seem to think that Harold is innocent and is taking the heat for the teachers."

"I read the *Morning Star* every day. Working at the school isn't enough for me."

"Did you see that long letter in the New Haven paper that Dewey wrote?"

"Yes. Dewey has somehow become the leader of Harold's supporters."

Tish put her forefinger in her wide-open mouth, made a gagging noise, and then said, "Give me a break."

Patty turned to her friend as they continued along. "So you and Dewey aren't seeing each other anymore?"

Tish shook her head. "Been there. Done that."

"Did you like him at all?"

"I guess. In a way. We always had a good time when we went out, but somehow, and I really don't know how or why, the relationship just never seemed to develop." She paused. "Maybe he met someone else who doesn't have kids. You know a lot of guys aren't interested in having a ready-made family. That could have scared him off."

"I'm sorry it didn't work out for the two of you. Dewey is a really nice guy. He's been a good friend to me. Of course, he's way off base about Harold, but remember from his point of view, Harold is an innocent man. And he must be aware that his support for Harold is killing his own chances for promotion in the school system."

Tish's voice became louder. "You can defend Dewey all you want, but I think I got to know him pretty well during the time we dated. In my opinion, he and Harold are cut from the same cloth."

Patty looked surprised to hear the criticism of Dewey as Tish went on. "Oh, Maybe I'm not being fair. Maybe I'm just mad because he stopped calling me, but it just seems to me that there's more to Dewey than meets the eye."

"What do you mean by that?"

"Oh, I don't know. He's just" Tish held back what she was about to say, and quickly changed the subject. "But getting back to the test tampering, how about all those charts and graphs and statistics that the *Morning Star* keeps publishing. I can barely understand them, but Rick says that they prove that the tampering did occur, as if we didn't already know it." She paused. "It must be hard for you knowing that Harold is guilty."

"It is hard. The teachers are always talking about it in the lounge, and I feel like standing up and yelling, 'He did it. I saw him change the scores. He's guilty,' but of course I don't. I'm under strict orders from John Larraway not to say a word to anybody else."

"And I won't say anything."

"I know you won't. I trust you and Rick."

"It is hard for me to keep your secret when it's the biggest story in the history of Hastings, but you know I will. And the silver lining of this particular cloud is that at least it gives me an excuse to talk to Rick. He's the only other person that I can discuss it with, and you better believe, that I make sure that we do."

They had reached Stadler Park and walked in silence for a few minutes. Then Tish said vehemently, "I hate that little worm Harold. He could get away with everything. He's got most of the people in town on his side."

"He certainly does have a lot of believers," Patty commented, her voice resigned.

"Have any of the parents asked for your opinion?"

"Not really. They haven't asked. I guess they just assume that all the teachers support Harold. I did have a close call at the supermarket around the corner from the school last week. I was wheeling my grocery cart out to the parking lot, and two parents stopped me and handed me a flyer for a rally to support the school. They also told me that I'm welcome at any of the teas and coffees that they're holding to discuss the tampering. I felt as though I were being held hostage as I stood there listening to one of the parents arguing that the superintendent had set up Harold, and the other insisting that the testing company had made a horrible mistake. They wanted to sign me up for some committee that Dewey is chairing, and I was only able to break away by saying that my perishables were melting. After that experience, I've asked Noah to do all of the shopping for a while. I don't feel like debating Harold's guilt or innocence in a parking lot."

They had reached the duck pond, and Patty bent down to pick up a small stone and tossed it into the center of the water. For a few moments the two of them watched the concentric circles before moving on into the park. Patty seemed lost in thought. Then she said, "You know it's funny. Do you remember that thing about throwing a pebble into a pond — how everything is affected and everything changes?"

Tish nodded and Patty went on. "I was just thinking. I was right here in the park last September, the day of my interview. I was thinking how my interview affected so many things. First I was interviewed, then I was hired as a teacher, then I caught Harold changing scores, and now all over the whole country people are reading about the test tampering at Island Brooke School in Hastings, Connecticut. Just think, if I hadn't been hired, there never would have been a test tampering scandal. Harold probably would have gone on his merry way and would never have been caught."

"You're right." Tish nodded in agreement. She stopped for a moment and then added, "I wonder what's next? You know, one thing leads to another. I wonder what the test tampering scandal will lead to."

"What could be next? Harold has been stopped. That's the end. Period. Nothing else."

"Well, Maybe you can make some money selling what you know to one of those tabloids, or they can make a Movie of the Week out of your story."

"No, I'm not interested in making money. I just want the whole thing to go away. I don't want my name in the paper. I don't want to be known as the teacher who blew the whistle on Harold Trelawney. I just want to teach school."

The two had reached the end of the gravel road, and Patty stopped for a minute to survey the open terrain. It was a pale, washed day, and the rain during the night had swept away most of the remnants of the winter's snow, but there were pockets of white here and there in the fields. In the distance the branches of oaks, maples and white birches were starkly silhouetted against the sky. The air was slightly damp, but cool and invigorating. She took a deep breath.

"I love the four seasons, " she commented. "Every season in Connecticut is so beautiful." She paused, "I feel sorry for all those people in San Diego who have the same, bland perfect weather day after day."

"That was a joke, right?" asked Tish.

"Well partially."

Patty turned to go back, still admiring the surroundings and noticed after a few seconds that Tish was not walking with her. She looked back to see her friend standing in place.

"How far do I walk every day?" Tish asked.

"Two miles."

"And how far is it from my house to Rick's?"

"I'd say about a mile. Or a little less."

"So if we go all the way to Rick's and back, that will take care of my two miles for the day." She paused. "Let's go to Rick's." She spoke as though she had just thought of it.

Patty looked closely at Tish. She had been so caught up in her own thoughts that it hasn't registered how colorfully attractive Tish looked in a new hot-pink sweat suit and a leather patchwork jacket opened to expose the fullness of her figure. She was wearing subtle makeup, and her chestnut hair was appealingly tousled from the fresh winds.

Patty groaned out loud. "Girlfriend, you planned this. You planned to go to Rick's all along. You planned to catch him before he goes out. That's why you wanted to walk so early this morning." She then chided her friend in a kidding tone. "Tish, we are going to have to find one of those twelve-step groups for you. What do they call them? Co-dependents Anonymous or something like that. Your feelings for Rick are starting to border on obsession."

"Guilty as charged," Tish admitted, "That's me. A co-dependent." And then, more softly, "Or it could be that Rick and

I are soul mates, and he just doesn't know it yet." She paused. "Well, are you game? How about walking to Rick's?"

"I do feel as though I'm playing right into your addiction, but I guess one time won't hurt. Rick will probably have fresh-brewed coffee ready, so we can sit down with him and have a cup, and chat. I haven't heard from him lately, and I like to keep up with his life."

The two crossed a plank bridge at the opposite end to leave the park and continued under the interstate and out to the Post Road where they waited for the steady, rumbling traffic to thin. They then darted across the busy road and entered the expensive and prestigious area of Hastings known as Seaside. Side by side they walked down Flanders Road past the sprawling campus of an exclusive day school on one side and on the other side, a large vacant lot, posted with the distinctive red, white and blue metallic placards of Vera Miller Realty. They walked for about a quarter mile and then turned right onto Seafarer Drive. It was Rick's street, an elegant area of architect-designed houses set back from the road on multi-acre lots with mature plantings. High stone walls, log fences, decorative boulders, and groves of trees separated the wide lawns from the street, and glimpses of red clay tennis courts and covered pools could occasionally be seen in expansive backyards while late model BMWs and Land Rovers sat in driveways.

"I'm always amazed when I come to this area, " said Tish. "We're really not that far from the Post Road, yet it's so quiet and peaceful here." She went on, "Even the air seems richer. What do you think?"

"No question," answered Patty, wondering what kind of people lived in houses like these, and how had they made their money.

Tish went on, "I'm surprised they even let Rick live here since he does have the smallest house on the street." Rick's house was coming up, a two-story contemporary made of brick, redwood and leaded glass.

"The closer to the water you are in Seaside, the more expensive the house is," volunteered Patty.

"So Rick's about half way there, but he does have that marsh. That probably counts for something."

As they neared Rick's house, Patty saw his sleek dark Lexus in the circular driveway and started walking faster, and then immediately after saw a second car, a classic Jaguar, British racing green in color. She stopped in mid stride.

Tish also came to a standstill, and for a moment her face held no expression. Then she spoke, her voice uncharacteristically subdued. "It looks like Rick has company."

"Yes, it does," Patty, said.

"And," continued Tish looking at her watch and throwing back her shoulders, "since it's only 8:25 in the morning, it's fair to assume that this company spent the night."

Patty nodded, and trying to make light of the situation said, "Houston, we have a problem."

There was a silence, and then Tish scowled in frustration. "OK, I give up. Rick, you win. You with your sensitive man of the nineties personality, all your money and your upscale shopping center and everything else you have. You can take it and stuff it. I've had it." She made two quick gestures. "This is for you, and this is for the horse you rode in on."

They left Seafarer Drive at a fast walk and turned left onto Flanders Road. Reaching the Post Road, they waited and then crossed, and finally Tish spoke, "I know who he's been seeing."

"Who?"

"His ex-girlfriend. Jordana something or other. Jordana Sumner."

"Who told you?"

"No one, really. We have caller ID at the office. Duh. I finally checked it and got the name of the woman who's always calling Rick. Jordana Sumner. . Of Greenwich. When I mentioned her name to one of the other agents, he told me that Jordana and Rick were once engaged."

"Right, Jordana Sumner." Since Tish had found out about Jordana on her own, Patty no longer felt held to her promise to Rick.

"You know her right?"

"Not well. They were dating for about a year and that was years ago when I was in college. I only met her a few times."

Tish pondered this as they crossed the narrow wooden bridge back into Stadler Park. "And what does Jordana yada yada look like?"

Patty wondered if she fib a little, and tell Tish that Jordana really wasn't that pretty. If fact, she could tell her that Jordana was plain. But why hide the truth? Rick was completely out of reach. It would be better if Tish knew everything.

"She looks like Snow White."

"Snow White," echoed Tish.

"Snow White."

"You mean the fairy tale character?"

"Right, what was it, skin like the snow, hair like ebony, lips the color of blood, something like that. That's what Jordana looks like, and" — she paused — "eyes as blue as the — what's a good cliché — the sky."

"And the rest?"

"She's petite. Five one or two, and very pretty."

There was a pause before Tish spoke. "You might know he'd be with some doll. This makes it final. It's over. I can't spend my whole life fantasizing about Rick Miller."

The two walked in silence through the park, Tish, stony faced. Patty finally suggested, "Do you want to jog a little?"

"Might as well. I didn't want to be sweaty when I saw Rick, but that doesn't matter now." She broke into a slow jog and then quickened her pace. "C'mon Patty. I'll show you what running's all about. Race you to my house for coffee."

Fifteen minutes later, Patty followed Tish into the kitchen of her saltbox. She slipped off her jacket and settled herself into a cushioned chair while Tish opened a new can of coffee. Patty took a deep breath of the pleasing aroma in the air while Tish busied herself at the counter, and then stood, arms folded under her breasts, waiting for the percolator to stop gurgling.

"I guess I have to accept it," Tish sighed. "I'm just not lucky in love."

"How about your husband Ed? You must have been lucky with him, at least for a while."

"I suppose I was for a while," she said wistfully. She looked down at Patty, "You never met Ed, did you?"

Patty shook her head.

"At UCONN my friends thought we were mismatched right from the start. I know it's hard to believe, but I ran with a really popular crowd when I was a freshman, and Ed was a senior, like this complete nerd. All he wanted to talk about were computers and dot com stocks. My girlfriends called him Mr. Ed." She paused. "You know, the horse."

"You married him. You must have been in love."

"I was. I thought he was really cute in an awkward way, and for the first few years it was wonderful. And we had the two sweetest babies. First Amy, and then ten months later, another little girl. Ed insisted on naming her Zoë. He said that two kids were enough. That was it — Amy and Zoë. A to Z. I would have loved one more, a little boy, but Ed said, 'No way,' so I settled. Then I got into the catering business and that took up a lot of my time. I'm not sure when Ed started cheating on me. I know he began to make oodles of money with his computer, and those dot com stocks he invested in went through the roof. And at some point, he must have decided to have all the fun that he had missed in high school and college. He got a new haircut, a new wardrobe, and contacts. Then he started working out. The working out should have been the signal to me, but I missed it. Of course, I was busy myself. Busy ballooning up. Back then the high point of my day was a bubble bath with Russell Stover." Tish forced out a laugh.

"How long has it been since you and Ed broke up?"

"Almost three years." She pointed toward the front door. "He stood right there with his hanging suit bag over his packed suitcases. He was leaving and even then he wanted to control my life. He put three of his fingers out and said, 'Tish,' she deepened her voice, mimicking him, 'I have three pieces of advice for you.' She held out three fingers and ticked them off. 'One, sell the house, two, go back to Providence and three, for God's sake, lose some weight.' And little fool that I was, I was all ready to do what he ordered." She paused, "And that's how I met Rick."

"How?"

Before answering, Tish poured coffee into two double-eared brown ceramic mugs and added low fat milk. She placed one mug before Patty and then sat down and drank from the second.

"Through the yellow pages. Vera. Miller Reality. It had the biggest ad, and it was right there in Hastings. I called and got Rick. I told him that I wanted to sell my house right away, and he said that he'd be over the very next day. I watched him pull up in his car and walk around and look at the house, and I thought he even looked something like Ed, but thinner and more attractive. When I went to answer the doorbell, I got kind of embarrassed because my eyes were swollen from crying, and my face was all red and puffy. But I realized right away that unless he had a poster of Mountain Girl on his bedroom wall, he wouldn't even see me. So I showed him around and finally he asked why I was crying. It seemed easy to talk to a complete stranger, so we sat down and I told him everything. And when I had finished he handed me his card, and said he would be happy to sell my house for me, but not then. He told me to see a good divorce lawyer, and to take some time to think over what I wanted to do. And when I did think it over, I realized that I wanted to stay right here in Hastings. Amy and Zoë were in the seventh and eighth grades at middle school and I didn't want to uproot them. So I stopped by his agency to thank him a few weeks later, and one thing led to another, and he told me that he would hire me if I got my sales license. So I gave up catering, went on a diet, lost thirty pounds, and started to work for him last year."

"So that's how you got into real estate."

"Yes, and that's how I fell for Rick. And you know, Patty, it's funny how our lives are entwined."

Patty absently stirred her coffee. "What do you mean?"

"What you said when you tossed that stone into the duck pond is true. Things are all connected. When I heard that Mr. and Mrs. Remack down the street were retiring and moving to New Mexico, I went right down there and got the listing. And then I took a call at the agency from a pilot named Noah Bass who was looking to buy his own home. And then I started taking the studly Mr. Bass around looking at houses. He liked the cape right away. Made an offer. And now I'm thinking, if I hadn't met Rick, you wouldn't have met Noah. At least you wouldn't have met him that night at Rick's Open House."

"Rick's Open House. That certainly was a red letter day for me."

"For all of us. I remember how you looked when you walked in. I really envied you. So slim. I felt like a real porker when Rick took me over to you."

"Tish, stop putting yourself down."

"No, it's OK. I know I don't look like that anymore. And I appreciate all the encouragement you've given me. But that's finished now. It has to be. I've had a crush on Rick for almost two years, but I just have to get over it. It wasn't meant to be. I guess every time Rick looks at me, he still sees the same old divorced reject, the same old chubbette. And I'd be foolish to think that I could ever compete with Snow White."

Tish laced her fingers around her cup and stared into her coffee for a long time.

Patty finally broke the silence. "So what are you thinking?"

"I'm thinking that I'm thirty-five years old, and I'm tired of being a single parent. I want a man in my life. A real flesh-and-blood man with the emphasis on flesh. And it may not be the politically correct thing to say, but I want to be married again and have a couple more kids." For a moment, Tish looked like she might cry.

"Guys are interested in me, you know. I'm not a complete washout. But Rick is holding me back."

Patty raised her eyebrows and Tish went on to explain. " I don't mean that the way it came out. I guess it's not Rick holding me back. It's me. I can't seem to get interested in any other guy because my feelings for Rick keep getting in the way." She made a little humming sound. "So I'll just have to get over him. From now on, I'll just have to put him out of my mind and be very businesslike in the office. If that doesn't work, I'll have to give my notice and find a job at another agency. Hell-o? What am I saying? I'll find a job at another agency first, and then I'll give my notice. You know something? I'm an asset at Vera Miller Realty. I'm good at what I do. When I'm gone, that's when Rick will be sorry. That's when he'll miss me. That's how men are."

Chapter 33

Noah came in through the garage, his arms filled with heavy bags of groceries, and the mail. He dropped the mail on the kitchen table, and set the bags of groceries upright on the kitchen counter. "Patty, I'm home," he called. When there was no answer, he walked to the foot of the stairs and could hear the shower running.

He called louder. "Patty, I'm home. I did all the shopping."

By the time Patty came downstairs smelling like strawberries, wearing a robe, and with her head wrapped up turban-like in a towel, he had put all the groceries away, and was sitting at the kitchen table, his dark eyes narrowing and his eyebrows slashed as he read a letter. Patty saw his frown and asked, "What's wrong?"

"The airline is giving notice that some pilots will be laid off. Furloughed, actually. That's what they euphemistically call it. Furloughed." He seemed deflated.

Patty was surprised. "Do you think you'll make the cut?"

"I hope so. But it sure won't be any fun waiting to find out." He paused. "And here's a letter for you. From Hastings Public Schools. I hope your news is better than mine."

Patty opened the letter and read it silently. Noah looked up.

"What?" he said watching her face.

"It's a form letter from John Larraway addressed to all the teachers at the school. The town has hired the Abeles-Mack Detective Agency to investigate the test tampering at Island Brooke. The agency is going to interview a number of teachers at the school. Larraway wants me to call the agency and make an appointment for an interview. He's even written a personal note on the bottom." She read it aloud. "*Patty, I know this will be hard for you, but it's important. Everything you say will be kept in the strictest confidence. Please call the Abeles-Mack Agency as soon as possible.*"

Patty snorted in disgust. "He's also kind enough to provide two telephone numbers for the agency. Doesn't this ever end?"

"Are you going to make the appointment?"

Patty took the letter and put it behind the frog magnet on the refrigerator. "I don't know what I'm going to do. I want to think about this for a while."

Chapter 34

The next morning in the staff room Eunice read aloud from the newspaper. *"A local detective agency has been hired to interview staff at the award-winning school in an attempt to gather further information on the question of test tampering."* She left off reading and threw the paper down in disgust.

"I don't think we teachers should cooperate. I know I won't."

A few teachers nodded their heads in agreement with her as she got up and flounced out of the room. Dewey, standing by the coffee pot, came over to Patty sitting on one of the sofas. "This whole thing is killing Harold. It breaks my heart to see what Larraway is doing to him. I'm so angry." He bunched up his hands and released them. Then he said, "You know about the emergency faculty meeting right after school, right?"

Patty nodded.

"We're going to discuss this detective agency and make some decisions about what we all should do. Harold is going to talk to us about our options. You wouldn't believe what's been happening at this school. Some of our teachers actually believe that Harold is guilty. We've got to stop this, talk to these people, convince them. Harold needs his whole staff behind him, 100 per cent. I know I can count on you."

Patty just stared at Dewey and made a noncommittal noise in her throat, but he didn't seem to notice.

By 3:45 p.m. that day, all the Island Brooke teachers sat in the library-media center, their faces serious and expectant, waiting to hear what their beleaguered principal had to say. Harold, his familiar face looking drawn, stood up before the group. His suit, a quiet brown check, looked expensive, but he had lost weight and the jacket hung loosely on him. He also seemed to have lost his air of importance, and he appeared nervous, twisting his wedding ring round and round, and clearing his throat repeatedly before beginning.

Once he began to speak, his voice held its usual authority. "I want to thank you for your support during these difficult times — and I want you to know that I support you as much as you support me. And by you, I mean primarily the fine third, fourth and fifth grade teachers who are the targets of these spurious charges. We have to stand together to face down these lies they're telling about the school. Most of you have risen to the challenge and are weathering the storm. Most of you. Unfortunately, I understand that a few of you are being influenced by all the negative information that is being passed around. Some of you are even questioning whether I could have changed the scores. The answer to that question is" There was a beat in time. "No." Another pause. "You all know me. You know I could never be involved in something dishonest like this. And I know all of you. I can't believe that any of the teachers at this school would have anything to do with changing test scores." He then held aloft a copy of the *Hastings Morning Star*, and his voice became strident. "And this poor excuse for a newspaper. The editor and all the reporters should be tarred and feathered for their virulent attacks on our school. They're vicious people. Malicious people. I would never suggest to you teachers what you should or should not read, but—" At this point, Harold seemed overcome with emotion and turned away for a moment.

Dave Mendel, one of the fifth grade teachers raised his hand. Harold noticed and pointed at him. "Dave."

"Many of us have received the letter from the superintendent requesting that we go for an interview with the Abeles-Mack Agency. We don't know what to do about this interview."

Eunice, livid, snapped out, "Interrogation, not interview."

There was a sprinkling of applause at Eunice's remark, and Harold's head snapped up at the support. He then went on to talk for several more minutes, his voice more confident, his words now flowing easily in defense of himself and the school.

When Harold was finished, Dewey raised his hand and was called on. "I was also asked to contact the Abeles-Mack Agency. This whole thing seems to be turning into a witchhunt. I don't know what to do either."

Harold answered, "Dewey, I don't know what to tell you. Let your conscience be your guide."

Eunice again called out, "I'm supposed to go too, but I'm going to refuse." Her tone was indignant.

Ellen's voice came out loud and clear. "I don't think we can refuse."

Harold gestured irritably. "Unfortunately, I believe that Ellen is correct on this." He stopped abruptly as though he could not continue. Then he said, "I know I have been scheduled to meet with them too. This is all a nightmare for me. I'm beginning to feel like that security guard in Atlanta who was unjustly accused of the Olympic bombing. What was his name?"

Marielle shouted "Richard Jewell," from the back of the library. Some of the teachers turned around to look at the woman who in the past had always been seated at the front of the room next to Harold. Now she was sitting in the closest seat to the door, with Sue at her side.

"Right. Richard Jewell. I'm the Richard Jewell of Hastings."

Marielle stood up at that moment and left the room, and more than a few teachers looked back as the library-media center door opened and closed. Eunice glared at the closed door for a moment, and then transferred her stare to Sue who returned the look.

"That agency is going to check fingerprints on the test. What will that prove?" Dave Mendel asked in a bewildered voice. "Of course our fingerprints are on the tests of our students."

Dewey answered for Harold. "That's right, each teacher's fingerprints will be on his or her own students' tests, but nobody's fingerprints will be on all the tests. That's what they're looking for. So when you think about it, it could be a good thing that they're checking prints."

Harold looked thoughtful as he gnawed at a hangnail on his little finger, and a silence stretched out. Then he spoke, "Well, remember, sometimes I kind of sort through the tests, and I like to put them in alphabetical order. It wouldn't be unusual to find my fingerprints all over them, so fingerprints don't really prove anything."

Eunice called out in support. "That's right. Fingerprints don't prove anything."

There were many murmurs of agreement throughout the room although knowing looks had appeared on a few faces.

Lauren Siegel raised her hand. "This whole controversy is hurting the kids." She went on to review how a few of her second grade students still thought that they were to blame for all the problems that the school was having even though she had taken a great deal of class time to explain that they were not involved in the testing.

Harold heard her out, and then commiserated. "I agree with you, Lauren. That is the saddest part of the whole test tampering fantasy. These lies about the tests are hurting our kids." His eyes welled up with tears for all to see.

In her seat Patty tensed up, thinking back to what she had seen on that Wednesday evening in January. How long can Harold Trelawney continue with this charade of innocence? she asked herself. How can he just stand there and lie and lie?

Harold sighed heavily, and then asked, "Are there any other comments or questions?"

The room was still.

"Again I thank you for standing together with me to defend our school. And I remind you that the most important thing is that we stick together. That we all keep on the same page. If you're called into that agency, tell them that no one at the school could have changed the scores. I pledge to all of you that this whole mix-up will be resolved in due time, and that we'll all be vindicated in the end."

Abruptly, Harold sat down next to Dewey, and they began to talk in low voices as the teachers rose and started flowing out of the room. Patty and Ellen were into their own thoughts and descended the stairs together in silence. Ellen finally spoke as they reached the first floor. "I don't know how Harold can stand this pressure he's under. I don't like the way he looks. I'm worried about him. He's keeping to his office too much, and I've heard how he made no move to shut down the PPT where that Mrs. Post came in and started shouting. I hope this whole thing doesn't drive him to do anything."

"What?" asked Patty, taken by surprise, and not quite catching Ellen's meaning.

"I hate to say take his own life, but he is the principal here. Captain of the ship. That kind of thing. He can be blamed for the test tampering even though I know he could never have changed any scores."

Patty felt a deep sense of unease as for the first time the thought of Harold committing suicide entered her mind. Once again, she silently chastened herself for making that hasty telephone call to her father on that fateful evening. As she and Ellen left the building by the side door, Sue rushed from behind to catch up, and they walked toward the parking lot three abreast. Ellen immediately turned to her. "I see you're thick as thieves with Marielle. What's going on with her?"

"Oh, Marielle had a real epiphany when the test tampering information broke. She's had an inkling for years that the math test results were out of line with student achievement, but could never dream that anyone would change scores. Once she heard about the cheating and read all those statistics, she told me that, of course, someone has been changing scores. And she thinks that Harold is the only person who could have done it."

Ellen gave her a scathing look, and Sue moved away toward her car. Then from a distance Sue flung back a defiant comment, "And I think so too."

Ellen's face was set in anger as she came to a halt in the middle of the driveway and turned to Patty. "Do you think anyone could have changed the test scores?"

The question caught Patty by surprise, and she struggled to think of a diplomatic way to answer Ellen's question without actually lying. On more than one occasion, she had toyed with the idea of telling her mentor the whole truth — leaving nothing out — but on reflection and discussion with Noah had been reluctant to disobey what had been a direct order from the superintendent of schools. And now she was on the spot, as Ellen looked right at her face waiting for an answer.

Patty shifted from one foot to the other in a self-conscious way, and began, "I'm not quite sure—" when the loud honking of a horn interrupted her in mid sentence. A car full of teenage boys had just braked on Emerson Street at the foot of the driveway to the parking lot, and as the driver gunned the engine, Patty could hear loud calls but at first couldn't make out the words. She turned to see a boy with a wispy mustache leaning out the front window of the car, and then she understood what he was chanting. "Island Brooke cheaters. Island Brooke cheaters."

"Island Brooke cheaters. Island Brooke cheaters. Island Brooke cheaters," the other boys called out in childhood rhythm, as they waved their arms out the window and grinned wide open grins at the two adult women standing in the school driveway. The shouting continued for a few moments, until

Ellen took two steps down the driveway toward them, and then amid hoots and hollers, the car revved up and screeched away, speeding down Emerson Street.

Ellen stopped walking and glowered at the departing car. She then shook her head. "It's kids like that who give teenagers a bad name. I don't know about you, but I've had just about enough of this for today. I'm going home. See you tomorrow."

Patty called, "Goodbye," after Ellen, and did a half-sprint to her car, thankful that the teenagers had gotten her off the hook, and yet wishing that she had had the courage to disobey the superintendent and tell Ellen what she had seen that Wednesday evening. As she drove home, she found herself doing what she seemed to be doing more and more — pondering her options. Should she go to that detective agency and tell what she had seen Harold doing — or should she refuse any further involvement in the matter? Finally, hoping that some music would take her mind off her untenable situation, she switched on the car radio and pushed in the button for what she thought was a classical music station. Instead, she found herself listening to a local talk show, and she heard a caller to the station asking, "What game do Island Brooke students always play at their birthday parties?"

"I don't know," said the host, already laughing. "What game do they play?"

"Erase the tail on the donkey."

There were loud guffaws as Patty snapped off the radio, and again mulled her choices over. Nothing in her life had ever prepared her for a situation like this. Hammered by conflicting emotions, she tried to look at her position from every angle, but the more she thought about it, the worse she felt. It just wasn't fair. The town of Hastings was split just about in half, the teachers were falling into factions, and now even the children had become the objects of derision on talk shows. And she was the only one who held the key. She was the only one who could bring an end to all the controversy, which had infected the town. As she pulled her Mustang into her driveway, she had finally made the decision that she would go to the detective agency and tell what she knew. She had to point her finger again at the one person who was responsible for the cheating. Harold. When she walked into her kitchen a few minutes later, she took John Larraway's letter from behind the frog magnet on the refrigerator, and taking no pleasure in what she was about to do, called the first of the two numbers for the Ableles-Mack Agency.

Chapter 35

Patty's appointment at the Abeles-Mack Agency was set for 1:45 the Thursday before Easter which was an early dismissal day in Hastings. That day she left immediately after school, went home to pick up Noah for moral support and then drove to the address she had been given. The agency was located right off the business section of town, only three blocks from Island Brooke School, on a small side street that Patty had never heard of before. She slowed as she drove down the street, checking the numbers of the cookie-cutter two-family houses against the address in the letter.

"This must be it," said Noah, as she slowed at a large white two-story house with an open porch on each floor. It was freshly painted and looked more like a home than an office of any kind.

"Is this address wrong?" Patty asked. "This doesn't look like a detective agency."

At that moment Noah noticed a small brass plaque with raised letters reading *Abeles-Mack Agency*, set inconspicuously in the picket fence. "No, look there on the fence. You can hardly see the sign. This is it all right. " He pointed it out to Patty.

"Very discrete," she said. "So this is the place. OK. We're supposed to park in the back and ring the back doorbell."

She guided her car up the side driveway and came to a narrow backyard, which had been completely blacktopped over, and divided into parking spaces by painted diagonal yellow lines. There were half a dozen cars already there, and Patty parked away from them, carefully allowing space on each side of her for future vehicles. They both got out of the Mustang, and Noah walked around to her, and gave her a hug. " How do you feel?"

"I can do this," was her answer.

"C'mon. Let's get this over with. We'll be out of here in an hour," he assured her.

They then walked along the sidewalk together and up the back steps. Patty straightened her spine as she rang the doorbell, and within a few minutes, a woman who had apparently been expecting them opened the door. The woman was about Patty's age, thin, and casually dressed in baggy, dun colored slacks and a matching cotton sweater layered over a white blouse. Patty introduced herself and Noah, and the woman stuck out a thin arm and a hand with long, French-manicured fingernails. She shook hands with the tips of her fingers.

"Toni Soffel," she said. Her features were pinched, but pretty, and she had a cloud of brown hair curling outward over her shoulders.

"Come right in." She led them down a narrow corridor that was very quiet and smelled distinctively of paint. They passed several doors which were closed and unmarked, and Toni continued on to the end of the hall. She finally stopped, opened some heavy wooden sliding doors and ushered them into a large room, which looked to Patty like a living room of a home. There was a blue-flowered area rug, a sofa covered with a bright blue slipcover, several wingback chairs and armchairs, bookshelves built into the wall, and flowered chintz drapes. Patty could see a small kitchen beyond. Patty and Noah sat down together on the sofa while Toni closed the sliding doors tightly.

"Did you have any trouble finding us?" inquired Toni.

"No, the directions were fine," answered Patty.

At that moment the wooden doors, which had just been carefully closed, slid open and a tall man clad in a button-down shirt, a tie, and an open cardigan with leather patches on his elbows entered. His eyes on Patty and Noah, he reached behind him to close the doors. He appeared to be in his forties and was nice-looking with a salt-and-pepper crew cut, and a brush of a salt-and-pepper moustache. He had a ruddy complexion, which spoke of the out-of-doors, which Patty thought was good, and a tight smile, which seemed plastered on his face, which Patty did not like at all. There was something robotic about his walk as he headed toward them.

"Ex-cop or ex-marine," Patty whispered to Noah as the man approached them. He shook hands and introduced himself, "Brian Heyhal." He had a deep, modulated voice.

Toni had gone to the kitchen and could be seen standing at a stove, watching a small bright kettle. She turned and called into the living room, "Herbal tea, anyone? I've got Red Zinger. Celestial Seasonings. No caffeine."

Patty and Noah both called back, "No, thanks," and Brian shook his head, and sat down. Toni continued heating the water for what seemed like an interminable time. There was no conversation with Brian Heyhal until finally the kettle began to whistle. "All right, " he said as he turned to watch Toni put a tea bag into a large mug, and pour the water. All eyes were on Toni as she came back into the living room area and placed her steaming drink on a coaster on the coffee table. She then sat down in a green wingback chair.

"Sorry," she said. "A watched pot."

"All right, we're ready," said Brian, turning on a small tape recorder, which Patty now noticed on the coffee table. He also produced two yellow legal pads, and handed one to Toni.

"Ironic," whispered Patty to Noah. "It's the same type of legal pad that Harold was using that night."

Brian's eyes settled on Patty, as he pressed a button. She took a breath and sat upright, waiting for the first question.

"Mrs. Bass, do you understand that this interview will be recorded?" Brian began in a formal tone.

"Yes, I do."

"Yes, and do you also understand that you have the right to have an attorney present?"

"Yes."

"And you have waived that right?"

Patty's voice broke nervously. "Yes, I have, but my husband is here with me." She reached over and touched Noah's arm.

"And your husband's name is Noah Bass?"

"Yes."

He gave the date and time, and went on. "My name is Brian Heyhal, my associate Toni Soffel is here with me, and we are interviewing Mrs. Patricia Bass. Her husband, Noah Bass, is also present."

At that point, Noah interrupted. "We have been told that any information given today will be held in the strictest confidence. Is that true?"

"Yes, it is. Anything that Mrs. Bass says today will not be released without her consent."

"You can call me Patty. It's easier."

"Thank you, Patty, and please call me Brian." Patty settled herself on the sofa, and for about the next thirty minutes answered much the same questions that John Larraway had asked her. Finally, Brian checked his watch, changed his tone and gave the ending time and date to the tape recorder. He then snapped off the machine and stood up. Patty, Noah and Toni also rose.

"Your comments will be typed up, Patty, and we will ask you to come in early next week and sign them in the presence of a notary public."

Patty nodded her consent.

"That's all then. Thank you for coming in today. And you too, Mr. Bass. Thank you."

"Thank you for coming in today," Toni Soffel echoed.

Patty straightened her skirt, and led the way to the heavy sliding doors, noticing immediately that they were not completely closed.

Brian reached ahead and opened the doors all the way, and started to usher the two of them down the corridor to the back door. Patty turned to see Toni hurrying down the hall without a backward glance.

Noah looked over to Brian and spoke to him. "I've already mentioned this but I want to be sure that all the information my wife gave you is kept confidential. Patty could not possibly continue working at Island Brooke if her role as a whistleblower ever got out."

Brian smiled. "I assure you that there will be no problem with that." He opened the back door, and said, "Goodbye," as they walked ahead down the steps into the sunlight. They heard the back door close and looked back. There was no sign of Brian.

Patty sighed in a dramatic way. "I'm glad it's finally over."

"Finally," Noah agreed as he moved ahead of Patty and unlocked the passenger door for her. He then went around and slid into the driver's seat. "How do you feel now?"

"Relieved. I'm now down on record, and I hope I never have to go through that again. Let the superintendent and the Board of Education decide what to do about Harold. I want to get on with my life." She paused for a moment as she got into the car, and then said, "OK. Enough of this. .Next stop. The supermarket. We have all our Easter shopping to do. I want to get a small ham for you, Dad, Brooke and Ilona. I'll make some manicotti for myself."

"Are Brooke and Ilona spending the weekend?"

"Just Saturday night. We'll have to pull out the hide-a-bed in the den."

"And Tish isn't coming to Easter dinner?"

"She's going home to Providence to be with her parents."

"How about Rick?" Noah asked as he started the car.

"I invited him, but he's dining in style in Greenwich this year. " She paused as she continued to think about her Easter menu. "And I'm going to make scalloped potatoes, and candied yams, and coleslaw, and cucumber salad. And let's get some chocolate bunnies for everyone. We can put them right on the kitchen. And some Easter breads and cakes. Oh, and hard-boiled eggs. Of course we have to color eggs. I always loved to do that with my parents when I was a girl." She paused to take a breath. "This will be our first Easter together. Let's think up some fun things to do." There was enthusiasm in her voice.

Noah started to pull carefully out of the narrow backyard. Patty suddenly let out a yelp, "Stop."

Noah stepped on the brake. "What?"

"That's Harold's car. That red Buick. Right in that space." She pointed.

Noah backed up and read the license plate aloud.

"That's his car," Patty insisted. "I know his license number."

"How could they have him scheduled at the same time you were here?" Noah asked, angrily. "Should we go back in and tell them off?"

"No, let's get out of here. We can call Brian from home."

Noah was in a rage, and as he drove home a shade above the speed limit, his hands were tightly gripping the steering wheel. Patty beside him looked miserable and kept shaking her head. Through the town and onto their street, Patty looked out at the familiar scenery, not really seeing it. As they pulled into their driveway, they saw Tish on their front porch ringing the bell. Tish waved and hurried down the steps to meet them, but as soon as the car had stopped, Noah was out of it and running through the garage and into the house. Pat signaled her to follow them.

"What's happening?" asked Tish, seeing Patty's agitation.

"I just had my interview, " Patty explained, "but as we were leaving the agency, we saw Harold's car. He was there at the same time I was. He could have heard everything I told the investigators, and it was all supposed to be so confidential. I trusted those people and they let me down."

Noah was already on the phone in the kitchen by the time Patty and Tish got in the house, and they listened while he used language that he usually didn't use. Anger had roughened his voice, but after about a few minutes, he seemed to settle down, but continued asking, "What do you mean? What kind of detective agency are you running? We were guaranteed that this would be all confidential. How could you possibly have Harold Trelawney there at the same time as my wife?" He seemed to be listening and then he held for a while. Then, he said, "It's still hard to believe. All right. All right, OK, here she is." He handed the phone to Patty.

She said, "Hello," and recognized Brian's voice.

"Mrs. Bass. Patty. I really apologize for what happened. Let me explain. Harold Trelawney was supposed to come in next week. He called late this morning and asked if he could come in this afternoon instead. One of my associates took the call and scheduled him for two o'clock today, not realizing that the two of you shouldn't be here at the same time. But," Brian went on, "I can assure you that it is impossible that Harold Trelawney heard any of your interview. He was met at the back door at two o'clock and taken immediately up to a room on the second floor." He paused as if considering and then went on. "I'll be completely honest with you. My associate did have to leave the room for a few minutes — he assured me no more than five or six — to take a confidential phone call. But when he returned, Harold Trelawney was still sitting there in the same place, and my associate is sure that Mr. Trelawney did not leave the room. There is no need to worry Patty. No need to worry at all There is no way that Harold Trelawney could know that you are the whistleblower."

Chapter 36

As soon as he opened the door to the old-fashioned barbershop, he realized that he should have waited one more week to have his hair trimmed. It was the day before Easter, and the place was crowded. With the first come, first served policy and only two barbers, he saw that he would have a long wait. For a moment, he just stood at the entrance, holding the door ajar and considering whether he should walk out and come back the next week. But it was a more than a half-hour drive back to Hastings, and he was here. He sighed and resigned himself. At least this would give him some time to try to sort things out. He walked into the shop and inhaled the smells of talc and shaving soap. He had always liked this place. He gave his name to the receptionist, hung up his windbreaker and walked over to the plate-glass window. For a long time, he stood there, looking out at busy downtown New London and watching the miniature candy-cane-striped pole going round and round as his problem went round and round in his head. There was no easy answer to his difficulties. Again, he sighed impatiently, and then turned to study his reflection in the lighted mirror that ran along one entire wall.

Time passed, and finally there were just two customers ahead of him. Bored with the wait, he sat down in one of the chrome and vinyl chairs, and started leafing through a pile of old magazines. Hunting magazines, girlie magazines — and then one of the true crime varieties was in his hand. Not his usual reading matter. He glanced at the cover and started to put it down when the word *Whistleblower* caught his eye. Whistleblower. Patty the whistleblower, he thought. He turned the pages and scanned though the article. He read about a young woman who blew the whistle on corruption in a governor's office in the Midwest, and a worker who contacted a newspaper about pollution caused by his company, and then a story about a famous bank robber who was turned in by an honest citizen. He read the whole article with interest.

Patty the whistleblower. He thought of Patty spilling her guts at the Abeles-Mack Agency. Closing the magazine, he leaned back and tapped his lip with the index finger of his right hand as he considered. The solution to his problem sprang to his mind. But he hesitated. Would it work? He had to be very careful. After all these years, he could still feel a shiver whenever he thought of Gill and Silverstone.

Debating in his head, he reviewed the pros and cons, and considered the obstacles. He had vowed that he would never kill again. But if he could kill Patty, and be one hundred percent sure that he could get away with it, now that was a different story.

One of the barbers called the man ahead of him.

He had no compunction about the killing itself — witness Gerry and Debbie — but the thought of prison terrified him. Capital punishment was even more horrifying although it was rarely meted out in Connecticut. Thank goodness for the bleeding hearts crowd, he thought.

But Patty was a whistleblower. She would fit nicely onto his list. First the bully, then the blackmailer, and now the whistleblower.

Just then, he heard his name called, and he dropped the magazine on top of the pile. Usually, he enjoyed the conversation and jokes of his barber, but today his mind was elsewhere as the man fastened a nylon cape around his shoulders. The barber picked up the scissors and comb, and said, "Stop me if you've heard this one. This monkey goes into a bar and orders a whiskey sour."

He was into his own thoughts. Patty was a whistleblower. Whistleblowers were punished. They should all be punished.

The barber's scratchy voice intruded. "He puts down a twenty-dollar bill, but when the bartender goes to make change, the cashier says, 'Who's that for?'"

"That monkey over there."

Whistleblowers were killed. They should all be killed. He tried to get back to his thoughts, screen out the stupid joke.

"Only give him a dime back. He won't know. He's only a monkey.' So the bartender gives the monkey a dime back, and the monkey doesn't say anything."

Whistleblowers should mind their own business. Anyone could understand that.

"So after a while, the bartender looks at the monkey and says, "You know you're the first monkey who ever came into this bar.' And the monkey says to him, 'Well, for nineteen-ninety a drink, I'm surprised that anyone comes in here."

The barber was now standing back and laughing loudly at his own punch line. He laughed along with the barber although he hadn't really followed the joke.

When his hair was trimmed, he thanked the barber and paid the receptionist. Then he went back to leave a tip in the barber's drawer, and saw that the man's attention was on the next customer. "This monkey goes into a bar."

Neither of the barbers, nor the receptionist nor any of the other customers who had come in after him noticed as he slipped the true crime magazine under his arm and walked away with it.

On the way back to Hastings, he drove at just under the speed limit in the right lane of I-95, windshield wipers and lights on against a sudden downpour, and thought about whistleblowers some more. He then did some planning — not unlike what he had done when he had been forced to take care of Debbie. He decided that he would draw up a plan as a mental exercise. Then he would take the first step. He could always abort if it seemed too dangerous for him. But how to set it up? At that moment, he remembered Marcetta Osborne and the annoying salmon-colored envelopes that kept appearing in his mailbox. Yes, it was corny, but anonymous letters would be part of his preliminary plan.

He slowed as he approached the Hastings exit, but at that moment realized that the large discount stores would be crowded on this day before Easter, and it would be the perfect time to be just one more anonymous shopper making last minute purchases for the holiday. But not here in Hastings. Further away. He accelerated by the Hastings exit, continued past the East Shore towns, and fought the usual heavy traffic over the Q Bridge to New Haven. By the time he had turned off the interstate onto Exit 39B in Milford, he had made a mental list of everything that he would need. A cheap manual typewriter should do it. And then some stationery and thin latex gloves. And yes — last but not least — he would need a tire iron.

Chapter 37

Patty didn't sleep well over the Easter weekend. Friday and Saturday nights were bad, but Sunday night into Monday morning was the worst. One thirty. Two thirty. Three thirty.

She still lay wide-awake. When she finally did fall asleep about four, and her alarm clock rang at seven, she woke up bleary-eyed and out of sorts. She considered calling in sick and spending the day in bed.

"It's up to you," said Noah. "If you're sick, Patty, you're sick."

"I'm not really sick," she answered. "I'm just exhausted from lack of sleep. This weekend has been torture. No matter what Brian Heyhal says, I have this awful scenario in my mind. I can just see Harold arriving at the Abeles-Mack Agency before two o'clock. Right away he notices my car in the parking lot. My Mustang is kind of distinctive, and Harold is the type who's very aware of his teachers' cars. I can just picture him sneaking down the stairs and standing out in the hall listening to me give my statement. He eavesdrops just long enough to learn that I'm the whistleblower and then scoots back upstairs."

Noah frowned as Patty went on. "And I've told you that those sliding doors weren't closed all the way. If Harold was standing out there, he must have gotten quite an earful. I can't shake the feeling that my scenario is true and that Harold knows that I'm the whistleblower. And if he really does know, there's no way I can continue to work at Island Brooke no matter how much I love my kids. I'll have to get in touch with John Larraway and ask for a transfer to another school."

"Do you think a teaching job will be available this time of year?"

"Probably not. But maybe I can take a job as a paraprofessional for the rest of this year."

"At that paltry salary?"

"I know it's a bad time with your possible layoff, but it's my only other option."

Noah still looked unhappy, but then said, "You know you may just be worrying needlessly. Harold might not have come downstairs at all. He might not have eavesdropped. You could be creating this whole terrible scene in my mind. I think what you should do is just play it by ear. See how he acts the next time you see him at school."

Patty seemed close to tears.

Noah put his arm around her, and said, "Honey, I love you and I support you in every way. If you want to quit your job, I'm fine with it. We'll handle it financially. I'll take care of you. I know I can get another job. There's always the insurance industry. " He leaned down and kissed her cheek, and then her lips. He kissed her again, harder, purposefully, and she kissed him back, relishing his warmth and enveloped by his strength. This was Noah, her Noah, the man who was the center of her being.

Finally, realizing that the clock had ticked away, and it was too late to call in sick, she quickly showered, dressed, and got into her car. As she drove to school on automatic pilot that day, her mind kept racing, going over and over her options. She told herself to calm down. She had to think logically about the situation that she found herself in. Either Harold knew that she had blown the whistle, or he did not. If he did, she would simply ask to be sent to another school. Surely John Larraway owed her something, and he would find her another job. On the other hand, if Harold did not know, she would just continue to teach at Island Brooke and avoid him as much as possible. And probably put in for a transfer for the next school year.

She arrived at Island Brooke just before the late bell for teachers, and as she signed in, Grace looked up and said, "No faculty meeting today. Harold will be out of the building all day long, and possibly most of the week too. He has meetings with the superintendent and that agency. They're really giving him the third degree. The poor guy."

Patty whispered a silent prayer of thanks and spent a happy day teaching children.

On Tuesday morning, Patty hesitated before she went into the main office. Finally, she opened the door and asked Grace the question, trying to keep her voice casual. "Is Harold here today?"

"No, he hasn't come in yet," Grace, answered. Patty waited until she got out into the hall before allowing herself to give a deep breath of relief. Going up to the teachers' lounge for a quick cup of coffee, she was sitting on one of the couches, discussing a coming third grade field trip with Ellen, when she heard Sue who was reading the paper call out, "There must be a whistleblower." As several of the teachers in the room got up and clustered around her, she started to read aloud from the front page of the *Hastings Morning Star*, her voice high with excitement. *"There are unconfirmed reports that an employee at Island Brooke Elementary School may have actually seen principal Harold Trelawney erasing and changing test score answers. Other reports indicate that this whistleblower reported this information to the superintendent of schools."*

"Does it say who the whistleblower is?" asked Shannon Cook.

Patty was incredulous at the published story, and then felt a wave of helplessness wash over her. She never should have gone to the detective agency. She should have known that her role as a whistleblower would come out. The secret could not be kept. Too many people knew about it. Wishing she could get up and escape out the door, she put her hands in her lap and waited for the blow to fall. There was a breathless silence in the room as Sue skimmed through the article searching. Finally, Sue said, "No. No, it just says that there might be a whistleblower, but it doesn't give a name." Patty let out an audible sign of relief, which she quickly covered up with a fit of coughing. The teachers in the room all seemed to be all talking at once when Dewey's voice with an uncharacteristic edge to it loudly cut across the flood of conversations.

"This is a sick joke. No one at this school could be a whistleblower. It's some kind of journalistic ploy. The story has been dying lately. They just want to sell more newspapers.

Just ignore it. We all know that Harold is innocent. There is no whistleblower because there was no test tampering."

Several people concurred, and as the last before-school bell rang, Patty joined the crowd of teachers leaving the room. The whistleblower story quickly spread through the building, and before morning exercises were completed, at least three teachers had stuck their heads in Patty's classroom and asked if she had heard the news. All morning, the newspaper story was at the back of her mind, and at lunchtime, she saw clusters of teachers in tense conversations in the halls and in the cafeteria and knew they were talking about the whistleblower- and wondered how long it would be before her identity was known.

Patty's dismay was increased when Harold, his face stormy, appeared in the playground right at the end of third grade lunch-recess, and seemed to be headed in her direction. Turning quickly, she led her class into the building, glad that she had avoided a face-to-face meeting. The rest of the afternoon seemed unusually long, especially since she now knew that Harold was in the building. Then when she glanced out of the front window at three o'clock, there was more bad news. TV crews were setting up again, parents were crowding together on the sidewalk in packs, and a policeman was standing at the end of the driveway to the parking lot. The whole frenzy seemed to be starting all over again. She watched them for a few moments and then turned back to her third grade class, twelve boys and twelve girls hard at work with math manipulatives in a cooperative exercise. Most heads were down, absorbed in the assignment — blond hair, brown hair, black hair, one reddish-brown and one bright red. There was a low murmur of voices as they worked together. Patty started going down the aisles, offering help here and there, when she heard Ellen from behind her call in her professional voice. "Mrs. Bass, would you come out here for a moment, please?"

Patty walked out in the hall to her friend who immediately asked, "Did you see the gauntlet we have to run today? The newsmen are back."

"I just noticed, but thank goodness the kids haven't."

"That story about the whistleblower in the *Morning Star* will start them up for a day or two. They probably want to ambush him — or her on — the way out." Ellen laughed lightly. "What a joke. There's no whistleblower."

Patty cringed at the comment and returned to her room. At dismissal time she walked her class to the main office where they were picked up by the bus monitor, and seeing no sign of Harold in the office, quickly dashed in and signed out. Then she hurried back to her room, intent on leaving the building as soon as possible, but just as she was crossing her threshold, Dewey came through the swinging doors of the cafeteria and followed her into her classroom. He was shaking his head, and Patty could see that he was upset.

"I've just been talking with Marielle and she apologized." Patty wasn't sure what Dewey was talking about, but he went on to explain. "She's convinced herself that Harold altered the test scores, but she said she's sorry that she ever told Sue. Sue has been blabbing it all over the school, and now a lot of other teachers have turned against Harold. I asked Marielle if she could go on record taking back what she said, but she refused to do that. She just said that she wouldn't discuss the whole issue anymore, but as far as I can see, the damage has already been done."

Dewey made a helpless gesture. "There's a whole group of teachers now who have turned against Harold. Most of the teachers in the fourth and fifth grades. A couple of the specialists. Some of the younger teachers. I feel so ineffective. When I talk to them, I just can't reach them." He frowned and stood silently for a moment, giving Patty a chance to look at her watch. He saw the glance, and said. "I guess you're in a hurry to leave today. I'll see you tomorrow," and quickly left the room, leaving the door open.

Patty immediately started getting her books and papers together, ready to go home. In her haste, she dropped some papers on the floor, and spent a precious minute picking them up and thrusting them into one of her folders. Just as she was zipping up her windbreaker and preparing to leave, she heard footsteps clapping down the hall. To her ears it sounded like Harold. She felt a moment of panic, and then tried to shake it off.

Of course it wasn't Harold, she silently reassured herself.

But her fears became real as she watched Harold walk into her room. He was wearing flannel trousers, an Oxford-cloth shirt, and his tie was hanging down unknotted and uneven, giving him an uncharacteristically rumpled look. He did not approach her, but went right over to the windows, which looked onto Emerson Street and stared out at the assembled newsmen and the crowds of parents and children. Patty was looking at him in profile and could see that his face looked strained and he kept tightening his heavily muscled shoulders, the chords of his neck bulging. He stood transfixed for a few minutes without saying a word, but the time seemed endless to Patty as she appraised his powerful physique. He then shook his head from side to side, and he seemed to be speaking through clenched teeth when he finally spoke. "Look at them, Patty. Look what's happening here. You would think that someone at this school had committed a murder. What do you think? Is test tampering as bad as a murder?"

She recoiled at his words and his tone of voice, but could think of no response. Harold changed his position at one point and on guard she reacted with fear, edging away from him, poised to run and give a power yell if he made any threatening move toward her. The minutes ticked by, and she felt she should say something — anything — but her mind was a blank. Suddenly, Harold turned and took a few quick steps toward the middle of the room, blocking her way to the door. He put his hand up to the frames of his glasses, and he gave her a long stare. She was looking right at him, and could see veins pulsing in his temples and lines on his forehead that she had never noticed before. Patty worked at keeping a look of polite interest on her face while inside she was shaking like a leaf, wondering what she would be able to do if he made some kind of attack on her.

Harold seemed about to speak again, but then without further words, he turned and left the room. Patty had been holding her breath, and took in great gulps of air as soon as he was gone. She just stood by her desk for a few minutes unsure what to do. Finally, she walked over to the door and checked up and down the hallway. She could see a group of teachers standing down by the main office, listening to Dewey who was gesticulating with his hands as he talked, but there was no sign of Harold. She quickly grabbed her books and folders and left the building by the cafeteria door, circling around the back of the school to the parking lot. She held her breath until she was safely in her car, and then she pushed the lock down and sighed in relief. The policeman in front of the school made way for her through the line of reporters, and as she slowly drove by them, turning her head away from their calls, she was glad to hear that they were not shouting out her name. When she reached her house, she drove into the driveway and turned off her car, and sat there immobile with her head in her hands. When Noah came home five minutes later, she was still draped over the steering wheel.

Chapter 38

Once in the house, Patty told Noah about Harold's strange visit to her classroom. "I think he actually came to my room to threaten me or attack me. Then he realized that there was a policeman out in front and a lot of teachers still in the building, and he held himself back. There's no question in my mind now. He did overhear me at the Abeles-Mack Agency. He knows that I blew the whistle on him."

"That's it," said Noah. "You're out of that school. You'll have to call John Larraway tonight at home and tell him what happened. See what he has to offer you." Patty called the superintendent at home twice that evening and left two messages on his machine. When he hadn't returned her calls by nine o'clock, she was starting to feel desperate. After she had made a few fruitless attempts to reach Jim Politano, she turned to Noah. "I think I'll give Dewey a ring. He's always on top of everything so maybe he knows of some teaching vacancy in town." Dewey answered the phone right away, but before Patty had a chance to tell him that she was leaving Island Brooke, and was looking for another job, he said, "I'm going to be Queen for a Day for the rest of the week."

"What?" asked Patty, not understanding.

"Oh, that's just an expression." He went on, and the pain in his voice was obvious. "I'm going to be acting principal for the rest of the week. Harold won't be in. They've got him tied up meeting with the Abeles-Mack Agency again and with the superintendent. I just got off the phone with him, and he told me that Larraway has ordered him not to set foot at Island Brooke for the rest of this week. He's been assigned to Central Office."

Patty got off the phone quickly, and told Noah the news. He listened and then said, "I still don't think you should go to Island Brooke tomorrow." But Patty did go to school the next morning, and it was just as Dewey had said. He was acting principal for the rest of the week in Harold's absence, but it was a difficult few days for everybody as rumors that Harold had resigned or been fired flew from teacher to teacher. Patty was glad when the week was over, but upset that John Larraway had still not returned her calls.

When she got home from school that Friday afternoon, she parked in the driveway and walked over to the mailbox to pull out a stack of bills, letters, flyers, and a copy of her monthly running magazine. Balancing her school materials and the mail, she went into the house through the garage, and then on to the kitchen dumping everything on the counter as she slipped off her heels. As she ran water into the teakettle and put it on the burner, she was truly grateful that she has gotten through the week, but wondered how much longer she could work at the school, fearing Harold as she did. She has been lucky the last few days, but could see the rest of the school year scrolling out before her. Almost all of April. The long month of May. Over half of June. She caught a glimpse of herself in the cabinet mirror as she reached for her mug, and noticed that she had a tired, harried look about her. The whole situation was taking its toll. She made her decision at that moment. It was no longer worth it to her. She could no longer continue to play *Hide and Seek* with Harold in this way.

The superintendent had still not returned her calls. So much for gratitude. But she would call him again that evening. She would also call Jim Politano to see if he could help her. If all else failed, she would just have to submit her resignation. She would not return to Island Brooke the next Monday when Harold would probably be back. Patty put on the kettle for tea water, and sorted through the mail. A letter from Hastings Public Schools caught her eye. She opened it first and skimmed it, and then read it more slowly in astonishment. It was a form letter addressed to:

Teachers of Island Brooke *School.*

Harold Trelawney has decided to take a leave of absence for medical reasons. Samuel Pepen, former principal of Thayer School, will replace him for the rest of this school year. There will be a brief faculty meeting at eight A.M. on Monday to meet the new principal.

"Oh, thank God." Patty laughed out loud, almost giddy with relief. She did a half turn, and punched her fist into the air. "*Yesss.*"

Still caught up in the wonderful, welcome news, she picked up a gray business-size envelope with her name neatly typed, and then turned it over to find no return address. Her mind still on the first letter, she tore the side of the envelope, dropped it on the counter, and unfolded the one-page letter.

Dear Whistleblower,

You should be ashamed of yourself. You know Harold is innocent.

Take good care of yourself,

W. Sutton

Although Patty was reading the words, they made no sense to her at first. The message seemed distant, remote from her life as a wife and teacher, and for an instant she just could not interpret them. Then realizing their meaning, she gave a gasp and almost stumbled against the kitchen counter. All the color drained from her face.

"Harold," was all she could say. She let go of the letter as though it were burning her fingers and dropped it onto the counter. The ringing of the phone and the simultaneous shrill of the teakettle jarred her, and she jumped back and then quickly took the kettle off the burner, but made no move to answer the phone. The phone rang again, and then three times, four times. After the fifth ring, she could hear Noah's recorded voice saying, "We can't come to the phone right now. Please leave your name and number and we'll get back to you." Then a beep and then Tish's voice, "Patty, pick up, I know you're there. I saw you drive by." Her friend's voice sounded almost childlike with pleasure.

Patty reached over and picked up the phone. Tish spoke without any greeting. "I'm going out to supper with Rick tonight. Not a date, a business meeting, but can you imagine after all this time? I've put out a few feelers at other agencies, and it must have gotten back to him. He probably got the message that I was writing him off, and he didn't want to lose me. Men are like that. They always want what they can't have." Tish rambled on in the same vein until Patty's mechanical answers got through to her. She finally stopped gushing and asked, "Is something wrong?"

Patty picked up the letter and read the brief contents to her friend.

"Oh, Patty, how awful." Tish's voice reflected concern. "I'll be right over."

Within a few minutes the front doorbell was ringing, and Tish was there. Patty let her in and handed her the letter as they walked into the kitchen. Tish read it silently and looked up with a frown on her face.

"I bet that little worm Harold sent this." She reached over and hugged Patty who had a disoriented air about her.

Patty just shook her head. "That was my first thought too. But is it possible? Can I really picture him sitting down and writing something like this?"

"Could you picture him sitting down and changing test scores until you caught him at it?"

"No, I guess you're right. And the way he acted at school Tuesday afternoon — coming into my room and mentioning a murder. He scared the life out of me. I'm sure he had some thought of confronting me or attacking me, and then thought better of it. He must have decided that he could get back at me by scaring me with this letter. And I have to admit that he's successful. I am scared."

"And what's this line about take good care of yourself. Is that supposed to be a threat of some kind?" Tish asked.

"I don't know. I just don't know."

"Is this the envelope the letter came in?" asked Tish picking it up.

"Yes."

Tish carefully checked the postmark. "Mailed right here in Hastings. Yesterday. " And then, she asked, "What time is Noah due home?"

"About seven, but you don't have to stay till then. You have a supper engagement with Rick, right?" She moved away from Tish, nervously turned around in circles and then sat down.

"I can cancel out on that, no problem," Tish loyally said. "It's not even a date, just kind of a meeting to discuss some properties that are coming up."

"No way," Patty responded, declining Tish's sacrifice. "I don't need you to baby-sit me. Noah will be home in the early evening. After all you and I have been through to get you and Rick together, you're not going to cancel out now. What time is he picking you up?"

"At six at my house."

"Stay till five, and then go and have a great time. I just need to be with you for a while. This letter has really knocked me for a loop."

Tish sat down at the table and read the letter again. "I wish I could put a face on the person who typed this. I know it's probably Harold, but I suppose it could be someone else."

Patty was glum when she spoke. "I keep thinking of all the teachers at school, and all the parents. And even the newsmen out in front of the building. Anyone could have sent it. But it's more likely that Harold sent it or Eunice or even Dewey."

"Or even Harold's wife, Ann Marie," said Tish. "Now there's a real possibility. I once read that women are more likely than men to write poison pen letters. So Ann Marie Trelawney might have sent it."

Patty just shook her head in consternation as she added, "Or someone from that detective agency. Like that Toni."

The two pondered over the letter, discussing who could have written it. Finally, Patty noticed the time, "Tish, it's after five. You're going to be late for your supper with Rick. Get out of here." Tish jumped up and ran for the door. "I'll call you tomorrow. Tell you all about it." She was gone and Patty was left alone in the house. She held the letter in her hand for a long time, and tried to picture someone sitting at a desk or table typing it. Harold's image kept coming to mind. Harold, the nationally known educator who was now in disgrace because of what she had seen and reported.

Finally, she took the letter and tucked it away in a kitchen drawer.

Chapter 39

The library that next Monday morning seemed just like a wake. There were serious expressions on the faces of all the teachers, and a few were fighting off tears. Ellen looked as though she had lost her best friend and had even forgotten to save Patty a seat. Dewey, seeing Patty looking around, waved her over and pointed to an empty chair next to him at the front. Patty was grateful for the seat until she realized that she was sitting right next to a tearful Eunice who was incongruously garbed in a bright tangerine-colored sweater dress. They exchanged polite greetings. At exactly eight a.m., John Larraway and a short fireplug of a man with a full head of black curly hair going gray came in the door. The unfamiliar man seemed ill at ease as they walked to the front of the room and turned to face the teachers.

The superintendent addressed the group briefly, skimming over the test tampering scandal and Harold's abrupt decision to take a leave of absence for medical reasons. He then said, "I've called Sam Pepen out of retirement to run this school till the end of this year. Sam, will you say a few words?"

Sam Pepen, still looking as though he were present against his better judgment stepped forward, and let his eyes sweep around the library-media center. He considered the many unsmiling faces, and nodded at the few teachers whom he knew from his long years in the school system. He had been enjoying his retirement, and had only agreed to take on the job because of his friendship for John Larraway and his concern about the scandal at Island Brooke. But now that he was actually here in the school, he was uncomfortable at the funereal atmosphere, and decided that his wife had been right when she had advised him not to take the superintendent up on his offer.

With a poker face, Sam quickly got his short speech over with. "We have about nine weeks left in the school year, and I know all of you will continue to provide the best possible education for the children here at this school. I would like to meet with each of you personally for about fifteen-twenty minutes during the next week. Please make an appointment with Grace Reilly. Also, during the next few days, I will be coming around to the classrooms to meet you and the children."

Patty glanced around the room as he started to finish up. Angry faces. Sad faces. Satisfied faces. When Sam finished talking, he and the superintendent immediately left the library-media center. Many of the teachers started to file out, but Dewey and Patty remained seated as Eunice began to speak, anger in her voice. "They can put in a new principal, but we don't have to like it. We can do a lot of little things to make it hard for this Sam Pepen. We can really stick it to him. No one can replace Harold."

Patty was taken aback at Eunice's words, and her old dislike of the woman surged up. She started to speak up, but Dewey was ahead of her. "I know you don't mean that, Eunice. We can't do anything like that. The bottom line here is the education for the kids. We can't do anything that will hurt them. We can still fight for Harold, but everything has to be above board."

Eunice seemed chastised by Dewey's comments, and without another word, abruptly got up and walked away stiff-legged and embarrassed. "Good for you, Dewey," said Patty. "Good for you." Later Patty was to spend some time thinking about what Eunice had said, and that evening even discussed with Noah the possibility that Eunice might be the person who had sent the upsetting whistleblower letter to her.

Chapter 40

By the time April vacation approached, all the teachers had become used to Sam's booming voice barreling down the hall, and some measure of balance had been restored to the school. Patty was bone-tired, weary, both physically and emotionally, and was looking forward to the week off, just to sleep late and do nothing. On the Thursday morning before vacation started, she was sitting at her desk reviewing her lesson plans for the day, and looked up to see Dewey coming into the room. He stood over her with a stack of flyers in his hands.

"Did you hear what happened at the Board of Education meeting last night?" he asked. There was sarcasm in his voice.

She shook her head. "No, what happened?"

"The geniuses on the Board made the decision that Harold would not be returning to Island Brooke in September under any circumstances. They won't even let him come back to the school to say goodbye to the kids and the teachers. They may be offering him some administrative position at the middle school, but even that isn't assured. I talked to a lot of parents on the phone last night till all hours, and we all want him back here where he belongs. We're all going to get together and fight this. Parents and teachers together. We're having a rally next Wednesday to support Harold. Are you going to be in town?"

Patty hesitated and then lied with a straight face. "Dewey, I'm sorry. Noah and I are getting away for a few days." She paused and thought fast. "We're going to Manhattan to catch some plays. We've never been in the city together, and I'm going to show him the real New York."

Dewey looked disappointed, but he then counted out some flyers and put them right in front of her on her desk. "Well, anyway, if you can't be at the rally, you can at least pass these out to your students today or tomorrow. These are for the children, but just make sure they take them home."

Patty looked down at the top flyer and read:

Mr. Trelawney will not be retuning to Island Brooke School for some time. This is a sad experience for all of us, and I know all you children will be thinking of him. Often, difficult and confusing things happen in our lives, and it requires very hard work to make sense of them. We all know that Mr. Trelawney is a good person. We all know that he is innocent of the charges against him. We all know that he has been falsely accused. We all know that some bad people have made up stories and lied about him. Your teachers will explain this and discuss this with you. Your teachers will also help you write letters to Mr. Trelawney to tell him how much you miss him. When you get home, you can tell your parents how sad you feel that Mr. Trelawney is no longer your principal. Perhaps, they can get together and do something about this terrible injustice.

When Patty looked up, she found herself staring at Dewey's patterned red tie so that she could avoid his face. In an effort to give herself time to organize her thoughts, she nodded her head up and down a couple of times. When she thought she could speak without stuttering, she asked, "Has Sam Pepen approved this?"

"No, he hasn't, but we have to do the right thing." Dewey smiled his usual smile, turned, and headed for the door.

Patty read through the flyer again, and then slipped the whole pile into the waste paper basket beside her desk.

Chapter 41

When Patty got home from work that day, she found Noah in the kitchen sitting at the table, leaning on his arm, his fist pressed to his temple and a frown on his lean face. Their checkbook and a stack of bills were in front of him. He furrowed his brow even more when she slid into the seat across from him and said, "I'm on vacation next week, and you're off in the middle of the week. How would you like to spend a couple of days in New York City? Take the train in? Stay at a hotel? See some plays?"

He shook his head with a lack of enthusiasm. "I don't think so. This fifteen-year mortgage is killing us. With my job up in the air, it's not a good time to spend the money."

When Patty made no response to his comment, he took a closer look at the dark smudges under her eyes. He then got up, and went over to her, and gently stroked her cheek with the back of his hand. As he leaned over to kiss her forehead, he said, "You know the last few months have really been rough. I think we both need a change of scenery."

Patty slipped her hand beneath the buttons of his shirt and felt his heart beating. This is the man I love, she thought. This is the man who will always keep me safe.

Chapter 42

Patty loved the rocking rhythm of trains, and as soon as Metro-North pulled out of Union Station the next Tuesday morning, she could feel the tension of the last few months start to peel away. She sat back and closed her eyes. Noah reached for her hand and squeezed hard. That felt good. She felt good. And the closer the speeding train got to New York City, the better she felt. By the time Patty could look out the window and watch the approach of the familiar jutting skyline of Manhattan, she felt that she was on another planet. She was away with Noah. No one else knew where they were. No one could find them. No one could call them. No Harold. No Dewey bothering her to attend rallies or pass out letters to her students. It was heaven.

Soon the train was rushing with a roar into the dark tunnel that led to the station, and within minutes she and Noah were walking through the huge cavern of a hall that was Grand Central Terminal. Patty was in her element. Hundreds, thousands, of anonymous people swirled around her, hurrying in all directions, many with luggage or briefcases in their hands. The buzz of conversations in scores of languages and accents was everywhere, while the concourse echoed with almost-constant calls for trains coming and going. Patty looked up at the high vaulted ceiling bright with the painted signs of the zodiac, and remarked, "Look how clean everything looks. What a welcome this is. I'm so glad we came. Every time I come back to New York, I remember how I loved living here."

There was a delay while Noah found a cab on Lexington Avenue, and then they were riding in stops and starts through dense streets clogged with traffic, Patty relishing the sights and sounds of the great city where she had lived six years of her life. It was all familiar and so sweet to her — towering buildings crowding almost onto the streets, the sidewalks filled with pedestrians rushing in random packs, the brightly lighted marquees and storefronts, the fountains and pocket parks, the chaos that was part of city life. She even welcomed the strident and ever-present grind and rumble of traffic, punctuated by an occasional siren. And then they were in front of their hotel, and Noah was paying the driver while Patty gawked up like a tourist at the skyscrapers of steel and smoked glass that made the city seem like a sculpture garden.

Check-in at the hotel was fast, and then they were zooming up to the twelfth floor in a wood paneled and brass elevator, Patty feeling her stomach left behind. Their room was small but bright with fresh flowers and bold purple, red-orange and yellow plaids running through the drapes and the bedspread. Patty didn't even bother to unpack, deciding to just live out of her suitcase for the next two days, while Noah, true to his nature, took the time to hang his suit, set his shirts neatly in a drawer, and line up his razor, shaving soap, their toothbrushes and the other toilet articles in a precise row on the bathroom counter. Patty sat on the bed, bounced up and down a few times to test it, and then settled back and propped herself up against the pillows. She reached for a complimentary issue of *New York Magazine* on the night table, and began to page through it, checking off tourist attractions with a pen. After a few minutes she felt Noah's gaze on her, and looked up to see him framed in the bathroom door watching her. His olive chinos were creased from the train ride, and his white shirt unbuttoned at the throat was brilliant against his tan. His face was unshaven, and his body looked lean and hard. She felt a surge of joy as she looked at her husband.

"Are you going to call Brooke and Ilona and let them know we're in the city?" he asked.

Patty shook her head and gave him an intimate smile. "No, I don't think so. They've both been after me to come down and visit, so I'm sure they'll invite us over if I call. But, frankly,

I'd like these few days just for ourselves. Actually, I'm kind of thinking of this trip as a second honeymoon."

"Sounds good to me." He returned her smile. "OK. So what are our plans?"

"I'd like to see three plays."

"How can we see three?" he asked. "We only have two nights here."

"One tonight. Two tomorrow. Don't forget Wednesday matinee," she explained. "Then squeeze in the Museum of Modern Art somewhere. I haven't seen *Starry Night* for a couple of years."

"That's all good."

"And," she continued, "Maybe we can even have a lunch to remember at *Cipriani's* on Thursday before we catch the train home."

He frowned a little. "I suppose. If we watch our budget. I don't want to run up too many big bills on our credit cards."

She went on. "The most important thing is to get the theater tickets. How about we walk over to Times Square now and pick up some twofers? Then we can get a slice and a coke somewhere."

"OK," he responded, glancing at his watch. "We probably should get going or all the good seats will be gone."

"We probably should," said Patty, taking another long look at him framed in the doorway. His eyes were dark, so dark.

"Right now," he added, a half smile on his face.

"Yes, right now," she agreed as she slipped off the bed. She crossed over to him in a few light steps, and reached up to touch his hair. He kissed her lightly, and then drew her into his arms.

Chapter 43

When they returned to Hastings late Thursday afternoon, Noah went right out to the post office to pick up their mail, while Patty called Tish to tell her all about the New York trip and how rested she was feeling. But all Tish wanted to talk about was Rick. In a rush, excitement in her voice, she broke her news, "Rick's confided in me. He told me all about Jordana. He told me the whole story way back to their first meeting. Did you know that she was working at the Yale Art Gallery when he met her? Now she's at the Metropolitan in New York City." Tish talked non-stop for almost five minutes, and just when Patty thought she would get a word in edgewise, Tish ended the conversation abruptly with, "There's a FedEx man at my door. Talk to you later."

When Noah came in with an armful of mail that had accumulated over the last three days, he poured everything out on the kitchen counter and went over to open the refrigerator. Her mind half on their recent trip, Patty went through the mail. There were large manila envelopes, bills with cellophane windows, flyers, magazines, junk mail and some letters. Later Patty would wonder what state of denial she was in when without concern she opened a gray business-size envelope with her name and address neatly typed. When Noah turned back to her with a can of beer in his hand, he saw that Patty's face was scrunched up and that she was holding a letter away from her body. He frowned and reached over to take it from her. He read it aloud.

Dear Whistleblower,

Running away for a few days won't solve the problem. You know that Sam can't replace Harold. Tell the truth.

Meanwhile take good care of yourself,

W. Sutton

"I never thought." Patty was stammering and nervously pushing the hair away from her face. "I just opened it without thinking. We had such a wonderful time in New York that the other letter went right out of my head." She was close to tears as Noah put his arm around her and looked at the postmark. They then studied the letter together.

"Who knew that you were going to New York?"

"Just about everybody at the school. I made a point of talking about it in the teachers' lounge last Friday so that I would have an excuse for not going to that rally."

"Could Harold have known?"

"Easily. Dewey is always over at Harold's. He probably has his own key to the house by now. I know he tells Harold everything that goes on at the school." She paused. "And now that Harold is on medical leave, he must just sit at home thinking of ways to get back at me for ruining his career."

With a sudden move, Noah reached for the letter, crumpled it in his hand and threw it into the bottom of the waste paper basket. But Patty reached down and retrieved it, smoothed it out and put it on the counter.

"Do you think that I should call the police?"

Noah shook his head. "If you go to the police, then even more people will know about it — and I don't know that they could do anything. The letters aren't really threatening."

"They're threatening to me. I feel so violated. Somebody out there is just chipping my life away. I dread the thought of seeing my name in the paper. What do you think I should do?" she asked miserably.

Noah scratched at his chin and didn't answer right away. His usual self-confidence seemed to have deserted him. Patty stared at him as he wrestled with the problem. Finally, he spoke, "I think we have to keep these two letters in perspective. Harold or some other coward is sending them to you to upset you. But we can't let two letters change our whole way of living. I think we should just go along and do the things we would ordinarily do." He paused for a moment and then said, "Let's hold off on contacting the police and see what happens. After all, there are no physical threats, and names will never hurt you." Although Patty didn't totally agree with Noah's reasoning, she tried to put her anxiety about the two letters aside and tell herself that he was right. The letters shouldn't stop her from doing all the things she wanted to do. As they were going to bed that night, they discussed the letters once more, and the last conscious thought that Patty had before she fell asleep was that names will never hurt you.

Chapter 44

The next morning was ideal for running — cool and sunny with strong shifting winds and only a few fat white clouds scudding across a blue sky that was glorious. Noah had left for the airport just after seven, and by seven-thirty, Patty was sprinting at a fast pace along the wooded paths in Stadler Park, her head inclined away from the winds, strands of hair brushing across her face, shoulders, arms loose, and her mind a floating place of white light. Abruptly, a loud crack cut across her consciousness, and brought her back to the woods. She immediately slowed down and then came to a halt. She turned to look around behind her but could see nothing but the movement of the leaves all tossed first in one direction and then the other by the winds. She was sure that there was no one else on the path. She took a few irresolute steps and then stopped again to look back and then quickly forward, thinking that the noise must have been a car backfiring somewhere on Parkway Drive — and certainly not a gun shot. As she thought herself foolish, she suddenly saw something or someone down the path. She asked herself, could that be a man outlined against the trees? No, it was only a shadow.

Torn out of her complacency, Patty suddenly realized the vulnerable position she was in all alone here in the woods. The image of Harold waiting in ambush at one end of the path or the other popped into her mind. Don't panic, she cautioned herself sharply. Seeking an escape route, she looked to the sides of the trail and saw that her way was blocked by the steep rise of an escarpment on one side, and trees shouldering together with prickly bushes and dense undergrowth on the other. The familiar course with its canopy of overreaching branches and tender young leaves quite suddenly looked to her like a tunnel, a tunnel with only two exits. She felt the prickling of danger, and started looking wildly up and down the path, ready to run one way or the other at the first sign of Harold. Her heart began to strum as she considered her two choices. Don't panic, she told herself again. A few seconds passed, and then she did panic, choosing randomly, breaking into a fast run the way she had been going, toward the opposite end of the park. By the time she passed the plank bridge near the Post Road, she was sweating heavily, her lungs burning.

She sped off the path, and took the gravel road back to the duck pond, keeping to the middle, her eyes searching the fields and woods as she labored by at her top speed. By the time she had reached the safety of the tennis courts on Parkway Drive, she was gasping for breath and her nerves were stretched to the breaking point. She stopped at the water fountain and drank deeply and for a long time, wondering what she was going to do about Harold. She did make one decision. She would never run alone in Stadler Park again.

Chapter 45

When Patty woke up on the morning of her birthday, she could hear a steady rain spattering against the bedroom window. She looked across at Noah who was lying on his side turned away from her and just stirring from sleep. Moving over, she spooned herself against his back, gave a deep sigh of pleasure and sang softly in his ear, "Happy Birthday to me. Happy Birthday to me." He woke up immediately. Later, Patty and Noah went to the window and watched the rain slant down into their back yard. A long roll of thunder rumbled somewhere in the distance, but they saw no lightning. "What a great day to spend the whole morning in bed," Patty said, "and this rain will really put a crimp in the plans that Tish and Rick have made. No eating on Rick's patio today."

"Do you want to cancel out on your birthday party?" Noah asked mischievously as he put his arm around her.

"No way. I guess we'll eat in Rick's pristine dining room. I don't think he's used it once since he bought the house last year."

"And what's happening with Rick and Tish? They seem to be together all the time now."

"They are together all the time now," said Patty. "Tish is really making progress with him although she tells me that they're just best buds. He cries on her shoulder whenever Jordana slaps him down."

"The bozo ought to open his eyes and really look at Tish, and he'll soon forget about that little snob from Greenwich."

Patty nodded in agreement as she led the way down to the kitchen for coffee. They spent the next hour or so stretched out on the living room rug reading the Sunday papers and trading kisses. Just before noon, they were turning onto Seafarer Drive and admiring the beautiful homes set back and shielded from the road. It had stopped raining, and as Noah switched off the wipers, he said, "Rick certainly has a great address. This is one of the nicest streets in town." He paused. "Would you like to live here Patty?"

Patty didn't answer right away because she was looking into the mirror on the back of the sun visor and fussing with her hair, which had drawn into tighter curls because of the humidity. She combed the curls as they rode, making them tumble to her shoulders. She turned to Noah and answered his question. "No, I think I'll stay right where I am. I love our house. It really has that lived-in look. Rick's house is an architect's dream, but I sometimes get the feeling that I'm in an expensive furniture store when I'm there. I think it needs a woman's touch." She smiled. "Tish's touch."

"And why are Tish and Rick giving you a brunch for your birthday? What about a dinner?"

"They couldn't find a menu. Rick and I are both vegetarians, so we don't eat meat or chicken. You don't like fish. And my father is complaining about his teeth, so Tish decided that a vegetarian brunch was the easiest."

By that time they had reached Rick's house and pulled into the Belgian block driveway. There were puddles on the street, and the shrubbery and flowers in his yard were wet and new looking.

"Look at that." Patty pointed to a mass of silver balloons and a giant birthday card held by a plastic bear hanging from the front door. The card proclaimed, *Happy Thirtieth Birthday, Patty.*

"That's Tish's work," Patty laughed. "She wants the whole world to know I've reached the big 3-0."

Rick greeted them warmly at the front door and with a proud sense of ownership led them through the small entrance hall, which opened into a long living room with walls of old brick and leaded glass. The room was bright and airy with a cathedral ceiling, skylights, and an open staircase to the second floor. There was an elaborate entertainment center, a stone floor-to-ceiling fireplace, and low, modern furniture textured in varying shades of red, gray and navy. Handmade tribal rugs in bold colors covered the hardwood floors, and framed black and white photographs lined the rough stucco walls. Patty looked around and smiled at this tangible proof of her cousin's success, and then took a breath and sniffed the air redolent with the smells of coffee, cinnamon and nutmeg. She followed her nose and walked across the stretch of living room to the open stainless steel kitchen, which was separated only by high broad shelving and counters. Tish, dressed in a beige crochet dress with a tight bodice was just taking a rack of cinnamon buns out of the oven. She seemed overdressed in pearls and heels.

"Tish, you look like one of those perfect housewives in one of those perfect sitcoms from the fifties."

Tish gave a raffish grin as she set the buns down and said, "Don't you wish?" Patty checked the kitchen counter lined with plates of thinly sliced smoked salmon, cut up fruit, a green salad, potato salad, cheese, eggs and the fixings for omelets, a basket of bagels, and now the hot cinnamon buns as Tish poured two mimosas into crystal glasses. She handed one to Patty and drank from the other. She then gazed at Rick watching his every move as he walked to the front door, and then stood in conversation with Patty's father who had just come in. Tish gestured toward Rick with her glass. "Well, Patty, it looks like it's going to work out after all. What's that song about saving the best for last?"

Patty hummed a few bars of the song, and then asked, "Are Ellen and Al coming?"

"No, they called. They couldn't make it, but they sent flowers."

Patty nodded. "It seems I can never meet Al. We've had plans to go out for dinner a couple of times with them, and he always has to work at the last minute."

"I'm sure you'll meet him at some point. And look at it this way. He's keeping Hastings safe for us." She gestured toward the baskets, plates and trays. "I have to made the omelets last minute so would you help me cart this other stuff?" The two of them spent the next few minutes carrying food into the dining room where Patty gazed with pleasure at the work that Tish and Rick had done. They had gone all out. The room was festive with several bouquets of fresh flowers and pink and white streamers, and the table had been set with tall pink candles, and Rick's best white linen, crystal, silver, and delicate white china. A bottle of champagne in a silver ice bucket graced the sideboard.

Tish was quick with the cooking, and soon called out to the three men, "Chow time, cowboys," and served the omelets individually as Rick opened the champagne and poured. Everyone was hungry, and conversation was sporadic as they ate — Noah expressed interest in the real estate course he had just started — Rick said that there had been some inquiries about the farm now that the asking price had been lowered — Patty's father talked about the high taxes in the state — but there seemed to be one subject just below the surface which everyone was waiting to discuss. As they finished up with coffee, Patty's father finally broke the ice.

"How are you teachers doing at Island Brooke with that new principal?" he asked as Tish and Rick started to clear the plates.

"Oh, Sam is great and most of us love him. He's won almost everyone over. Now it's just as though he's always been there." She paused, "Of course, we still have an awful lot of dissension as more and more teachers realize that Harold is guilty. Teachers who were best friends aren't even speaking, and some who never got along can be found in a corner either dissing Harold or praising him to the skies."

"And I can't believe that I saw Dewey on a local TV station last night," Tish cut in. "He really has become the leader of the pack. He was on some kind of panel discussing the school and defending Harold. I've never seen such a change in a personality. When I dated him, he was so quiet, serious, kind of like an Eagle Scout. Now he's a rabble-rouser." She looked at Patty. "How do you mange to get along with him on this test tampering thing?"

"I never discuss the test tampering at all. If I'm in the teachers' lounge and someone brings it up, I either start reading the newspaper or leave. Dewey is so touchy. I'm lucky that he just assumes that I'm in the pro-Harold camp because I hang around Ellen, and she's one of Harold's biggest defenders." She sighed. "And you've probably heard that Harold's lawyers have tied up all the interviews from the Abeles-Mack Agency. The school board isn't going to be able to use them to make any decision on who actually did the tampering. I think if Harold does leave the system eventually, the town will have to pay him off. Especially since he comes from a family of lawyers."

Noah shook his head. "And it's hard to believe that my bride played a key role in all this."

"Don't remind me," she said, covering her eyes with her hand. "I'm trying to forget about the whole thing. It's been months and months now since I first caught Harold changing scores. And there just doesn't seem to be any light at the end of the tunnel. Hey, let's talk about something more pleasant. Like this chocolate cake with what looks like a hundred candles that that Tish just brought in."

After Patty silently made her birthday wish and blew out the candles, and more coffee and the homemade birthday cake were served, Tish called out, "Time to open presents."

The five of them got up and filed out into the living room where three gaily wrapped packages and an envelope with a pink stick-on bow were set on the gray linen sofa at the end of the room near the kitchen. Patty pushed aside some throw pillows, took the place of honor on the sofa and opened the presents quickly, tearing off the ribbons and wrapping paper and handing them to Tish. Inside the first box was a chunky gold bracelet from Noah. Patty put it on her wrist, and Noah snapped the clasp. "Just my size and color," she said. "There's something else, birthday girl," said Noah. "A gift that keeps on giving." Patty unwrapped a small piece of paper, which read, "*IOU* one *tomato garden to be planted over Memorial Day Weekend. All My Love, Noah.* Patty's eyes sparkled as she raised her mouth for his kiss.

Patty's father had given her a new can opener. "Something practical," he said. "I heard you saying last week that you were having trouble with yours." Rick's present was a very generous gift certificate from the bookstore in his shopping center. Patty opened the last package and found two creamy-white cotton T-shirts from Tish. Both were lettered. The first read, *Rydell High School*, and the second read, *Don't trust anyone over thirty.*

"Thank you friend," said Patty, "and thank you for mentioning my age once again." Tish scrunched up her face at Patty and then looked over and winked at Rick.

"I'm leaving for Florida next week" Patty's father abruptly announced. "I'll be back right after the fourth of July. Then I have some loose ends to tie up. And if everything works out, I'll have Rick sell my house."

"Dad, I told you once before, nobody, but nobody, goes to Florida in June," Patty teased.

He smiled indulgently at her and kissed her on the cheek as Noah came over to them. The two started talking about the high taxes in Connecticut, and Patty looked around to see Rick going back into the dining room. She turned and followed him. He was standing at the dining room window, and looking out at the patio where they were supposed to have eaten that day. Patty walked over to stand beside him, and they both looked over his good-sized backyard. The sun had come out and the burnished greenery of the yard glistened. Beyond they could see a peaceful yellow haze over the low sweep of grasses and cattails in the marshland that adjoined Rick's property.

"I envy you this view," Patty said. "I love the marshland. It's so full of life."

Rick made no comment to answer hers, and Patty turned to look at him. His face had a distant, longing look, and when he finally spoke, there was sadness in his voice. "It would be a lot nicer if I had someone to share it with."

"What about Jordana?"

He answered slowly. "She's not sure anymore. She may have met someone else. Nothing is sure at this point." Before he had a chance to go on, Tish came in to clear the cake plates from the table. Her face was flushed from her exertions in the kitchen, and she had recently lost a few pounds. Patty thought that she had never looked more beautiful. Tish took one long look at their serious faces and said, "Oh, sorry, cousins' conference. I don't want to interrupt," and she walked out again.

Patty saw Rick turn his head to stare at Tish as she left the room, and she resisted the impulse to interfere. Now that Jordana had once again revealed her true colors, Rick would surely be able to see that Tish was worth ten of his ex-fiancée. Things were working out after all.

When they went back into the living room, Patty's father was preparing to leave. Patty thanked him again for his gift, put her arm around his shoulder, and then turned to the rest of the group. "The people I love most in the world are here today. I feel so lucky to have you all. Dad, Rick, Tish, and of course, my Noah." She looked at each in turn. "I want to thank you all for this wonderful celebration, and now I'll repeat my birthday wish so that you all can hear it."

"No, don't tell your wish," Tish called out. "That's bad luck. It won't come true if you say it out loud."

Ignoring Tish's protests, Patty held up crossed fingers and tempted the fates. "Here's my wish. I want the five of us to be right here at Rick's house next year to celebrate my birthday.

All in good health. And I want to sun to be shining so that we will be able to have my thirty-first birthday party out on Rick's patio." As she looked into the smiling faces of those so dear to her, Patty had no way of knowing that her birthday wish would never be realized.

Chapter 46

Later Patty gave Tish some help in the kitchen and then walked back to the living room where Rick and Noah were talking about burglar alarms. "I probably should get one," said Rick. "For example, that red Buick that just went by so slowly. Probably some poor guy trying to find an address, but on the other hand it could be someone casing the street in the daylight. I understand the police still haven't been able to catch that burglar who's been working the East Shore."

"What red Buick," asked Patty, suddenly alarmed.

"Just some car who's lost, I'm sure." Rick spoke with a smile.

Patty's face had gone white. "Did you get the license plate number?"

"What's wrong?" The smile had faded from Rick's face.

"Harold has a red Buick."

"Whoa, Patty. I'm sure it wasn't Harold, but if I see it again, I'll go out into the street and get the number." He paused. "I'm getting to hate Harold Trelawney." He looked at Noah, "I don't know how you and Patty can be so temperate about this whole whistleblower letter thing."

Noah frowned and looped his arm over Patty's shoulders. "I wish there was something we could do, but our hands are tied since we don't know for sure that Harold is sending the letters. Patty thinks it's definitely Harold, but it could be his wife, or one of his friends at school — or it could be several other people. It's making Patty paranoid. She's even cut way back on her running. She's afraid to be in Stadler Park alone because she thinks that Harold will jump out of a bush at her."

Rick thought for a moment and then looked at Patty. "Tell you what. I'll start carrying my running clothes in my car. If you want to run after school, give me a call at the agency, and I'll come over in the late afternoon. You're right not to run alone in Stadler Park. Once you're on those running paths, it can seem like the wilderness."

"And we're even getting some crank calls now," Noah added.

"Get Caller ID," suggested Rick. "I have it at my office, and it's great."

On their way home, Patty and Noah saw two red Buicks, and both times pulled over to look closely at the drivers. The driver of the Buick at a gas station on the Boston Post Road was an attractive young woman wearing a baseball cap turned backward. When she saw Noah looking over at her, she smiled invitingly until she noticed Patty and then turned away. The second car was overfilled with teenage girls who didn't look old enough to drive. When Noah took a right off Parkway Drive, he reached across and squeezed Patty's shoulder. "It was probably one of those two cars. See, it wasn't Harold after all."

That evening the phone rang, and Patty picked up. "Hello." There was no answer. "Hello." There was only breathing on the line.

Noah reached for the phone. "Hello." The line was disconnected. When the phone rang a few minutes later, Noah answered it. Again, no one spoke, and Noah slammed the phone down, and took it off the hook. Exasperated, he said, "I'm taking Rick's advice and calling the telephone company tomorrow. We're getting Caller ID. If Harold's number shows up just once, we'll know for sure that he's the one behind this campaign. I'm not going to put up with this anymore. I'll go over there to his house, and the two of us are going to dance. I don't care how old he is."

Worried about the red Buick on Rick's street and the two crank calls, Patty had trouble falling asleep that night. When she finally did drift off, she dreamed that she had gone back to Island Brooke School one night and was looking for something that she had lost. She wasn't quite sure what it was, but as she walked through the parking lot, she could see Harold's car parked in the *Reserved for Principal* space, and thought that he could help her find it. Then she went inside by the side door, and saw that there were two men in the office. At first she didn't recognize either of them, and then realized that one of them was Dewey, but it didn't quite look like Dewey. Then the other man turned around, and stared right through the glass windows at her, his face unusually large, almost bloated. It was Harold. In her dream, Patty suddenly knew that she was in danger, and somehow realized that she would be safe if she could get into her classroom. As she walked down the long corridor to Room 105, she could hear footsteps behind her synchronizing with her own, but when she looked back, she could see no one. She started to run but the familiar hall seemed to have become a long, long street, and when he finally got to her classroom, it was locked. She had forgotten the key, but she pulled at the door, hoping it would somehow open. The footsteps were now getting closer, but it was still too dark to see a face, yet Patty could see an arm reaching out for her.

Through her fear Patty suddenly thought, "I'm dreaming," and fought her way up through layers of sleep to consciousness. Opening her eyes in her dark bedroom, she could hear the soft sounds of Noah asleep beside her. Her heart was beating wildly and she was afraid, but she knew that he had to fly the next day and she didn't want to wake him up. She lay still for a long time listening to Noah's regular breathing and thinking that now Harold was even invading her dreams.

Chapter 47

Rick was as good as his word and that next Saturday, they were running on the paths through Stadler Park. Rick was holding back and allowing Patty to take the lead, and she was pushing her body, feeling the pain, running with intensity as though she could outrun all her problems if she ran fast enough. Moving like professional athletes, they flew over the path and trampled at high speed across designs dappled by sunlight leaking through the leafy canopy overhead. Walls of green trees flashed by, and she turned for a moment to look across to see her cousin as nothing more than a blurred shadow against the sun. Patty could feel the beads of sweat on her back and under her arms and finally, she led the way off the course and they both were bent over, hands on their knees, gasping and gulping air, struggling for breath.

"I'm glad you got that out of your system," said Rick finally, taking ragged breaths. "I had trouble keeping up with you."

"I'm sure you did," answered Patty sarcastically when she was able to speak. "I could see that you were having a problem." They walked slowly by the light-mirrored duck pond, still breathing hard, not ready for conversation until after they had plodded up the hill and drunk their fill at the water fountain.

"I'm so glad you could run with me today. I haven't run at all in a month. I'm afraid to come down here myself. I'm even afraid to use the course at the high school or run along Hastings Beach. I keep thinking that Harold is going to be there waiting for me. I'm becoming a nervous wreck."

Rick winced in acknowledgement of Patty's distress. "This whole situation with Harold has gotten way out of hand." He then asked Patty the question she had been asking herself. "If you could do it over again, would you blow the whistle on Harold?"

Patty answered immediately. "No way. I don't even have to think about it for a second. I would just forget what I saw. Or maybe if I felt I had a moral obligation, I would use some kind of intermediary to warn Harold to stop the cheating, but no way would I go to the superintendent." She paused. "And don't forget, I was really forced to do that because of Jim Politano. I'm no hero. I'm just a regular person, a school teacher, trying to get along, and this whole thing has turned into a major headache for me. It's even affected my relationship with Noah. As I've become more and more anxious, his personality has changed too."

"And how about these letters? I've been wondering. Is there anything else you can do to find out who's sending them?"

Patty shook her head. "I'm not Nancy Drew, Rick."

Rick nodded.

The two crossed Parkway Drive, walked down the two quiet side streets and past the campus of the technical high school, and then they were at Iron Weed Road. Rick gave Tish's house a long look as they passed by. He then turned back to Patty. "I still don't understand why you haven't gone to the police about those two letters."

"What could the police do? The letters aren't even threatening, just annoying."

"I don't agree with you. I think they are threatening. Someone is thinking about you and not thinking very nice things. Someone is going to some trouble to write and send them. The writer must be aware of the effect they're having."

Patty had no answer, although she thought that Rick was probably right. By this time they had reached the front of Patty's house and Rick stopped for a moment. "I'm glad Noah took my advice and started that real estate course. It's a great second job for a pilot. And I'm sure he knows he'll always have a job at my agency if he's laid off."

"It was nice of you to suggest the course. That thought of a furlough from the airlines has hit Noah like a ton of bricks.

I've never really seen him so bummed out about anything. His father was laid off once when Noah was very young, and things were really rough for his family for a while. The experience must have traumatized him."

"I don't think Noah has cause to worry. He's bright, and he's good with people, so I'm sure he'll do well in whatever he does." Then he turned toward his darkly gleaming Lexus, which was parked in the driveway while Patty walked over to get the mail.

"If Noah has any questions about the course, have him give me a ring," Rick called. "And the two of us should run more often. Be in touch."

" Do you want to come in for a drink or something to eat?" Patty called out at the last minute as Rick opened the door of his car.

He shook his head. "No, I told Jordana I'd call her tonight, so I might as well go home. That's one of the advantages of being the boss. You can take off when you want to." He laughed. "As long as you don't do it too often."

"Are you seeing Jordana tonight?" Patty asked as she opened the mailbox at the head of the driveway and reached in.

"No, as a matter of fact, Tish and I are thinking of going to the movies. Would you like to join us?"

"Two's company. Three's a crowd," Patty called, smiling as she drew out the mail and closed the mailbox. She was not looking at the mail in her hand. She was looking at Rick, and from a distance, she thought she saw a slight smile on his face.

"Tish and I are just good friends," he said, about to lower himself into his car. At that exact moment, Patty looked down and saw the gray business-size envelope right on top of the rest of the mail and let out a yell. Rick stood up and looked over at her.

"What's wrong?" he asked, and then saw her holding the letter up in her hand. He ran over and watched her tear it open.

Dear Whistleblower,

Happy Birthday. Do you think Harold will have a happy birthday this year?

Meanwhile promise you'll take good care of yourself,
Willie Sutton

Rick looked quickly up and down the street. Then he put his arm around Patty's shoulders in a protective gesture and propelled her toward the house. "Come on. Let's get inside. We don't know where the nut is. He might have a rifle pointed at us right now." Patty hurried alongside him, looking ahead to the safety of the house. They were inside within seconds, and Rick slammed the door. They walked through into the kitchen and Rick looked at Patty. "Where are those other two letters?" Patty brought the first two letters out of her kitchen drawer and put them with the third. "This one is signed Willie Sutton," she said.

"Willie Sutton. For some reason, I think I should know that name. It's not the same as the first two, is it?" asked Rick.

"No, let's see." She unfolded the first two letters. "It was just W. Sutton. Now it's Willie. He must feel that he's becoming a friend. I wonder what kind of sadistic game Harold is playing with these names."

Rick picked up the three letters and quickly read them. He shook his head as he handed them back to her.

She folded the three letters and put them in a kitchen drawer. "Thanks for hustling me in. I felt wobbly on my feet when I saw that letter."

"Anyone would." He got up and crossed the room to look out the kitchen window to the back yard. Then he closed the curtains, and realizing that she needed something to do, said, "How about some coffee?"

An hour later, Patty was pushing Rick out the front door. "I don't have to go," he said. "I can stay until Noah calls, at least."

"No, you told Tish you'd take her to the movies, so take her."

"OK," he finally agreed, and as he left, he called back, "Let me know if you decide to go to the police. I'll go with you if Noah isn't around."

When Noah called that evening, Patty recounted what had happened and read the third letter to him. "The name is different this time. Willie Sutton."

Noah repeated the name. "Willie Sutton. Willie Sutton. Sounds familiar somehow."

"That's what Rick thought. Do you recognize the name?"

There was a brief silence on the line. "No, I thought it rang a bell, but no. Never heard of it. I've never heard of Willie Sutton."

"Rick thinks that this letter is the last straw. He thinks that I should go to the police."

Again there was a silence and then Noah said, "You're the most precious thing in the world to me. Go to the police."

Chapter 48

With her decision made, Patty called Ellen as soon as she hung up with Noah. When Ellen answered on the first ring, Patty asked, "Expecting a call?"

"No. Hi, Patty. I was just passing by when it rang. So what's doing?"

"Ellen, do you have time to hear something? Something really important. Something confidential. Something that you can't repeat. "

"Sure. Shall I sit down?" She laughed.

"You'd better." Then Patty paused to gather her thoughts. "You know that rumor about a whistleblower? Someone who saw Harold changing test scores and turned him in?"

"Yes, but we know it's not true."

"That what you think, but I can tell you that the rumor is true because — I'm the whistleblower. I went back to school one night in January and saw Harold changing test scores. I reported what I saw to the superintendent of schools. That's how he knew to check the tests for erasures and changes."

There was a dead silence and then Ellen said, "You're kidding right?" Her voice was guarded and she sounded as though she were waiting for the punch line of some unfunny joke.

"No, I'm serious, and that's why I'm calling. Since early April I've been getting letters addressed *Dear Whistleblower*. The third one came today. I need to see Al or some other detective. Somebody has to do something to stop the letters and find out who's sending them. They're scaring me."

Ellen's voice was still disbelieving. "You actually saw Harold changing scores and never told me?"

"I couldn't," Patty explained, making her case. "John Larraway gave me orders. I couldn't tell anyone. I was sworn to secrecy. Let me tell you what happened." Quickly, Patty went over the events of that Wednesday evening in January. Ellen listened without interruption until Patty had finished.

Then she said, "It's a good thing I am sitting down. I can hardly believe it. What an actor that Harold is. I believed every word he said, crocodile tears and all. I feel like such a fool. I've gotten into so many arguments in town about him. All my friends say I'm part of the cult at Island Brooke." She paused.

"Do you want to talk to Al? He's here for a change. I'll get him."

A few minutes later, a man's voice was on the phone. "Patty, this is Al. Ellen has talked about you so much that I feel I know you. She just filled me in. She said that you're the one who blew the whistle on the test tampering at Island Brooke. Is that true?"

"Yes, I went back to school one night and caught Harold changing scores. I've been dying to tell Ellen, but I couldn't. I was under directions from the superintendent of schools. Today I received a third letter addressed 'Dear Whistleblower' and I'm all in knots about it. I can't be 100 per cent sure, but I think that Harold Trelawney is sending them."

"Can you come to the police station tomorrow morning about nine to give us a statement?"

"You're working on the Memorial Day weekend?"

"Yes. I'll be there."

"Then I'll be in."

When Patty hung up the phone, she called Rick at home, and left a message on his machine. Later that night, he returned her call. And when she explained that she was going to the police station the next day at nine, he said, "I'd be happy to go with you." She could tell he had put his hand over the receiver, and he came back on in a minute. "Tish will go too. I'll pick you up about eight-thirty in the morning. I think it's time and past time to do something about those letters."

Chapter 49

The Hastings police station was a long two-story concrete building with small recessed windows, and the look and feel of a bunker. The next morning, just before nine, Patty, Rick and Tish were walking through heavy-duty doors and past signs, which read *No weapons beyond this point.* The lobby seemed barricaded from the outside, and was separated from the office by a partition of bulletproofed glass, and Rick had to pick up a telephone to identify himself to the uniformed policeman and explain their business. While Rick talked on the phone, Patty had time to look around at the signs on the institutional gray walls, *Buckle up. No exceptions. It's the Law,* and remark in a tone of lightness that she did not feel, "Even The Terminator would have trouble getting in this place."

Once they were buzzed inside, they stood rather uncertainly in this unfamiliar place for a few minutes, until Al Cherry appeared through a door marked, *"Private,"* attired in a sports jacket, white shirt and well-pressed trousers. He was a tall, wiry man with dark skin and dark hair going gray at the temples, and Patty was surprised to see when he turned toward her, eyes as blue as her own.

Patty introduced herself and then Rick and Tish. Al then led the way through the brightly-lit squad room through one door and then to a small cubicle which had a metal plaque reading *'Detective Alvin Cherry'* on the door. Inside was a small, no frills office with an acoustical tile ceiling and glassed-in walls papered with flyers, framed photographs, commendations, and diplomas. He offered them gray metal folding chairs in front of his desk, busy with a laptop, printer, phone, scattered file folders and an in-tray heaped high with papers. As he slipped his jacket off onto the back of his chair, Patty could see an automatic on his hip.

Al sat down and began by looking at Patty. "What you told me on the phone sounded kind of hokey. Do you want to start from the beginning and tell me how all this happened?"

Rick answered instead. "Detective, what Patty has to tell you is very confidential. Only a handful of people know about it. She doesn't want it to get around. And actually the superintendent of schools has directed her not to talk about it."

"The superintendent of schools has no right to do that. But if it will make you feel better, Patty, I will keep this as confidential as we can. But I do have to discuss it with my partner. I'll call him in later so that you can meet him."

Everyone then looked at Patty as she poured out the story, which she had now told so many times. She ended with, "I don't know for sure who is sending the letters, but I think it's Harold Trelawney. I think he overheard at least part of what I said at the Abeles-Mack Agency. He knows I'm the person who brought him down, and this is his nasty way of getting back at me."

Al listened attentively to what she had to say, and made notes as she talked. He then asked, "Did you bring the letters?"

Patty nodded and produced them from her purse. They were in a manila envelope. She handed the envelope across the desk to the detective who shook the letters out onto his desk.

"And I suppose these have been handled by a lot of your friends and family?"

Patty nodded.

"We'll have to get fingerprints on everybody so that we can rule some prints out, but we can assume that whoever wrote them took care. But we'll check anyway." He read the three brief messages and then laughed out loud. "So Willie Sutton is writing these. I thought he was dead."

"You know him?" Patty was incredulous. "Is he a famous person or someone you knew personally?"

"A famous person, or an infamous person is more like it. Willie Sutton was a bank robber who had a special talent for breaking out of prison. The press made him something of a folk hero, kind of a lovable bad guy, and a lot of people loved reading about him. Once he was asked why he robbed banks, and his famous answer was, 'That's where the money is.' When he was finally captured for the last time, it made the front page of just about every newspaper in the country."

"How was he captured?" Tish asked.

"Well, you could say that a whistleblower turned him in although the circumstances were a little different, and I'm not sure the word was in common usage at that time. But I do see the connection. Some honest citizen was riding on the subway and looked across and recognized Willie. The honest citizen turned him into the police, and that was the end of Willie's life of crime. He died in prison."

"So the name 'Willie Sutton' does have something to do with whistleblowers," said Patty. "That must be why Harold signed that name."

"That's probably it," said Al." Let me handle it this way. I can hang onto these letters and have them checked for prints. We can look for the person who sent these to you, but I'm not sure what kind of crime we can charge him with. I'm not sure these letters are threatening. I know Ellen told me I better make things right for you, or I'll have to answer to her." He read the letters again. Then he picked up the phone and spoke briefly to someone. Within a few minutes the door swung open, and a big man dressed in shades of brown came in. He had a bull neck and sun-streaked dark blond hair combed straight back from his forehead. The man swaggered over to Al's desk and plunked himself down on the edge without making any effort to greet Patty, Rick or Tish.

"Patty, Tish, Rick, I'd like you to meet my partner, Gene Hanlon. Gene, this is Patty Bass. She works with Ellen at the school. And this is her cousin Rick Miller, and her friend Tish Jackson. Patty's been receiving some hokey letters and she wants us to look into it for her."

Gene Hanlon gave only a perfunctory nod in response to their greetings, and Patty immediately recognized him as one of those policemen who believe in keeping distance between themselves and the public they are hired to protect and serve. When he read the letters, his face did not change at all. Patty was waiting for him to say something, but he made no comment. Instead, he only stared over at her and seemed to be sizing her up. Uneasy under his gaze, she finally turned back to Al and asked, "You said that Willie Sutton was turned in by a honest citizen who was a whistleblower. How did the whistleblower make out?"

There was a fractional pause as Al and Gene exchanged glances. Then Al said, "The whistleblower was killed. That's why I'm taking these letters seriously."

Patty shuddered and turned to look at a gray metal cabinet in the corner of the cubicle, finding her eyes on a standing photograph of a younger Ellen beside two small boys.

"Oh, by the way, just for background information, Patty, who would profit if you were to die?" asked Gene speaking for the first time. His voice was raspy from cigarettes but not unpleasant.

"What do you mean?" inquired Patty, surprised by the question.

Al tilted his chair back and followed up on the question. He spoke in a casual way. "In the unlikely event that the letter writer is planning to take some kind of revenge on you, who would profit from your death?"

"Why nobody would profit," replied Patty, confused. "I don't have any money. Actually my husband and I are just starting out. We have a lot of debts, and there's a chance that he may be laid off from his job this summer. So nobody would profit."

"You have a house," Al pointed out.

"Yes, we do, but we don't have much equity in it. My husband bought it just over a year ago, and really the bank owns most of it."

"How about family money?"

"No, my father was a schoolteacher until his retirement so you can forget about thinking I'm some kind of heiress. And Noah comes from a middle class family too. There are no stocks and bonds in our family trees."

"How about insurance?" Al persisted.

Patty felt on the defensive. "Well, yes. I have some from school. About $50,000, and I did take out $150,000 more last fall when my husband took out a lot. He's a pilot. He always says that it's the safest way to travel, but you never know. He wanted me protected just in case. And the insurance was so cheap that I took out a policy on myself."

"So you have $200,000 worth of insurance. And who's the beneficiary?" asked Gene.

Patty showed the slightest hesitation in responding, and then said, "My husband, Noah." She could see where the conversation was leading, and she didn't like it.

Rick jumped in. "Wait a minute. I think we're getting off topic here. We're talking about letters that Patty has been getting, not life insurance." He seemed angry, and Patty silently thanked him for coming to Noah's defense.

She spoke up, "I really don't think life insurance or any other kind of insurance has anything to do with my problem."

"We need all the background we can get, and we just need to rule things out," said Al, sounding to Patty like one of the detectives on *Law And Order*. "One more thing. You probably know that Ellen and I are going to Europe in three weeks just as soon as the school year is up. We'll be away for ten days. If anything happens while I'm away, give Gene here a call." Gene nodded and reached into his pocket with nicotined fingers to produce a card, which he handed to Patty. "My number's on this. Call me if you have a problem." Patty took the card and slipped it into her bag.

They all got up at once, and as Patty, Rick and Tish turned to leave, Al looked once more at the letters, shook his head, and for the third time repeated the word "Hokey."

Chapter 50

Sam Pepen was having breakfast with his wife on the morning of the first day in June. He drained his cup of coffee, raked his fingers through his black and gray curls, and pushed his chair back from the table with a grating sound. He then went over to the *Sierra Club* calendar, which was hanging on the kitchen wall opposite the table and flipped the page from May to June. He looked at the days ahead and counted out loud, "One, two, three, four, five, six, seven, eight, nine, ten, eleven, twelve, thirteen." He then took a pen out of his inside jacket pocket and circled a date on the calendar.

Judy Pepen, a matronly-looking woman of generous proportions who had been his wife for almost forty years, looked up from her breakfast of oatmeal and orange juice and asked, "What are you doing, Sam?"

"Counting the days left in the school year."

She laughed, "You've never done that before. You're just like a kid. I didn't realize that principals counted the days left."

"Well, this one does. John Larraway really owes me big for what I'm doing. Thirteen more school days and one week beyond that. I've never worked under such pressure in my life.

The air at the school is so thick with tension, that you have to labor to walk down the halls."

"Because of the Island Brooke parents?"

"No, not the parents. The parents aren't the problem. They're not really so bad because they're almost all on the same side of this thing. They all think that Harold is innocent. It's the teachers. They're split right down the middle at this point. Half of them think that Harold is innocent, and the other half think he's guilty. My worst fear is that some of them will get into a fist fight right in the teachers' lounge."

She raised her eyebrows, "Is it really that bad?"

"Worse," he answered. "My reading specialist in particular is a troublemaker. A couple of weeks ago he came in with a big cardboard box labeled, 'Letters for Mr. Trelawney.' Then he went around to all of the teachers and asked them to have their students write letters to Harold. Can you imagine such a thing?"

Judy Pepen clucked in disapproval. "How did the teachers react to that?"

Sam sat back down. "Just as you might expect. Some of them were enthusiastic, some acquiesced, and some downright refused. It caused a lot of dissension." He started to eat his oatmeal. "Then last Friday he came into school with a petition to get Harold reassigned back to the school in September. Again, some teachers jumped right in, but others wouldn't sign. Right now the tension in the building could be cut with a knife."

"Who is this guy?"

"His name is Dewey Willis. He has a wonderful reputation as a reading specialist. Actually, I believe he was slated for a big promotion in the system, but once this scandal broke, he ended up on the wrong side of the dispute as far as the superintendent was concerned. He does seem to be going off the deep end. I hear he's always over at Harold's. He eats there. Probably sleeps there half the time too."

They ate in silence for a few minutes, and then Judy asked, "There's one thing I don't understand. Why didn't someone realize before this that the Island Brooke scores were out of line?"

"I've wondered about that myself. Now with 20/20 hindsight, it seems that someone should have known that the scores were inflated, but remember Island Brooke always had a lot of Yale professors living in the district, and we can assume that their children would do well on tests. Also, with open enrollment, many of the brightest kids from all over Hastings were registered at Island Brooke." He stood up. "But I do remember how frustrated the my teachers used to be when the standardized testing results came out. My staff was as hardworking as the Island Brooke staff, and each year they were so disappointed that their students didn't do better."

Judy just shook her head. "And it all had to do with test tampering."

"Anyway, I just have to get through the next thirteen days, and then things will calm down. Once the kids are gone, the atmosphere will relax. That one extra week won't be bad. I don't think I could take it any longer than that. It's all too much for a man my age."

"All right. You've convinced me. You're having it rough. I can see why you're counting the days. But it will be all over before you know it. You should be able to finish up the year without any more upheavals. Then we'll just get in the car and go to Lake George."

Chapter 51

When Patty got to school that same day, she looked at the calendar and did exactly what Sam Pepen had done — counted the days left in the school year — and with a red marking pencil circled the Thursday that was the last day of school. Then she circled the Friday of the following week, the day she and Noah planned to fly to Idaho. She was really looking forward to staying with his family. She had talked to her in-laws on the phone numerous times, and she was anxious to spend some time with them.

Chapter 52

He was watching the water lap up against the brown-black pilings, and listening to the gulls make their odd cries as they searched for food. It was just before eight o'clock in the morning, and, except for the ferry on its way to Montauk, the glistening surface of Long Island Sound was deserted. He checked his watch. The man who rented boats was due at eight o'clock. He wished the man would get there. Not that he was planning to go out on the water that day, but he did need the information about renting a boat His preliminary plans had all gone well, but now he had decided that the only safe place for the typewriter was at the bottom of the sound. It was a lot of trouble to go to, but he couldn't afford even one mistake.

As he walked back down the dock to the blistered plywood shack, he checked off the details in his mind one by one. He had purchased the typewriter and the stationery at two different discount stores the day before Easter, and paid cash. There was no reason why anyone should remember him. No problem there. He had sent three letters to Patty, and one to the *Hastings Morning Star* to keep the pressure on her. He was well aware of the advances in DNA testing, but there should be no problem with any of the letters. And the left over gray stationery could easily disappear. But the typewriter was another matter. He couldn't be sure that a microscopic sample of his blood or his saliva or his hair or a thread of his clothing wasn't curled somewhere up under one of the keys. And it was just his luck that the top cop in Connecticut was one of the world's most accomplished forensic criminologists. He could just imagine the famous Dr. Henry Lee finding one follicle of his hair on the typewriter which some kind soul had pulled out of a dumpster, and using it to reconstruct his whole plan. There was no way around it. The typewriter had to go into Long Island Sound.

He sighed as he wrenched his mind back to the task ahead of him. He knew that he had to make some hard decisions, and he knew that he had been delaying the final step. He hoped he wasn't losing his nerve, the edge that he was so proud of. But he had to face facts. Apparently, killing Patty wasn't as easy as he thought it would be. But he really shouldn't blame himself. After all, he wasn't some kind of psycho who went around killing indiscriminately.

He reassured himself that he had already committed two perfect crimes, and now just about everything was in place for the third. There were a few logistical problems, but he knew that he could work around them. And of course, now there was a time limit. Patty had to die soon. He needed a tentative date. He glanced at the *People's Bank* calendar tacked to a grimy corkboard on the door of the shack, and with his finger tapped June 17. He laughed. Now wasn't that appropriate? It was the last day of school.

He looked over the bobbing twelve-footers for a minute, and then heard the voice, coming up behind him. "Been waiting long?" As he turned to the man who rented boats, he was smiling his practiced smile.

Chapter 53

In the teacher's lounge that day, everyone was talking about Dewey and his appearance the previous evening on a local talk show. "He was wonderful," Eunice gushed. "His defense of Harold was inspired. How did he put it? 'This is the greatest injustice since the Dreyfus Case.' I never realized that Dewey had so much emotion beneath the surface."

When Dewey came into the room a few minutes later, the teachers who supported Harold roundly congratulated him. A few other teachers continued correcting papers or planning lessons without comment, making it only too plain where they stood on the issue.

"How are you doing with the petition?" Eunice asked him. "Has everybody signed?"

"No, some teachers have refused, and I can't seem to get hold of some people who support Harold. They're never around when I'm carrying the petition." He laughed. "It's almost as though they're ducking me."

Patty was one of the very people that Dewey had in mind. She has been avoiding him for the last few days, sticking to her room, and trying to make herself invisible in the school. She and Ellen had even started eating lunch in her classroom instead of the teachers' lounge. That day, as usual, they were talking about Harold.

"How do you think he got started?" Patty asked. "How could he have crossed the line?"

"Al and I have discussed that a few times, and there's no easy answer. The only thing we could come up with was that he's probably like a cashier who steals a few dollars from a cash register. When he gets away with it, he takes more, and before long, he's taking big bills. Maybe that's how Harold got started. Just changing a few scores at first and then more and more to keep up his reputation."

Patty took the last bite of her sandwich and nodded.

After lunch Ellen stopped in the teachers' lounge for a few minutes to read the newspaper and almost saw Sam's worst fears realized. As she sat at one end of the table, she could hear Eunice at the opposite end defending Harold. Ellen then heard her say, "I've applied for a transfer out of this school. If Harold isn't here, I don't want to be here." Behind her on the couch, Ellen could hear Sue talking to Julie LaVoie. "I got a call last night from a friend in Los Angeles. She said the test tampering scandal here in Hastings was discussed during news broadcast yesterday, and the anchorman seemed to be blaming the teachers. I'm going to write a letter of protest to that station. Harold is as guilty as sin." Sue's last words cut across an unexpected silence in the room, and Eunice heard them. She got up from her seat and with hands on her hips walked right over to Sue. "I don't think that you should be saying things like that at school. It isn't professional." Her gravely voice had turned shrill.

Sue's face was determined as she stood up, and faced down the woman who had taken Harold away from her. "As far as I know Eunice, this is a free country. If I want to discuss this with a colleague, I don't think it's any of your business, and it certainly isn't your place to eavesdrop on my private conversations." After a moment of stunned silence, a few teachers got between the two, and Eunice went back to her seat in a huff. Ellen, still seated at the table, looked around and said to no one in particular, "This party is getting rough. I'm glad this school year is almost over."

Dewey with the petition finally caught up with Patty later that week. She was sitting in her classroom before school correcting a stack of spelling papers from the previous day. She looked up as Dewey approached her desk, complaining, "Linda Hicks won't sign the petition to bring Harold back. She told me she's just a first year teacher and doesn't have tenure. She's afraid of some kind of retribution from the superintendent."

Patty put down her marking pencil and began to finger the base of a ceramic vase on her desk, her mind racing to think of a plausible excuse not to sign and at the same time not alienate Dewey. Then she looked up. Dewey was handing her the petition and a pen, and in a reflex action, she started to take them. Then she stopped, shook her head, and waved him away. She couldn't sign the petition. "I'm sorry, I can't." Her voice cracked, and she shook her head from side to side. Afraid to be candid and still trying to preserve her friendship with Dewey, she weakly said, "I'm a first year teacher. I don't have tenure either."

Patty couldn't read the emotion that crossed Dewey's face, but his words were harsh. "You're kidding, right? You haven't gone over to the other side too, have you?"

Patty shook her head again and started to reach out her hand to him in friendship. Then, just for an instant, his veneer of affability seemed to slip away, and she saw anger, real anger, in his face. He stood there for a few moments glaring at her. Then without further comment, he wheeled around and left the room. His anger was so unexpected and so out of character that Patty wondered if she really had ever known Dewey at all.

Chapter 54

The last regular faculty meeting of the year was held right after school the next Monday. All the teachers in the library-media center looked spent as Sam Pepen called the meeting to order. "This will be the last faculty meeting of the school year," he announced, and then waited for the spontaneous applause from the assembled teachers to die down.

"There are three more days of school, actually two and a half when you consider that the students will leave at one on Thursday. As soon as the buses roll out, you may leave. I would like to see the school clear by 1:20." Again there was scattered applause.

He went over some housekeeping matters in detail, and then said, "Let's review the schedule for Thursday. As you all know, the cafeteria will not, I repeat, will not be operating that day, so teachers and students will have to brownbag it. Notices to that effect will be going home tomorrow. Some teachers have come to me and asked if they could provide a special lunch for their kids. That's fine with me, but remember to check health records for allergies."

"How about peanut butter for everybody?" someone at the back called out with a laugh.

"Not funny," said Sam without a smile. "This is serious. Again, please check the health records. We don't want some child with an allergy leaving the school on Thursday in an ambulance. We've had enough bad publicity this year. If you do bring in lunch or some special treat for the kids, make sure to get signed permission from parents."

"Will lunch be at the regular time?" Sue asked.

"Yes, let your kids eat at their regular time in your classrooms. Then, you may either take them out for recess or just keep them in their rooms. I know there's plenty to do.

They can clean out their desks and help you take down bulletin boards, or just play board games. That's up to each of you. The school will be open this Friday and most of next week, so if you have to come back for some reason, you will be welcome. I'll be here until Thursday of next week. One week after the close of school for the students."

He glanced down at his agenda. "Also, as decided by teacher vote, there will be no end-of-the-year party this year. If any of you teachers want to get together on Thursday afternoon, that's up to you. But again, no formal school party this year."

Marielle raised her hand. "Any chance that you'll return to us in September?"

Sam's rollicking laugh was the only answer needed. He then went on to say, "The name of the new principal should be announced within the next couple of weeks. I'm sure you all know that the Board of Education has announced that Harold will not be returning to Island Brooke under any circumstances. There have been some rumors that he would be offered an administrative post at one of the middle schools or the high school, but that is still up in the air."

He wiped his brow, and then he said, "I don't want to keep you today. I just want to thank all of you for pulling together with me to keep this school afloat since early April. You have been a great staff and have answered far above and beyond the call of duty. I was recently complaining to my wife about how tough it was working here, but now that my tenure as acting principal is coming to an end, I am very glad that I took the superintendent up on his request. I feel fortunate to have worked with you, even for this short time, and will always value my brief stint at this school. Since I will not be returning to Island Brooke, I will say a formal goodbye today although I'm sure I'll be talking to all of you over the next few days. I will be returning to my peaceful life in retirement a week from Friday, but I will always remember how you teachers came through for the children despite the frenzy outside, literally outside this building. Thank you all. And enjoy the next few days. No more faculty meetings. Again, I hope you're all out of here by 1:15 on Thursday."

Marielle was the first one to rise and begin clapping, and then all of the teachers on the Island Brooke staff rose to their feet and applauded the man who had taken the tough job of replacing Harold Trelawney in the time of crisis for the school. Later as Patty walked out of the library-media center with Ellen, she turned to her mentor and said, "I thought this school year would never end. This is the first time that I can really believe that we're going to make it. But I hate to lose my kids. I love each and every one of them. I think I'll give them a special treat for lunch the last day. Maybe pizza."

Chapter 55

The next Wednesday at the end of the day, Patty literally ran into Dewey in the main office. Since her refusal to sign the petition, he had taken pains to avoid her in the school. He no longer stopped in her room in the mornings, and when they passed in the hall, he averted his eyes or merely nodded. On the occasions when they had to speak, he had conducted their business quickly and in purely formal tones. Yet within the last day or two, Patty had seen him skulking around the hall near her classroom, but when she had started to approach him in the hope that they could talk out their differences, he had hurried off.

That afternoon Dewey was standing between the central counter and the mailboxes, holding the 'Letters for Mr. Trelawney' box in his hand. As Patty squeezed by to get to the sign in-sign out book, he stepped back, apparently accidentally, and she knocked into him. They each quickly apologized and then he asked, "Do you have any letters for Harold?" There was something abrasive in his voice that Patty didn't like, but she choked back a sharp retort, and merely answered pleasantly with even tones, "No. Sorry. We haven't had time. Last minute rush. The kids have been so busy. Finishing up and everything."

Because of Dewey's position, he was still blocking the sign-out book, and she found herself looking right into his face. There was something challenging in his half-smile, and his new colored contacts made his eyes a startling blue. "I just thought you might have," he went on, those blue, blue eyes never leaving her face. "Harold will be out of town for a couple of days, but I'm going to take this box of letters home today and give it to him this weekend when he gets back." Patty just shook her head, and tried to act casual as he moved aside so that she could sign out. She then beat a hasty retreat out of the building and home to Noah.

Noah had his last real estate class that Wednesday evening, so Patty planned an early supper. Just as they were finishing up, the front doorbell rang. When Patty went to the door, she found Tish looking tanned and jaunty in a short white tennis dress with a pleated skirt, pompom socks and spotless white tennis shoes.

"Do I have good news for you," Tish said. Patty could sense her excitement as they walked into the living room. Patty slipped into an overstuffed chair while Tish remained standing. "I can only stay a minute," she said, "but this couldn't wait."

"Since you're all in white, I guess you're here to announce that you and Rick are getting married."

Tish smiled. "Not yet. I wish, but we're not quite at that stage yet. He's still pining for Snow White." She greeted Noah who had heard her voice and come in from the kitchen. "I'm glad you're home too. I have the best news for both of you." She had a cat-ate-the-canary look on her face when she went on, "Guess what I've found out? Harold and his wife have just made an important decision. They're selling their house and moving to Seattle."

She got the amazed and happy reactions she was expecting.

"Are you sure?" asked Patty and Noah in unison.

"Positive. Harold called the agency first thing, and Rick went over there this morning and they talked for a while. Harold and Ann Marie have had it with Hastings. Harold is resigning from Hastings Public Schools next week. He's decided to take his life in an entirely new direction. Apparently, he has some investments that he's going to follow more closely, and he's also planning to go into the antique gun business. And the best part of the news is that they want to put their house on the market right away. Sometime next week, the two of them are flying out to Seattle to stay with their daughter while they look for a condo. They're not planning to wait on anything. They're leaving all their furniture. Once the house is sold, they'll have everything shipped out. Harold told Rick that they'd be leaving as soon as he takes care of some unfinished business."

The weight of the world seemed to lift from Patty's shoulders.

"So did they sign the contract with Rick?" asked Noah.

"No, there wasn't time. They had to leave for Boston this morning — some big family affair — so they couldn't do it today. But they'll be back on Saturday, and Rick has an appointment to appraise the house and get their signatures on the dotted line over the weekend."

"This is so perfect," said Patty to Tish. "The school year is ending tomorrow. Harold is leaving town. We're going on vacation to Idaho next week. Noah didn't get laid off after all, but he thinks he might go into real estate part-time anyway. Everything has worked out." She paused. "And one other bit of news from Al Cherry. He called late this afternoon. He told me that the three whistleblower letters weren't computer-generated.

They were typed on a manual typewriter. Also, the stationery was medium quality. As if I care. And they couldn't find any unidentified fingerprints. Harold must have worn gloves when he touched them."

"Well, at least you won't be getting any more of them. Harold must feel he's done as much as he can to upset you," Tish said with a smile.

The three of them talked for a few minutes more about the Harold's decision. Then Noah commented on Tish's attire. "I see you're dressed for tennis, Tish. I played a lot in college. I didn't know you played."

"I don't. At least not well. I'm just a beginner and Rick is too. We're going to learn together. We're playing at the high school courts tonight, and then—" she stopped in mid-sentence and did a comic bump-and-grind.

"Tish, what do you have in mind for tonight after tennis?" laughed Patty as her friend started to leave.

"I'll never tell," was Tish's exit line.

Noah sank into a squashy chair opposite Patty. "Well, that's a relief. Harold is leaving town. So the reign of terror is over. No more letters from Willie Sutton. No more phone calls with nobody there. I hope Harold doesn't change his mind."

"No, I don't think he will. The Island Brooke parents still support him, and he has some of the people in town on his side, but he's an outcast with a lot of people. I don't know how he can walk down the streets of Hastings and hold his head up."

"What did Tish say? Harold and his wife are spending the next couple of days in Boston?"

"Right. They're both from the Boston area."

"Is he still officially working for Hastings Public School?" asked Noah.

"Yes, he's on medical leave." Patty thought for a moment. "You know now that it's almost over, I can see that for Harold this whole thing is kind of like a Greek tragedy. He was so high, and now he's so low. He had that one flaw. Arrogance.

Hubris. Is that what they call it? I remember how he was the day he interviewed me last September. He was sitting on top of the world. Nationally known. Turning down jobs. And now he's practically being run out to town. In a way I could almost feel sorry for him."

"Not with those crazy letters he's been sending you. He's made our lives miserable never knowing what the mailman will bring. I hate what he's done to you."

"You're right," Patty said in agreement.

As Noah was leaving the house for his real estate class a few minutes later, she called after him, "What time will you be home?"

"I'm not sure. I think everybody might want to go out to a diner after class to celebrate, so let's play it by ear. Don't wait up if you're tired."

When Noah was not home by ten, Patty went to bed. She wanted to be completely fresh for the next day. The last day of school. June 17.

Chapter 56

That same evening at ten o'clock, Harold, fully clothed, lay on top of his bed talking on his cordless phone and staring into the darkness.

"Do you still love me?" he asked.

When Eunice answered, there was indignation in her voice. "Of course, I do. I've proved it to you over and over. How can you even ask such a question?"

"Canceling out on me at the last minute like this. I would be at a big party in Boston right now if you hadn't called this morning."

"I couldn't help it. Everything was set. David was supposed to be meeting with his assistant managers at the restaurant tonight, but he just delayed and delayed, and finally, about twenty minutes ago, he called in and postponed the meeting till next week."

"Where is he now?"

"He's out with my father getting ice cream at Baskin-Robbins."

"When will I see you?"

"When is Ann Marie coming back?"

"Not till Saturday."

"Tomorrow afternoon looks good. We have early dismissal because it's the last day of school." She laughed as she realized that she was talking to the man whose name had been synonymous with Island Brooke School. "As though you of all people don't know that."

"What time can you be here?"

"By 1:35 or so."

"That's fine. I'll plan my day around it." He paused "How is school going this week?"

"Terrible. I've told you the whole place has fallen apart since you left. The kids aren't learning a thing." He didn't speak, and she went on. "I'll be glad when this year is over. You know I've applied for a transfer to another school. There's going to be a third grade vacancy at Soderholm. I hope I get it. I just can't take it anymore at Island Brooke. All the backbiting. Most of the Island Brooke teachers are so shallow. They have no loyalty. It's becoming more and more uncomfortable for me. Sue's the worst of all. She just goes around gloating. I almost got into another fight with her in the teachers' lounge today. She started talking about how your scores went way up when you were a second year teacher. She said you made everybody else in the school look bad. She was hinting that you've been changing test scores for years. I felt like going over to her and pulling that dyed red mop off her head."

There was rectitude in his voice when he spoke. "My scores did go up my second year of teaching. Because my students worked hard and I worked hard." He thought back to the first time he had changed the test scores — the day his best student had come in out of a sick bed to take the standardized tests. Worried about how illness might affect her performance, he had adjusted her scores — and then a half-dozen others.

"Sue thinks she's so brilliant. She said she's analyzed the scores. She was saying that you generally left the high scores alone. You changed the average ones to above average, and the low average ones to average."

Harold worked to control his anger. Then, he responded, "If Sue knows so much about it, maybe she changed the scores herself."

Eunice laughed. "She also said that you turned down that big job in the state department of education because you knew the scores would nose dive if you left."

His laugh wasn't pleasant. "Sue has a very active imagination. She should get a life." He was wondering how Sue had figured it out. He had been like a man riding a tiger.

"She really seems to hate you making up stories like that. Are you sure you never had an affair with her?"

"Absolutely not," he lied. He then went on, "What else is new at school?"

"Well, I'm not the only one who wants to get out of Island Brooke. Quite a few of the teachers have asked for transfers. I guess about twelve."

"I still have that many supporters at the school then?"

"Well, to be perfectly honest, some of the ones who are leaving don't support you at all, but they just don't want to work at Island Brooke any more. Too much notoriety."

Harold's voice was strained. "Thank you for sharing that with me."

Eunice regretted her perfect honesty, and sought to change the subject. "Oh, and there's talk about that whistleblower thing again. How did that stupid rumor ever get started?"

"No idea. That Abeles-Mack Agency kept asking me about Wednesday evening of test week. I think they were trying to imply that someone was in the building and saw me changing scores that evening. But that's ridiculous. That was the evening I had a long, long conference with some parents, the Osbornes, and remember, then you came to the school at nine. So believe me, test scores were the last things on my mind."

"Could someone have been in the school that night? Someone that you didn't see? And that person saw you doing something that made them think that you were changing scores? Do you think that someone could have been spying on us?"

"Of course not. I had the all the doors locked."

Eunice kept on talking, but he drifted away, thinking of that Wednesday in early January. He remembered that day so well. Ann Marie had a 7 o'clock meeting at her own school, and he had reserved that whole evening for changing standardized test scores. The call from Marcetta Osborne in the late afternoon had changed some of his plans. She had insisted on dropping by for a few minutes at about seven to show him some posters for the upcoming school auction. She had said that she had only a few quick questions about the layout, and he only needed to take a peek and give her an answer. He had reluctantly agreed because she was the co-president of the PTA, but he had made it clear that he had a lot of work to do that evening and could only give her a minute. He remembered walking through the building at six. Everyone was gone. Even the custodian. He had then done an all-call. Sure that nobody was in the building, he had locked the side door. Alone in the school, he had felt safe. He had then taken out the third grade standardized tests and erased and changed answers till almost seven. Then he had parted the drapes in his office and watched the Osbornes drive up and park. He remembered going to the side door prepared to look at the posters and answer Marcetta's quick questions. But the Osbornes had insisted on coming in. The three of them had gone into the main office and talked for about five minutes at the central counter. He remembered how nervous he had been because all the tests were right out on the table in his office, but fortunately Marcetta and Bill had made no move in that direction. When he let them out a few minutes later, he distinctly remembered locking the side door.

As he went back to the office, the phone was ringing and he had hurried to catch it, thinking that it might be Eunice, firming up their plans for that evening. It was Eunice, and he had sat down and worked on the tests while he talked to her. After he hung up, he had worked till almost nine. Then he had parted the drapes and seen Eunice's car already in the parking lot right beside his. She had come a few minutes early. He had been in a rush then, hurrying to put the tests away so that she would not see them. By the time he got to the side door, she was coming up the sidewalk.

He realized that Eunice has asked him a question. "What?" he asked. She repeated, "How were you able to get out of going to Boston?"

"There was no problem about it. Ann Marie was upstairs in the shower when you called this morning. When she came downstairs, I put on a big act and told her that I was having a stomach problem. I said I just wasn't up to the car ride to Boston. She wanted to cancel out too, but I talked her into going. I told her at least one of us should be there for her nephew's graduation party." He paused. "To tell the truth, I wasn't wild about going anyway. Some of Ann Marie's relatives have been giving me funny looks ever since the test tampering story hit the news."

"How about your own family? Are they all still supporting you?"

"Of course. Ann Marie. My daughter. Her husband. My mother. My sister. They know I could never be involved in cheating." He paused. "But I'm glad that my father isn't alive to see this whole test tampering mess."

"I met him once when I first started teaching at the school. He seemed nice."

"He wasn't nice. He wasn't nice at all. He was an obstinate and autocratic man. Roland Trelawney. Judge Roland Trelawney. A legend in his own mind. I was never good enough for him. My sister Becky was always a brilliant student, and he never let me forget it. I got decent grades, even honors, but I could never measure up."

"So you didn't get along?"

"That's putting it mildly. We never got along at all. From the time I was in elementary school, he was always on my back. And he was furious when I went into teaching instead of law." Harold paused. "But he sure changed his tune over the years when Island Brooke won all those accolades. Actually, I think he became quite proud of me although he had trouble admitting it. But he would never understand this whole controversy. The accusations. The lies. The venom."

"This whole thing is such a farce. What do you think set Larraway off on the standardized tests?"

"I have no idea."

A silence stretched out.

"Well, I'd better get going. I don't want David to find me on the phone when he comes home."

"Smart girl." He paused. "I have something to tell you. Ann Marie and I have just made an important decision."

"What decision?"

"I'll tell you tomorrow."

Her tone was petulant. "You want to keep me hanging till then?"

"I'd rather tell you in person."

"I hate it when people do that."

"I'm sorry. I probably shouldn't have mentioned it, but I do want to tell you in person."

"OK, I guess I can wait," and then, "I love you."

"I love you too."

"I'll be there tomorrow at 1:35. 1:35 on the dot."

"I'll be waiting."

He hung up, sighed, and again thought back to that Wednesday evening in January. In his mind's eye, he could still see Eunice coming up the sidewalk toward the door. But then there was the part he couldn't remember. Was the side door locked? He thought so, but he couldn't be sure. Could there possibly be a whistleblower? Did someone get into the building that night and see him changing scores? He thought of Sue Strauss. She would be the one. Or Marielle Rossamondo who had turned on him. If there really was a whistleblower, it had to be one of them. Or was the whole whistleblower thing some kind of ruse to get him to confess? If so, he hadn't fallen for it. He had outsmarted them since he still proclaimed his innocence to all who would listen. And at least half of the town still believed him.

As Harold lay there, he heard a noise from downstairs. Familiar with the sounds of the house, he gave a start and sat up.

Had that been a door closing? he asked himself. Had Ann Marie come home for some reason? If so, thank goodness Eunice did cancel out. It would be a disaster if Ann Marie ever found out about her, especially now that the affair was just about over with his move to Seattle. But that had sounded like a door closing. Could someone have broken in? There was something about burglaries on the East Shore in the paper the other day. He felt a spike of fear at the thought of an intruder in the house.

He got out of bed and snapped on the lamp on the night table. He picked up the phone and dialed 9-1. Then he stopped his finger from pushing in the final digit — and disconnected.

He thought of a police car with sirens blaring racing through the night to his house, and his neighbors crowding at their windows to see what else could be happening to Harold Trelawney. The incident would probably even make tomorrow's edition of the *Morning Star.* With everything else, he didn't need that. He had already had enough publicity to last a lifetime. The noise he had heard was probably nothing, and he didn't need people talking about Harold Trelawney, the old maid, who hears suspicious sounds in the night and calls the police. On the one chance in a thousand that a burglar had broken in, he would take care of the matter himself. He was an expert with handguns, and he could handle the problem.

He opened the drawer of the night table, and reached for his Smith and Wesson revolver. Carrying the weapon in front of him, he put on some more lights, walked down the hall and descended more than halfway down the winding staircase. The first floor was in darkness. He listened. The house was almost silent. Just the steady beat of the grandfather clock in the entry hall. He took the last few steps, stood in the flagstone entry hall and listened again. Nothing. He had been holding his breath, and he exhaled. All right. Just as he had thought. A false alarm. It was nothing. He was about to go back upstairs when he looked down the hall and noticed a wedge of light under the door of his den.

He was sure that he had shut off all the lights in the house because he was expecting Eunice. Could someone be in there?

He walked silently down the hall and heard the hum of his printer. He tiptoed slowly, turned the handle and pushed the door open. A man, wearing a watch hat of some kind and latex gloves, was sitting in front of his computer, just taking a paper out of the printer.

What kind of burglar was this? Harold asked himself.

"Turn around and put your hands up," he said calmly with his principal's voice. The man spun around, looking very surprised and struggling to regain his composure. A puzzled frown spread over Harold's face when he saw who it was. Then he lowered his revolver and strained to see what was written on the computer screen. The message began, "Dear Whistleblower."

Chapter 57

Patty had phoned Jimmy's Flash Pizza and arranged for five large pies to be delivered at 11:15 on Thursday, her last day. At 11:30, lunchtime had arrived, but there was no pizza. She was starting to feel panicky, going to the door every other minute to check the long corridor. By the time it was 11:45, she decided to go to the main office and call the pizza restaurant to find out what had happened to the children's lunches. She walked over to Ellen's room and called in to her.

"Mrs. Cherry, would you keep an eye on my class. I have to go down to the office to see why the pizza hasn't been delivered. My kids are starving."

Ellen nodded and Patty started up the hall just in time to see a group of men come in the side door and walk purposefully toward the main office. She recognized John Larraway, towering above them all, and started to wave, but then realized that he was not looking her way. She also thought she recognized the burly figure of Gene Hanlon, Al Cherry's partner. When she got to the main office, she saw the group just closing the door of Sam Pepen's private office.

"What's going on?" she asked Grace.

"I don't know. Sam's been calling back and forth for the last hour, and the phone's been ringing off the hook. There's some kind of big problem, real big, but I don't know what it is."

"That was the superintendent, wasn't it?" asked Patty.

"Sure was. Can't miss him," was the response.

Patty walked over to the telephone on the counter. "I have to call Jimmy's Flash Pizza. They're late with my kids' lunch. Do you have a phone book?"

Grace reached in her desk drawer and pulled out a thin Hastings phone book. Patty started to take it, but through the window at that moment saw a truck with the large red letters spelling out Jimmy's Flash Pizza stenciled on the side, parking in the fire zone.

"Oh, they're here. Better late than never." She handed the phonebook back to Grace, pulled out her wallet and took out the exact change plus a tip. She met the pizza man at the door, and within seconds was rushing down the hall with a stack of flat, white boxes in her arms.

By one o'clock, the children were lined up, many crying at leaving their teacher, and Patty's desk was piled high with wrapped boxes of what various children had proudly told her contained chocolate candy, writing paper and dusting powder. As Patty waited for the last bell of the school year to ring, she gave each of the children a hug. The all-call went on at that moment and Sam's voice came over the PA system.

"There will be an important faculty meeting promptly at 1:15 in the library-media center today. Attendance is mandatory. This includes all teachers and paraprofessionals. All staff. Again, this is mandatory. There will be an emergency faculty meeting promptly at 1:15."

On the way down to the office with her line of children, Patty looked at Ellen and mouthed, "So much for Sam's promise. Teachers can leave as soon as the kids are gone." She then went back to her room, packed together some of her things and started heading for the library-media center. Ellen joined her, and they hastened up the stairs together.

"Sam said no more faculty meetings. I wonder what this is about," said Ellen.

"Do you think it's to announce the new principal?"

"Could be," Ellen said, "but Sam shouldn't have made a promise if he wasn't planning to keep it. I want to get home. Al and I are flying out of Bradley early this evening, and I have lots to do."

Walking down the second floor corridor, they were joined by other teachers grumbling about the unexpected meeting.

The meeting did not start promptly at 1:15. It was almost 1:30 when Sam flanked by John Larraway entered the room. Sam stayed in the back and sat down at one of the long tables as the superintendent of schools walked directly to the front of the room and raised his hand for silence. There was instant quiet. The teachers were itching to get the meeting over with and get home. But the superintendent, grim-faced and nervous, did not begin. Instead, he stood awkwardly massaging his chin with his hand and straightening his shirt collar. Then he steepled his hands in front of him as though he were about to pray. There was shifting and an undercurrent of impatience in the room. Someone coughed. Glances were exchanged. Feet were jiggling and shuffling. Patty heard Eunice across the table from her say under her breath, "C'mon. Let's get this show on the road." Finally the superintendent began in a loud, clear voice.

"I have some tragic news for you. Some shocking news." He paused and there was another uncomfortable silence, but the restless movements had stopped. All eyes were fixed on the superintendent.

"I thought it better to tell you here at school than to have you hear it on the radio on your way home. I have some terrible news." He paused again, and there was minor shuffling in the back of the room. "Terrible news." There was now total silence, and the teachers seemed to be holding their breaths. "Harold Trelawney was killed by a burglar sometime last night."

A shock went through the room, and then a chorus of gasps There were looks of disbelief, and cries of "Oh no." For a second or two Eunice looked pole-axed. Then she crumbled across the table and began to sob. From the side of the room someone asked, in a loud voice, "Did he say killed?"

The superintendent put up his hand for silence and went on. "We don't have too much information on exactly how this happened. Apparently, Harold and Mrs. Trelawney were planning to spend a couple of days in Boston. At the last minute, Harold felt ill and did not go. They had an arrangement to speak on the phone at eight this morning. When Mrs. Trelawney called at eight, she got no answer. She then called at intervals of fifteen minutes, and became so concerned at ten o'clock that she phoned one of her neighbors, and asked him to go check on Harold. The neighbor found that the back door to the kitchen was broken in and immediately called the police. They arrived very quickly and found his — " He changed what he was about to say. "The police found the house had been ransacked, and there was evidence of burglary."

Again, the superintendent hesitated. "I know that many of you were very close to Harold and will have difficulty dealing with this tragedy." Several teachers were now openly crying, and their sobs filled the room. "There will be grief counseling available at the high school for teachers and students. I also know that some of you had planned to come in tomorrow or next week to clean up and organize for the next school year, but that will not be possible now. I am going to close this school as of two o'clock today. I am doing this to avoid another media circus in front of this building. I believe that I will be able to open this building sometime after July fourth, but that is subject to change. I have nothing more to say at this time other than this is the most tragic incident in a series of unfortunate occurrences, which have plagued this school since January of this year."

Marielle half in tears called out, "But how could something like this happen?"

The superintendent shook his head. "I don't know. I'm sorry, Marielle. I don't have any more information, but I'm sure the press throughout the country will feast on this. And as we speak, this information is being released to them, so I would advise all of you to get out of this building and to your cars as quickly as possible."

He left the front of the room and made his way toward the door. He then stopped. "One more word about transfers. I know that a number of you have requested a transfer to any other school in town. Please call my office next week if you are serious. First priority will be given to faculty of this school, so identify yourself as a teacher at Island Brooke. I am very sorry. I have no further information to give you and nothing further to say. I am very sorry. Very sorry." He turned and went out.

The teachers, bewildered, stunned, frightened, many in tears, were starting to rise from their chairs and start toward the door. Patty was one of the first to get up. She gave Ellen a hug, and started over toward Dewey. All her old feelings of friendship for him had come back with the tragic news, and she wanted to reach out to comfort him. She could imagine how he felt at the news of Harold's death. He was still seated, and as she approached, she could see that his face looked very still. Suddenly, she recalled her role in the test tampering scandal and felt like a hypocrite. Thinking that she had no right to intrude on his sorrow, she turned on her heels and swiftly left the room.

At the corner of his peripheral vision, Dewey had seen Patty's approach and then her hasty exit. He got right up and went after her, but teachers crowding out the door blocked his way, and by the time he got to the top of the stairway, he knew he could not catch her. He stopped at the window on the stairwell and watched her cross the parking lot, get into her car and drive out of the lot. He craned his neck to watch as she turned her car onto Emerson Street. A strained expression distorted his features as he castigated himself for not catching Patty before she left.

Chapter 58

Noah watched the accounts of Harold's death on local and national newscasts that evening. Too upset to even look at the television, Patty secluded herself upstairs in her bedroom and took calls from Tish and Rick, and then her father and Aunt Vera in Florida. Shortly after seven o'clock, Brooke called from New York City. "Patty, I just heard about your ex-principal's murder on the news. How horrible. You must feel terrible."

Patty made a quick decision, and began, "Brooke, you don't know how terrible. I have to tell you something, but you've got to promise to keep it all to yourself." She then poured out the whole story starting with her trip back to the school that January evening. She talked to Brooke for a long time, almost two hours, and when she finally hung up, she felt enervated, physically exhausted, and ready to fall asleep. But the phone kept ringing, and finally she just reached over and pushed it off the hook.

Chapter 59

Patty tossed and turned during the night, and woke up exhausted. Then the horror of Harold's death hit her, and she dissolved into tears. Later, she went downstairs to the kitchen where Noah was sitting at the table reading the New Haven newspaper, with a cup of coffee and the still-folded *Hastings Morning Star* at his elbow. "What does it say?" she asked in a choked up voice.

"It's an ugly story," Noah answered. "The police think that Harold came downstairs with a gun and surprised the burglar in the den. That's where Harold's body was found. It looks like the burglar somehow distracted Harold, and knocked him out with one of those heavy wrestling trophies I told you about. Then the burglar killed Harold with his own gun. The gun and the trophy were missing and it can be assumed that the burglar took them with him when he left."

Patty reached across the table, unfolded the local newspaper, and the huge headline *Burglar Kills Principal* leapt up at her. A photograph of Harold was prominently featured, and the entire front page was taken up with the news of Harold's death and a sidebar rehash of the test tampering scandal at Island Brooke. Patty read the entire paper, devouring the news and then slapped the paper down. It had been worse than she had expected. She looked across at Noah.

"This is so tragic. I had to read it once, but I don't want to read anything else about Harold's death. I just can't bear it. I was planning to cancel both newspapers next week when we go to Idaho, but if you don't mind, I'd like to call up and cancel them today."

Noah reached across the table and held her hand for a moment. "I don't care, honey. I can always buy one at the airport if I want to read something, but I think you're right.

This has hit too close to home. Harold was your principal for most of the year."

Patty's words came out in a rush. "I think it's even closer than that. You may think I'm crazed because of everything that's happened, but I just know that Harold's death is connected somehow to the whistleblower letters."

Noah shook his head. "No, Patty, no. A terrible thing has happened to someone you knew, but you can't let your imagination run wild. Harold's death has nothing to do with those letters you've been getting. And certainly nothing to do with you."

Nothing to do with you. Patty didn't agree with Noah, but she held her piece. Noah just didn't understand how she was feeling. The days had become long and fearful. So many terrible things had happened that she had started looking over her shoulder, and wondering what other awful thing lay ahead.

The ringing of the phone interrupted her thoughts. She got up to answer it. The caller didn't identify himself, but Patty immediately recognized Dewey's voice. "Patty, I feel so bad about this. I don't know what I'm going to do." His voice sounded muffled as though he might be crying.

"Dewey, I'm so sorry. I know how close you were to Harold. This must be so hard for you. What a tragic waste. How could something like this happen?"

"I don't know. Crime is out of control in this country when a man isn't safe in his own home." There was a pause. "A lot of teachers called me last night and this morning to ask about the funeral. I didn't hear from you, and I didn't know if you've been trying to get me."

"Uh, no. I didn't call."

Dewey didn't seem to notice her response and went right ton talking. "Harold's funeral will be in Boston and it will be private. Family only. Ann Marie made that decision to avoid a carnival atmosphere. So no teachers will be attending. Except me of course."

"That's only right. You were Harold's best friend and really stood by him."

"We will be having a memorial service right here in town on June twenty-ninth. Considering the tragic circumstances, I'm sure the superintendent will unbend and let us use the high school auditorium. I imagine that hundreds of people will attend. I know I can count on you. "

There was a brief silence as Patty calculated. "June twenty-ninth. Oh, Dewey, I won't be able to come. Noah and I are leaving for Idaho next Friday. We'll be gone for two weeks. We won't be home till the second week in July."

When Dewey spoke again, there was a note of desperation in his voice. "Can't you change your plans and go a little later?"

"Dewey, I'm sorry. Our trip is planned around Noah's vacation time. We can't make a change."

The telephone wires seemed to hum with the silence, until Dewey spoke again, his voice now even more strained and little more than a whisper. "Well, I guess you've made up your mind. You really never supported Harold when he was alive so why should you go out of your way for him now that he's dead." The phone was disconnected at that point, and Patty found herself listening to a steady dial tone in her ear. As she gently replaced the phone on the hook, she started to cry, not for Dewey and not for herself, but for the poor flawed man who had been killed by a burglar. Noah stood up and held out his arms, and she went into them for comfort.

Chapter 60

O'Heffernan's Chowder House was famous, one of the best restaurants on the East Shore. Housed in a free standing brown-shingled building set back from a working wharf near Hastings Beach, it was known all over southeastern Connecticut for its fresh seafood and Maine lobster. Patty, Noah, Tish and Rick had reservations for 5:30 that next Wednesday, and there was only a short wait before the busy hostess seated them at a corner table in the main dining room. They settled themselves and found the darkened atmosphere pleasant, if somewhat over-decorated with a nautical motif — cargo nets stretching across the ceiling, and carved figureheads, anchors and seascapes on the grained walls. A ship's lantern over their table provided light, and from her chair Patty was able to gaze out at the water through a porthole instead of a window.

Rick signaled to the young waiter with the John F. Kennedy hair, and ordered wine and only Noah demurred. "I'm driving tonight and flying all day tomorrow, so I'll pass." The two men then dominated the conversation and at length discussed the Red Sox's chances that year. When their chowder was served, the conversation turned to Noah's real estate course and his future in the business.

Rick, his face bright with sunburn, spoke with enthusiasm. "I think you'll enjoy sales. I know you'll like dealing with the public. A lot of people start out part-time in real estate and find they do so well financially that they go into it full-time. Look at Tish here. She gave up her catering business and now she must be making at least twice the money."

Patty looked across at her best friend who was nodding in agreement with Rick, and looking as though she would nod in agreement with whatever he said. The lantern was casting interesting shadows on Tish's face, and her eyes were enormous and bright with adoration — and riveted on Rick. His attention in turn seemed focused on her, and he leaned over occasionally to pat her hand and kiss her on the cheek. He went on to explain, "That's how I got started in the real estate business. I was working in a white-collar job in Stratford when my mother asked me to help out weekends at her new agency. Within a year I was making more money weekends than I was during the week, so I quit my job and went into real estate full time. You never know. You may decide to do the same, Noah, and the hours would be a lot better for Patty. It must be hard on her to have you away all those nights."

Rick then turned to Patty who seemed to be in a world of her own. Noticing that she had been unusually quiet and uninvolved in the conversation, he asked, "Thinking about your trip to Idaho?"

Noah answered for Patty. "I was hoping that this wouldn't come up, but it's not the trip. Patty didn't even want to come tonight. She just wanted to stay home and isolate. She has some half-baked ideas about Harold's death. She thinks that it has something to do with her. This whole thing has been preying on her mind, and she's been having trouble sleeping."

"But how can that be?" asked Rick, talking directly to Patty. "The newspapers have been saying that a burglar broke in and took a lot of valuables from the house. Silverware, firearms, jewelry. There was a whole list of things. It was just a coincidence that the person who was sending you those letters was killed. A horrible coincidence, I might add, but just a coincidence."

"I can't explain it." Patty's voice was weak. "I just know it's not a coincidence. Something is going on here. I can feel it."

Noah turned in his chair to face Patty. He spoke slowly and harshly, forming every word. "You're scaring yourself with those ideas. You're just feeling guilty because you blew the whistle on Harold. You feel guilty because he lost his job, and now he's dead. You've got to snap out if it or maybe we should think about some counseling for you when we get back from Idaho."

Patty flinched at the tone that she had never heard from her husband before, and both Tish and Rick looked over at him in surprise. There was a short uncomfortable silence. Then Rick said, "I don't know about that. There is such a thing as women's intuition. Patty may be right. I never considered it before, but maybe there is more going on than meets the eye." Patty welcomed Rick's support and was about to make a follow-up comment to back up her feelings when the young waiter appeared with their entrees, and the thought was lost. They lingered over dinner, and then Noah turned the conversation to the coming trip. "We're flying out the day after tomorrow. A few nights with my parents, and then we'll rent a car and tour Idaho. Patty has never seen the West so she's in for quite a treat."

"And you've never met Noah's family either, have you?" Tish asked.

Noah again answered for her, "Well, Patty did meet them, but only briefly. We got married so abruptly last August that they weren't able to have any real time with her, but I know she'll love them, and they'll love her."

As Noah raised his finger for the check, Rick and Tish exchanged intimate glances, and then he announced, "The food is great here, but tomorrow night I'm going to a place where the food is even better." He looked at Tish and winked. "Shall we tell them?"

Tish put her hand on Rick's arm in a proprietary way, and with a smug voice said, "I'm cooking Rick a gourmet dinner tomorrow night. And would you believe no meat? I won't say what I'm cooking, but I will mention swordfish and Gorgonzola cheese. And of course, strawberries and lots of chocolate for dessert."

At that moment the waiter arrived with the check, and Rick reached for it easily ahead of Noah, and insisted on paying.

"This will be my treat. You'll need all your ready cash for the trip. When you get back, you can take Tish and me out somewhere."

Noah shook his head, and good-natured squabbling over the check began. Dabbing her mouth with her cloth napkin and then tossing it onto the table, Tish gave Patty the high sign. "C'mon, Patty. Let's go to the ladies room while these two guys arm-wrestle over who's going to pay. We'll be right back."

In the ladies room they sat before the mirrored wall while Tish fussed with her hair and talked rapidly, excitement in her voice. "Ed is picking up the girls tomorrow morning and taking them to Cape Cod for the long weekend, so Rick and I will have the house to ourselves. It will be the first time that we'll have this kind of time alone. He's told me that he wants to go slow after his big disappointment with Jordana, but I think tomorrow night will be the night."

Tish gave a little squeak of pleasure and went on. "Listen to this day I've planned. All for myself. I'm walking my two miles and working out first thing in the morning. Then I'm going to that new spa for a half day of beauty. The whole works. Facial, manicure, pedicure, make-up. Then I'm getting my hair done and then I'm cooking the famous gourmet dinner." Her laugh rippled through her whole body, and there was a note of triumph in her voice as she went on, "Who would ever have thought? I wore him down. I did it. I did it. After all this time, I think Rick may be falling for me." She reached up, and slapped Patty's palm in a high five. "Here's to perseverance and patience. And here's hoping that tomorrow night with me will drive Jordana Sumner right out of his memory banks."

"What has happened to Jordana?"

"No idea, but Rick told me he's not seeing her anymore. And I don't care if she dropped him, or he just got tired of running after her." She paused. "Oh, and Dewey called me this afternoon to see if I would come to the memorial service for Harold next week. I told him I would. I haven't mentioned it to Rick yet, but if tomorrow night goes the way I want it to, I think he'll come with me."

"Dewey was devastated at Harold's death," said Patty. "He was so upset that he hung up on me when I said I couldn't go to the memorial service."

"I think he's calmed down. And listen to this. He told me that he won't be working at Island Brooke next year."

"Did that promotion finally come through for him?"

Tish shook her head. "No, somebody else got the job, but he has been promised a transfer to the high school." She stopped talking for a moment, and seemed to consider. "That means I can tell you something that I've wanted to tell you for a long time. Prepare yourself for this." She paused for effect. "I think Dewey is in love with you."

Patty opened her mouth. "In love with me?" She thought for a moment. "That's kind of hard to believe. On the other hand, that may be why he's been acting so irrational since I refused to sign that petition. But what makes you think that?"

"Remember when Dewey and I were dating last winter? Well, whenever we went out, and whatever we were talking about, he always seemed to steer the conversation around to you. I can tell you that it got pretty irritating."

"Why didn't you say something to me at the time?"

"I wasn't one hundred percent sure till I talked to him last night, and he kept bringing you up and up. And also to be honest, I thought about how hard it would be for you to work with him if you knew. Now that he's transferring to a different school, you probably won't see him much so it really doesn't matter."

"It's a good thing he won't be back at Island Brooke. I don't need this. I don't need one more thing to deal with."

"He also said that he wanted to see you before you went away on vacation. He wants to apologize for hanging up on you. He seemed to know that you were leaving the day after tomorrow."

"See me before I go away on vacation? I don't think so. It sounds like Dewey has his own agenda, but it's not my agenda. Actually, I've got lots to do tomorrow, and I'm feeling so sleep-deprived that I just might decide to nap in the afternoon. And after everything's that's happened in the last few months, I'm just not up to any emotional scene with Dewey. I think the best thing might be to let our friendship — if that's what it was — just wither away. I think at this point that it would be really awkward to see him."

Tish nodded in agreement, and rose, ready to return to the table. "And what's going on with Noah tonight? I never heard him snap at you like that before."

"I don't really know." Patty touched up her lip-gloss before getting up. "He has been on edge lately. I think just the possibility of being laid off by the airline got to him. He had thought his job was so secure."

"But his job is safe?"

"It looks that way. That's what he told me."

When Patty and Tish got back to their table, the deferential young waiter was thanking Rick and bowing himself away. The two men stood up, and Noah slipped his arm through Patty's as they headed for the front door. As they left the dining room, threading their way through a line of people who were waiting to be seated, a plump woman wearing a black and white harlequin dress broke away from the crowd and placed herself right in Noah's path.

"Noah? It is Noah Bass, isn't it? Remember me. I'm Jane Frances Moody. I dated your friend Hal Kinder in college."

Noah didn't appear to recognize the woman, but he smiled in a charming way.

"My name was Tolles then. Jane Frances Tolles. I was in one of your classes. Have you been in touch with Hal at all?"

Noah let go of Patty's arm as he spoke to the women, and she along with Rick and Tish was jostled through the crowd and did not hear Noah's answer. Noah joined them in a few minutes as they waited for him in the lobby of the restaurant.

"Who was that?" asked Patty.

"I have no clue," was Noah's response. "She said she went to college with me and dated someone in my dorm, but I don't remember her."

He quickly pushed ahead of the other three and turned back to say, "It's kind of stuffy in here with these crowds of people. I need some fresh air." Tish moved up and walked beside Noah, while Patty and Rick fell behind. Patty just had time to look back to see the plump woman in the harlequin dress staring after them with an annoyed look on her face. Rick had also stopped and turned to look. He took Patty's arm, and said, "Probably some ex-coed who had a big crush on Noah. He was a jock in college, wasn't he?"

"Yes, he sure was. Baseball, tennis."

"So that explains it. Noah stood out in her memory because he was a big star. He doesn't have any special reason to remember her."

"Probably," Patty agreed although the incident struck her as odd. She and her cousin walked out together.

It was getting late, but was still light when they arrived back at Patty's house for dessert.

Noah turned to Tish. "Come on. We'll run out to the backyard so I can show you how to take care of Patty's tomato plants while we're away."

"No problem as long as I get my fair share of them when they're ripe. I love tomatoes as much as Patty does." Noah and Tish went through the house and out the back door without stopping. Rick halted in the den and eased himself down into the Barco Lounger. "Mind if I watch TV until dessert is ready? I want to get all the baseball scores." He tilted himself back and reached for the remote control.

"Fine. I've just got cake, fruit and cheese. And coffee. Give me ten minutes to get everything together. I'll call you when it's ready."

Patty got the coffee started, and cut up some watermelon. She arranged the fruit artistically on a Wedgwood platter, uncovered the Brie, cut the cake, and set the table. She then stood by the counter waiting for the coffee to begin to perk. Glancing out the window, Patty saw Noah and Tish at the tomato garden near the post-and-rail fence, which served as a boundary and separated their yard from the neighbor's in back. As she watched, Tish appeared to lose her balance and almost fell. Noah reached for her and for a moment the two were in each other's arms before moving quickly apart. A strong possessiveness took hold of Patty for an instant, but then she laughed and said softly under breath, "Tish, it's a good thing that Rick didn't see that, or you'd be back on the outside looking in again."

A few minutes later Noah and Tish came into the house, laughing loudly with their arms casually around each other's waists as Rick ambled in from the den. They all sat down at the kitchen table, and Patty served the dessert and poured coffee into three cups.

"Who's not having coffee?" asked Rick.

"Me." Patty raised her hand like a schoolgirl. "I haven't been sleeping well since Harold's death, so I put myself on a caffeine-free diet." When most of the fruit and the cheese were gone, Rick and Tish stood up. They seemed anxious to leave.

"Guys, I won't see you until you get back so have a wonderful time," said Tish. She gave Patty and Noah kisses and hugs. Noah and Rick shook hands. Then Rick turned to Patty. "Enjoy the Wild West. And take care of yourself," he said emphatically as he kissed her on the forehead. He stepped back to take a good look at her, and for a moment, Patty felt as though he were put off by something that he didn't quite understand and was about to say more. But Tish was tugging on his arm, so he just gave

Patty an affectionate look and a smile, linked his arm through Tish's, and they were gone. As soon as they were alone, Noah walked over to Patty who was rinsing the few dishes at the sink and putting them into the dishwasher. "Patty, I want to apologize. I think I was a little short-tempered with you at the restaurant. I'm sorry. I don't know what came over me talking to you like that. I guess I'm just not myself."

Patty's face softened, and she turned to slide into his arms and burrow her face in his chest. "Your apology is accepted. I guess we've both had some rough times the last months, and we're both on edge. With everything that's happened, it's no wonder that we're not ourselves. We really do need that vacation. Two weeks away from Hastings will fix us up just fine." They hugged for a few minutes. Then Noah began to trace his finger along her neck. "I like your neck bare like this." He then leaned over and kissed her neck softly, just grazing it with his lips. His mouth was next to her ear. He murmured a question.

"The best offer I've had all day," was her response. She faked a yawn, and then in mock formal tones said, "My goodness, look at the time. Eight-thirty. Way past our bedtime. I think we should turn in now, Mr. Bass."

Noah flicked off the kitchen lights, and laughing they raced each other up the stairs.

Chapter 61

Patty was tired the next morning, her eyes lined from lack of sleep, but Noah seemed unusually alert. Ready to leave for the airport with his flight bag on the floor, he stood at the kitchen door to the garage looking lean and strong in his pilot's uniform and shook his noisy set of keys at Patty.

"I'll be home tonight, really tomorrow morning around two. I'll sleep till nine and then I'll do my packing. I'll have plenty of time before the flight."

"But I can pack for you," she protested, wanting to be helpful. "I know what you need to take. It'll be no trouble at all."

"No, absolutely not. Leave my things alone. In fact, keep out of my closet. I'd rather do every thing myself. Leave my things alone. I like things done a certain way, and only I can do them."

"All right. But look at this, Mr. Neat-Gene." She went over to Noah and smoothed out his white uniform shirt, which had bunched up. "There, now you look perfect." She looked up at him and thought that she had never seen him look quite so handsome before. She stifled a yawn. "See you at two a.m. I'll wait up if I can."

"No, don't do that. You haven't been sleeping well, and tomorrow's a big day. I'd just as soon find you fast asleep when I get home."

She bobbed her head in agreement. "OK, I'll try to get to bed early."

He smiled and kissed her goodbye.

Chapter 62

"It's the money, stupid."

He knew that his plan was brilliant and he would never be suspected, but at times he took perverse pleasure in imagining that the police had found him out, and he had been arrested for murder. He could picture two foul-mouthed detectives who looked amazingly like Gill and Silverstone leaning over him in an almost-bare interview room at the police station and screaming, "Why did you kill her?"

And he would answer simply, "It's the money, stupid."

"What?" the detectives would ask, and he would go on, "You don't really think that some wimp of a principal was going to kill Patty because she blew the whistle on him, do you? It's the money. It's always been the money. The whole whistleblower plan was just a ruse, a smokescreen. But I do have to give credit, where it's due. I had been trying to come up with some plan to kill Patty, but I was completely blocked. And then the whole test tamping scandal fell into my lap. I would never have thought of sending those asinine letters if it hadn't been for the test tampering scandal and Patty's role as a whistleblower. I can remember sitting in that barbershop in New London and finding that true crime magazine, and reading about the whistleblowers and especially Willie Sutton. I started to plan it all out then and there. I would send her a few whistleblower letters. Eventually, I knew she would go to the police, and the link with Willie Sutton would come out. And then I could kill Patty, and the crucial fact, the most important factor, was that I would never be suspected because the police would be looking in the wrong direction. They would be looking at Harold Trelawney. They would think that he killed her because she blew the whistle on him. The plan was perfect. Patty would be killed because she was a whistleblower. Everything was planned down to the smallest detail."

"And why did you kill Harold Trelawney?" they would yell.

"I had to. He caught me in his house writing a whistleblower letter on his computer." Then he would pause. "But I feel sorry about that, really sorry."

"You do?"

"Of course. I spent over two months setting him up, and then he was home when he should have been in Boston. Killing him almost spoiled all my plans, and I had to put off Patty's murder till another day."

The detectives would exchange glances, and he would go on. "It was horrible."

"You mean Harold's murder?"

"Yes. Just try to put yourself in my place. I was positive that Harold had gone to Boston, but I even took the precaution of driving around his house at about quarter to ten that night to make sure. The house was in complete darkness. I circled the block and parked on the next street and came across that big back yard of his. The house was quiet, and I had Harold's computer all to myself. I could hardly believe my good luck. The first three whistleblower letters were written on a typewriter, but I wanted to type the fourth letter on Harold's computer, and leave it on his hard drive for you to find. It was just one of the many clues I planned to leave to implicate Harold. Everything seemed to be working out so well, and I had just printed the letter when I heard Harold's voice say, 'Turn around and put your hands up.' The word 'shock' doesn't begin to describe what I felt. Harold was right there at the doorway with a gun in his hand. And he was supposed to be in Boston. He should have been in Boston.

As soon as he saw my face, he put the gun down, and I knew I had to think fast. I really didn't want to have to kill him. I was struggling to come up with some story, thinking I would act drunk, act crazy drunk. And then before I had the chance to say anything, Harold made the decision for me. Took it right out of my hands when he headed for the computer screen to see what I'd written. That did it. He was reading the letter, the letter that began 'Dear Whistleblower.' I had no choice. I couldn't let him live after that. I just got right up, brushed by him, and grabbed a heavy trophy off the shelf and knocked him out. And then I used his gun. But that meant I had to improvise. And I was like a mad man."

"How so?"

"I was afraid that some nosy neighbor had heard the shot and would call you people. Talk about working under pressure. I had to delete the whistleblower letter. Then I had to rush into the kitchen for some black plastic garbage bags and run around the house like mad grabbing anything that had value so it would look like Harold was killed by a burglar. Everything went into the bags including the trophy and the gun. Then I had to break in the kitchen door. I think I was back in my car and driving away within ten minutes after I killed Harold."

And then the two detectives would fade away, and he would walk out of the police station of his fantasy and come back to reality. Patty thought she was going on vacation tomorrow, but there was no way he could let her go to Idaho. Her time had run out. She wouldn't make it through the night.

Chapter 63

Although Patty was feeling tired, she was busy doing errands all Thursday morning — picking up cleaning, a trip to the bank and then to AAA for travelers checks, buying a paperback for the flight, doing a load of laundry and cleaning out the refrigerator. She then did all her packing, but was careful to avoid the spare bedroom where Noah's things were kept. Finally about noon, all her work was finished, but for some reason she felt jumpy — as though something important was about to happen. She finally decided that the flight the next day was getting to her. As a pilot's wife, she knew that it was foolish to be scared of flying, but she was afraid despite all of Noah's quoting of statistics. She tried to shake off her sense that something was wrong, but found herself walking aimlessly from room to room. Wandering into her living room, she sat on the padded seat of the bay window so that she could look out at her sun-splashed street and the houses opposite. Across Iron Weed Road she could see two preschoolers running through a sprinkler, shrieking and laughing under the watchful eyes of their mothers, and down the street there were a few older girls setting up a lemonade stand on the sidewalk. It was hot. A fine June day.

Stuck in the house, she prowled restlessly through the downstairs rooms for a few more minutes, and then abruptly realized that she didn't have to be a prisoner. Stadler Park would be crowded that day, and she could go for a run. She went upstairs and quickly changed, and unhurriedly jogged down Iron Weed Road and across the side streets to the park. Stadler Park was humming with activity, tennis courts full with players waiting, college students throwing Frisbees, senior citizens sunning themselves on striped deck chairs, lots of people in shorts and sleeveless shirts jogging and walking. She finally attached herself to some novice runners who were just starting on the trails, and spent the next half-hour in a slow jog. Then she passed some time standing at the water fountain talking to two high school boys in tennis gear who flirted with her and tried to persuade her to take up their sport. On the way home, she heeded the calls of the neighborhood girls who were sitting at a table in front of their house selling lemonade. She spent a few minutes drinking the most delicious lemonade she had ever had, and chatting with the girls about some young rock stars.

When she got home about one-thirty, she went right up to her bedroom to pull off her sweaty clothes, and immediately noticed that the light on her answering machine was blinking. There were two messages. She played back the first one, and heard Dewey's voice. "Patty, I owe you an apology for the way

I've been acting. I just haven't been myself recently, and I'd like to see you later today and talk everything out. I'll be home all afternoon. Please call." And then, Rick's voice sounding worried came on. "Patty, something peculiar just happened. Call me as soon as you can. We need to talk. Very important." Patty frowned and was just reaching for the phone to call Rick when it rang again. She checked the Caller ID and saw Dewey's name and number appear. She made no effort to pick up, but merely stood with her arms folded against her chest as she listened through his impassioned second message. "Patty, it's Dewey again. I do have to go out for a while after all, so I won't be home till about three. Please call me then. After three. Bye."

She thought about Dewey and all the conversations that she had had with him through the school year. She shook her head. She had no intention of returning his calls. She then pushed in the number for Rick's office. An agent answered, but within a few minutes, Rick's familiar voice came on the phone.

"Hi, Rick. It's me. What's up?"

Rick seemed to be having trouble choosing his words when he said, "Patty," and then again, "Patty."

"Yes."

"Patty, someone came in my office this morning."

His voice told her that something was wrong. "Who was it?"

"Do you remember that heavy-set woman at the restaurant last night? The one in that black and white dress. The one who seemed annoyed that Noah didn't remember her from college?" Rick went on without waiting for an answer. "She stopped in my office today looking for a map of the area. She's staying with friends and touring around the East Shore. She recognized me from the restaurant and started talking about Noah." He stopped again, and Patty could feel herself becoming impatient with his hesitations.

"Yes, yes, what did she have to say? I'm not jealous of Noah's old girlfriends in college. You can tell me."

"No, it's not that. Not that at all. It's just that she told me that she knew Noah well in college and couldn't understand why he snubbed her last night. Then she said, and this is when my phone rang and I picked it up, and it was an important call, so what she said was really garbled. About how her boyfriend had provided Noah with an alibi when he was questioned about something. I think it was a murder."

"A murder? Noah?" The thought was so outrageous to Patty that she laughed out loud for the first time since Harold's death.

"Right. Now naturally she wasn't saying that Noah had anything to do with the murder. I don't know. Apparently, something did happen. It was right at the end of their senior year — just before graduation. Or something like that." He went on to explain, "Anyway, she was only in my office for a few minutes, and she seemed kind of scattered, and I was on the phone, and then she hurried out before I had a chance to get all the details, so I'm not completely sure about anything." Patty detected concern in his voice, which trailed off awkwardly. She did not know what to say.

"And I just got wondering why Noah never mentioned it to us. I mean the three of us have gotten into some pretty heated discussions on capital punishment, and it just seemed odd to me that Noah never brought it up."

Patty again had no comment, so after a brief silence, Rick continued "And I had the strangest feeling when she was telling me this. I actually feel a chill run over me. And I was thinking about it, about how you and Noah have such a perfect marriage, and how well he and I get along, that it's almost as though we've known him all our lives. But then when I thought about it, I realized that a year and a half ago, none of us had even heard of Noah Bass." Rick's tone became light. "I wonder if he has any deep dark secrets under his hat."

Patty still had no response to make. She had always taken everything that Rick said seriously, but she couldn't bridge the gap between the Noah she knew and the Noah that Rick was speculating about. But then Rick laughed in a self-conscious way. "You know as I'm talking along here and listening to myself, I'm hearing how paranoid I sound. Last night Noah accused you of imagining things, and for some reason, I guess I'm pretty spooked myself."

Patty laughed to break the tension. "I'll tell you what. When Noah and I are driving through Idaho in a few days, I'll lead him around to the morbid subject of murder. I'll come right out and ask him if anything happened about the time he was graduating from college. I'll let you know what he says when we get back."

"I guess that's OK." Rick still sounded doubtful, but then went on. "When is Noah due home tonight?"

"Actually, he's not due until two o'clock in the morning. Tomorrow morning. "

"Well, how about this? Tish is cooking that famous gourmet dinner for me tonight. Would you like to join us?"

"You must be kidding. Tonight is for you and Tish. I'd feel like a third wheel."

"I guess you're right, but I do want to talk with you. I have to be at Tish's at eight. Will you be home tonight?"

"Sure, we're flying out tomorrow afternoon, so I'm hoping to get a good night's sleep for a change. I'm really exhausted. I'll probably go to bed early. About nine. Noah doesn't want me to wait up for him."

"Why don't I stop by before I go to Tish's? I can be at your house, say around 7:30." He paused. "I know I'm probably imagining things, but what you said last night at the restaurant about Harold's death has been bugging me too. Somehow our conversation was interrupted, and we never went back to it, but I'd be interested in hearing what you think. So I definitely want to get together with you and talk over a few things."

"Fine, I'll see you tonight then. See you at 7:30."

Attempting to digest Rick's words, Patty went downstairs to the kitchen. Lunch was light, a carton of Dannon's yogurt, some juice, and the rest of the fruit. As she ate at the kitchen table near the window and watched dust motes dance before her eyes, she went over the strange conversation she had just had with Rick and tried to dispel her anxiety. But she finally decided that Rick's concerns were on target. There was something bothersome out there. Rick had picked up on it, but actually, she was the one who had brought the subject up first during dinner at O'Heffernan's. She was the one who had sensed some kind of threat hanging over her. And she was the one who had been feeling nervous this morning.

As she brought the glass of juice to her lips, she asked herself, Do I now think I'm some kind of psychic?

No, not a psychic, she finally decided. But she had recently read that much of communication was nonverbal, and wondered if her unconscious had been picking up some subtle words or gestures from someone. Incongruent cues that her conscious mind couldn't read. For some reason, an image of Noah popped into her mind, and she thought how much his personality had changed over the last few months. Had she been picking up some subtle words or gestures from him? She laughed out loud and chided herself for the ridiculous thought. Finally, she just shook her head in exasperation, and decided that this was one more topic that she and Rick would discuss that evening, and that she and Noah would discuss on their trip.

Her lunch finished, she walked over to the drawer to look at the two airline tickets to Idaho. She took them out of their envelope, touching them, reading them over and over, and then with closed eyes tried to picture herself boarding the flight the next afternoon. Meeting Noah's family. Days on the road with Noah. Enjoying his home state. Just the two of them. The tickets represented a wonderful vacation that she had been looking forward to for some time. Yet for some reason, the happy images wouldn't come, and her unexplained jitters increased. A sense of foreboding settled over her, and, exasperated, she thrust the tickets back into the drawer.

Upstairs, she decided against taking a nap although she was tired, and instead made the bed and straightened the bedroom. Then spotting the paperback that she had bought for the plane, she spent the next hour and a half in a world of romantic fantasy sprawled out on her iron bed, her head against the pillow. She finished the book shortly after three-thirty, put it down, and then strolled out to the mailbox to pick up their last mail delivery before the vacation. The mail was heavy that day, and a glossy postcard from Florida was on top of the stack. She recognized her father's crabbed handwriting and read the message he had hurriedly written.

Having a great time. Even have a couple of lady friends. Will make a permanent move to Florida in the fall. Home right after the fourth of July. See you when you get back from Idaho. Vera sends her love.

Dad

Sorting through the rest of the mail, as she walked back to the house, she suddenly stopped and stared at one letter, which stood out. It was a gray business-size envelope with her name and address neatly typed. She turned it over. There was no return address. Her eyes sought out the postmark. Hastings. Patty tore it open. Again it was a short message.

Dear Whistleblower,

Bon Voyage. Meanwhile promise you'll take good care of yourself on your trip,

Willie

Patty almost stumbled in shock. Recovering quickly, she sprinted into the house, banged the door behind her, and lunged for the kitchen phone. In her haste to call Rick's cell phone, she pushed in the wrong number, and had to call a second time. There was silence and then a strange noise on the line. His cell phone wasn't working. She immediately called his office.

"Vera Miller Realty." An unfamiliar voice.

"Is Rick there? This is his cousin Patty. It's an emergency."

"Please hold."

Patty's fingers thumped nervously on the kitchen counter as she waited for Rick to come to the phone. A long wait. Finally, another strange voice. "Sorry, Rick isn't here. He's due back soon, or he may call in. Do you want to leave your number?"

"He's got my number, but can you tell him that his cousin Patty called? And it's an emergency. Even if he just calls in, please have him call me immediately."

Patty stood uncertainly in the kitchen for a few minutes, her mind whirling, trying to make sense out of the fourth letter. The phone rang. Before answering it, she glanced at the Caller ID to make sure that it wasn't Dewey again. It was Rick's office number. She snatched at the phone.

Rick's familiar voice. "Hi, I just got back to my office. They said you had called and said it was an emergency."

"Rick, I got another whistleblower letter."

He swore under his breath. "So you were right last night. It wasn't Harold after all." His voice took on a note of urgency. "This is the last straw. Call the police right now. Call your friend's husband, Al Cherry."

"Al and Ellen are in Europe. They won't be back till early next week."

"What's the name of Al's partner? Hanlon. Call him. The police have got to give you protection."

"Rick, the police are not going to send over an armed team in Kevlar vests to give me protection. That's not going to happen. We've been through this with them before. This letter has really knocked me for a loop, but this is just small stuff for them. They're dealing with that burglar who killed Harold, so they don't have time for me. Anyway, Noah and I are leaving for Idaho tomorrow. When we get back, we can handle this."

Rick's voice then ran on, sounding as though he could not stop himself. "And there's one more thing I've been thinking about. Does Noah?" He stopped, and then reworded his question. "Do you know anybody who owns a typewriter?"

"A typewriter? No, of course not. How low tech can you get? I'm surprised they even make them anymore."

"OK, I may be grasping at straws, seeing things that aren't there, but I'm back to what we were talking about earlier. Something is going on. I'm starting to feel like I'm looking at a big jigsaw puzzle, but half the pieces are missing. I can't really make out what the picture is, but I'm starting to get an idea, and I don't like it. I don't like that fourth letter, and I'm wondering if you're in some kind of danger from the person who's sending them. I hope I'm off base, but until we know for sure, we can't take any chances with your safety. I'll definitely come over at 7:30 tonight. I'm going to do some thinking about all this. See you tonight."

Patty stood at the phone for a minute feeling that she was at some kinds of crossroads, trying to decide if Rick had overreacted, or if she really was in some kind of danger. Her whole world seemed to be upside down, and now Rick was even harboring suspicions about Noah. She sat down on a kitchen chair, and considered her situation. She thought about the heavyset woman who had come to Rick's office. She thought about what Rick had said about a big puzzle. She then wondered if the two of them together would be able to put all the pieces together when he came by that evening.

At five thirty, Patty put a low calorie frozen dinner in the microwave and stood listlessly by the counter waiting for the beeps to tell her it was done. Then she poured herself a diet soda and sat down at the table. About a half hour later, she realized that she was staring into space, and the dinner was now cold and the soda was now warm. She pushed herself up, poured the soda into the sink, and tossed the congealed food into the garbage. The fourth letter had made her more nervous than ever. Also, the woman from the restaurant and the information about some murder kept running through her mind.

Thinking that a long, hot bath would relax her, she went upstairs to the bathroom, undressed, and started running hot water into the tub. She was just pouring bubble bath into the water when she thought she heard the slam of a car door. She stood in place, listening, and less than a minute later heard the front doorbell ring. Patty shut off the water, wrapped herself in a robe and went into her bedroom. She tiptoed over to the window and hiding herself from the street, peeked out through the blinds. Startled, she saw Dewey's car in the driveway. The bell rang again, and then a third time. Patty just stood motionless beside her bedroom window. Finally, she watched Dewey in shorts and a T-shirt, dark glasses hiding his eyes, walk to his car. Abruptly, he turned and looked up at her bedroom window, but she jumped back quickly, and was almost sure that he had not seen her.

When his car pulled away, she tried to fight off the strange new feelings that she had about Dewey. This was a man who for most of the school year had seemed like a good friend, but now she wondered if his friendship for her had really been nothing more than a mask for more erotic feelings. A mask she thought, and as she stood by the window, she wondered if Dewey was wearing any other kind of mask. Could he be the person who had sent the whistleblower letters? Could she be in any danger from him? No answers to her silent questions came, and she shook her head in confusion. She did know that Dewey was determined to meet with her that day, and seemed willing to go to unusual lengths to do so.

She started walking back toward the bathroom, and then stopped herself. Were all her doors locked? She suddenly had a vivid mental picture of Dewey coming back and just walking in on her as she took her bath. She decided she had to check the whole hour and hurried downstairs to make sure all the doors were secured — kitchen door to the garage, front door, back door from the dining room, and door to the cellar. All were doubled locked with a safety chain. After she was sure that she was securely locked in, she went around turning on all the lights in each of the downstairs rooms. Only then did she go back upstairs to the bathroom, and step into the tub. She ran more water till the bath was wonderfully hot and steamy, and sank back, submerged in a cave of bubbles.

Chapter 64

Hoping that her tension and fatigue would drain away into the water, Patty tried to clear her mind and just become weightless and relaxed, but she could not turn off her inner voice that insisted on reviewing the day's events, starting back when Noah had left in the morning. She remembered his words as he stood in the driveway. "Leave my things alone. Keep out of my closet. Leave my things alone." And the woman from the restaurant who had stopped at Rick's office with her story about some murder. And the fourth letter from an anonymous person who must really hate her. And now Dewey becoming more than a pest.

After a long while, Patty realized that the bath water had gotten cool so she got out of the tub and toweled herself dry on her way to her bedroom. The first thing she did was to turn on all the lights in the room. She felt safer in the light. She then changed into the first clothes that she found left in her bureau drawers, a pair of tan shorts faded almost white from frequent washings and the white T-shirt with *Rydell High School* lettered on the front that Tish had given her for her birthday. Remembering that Rick was stopping over at 7:30, she also put on socks and running shoes. Sitting on the side of her bed, she made one more effort to figure out what was going on, wondering if lack of sleep was interfering with her ability to think logically. She found herself coming back to Rick's question. "Do you know anybody who owns a typewriter?" but somehow she knew that what he had really wanted to ask was, "Does Noah own a typewriter?"

The word "Hokey" suddenly jumped into her mind. Al Cherry had used the word several times that day at the police station, and she was familiar with the word, and had used it, but she just couldn't define it. She should really look it up.

Noah had asked her not to go into his closet and by extension the room where he kept his things, but she now felt justified in disregarding his request. She now had a legitimate reason to go into the spare bedroom where their tome of a dictionary was kept. She got up and crossed the hall to the spare room, still used mainly for storage and for Noah's things. It was empty except for Noah's old wooden desk, a desk chair and his exercise equipment — a stationary bicycle and some weights. The dictionary was there on the desk. She opened it, and flipped through the pages till she found the word *Hokey*. It meant *contrived, fake. The* whistleblower letters were contrived. It was some kind set-up. Patty could picture someone sitting at a typewriter and deliberately writing the letters as part of some bizarre plot. But she could not see the person's face.

Jumpy and distracted, she scanned the room. She stood for a moment and then almost without consciously willing it, walked over to Noah's closet and pushed aside the louvered doors. The closet was Noah at his best — West Point neat. Shoes — sneakers, sandals, loafers, and three pairs of shiny dress shoes neatly lined up on racks. His uniforms, trousers, suits and shirts were carefully hung in rows. Patty went into action, pushing the clothing aside, looking through everything, rummaging through his pockets, opening boxes on the top shelf. She then dragged out his suitcases and went carefully through them, even checking the linings. She inspected an old faded gym bag, which was pushed behind the shoes. Nothing was amiss. Then she took the time to put everything back just as it had been. It was only then that she could draw a breath as she sighed in relief that she had found nothing, and realized at that moment that she had been looking for an old typewriter or some gray business-size envelopes and paper.

She smiled a little at her own foolishness, and thought how ridiculous she was to worry about the heavy-set woman who had talked to Rick. She then started to walk out of the room, but turned back to close the dictionary, speaking aloud to herself,

"Noah would kill me if he knew I had been looking through his things." After she closed the dictionary, she stared at the top drawer of the desk. On an impulse, she tried it, and found it locked. She looked in the obvious places, and after a minute of searching, found the key tucked into an almost invisible slit in the back of the leather-edged desk blotter. She reached for it, sat down, opened the top drawer and started to sift through Noah's possessions. Pens, pencils, rulers, scissors, paper, elastic bands, boxes of thumb tacks and paper clips, a bottle of correction fluid, note cards. Everything was neatly placed. She tried the right side drawer and found it hanging with concertina files and manila envelopes labeled *Mortgage, Homeowners' Insurance* and *Income Tax*. There was a third manila envelope labeled *Wills and Life Insurance*. The first drawer on the left held folders with copies of Noah's resume, some brochures from his airline, and two application blanks for employment.

The bottom drawer seemed to stick a little when she pulled it out. In it she could see only a red leather photograph album and an eight-by-ten framed photograph in a Lucite frame. She remembered the album from the previous summer when Noah had showed it to her. She remembered how they had laughed hard at some of his pictures. The album had been put aside and forgotten, and this was where Noah kept it. She sat in the desk chair, leafing through snapshots of Noah's life. An infant in a carriage. Baby pictures. A toddler holding a broom. Noah in grade school blinking and smiling into the sun. A self-conscious teenager holding a hockey stick, thin and short before he got his growth. His father, standing arms folded in front of a potash plant. Noah with his dark-haired mother whom he seemed to favor. Noah smiling at the camera with his friends. With a pretty sister in a prom gown. Noah in a school baseball uniform. Noah hunkered down with his father who looked like him, yet was only a pale copy in Patty's eyes. Noah playing tennis for his college team. Noah in college, attractive with his dark hair worn long. Noah and a curvaceous blond coed, an impish grin on her face as she held bunny ears in back of his head to make him look like a devil. Noah standing before a modest house. The whole family posing for a professional photographer. Noah in uniform looking his Air Force best.

Finally, Patty closed the album and picked up the single picture in the frame. She had never seen this picture, which had appaently been taken on the day he graduated from college. Noah was wearing a cap and gown and in the background a group of other graduates and a campus building could be seen. He was looking into the camera, but his eyes were shaded and indistinct from the tasseled cap he was wearing. Patty wished that she could see his eyes, and wondered what he was thinking that day as the camera clicked. She wondered if he was looking ahead to the future and thinking that one-day he would meet a woman like her. She traced her finger over his face and stared to slide the album and the photograph back into the drawer.

But something was stuck, and she reached in and pulled it out. It was a magazine of the true crime variety. Not Noah's regular reading matter, she thought. She put the magazine on the top and started to close the drawer. Then she realized that the magazine had probably been on the bottom before it got caught. Not wanting Noah to know that she has been looking through his desk, she decided to take everything out again, and put it back with the magazine on the bottom. As she held the magazine in her hand, she glanced more closely at the cover. The words *Whistleblower* and *Willie Sutton* were prominent.

But Noah had insisted, as they all had, that he did not know who Willie Sutton was. There was a moment of revelation along with pain that was more than a pain. Patty's stomach churned as she let the magazine slip to the floor.

Chapter 65

She saw herself as though from afar, a young blond woman looking down at a magazine and sitting stiffly in a second floor room of a house which no longer seemed safe. She saw everything as close and deadly still in the house even though she could hear the ordinary sounds of the suburban neighborhood through the screened windows — the shouts of children — a car passing somewhere on the street — the barking of a dog. Her mind seemed to be racing out of control as she now saw the whole puzzle that Rick had suggested. Could it be true? Could it be Noah? Noah — who had snubbed the woman from his college because she knew something about a murder. Noah — who had protested that he did not know who Willie Sutton was. Noah —who had a magazine about Willie Sutton hidden in his desk.

The person who had been sending the whistleblower letters now had a name and a face. She thought back. Noah had received word of his possible layoff in March. She had received the first letter early in April. She tried to picture him writing the letters, and the image came easily. In her mind, she saw him typing out the first of four letters addressed *Dear Whistleblower* — and then she saw him watching as she slowly fell apart. She knew that this wasn't just a cruel practical joke, but was something more menacing than that. Patty tried to think of a motive for his plan. The two insurance policies totaling $200,000 immediately presented themselves. Patty could not bring herself to think beyond that, but she now knew that she would not be boarding a plane with Noah the next day.

She looked at her watch so that she would know the exact time that her marriage had ended. It was six minutes before seven on Thursday, June 24, 1999. Noah was not due home for hours, but she had to get out of the house. In a very deliberate way, she closed the desk drawer, locked the desk, and put the key back into the back of the desk blotter. Then, carrying the magazine under her arm, she walked into the bedroom, sat on her bed, and picked up the phone. As she pushed in Rick's number, she glanced in the bedroom mirror and saw a strange woman sitting on her bed. The strange woman was hunched over, and looked very pale, as though she might be in shock. Her curly hair, still damp from the bath, tumbled to her shoulders in a disordered way. Patty pushed her hair back with one hand, and realized that she was looking at her own reflection.

The phone rang at Rick's house and his answering machine picked up. She waited through Rick's message and then spoke, "Call me please. It's an emergency. Call me, Rick. I need you." She then called Tish. The phone rang and rang, but there was no answer and no machine. Patty then called the number for Rick's agency. The phone rang a few times.

"Vera Miller Realty."

"Rick Miller, please."

"No. Sorry. Rick is gone for the day. He won't be in until tomorrow afternoon. Can I take a message?"

She left her name.

She called Tish's number again. The phone rang for a long time, but again not even the machine picked up. She thought of her father in Florida, and Ellen and Al in Europe. She tried Rick's home number again, and repeated her plea to the machine. She then sat on the side of the bed and stared at the items on her bureau which seemed suddenly sharp in relief and totally irrelevant - silver-backed hairbrush, jewelry box, makeup, perfumes, the paperback book she had read that afternoon, and the chunky gold bracelet that Noah had given her for her birthday. For a moment she felt a strange lethargy come over her, and thought how easy it would be to just lie down and be asleep when he came home as he had requested. What had his words been? "I'd just as soon find you fast asleep when I get home." She instantly fought off the depression. She would not make it easy for him. She would not be caught here in this house when he returned at two a.m.

Or was he coming home at two a.m.? she asked herself. He had made such a point of the time. Could he have made plans to come home early? To surprise her?

She knew she had to get out of the house, but her body seemed almost paralyzed with indecision as she sat there with her mind racing. Where should she go? She called Tish again. After six rings, she hung up. She swore softly, and the image of Brooke and Ilona in New York City came to her. She quickly punched in area code 212 and the familiar series of numbers. Brooke answered on the second ring, and Patty felt a wave of relief.

"Brooke, it's Patty, calling from Connecticut."

"Hi Patty from Connecticut. Good to hear your voice. When are you coming down to see us?"

Patty improvised. "Actually, I plan to be in the city tonight. I was just wondering what you're doing."

"Other than a date with Judge Judy, I'm completely free. Ilona and Kate are both away. Won't be back till Sunday night. If you're looking for a place to stay, come here. Spend the night. I've got room for both of you. I'd appreciate the company. I'm going bananas."

Patty whispered a low "Thank you, God," under her breath. And then louder to Brooke, " It's just me. Noah won't be coming. I'll be leaving my house in a few minutes. Don't look for me till ten, ten-thirty depending on traffic. It may even be later."

"No problemo. You know me. I'm a night owl. I never even think about going to bed till one or two. Take your time."

"Fine, I'll try driving right into Manhattan, but if I hit a lot of traffic, I may park at one of the stations in Fairfield County and take the train."

As soon as Patty got off the phone, she took a small night case out of her closet, opened some drawers and without taking the time to see that anything matched, threw in whatever was within easy reach — some underclothes, a cotton nightgown, a long floral skirt, a sleeveless sweater and a pastel blue sweat shirt. She put the chunky gold bracelet on her wrist, and picked up the night case, her bag, and the true crime magazine and hurried down the stairs through the den and into the kitchen. Standing before the door, she decided she had to let him know that she had outsmarted him. She took her assignment notebook out of her bag and wrote:

Emergency. Gone to New York City. Will call tomorrow morning.

On purpose she did not include Brooke's name, and she could not bring herself to write *Love, Patty*. As she stuck the note under the frog magnet on the refrigerator door, she froze at the sound of the wheels of a car on her paved driveway.

Noah?

Rushing to the den window, she was just in time to see a pickup truck driven by a bearded, pony-tailed man turning around in her driveway. An Irish setter, tongue lolling out of his mouth, had his head out the passenger side window. A deep breath. She then grabbed her keys, bag, night case and the magazine, and entered the large dark space that was the garage. She half ran to her car and then stopped, remembering to check the back seat before she opened the door. She then fumbled as she put the key into the ignition, recalling all the cars that wouldn't start again in countless horror movies that she had seen as a teenager. The motor turned over immediately. She backed out of her driveway, and headed down Iron Weed Road toward the center of town and the entrance to I-95. She was free and clear, she thought to herself. There was no way that Noah could stop her now.

As she passed Tish's house, she remembered that Rick would be arriving at her house in less than fifteen minutes. She slapped her hand against her forehead. She couldn't let Rick go to her house and find her missing, but she knew that she could not go back there to wait for him. She abruptly turned left at Tish's, swerving in front of a silver Pontiac coming up the street. The two cars just missed colliding and for a second she thought that somehow, illogically, it might be Noah, but then caught a glimpse of Dewey's face through the window, horrified at the near collision. Dewey blared his horn at her, but Patty kept right on going. As she approached Stadler Park, her eyes kept going to her rearview mirror, and then deciding to be doubly safe, she pulled over to look back and make sure that Dewey was not following her. She no longer had any concerns that he might have sent the whistleblower letters, but he was one further complication that she did not need at this moment. At first she saw no cars coming from Iron Weed Road, but then there was one pulling out. She watched, as it turned into a driveway halfway up the block. It could not be Dewey, she reassured herself.

She gunned her motor and speeded up, slowing for the left turn onto Parkway Drive paralleling the near side of the park and continuing on to the Post Road. She turned right on the main thoroughfare, and then onto Flanders Road, and then onto Seafarer Drive.

There was the slightest reddening in the western sky as she sped down Rick's street, but she took no notice. Her mind on Rick, she whispered aloud, "Be there. Be there. Be there." She held her breath as his house came up, and then felt sudden relief when she spotted his Lexus in the driveway. She quickly braked, switched off her engine and was up the front steps in a leap before her car had stopped rocking. She impatiently leaned on the bell. Rick opened the door within seconds, a questioning look on his face. He looked freshly shaved and showered and was casually dressed in a new-looking midnight blue sweat suit and running shoes.

"Patty, I told you I'd drop by at 7:30 before I went to Tish's. I was just about to leave."

She rudely pushed by making him back up, and entered the house. She wheeled around his modern living room walled largely by old brick and glass, and handed him the true crime magazine. He took the magazine without comment in an absent-minded way and moved over to sit down in a leather and wood chair. Worry lines appeared on his forehead as he read the cover.

"Where did you get this?"

"In Noah's desk. Locked away in the bottom drawer. I almost didn't see it."

"What's this article about Willie Sutton and a whistleblower?" Rick turned to the feature article and quickly skimmed it. He looked up. "Why would Noah have this?"

"The only explanation is that Noah wrote the whistleblower letters."

The lines on Rick's face deepened as he listened intently. He thought for a few moments, and then asked, "Did you find a typewriter?"

Patty sat down on Rick's sofa. "No, he must be keeping it somewhere else." She paused "Or maybe he got rid of it because he doesn't need it anymore. Maybe he's coming to the end of his long-range plans."

Rick got up with the magazine in his hand and walked back and forth along his long living room while Patty sat silently, waiting for him to speak. He finally stopped his pacing. Then he dropped the magazine on the coffee table and when he spoke, his hands were spread out in front of him, palms down. "I have to be clear about this. What we're saying here is that all the time we thought that Harold was sending the letters, it was Noah. It was Noah all along." He went on, speaking with difficulty. "And the reason he sent the letters was that he was planning to — harm you."

"Yes. And I'm not going to be in that house when he gets home. He's supposed to be home at two a.m. I left him a note telling him that I'm going to New York City, but I didn't tell him exactly where in New York City. I called my friend Brooke, and I'm staying with her."

"And what about your trip to Idaho?"

Patty laughed bitterly. "For some reason I don't think Noah had any intention of taking me to Idaho tomorrow." Her face twisted. "I think something was supposed to happen to me tonight."

Rick seemed visibly shaken when he spoke. "But why?"

"The life insurance. Not that $200,000 buys that much these days, but money has always been an issue for Noah. And he has been worried about his job at the airline. He told me that he was safe from the furlough, but now I don't even know if that's true. He may have even been laid off. I just don't know. I can't trust anything he's said to me." She fought back a sob, and went on. "I guess I'm just expendable. We've been married for almost a year, and he's probably ready to trade me in for a new model. Maybe he already has someone on the side. With his looks Noah can get a girl anytime he wants. And the uniform doesn't hurt."

"Patty, I can't believe this."

"I can hardly believe it myself. But this magazine." She pointed. "And the story you heard from that woman in your office today. And Noah made a big point when he left this morning. He told me not to touch his things."

"But you can't possibly drive to New York City in the condition you're in. I'll drive you."

"No way. You've got a big date. Remember?"

Rick thought for a moment. "You said you left a note for him saying that you went to New York City. That means you're safe staying right here in Hastings. As long as Noah thinks you're in New York, he won't come looking for you."

Patty thought for a minute. "You're right. And I know I'm not up to a drive to New York City right now. I'm so shaken I almost had an accident on the way here. No, what I can do is just drive down the Post Road toward New Haven and spend the night in any random motel — and go to the police tomorrow morning. I'll make someone listen."

"And tomorrow morning Tish and I will go with you."

With a sign of fatigue, Patty reached for a Hastings phone book that was on the coffee table, and turned to the M section of the yellow pages. Rick saw what she was doing.

"Patty, there's no point in going to a motel. Spend the night with Tish at her house." Patty considered his suggestion for a moment, and then shook her head. Rick frowned, and then his face brightened. "Then spend the night here. It's like a safe house. This would be the last place in the world that Noah would expect you to be — especially if I'm at Tish's." Patty followed his logic. "I'll park my car right out in front on Iron Weed Road so when he goes by at two he won't be able to miss it. When he finds your note, he'll think you're in New York City."

Patty nodded in agreement as Rick picked up the phone and called Tish. Patty heard him quickly tell her about the true crime magazine in Noah's desk and the fourth letter. He also briefly outlined what he had told Patty about the heavyset woman in the black and white dress. She then heard him say, "I know. I know. It is hard to believe. Almost impossible to believe. But it looks that way. It looks like Noah sent all the letters."

Rick was holding the phone out to her. "Tish wants to talk to you."

Patty took the phone to hear Tish saying, "I can't believe it. Noah sent the letters? Is it true? Why didn't you call me?"

"I tried to get you but your number just rang and rang, and you didn't answer. Your machine wasn't even on. I thought you had to run out for some last minute gourmet item."

"Oh," Tish screamed out. "The dinner. The dinner. You must have called at some crucial time when I was doing a lot of preparation. I turned off the phone, and I must have forgotten to put the machine on." She then asked Patty to repeat what Rick has just told her about the magazine and the fourth letter. Patty ended, "I left a note for Noah. I told him that I would be in New

York, but I'm thinking of spending the night here at Rick's, and going to the police tomorrow morning."

But Tish was there for her. "Honey, you can't spend the night alone. I have a gourmet dinner all ready to go and there's plenty for three. Come along with Rick. You can spend the night here, and Rick can go home. Or you can eat here and go back with him and stay at his house. "

There was a pause as Patty considered Tish's offer — the same one that Rick had made. But Tish had waited so long for Rick, and this was their night. She wouldn't interfere, especially since she was perfectly safe here. "No, Tish, I'll just stay here. I don't need either you or Rick tonight. It's like a safe house here. When Noah gets home, he'll read the note and think that I'm in New York City. There's no way in the world that he would imagine that I'm here."

Tish made the offer a second time. And then a third. "Are you sure? OK, you've convinced me that you're safe at Rick's, but are you sure you want to be alone at a time like this?"

"Absolutely, I'd prefer it. There are going to be some pretty drastic changes in my life, and I need some time alone to think about them. "

"I still can't believe this is happening. Why would Noah do something like this? What would he gain by all this?"

"How about $200,000 in life insurance? And the freedom to be a swinging single again."

Tish gasped. "No, Patty, no. It can't be."

"I hope you're right. We'll find out when we go to the police station tomorrow. I'd like you and Rick to come with me for moral support."

"Of course. No question."

After Patty had ended the phone call, Rick looked at her and asked again, "Are you sure you're OK? Tish and I can easily change our plans."

"I'm fine. I'll be fine here. You go on to Tish's. I just need this time alone."

"If that's your decision, I'll abide by it, but let's go all the way with this safe-house thing." He went to the back door and the cellar door and checked the locks. He then disappeared into the dining room, and when he came back, he commented, "This place is like Fort Knox." Then he held out his hand. "Do you have your keys? I'll put your car in my garage, just in case Noah should drive by. I can't imagine that he would do that, but let's go the extra step." Patty fished in her bag, pulled out her ring of keys and handed them to Rick.

"You might call your friend in New York to tell her you're not coming, " Rick called back as he went out the front door to move Patty's car. Miserable, Patty picked up the kitchen phone again and called Brooke. Again the phone was answered on the second ring.

"Brooke, Patty."

"Where are you?"

"Still in Hastings. I won't be coming to New York after all. Something has happened at home."

"Sounds like you and Noah have had your first big fight."

"Something like that. Look I can't talk now. I'll call you soon." Patty started to cry and hung up without saying goodbye.

When Rick came back in the house, he was carrying Patty's night case. She took one look at him and said, "How could I be so wrong about somebody?" She sat down, and closed her eyes for a moment as though that would change the reality of her situation. Seeing the pain in her face, Rick put his hand on her shoulder in a gesture of comfort and spoke softly. "We're going to get through this, Patty. Somehow we'll get through it. I promise you. I know everything will work out." He paused. "Come on now. Let's get you settled."

Carrying her overnight case, he led her up the open staircase to the second floor. She followed him meekly, her thoughts all a jumble. He stopped before the master bedroom. "You can use my room if you like. It's bigger."

"No, the guest room will be fine."

Rick led her past his home office to a small room at the back of the house and reached for the wall light switch. There was a wheat-colored carpet on the floor, and the room was minimally furnished with a single bed covered with a tan blanket, a modern blond dresser, one matching nightstand with a lamp and a phone, and a plump brown leather armchair turned to face a television set on a stand. A monochromatic seascape and a golden-yellow glass mosaic between the two windows were the only wall decorations. Rick set the night case down beside the bed and clicked on the bedside lamp. He then turned on the television and flicked through a few channels with a remote control until he came to an all-news station.

"You can have the run of the house, or you can just watch TV. That might help take your mind off what's happened. Are you sleepy at all?"

"I should be tired since I really haven't been sleeping well, but I'm wide awake. My mind is jumping all over the place, so I may have a problem sleeping again tonight."

"I have some sleeping pills. If you feel like it." He then gestured to his right. "The bathroom's over there. Did you bring a toothbrush and toothpaste?"

"No. I never thought of it. I just ran out of the house with the minimum."

Rick went into the bathroom, and Patty could water running. He came back with a new tube of toothpaste, a new toothbrush still in its package, a glass of water and a small plastic vial of sleeping pills. He put everything on the night table, opened the bottle of pills and shook a few out. He started to put the pills beside the glass of water and then, said, putting them in his pocket, "No, I'll leave the vial for you. You may need them later." He then walked to the door and tried the lock. "If you want, you can even lock the door." He fiddled with the lock and showed her how to use it. "The lock is new and sturdy All the locks throughout the house are. You'll be all right."

"You're giving me all the comforts of home. Sleeping pills and locked doors." The timbre of her voice shook.

Rick grimaced with sympathy. Then he said, "You know as we're doing all this, I suddenly feel foolish. I just can't believe that Noah is some kind of monster. There must be something, some reason that we can't think of for Noah to have that magazine."

Patty nodded dumbly.

Rick walked down the hall to his bedroom and came back carrying a small leather bag. "I have to go now or Tish's dinner will really be spoiled. Are you all right?"

"I'm fine."

"Tish and I can give you a call after dinner or even —"

"No," Patty cut him off. "I'm fine. Really I am. I need this time alone to think."

Rick nodded. "OK. Then Tish and I will be here about nine tomorrow morning. Be ready. We'll go right down to the police station and call Noah from there. Have you had supper?"

"Not really, but I'm not very hungry." Patty was now wishing that Rick would stop acting like a mother hen and just go on to Tish's. She knew she had a long night ahead of her, and she really was looking forward to being alone with her grief. She silently admonished herself for being so ungrateful for his overtures.

"OK, there's food in the fridge if you do get hungry. Half a bottle of wine too. Take anything you want." He glanced at the clock on the night table. "See you in the morning." Patty looked at the clock as the bright red digits fell to 7:50.

"Fine. I'll be ready."

Rick turned to go and then turned back. "Look, if Noah is innocent, he'll be able to explain everything with no problem. If not, he'll know that we're on to him, and he'll abandon any plans he might have."

"And I'll abandon my marriage," Patty whispered softly.

They both walked back out to the hall, and then he went down the open staircase. She stood at the top of the stairs as he paused for a moment by the front door. "Things will sort themselves out, Patty. You're safe here. Try to get some sleep." With a salute, he opened the door and was gone. A minute later, she heard the sound of his car driving away. A sense of depression washed over her as she went back upstairs to the guest room and locked the door.

Chapter 66

She stood at the bedroom window for a long time and watched the shadows take over Rick's backyard. For a moment her eye was caught by what seemed to be a movement in the heavy patterns near the marsh, and she imagined that someone was standing out there. She immediately thought of the persistent Dewey, but when she blinked her eyes, the figure was gone. No, it couldn't be Dewey. An illusion. It must have been an illusion.

Then the margin between dusk and night was crossed, and the neighborhood was engulfed in summer darkness. Because of the distance between the houses on Rick's street, she could see very few lights. She shivered and the expression that her father often used came to mind. Someone is walking over my grave. With that, she pulled the drapes tightly shut, quickly changed into her cotton nightgown, lay back on the bed, and attempted to watch the world news.

At first she tried to push back the image of Noah and made efforts to concentrate on the television program, but she soon saw that this was impossible. Instead, she found herself reviewing their life together since their meeting at Rick's Open House. Then she went over every detail of the test tampering scandal at Island Brooke. Finally, she found herself reliving each event of the present day. The programs on television changed one by one, but she still found herself caught up in her own painful memories of Noah as she kept asking herself the same question, How could all this have happened to me?

Finally, just as the ten o'clock news came on, the phone rang. Patty hesitated about answering it, but the insistent ringing convinced her that it was Rick or Tish calling to check up on her, so on the eighth ring, she picked it up. Tish said, "Hello," and she could hear Rick talking to her in the background.

"Patty, I just had to call. We feel so guilty being here when you're all alone there. How are you doing?"

"Hanging in. I've been watching TV, and doing a lot of thinking."

Tish talked for a few minutes more and then Rick took the phone. "We just wanted to see if you needed anything. We didn't wake you, did we?"

Afraid that Rick might try again to get her to join them or possibly even insist on coming back home, Patty loudly yawned into the telephone and made her voice sound sleepy. "Not really. I took a couple of pills, and I'm feeling very tired. I was just about to turn in."

"OK. We won't bother you again. We'll let you go to sleep."

"I think I'll take the phone off the hook."

"Fine. See you in the morning at nine."

"See you in the morning."

When Patty disconnected, she left the phone off the hook and listened to some annoying squawks for a minute. Then she lay back and continued to go over her plight, reviewing and reviewing and reviewing the illusion that Noah's love had turned out to be. Finally at eleven o'clock, she clicked off the television set, and got up to inspect the door. It was securely locked, and as Rick had said, the lock was new and strong. She flicked off the light. Curling under the light cover in the unfamiliar but comfortable bed, she willed herself to go to sleep, but found herself wide-awake, listening to the sounds of nocturnal life coming through the screened windows. She tried counting sheep, relaxing the muscles of her body one by one, regulating her breathing, but nothing worked. She felt as though she had just drunk a whole pot of coffee and could imagine herself lying awake all night until Rick and Tish came for her in the morning. Sleep would not come despite the fact that she had been operating on three or four hours of sleep a night for the past week and was physically exhausted. Tossing and turning, she avoided glancing at the clock. Time passed, and she just couldn't go to sleep.

She finally gave in and looked over, thinking it surely must be way after midnight. The numbers were just falling. 11:21. Something was keeping her awake. She tried to pinpoint what it was. Vaguely, at the corner of her mind, something was niggling at her consciousness. Some small piece of the day was out of sync. Something was not right.

"Something isn't right?" She spoke out loud and laughed without mirth into the darkness of the bedroom. Nothing was right — but yet there was something, some small thing bothering her like a pebble in her shoe. Something that had happened today. She went back over the day one more time, trying to identify the small part that didn't fit. Noah standing in the doorway shaking his keys at her. Her errands in the morning. The housework. The woman at Rick's agency. The fourth letter. Dewey ringing the bell. Dewey in his car as she pulled in front of him. The true crime magazine hidden in Noah's desk. The shadow in Rick's back yard. She felt a prickling of fear. Was it the shadow in Rick's backyard? Could that be it? Was it possible that someone had been out in the yard and was still out there, waiting for her to fall asleep?

She pushed the frightening thought away. No one could be out there. She had to stop thinking that way. She deliberately turned her thoughts back to Noah, and she tried to remember exactly what he had said as he stood at the door shaking his keys at her. She again wondered why he had made such a point that he would be home at two in the morning. Could he be home even now reading her note?

Chapter 67

She looked at the clock. The red numbers seemed very large and read 11:48. Patty snapped on the lamp, got out of bed, and checked the lock again. It was still new and strong and locked. She considered going to the window, pulling back the drapes and looking into Rick's backyard, but she knew she would see nothing out there but the darkness of the night. She slipped back in bed and was about to turn off the lamp when she glanced at the vial of sleeping pills and the glass on the nightstand. She hated sleeping pills. They always left her feeling dry-mouthed and out of sorts in the morning, and she felt so bad already. But she had to get some sleep. If she took two, she'd sleep soundly till Rick and Tish came for her. She sat up and reached over for the glass of water with one hand and the pills with the other, and accidentally brushed the receiver of the phone lying off its cradle. Her hands hesitated, and she stared at the phone for a full minute. Making her decision, she picked it up and called the familiar Manhattan number.

"Kehoe residence."

"Brooke, it's Patty again."

"Patty." Brooke was practically screaming. "What is going on up there in Connecticut? You sounded like you were crying the last time I talked to you. I called you right back, but just got your machine. I've been sitting here for hours chewing my nails. I called you again at nine, and then at ten-thirty."

"I'm not home. I'm hiding out at my cousin's house."

"Hiding out?" There was a pause. "Have you been getting more of those crazy letters?"

Patty hesitated for a moment, and then said, "Yes, I got one today — and it's hard for me to even say these words — but — but I think Noah has been sending them."

Brooke croaked out, "Noah," but made no other response, so after a silence, Patty went on. "I couldn't fall asleep, and I knew you'd be up. Do you have time to hear what happened today?"

"Are you kidding? I'm waiting with bated breath. Shoot."

After Patty recounted the day's events, she ended with, "That's why I'm here at Rick's."

"Aren't you scared to be there all alone?"

"Not at all. This is probably the safest place in the world for me. When Noah reads my note, he'll think I'm in New York City. He'll probably assume I'm with you, but I know he doesn't have your number so he has no way of checking."

"And we're unlisted so he won't be able to get it from Information."

"Right." Patty thought for a moment, and then her mind made a connection, which made her shriek. "Oh, no. He does have your number. The Caller ID. You called my house three times tonight, so your number will be right there on the Caller ID. Once Noah reads my note, he'll look and see the New York number and call you."

"Well, that's perfect. If he does call me, I'll tell him that we talked, and I'm sure that you're in Manhattan, but I don't know where you're staying. You know something. It's a good thing you called me back. If you hadn't called me, I would have told him that you had decided to stay in Hastings. Well, now anyway, we have our stories straight."

There was a long silence on the phone.

"Brooke, are you falling asleep?"

"No way. How could I fall asleep at a time like this? But you know, Patty, I think you may have jumped the gun on this. There could be another explanation for the magazine. I can't come up with one, but maybe tomorrow will be different. You know you really haven't given Noah a chance to explain everything. What evidence do you actually have? A magazine. An incoherent woman in your cousin's office. That's really not a lot to build a case on. It certainly wouldn't be enough for me to break up a marriage. I think you should wait until tomorrow to see what Noah says. Maybe everything will be good again."

Patty felt her heart lift at the possibility that all her suspicions were wrong. She so desperately wanted to believe that Noah really loved her and was not planning to kill her, but what was true and what was not? She couldn't tell. She couldn't think straight. She was so exhausted. She held the phone in one hand, thinking.

Brooke went on. "You said Noah would be home at two a.m. It looks like you'll be up anyway, so call him then and tell him you found the magazine and see what he says." She laughed in a stilted way. "Oh, by the way, to protect yourself, just in case, make sure you first tell him that a whole slew of people know about the magazine. Me. Your cousin. Tish. You can even make a good story better and tell him that you've even talked to the police tonight about it. If he should be guilty, he certainly won't try anything if he knows that everybody suspects him." They talked for a few minutes more, with Brooke giving advice and Patty almost ready to take it. Then they promised to be in touch the next day.

Patty looked at the clock again when she hung up. The red liquid crystal digits read 12:16. Thursday night had turned into Friday morning. Reconciling herself to a sleepless night, she left the lights on. She lay back down on the bed, now even more wide-awake than she had been. She was deep in thought for a long time, trying to put some rational order on the events of the day. She considered what Brooke had said, and tried to look at the facts from a different angle. She asked herself whether she could have jumped to the wrong conclusions. In her frazzled state of mind and with her lack of sleep, she might have taken some unrelated events and forced them together to imagine Noah's guilt. But he might actually be innocent.

A wave of emotion swept over her as she remembered all they had been to each other, and how loved Noah always made her feel. She let herself feel the great longing for him that she had been suppressing, and her feelings for him overwhelmed everything that had happened in the past few hours. There must be an explanation for the magazine, she decided. There must be an explanation for the woman in Rick's office. Fatigued, she drew a deep breath, and realized that she wanted to see Noah, not speak to him on the phone as Brooke had suggested.. She would go back to Iron Weed Road right now. She would be waiting for Noah when he got home from work.

Her decision made, she abruptly swung her legs onto the floor, pulled off her nightgown and dressed quickly. Taking her assignment notebook out of her bag, she wrote a brief note, *Going home to Noah. I don't think he wrote the letters and* put it on the pillow for Rick and Tish to find the next morning. She threw everything into her overnight case, slipped on the chunky gold bracelet, and hurried down the staircase to the living room, fishing in her bag for her car keys as she went. But she couldn't find her keys. She felt around on the bottom of her bag.

Where are my keys? she asked herself. And then she remembered. Rick had them. He had taken them to put her car away in his garage, and must have forgotten to return them. She sighed in frustration. This would make it harder. She would not be able to drive home to Noah, and she certainly wasn't going to walk or run the mile or so home at this time of night and possibly run into Dewey driving back and forth.

She would call Noah, and he would have to come and get her. She glanced at the kitchen clock. It was 12:43. Noah would be home in about an hour. Unless he was already home. She hurried over to Rick's kitchen phone and called her home number. When the recording ended, she left her message, "Noah, it's Patty. I didn't go to New York. I'm in Hastings. I'll call you again at two o'clock."

She felt she had made the right decision. She loved Noah. He loved her. She would call him again at two. He would explain everything. Together they would laugh about it.

Suddenly, the weight of recent events and her lack of sleep crashed down on her, and she felt so tired that she could barely stand. She shut off all the downstairs lights and sat down on Rick's sofa with its smooth soft cushions, waiting for two o'clock when she and Noah would talk everything out. There was a plastic-covered nightlight in the kitchen providing some illumination, but most of the downstairs area was in darkness or shadows. The silence was broken only by the background hum of the refrigerator. Patty felt so tired that she lay back for a minute. As she sank into the cushions, she now had to remind herself that she had to be up at two to call Noah. She could feel herself dozing off. In her dreams, Noah's plane was spinning out of control over Bradley Field.

Chapter 68

The sound of breaking glass woke her up with a start. For a moment, she couldn't remember where she was and struggled to rise. Gritty-eyed she tried to orient herself, but became instantly alert as she heard again the sound of glass clinking onto the kitchen floor. She looked into the darkness of the kitchen but could see nothing. Then she heard the sounds of the lock being turned and the kitchen door opening.

Burglar Kills Principal. The headlines from the *Hastings Morning Star* screamed into her mind as she thought of the burglar who had killed Harold. A ripple of horror ran through her body as she sensed a vague presence now in the kitchen. Patty crouched down on the sofa and then got back up, unsure of whether to try to hide or flee. Because of the cabinets that blocked her view, she could see an amorphous male figure in the darkness, a large dark shadow, but she could not recognize who it was. She looked at where the head might be and saw what looked like dark hair. She could see the illuminated kitchen clock from her position on the sofa. It was half past one.

Terrible thoughts popped into her mind as she looked at the clock, and remembered the Caller ID.The Caller ID. Had Noah come home early and checked the Caller ID? Had he recognized the number and realized that she was at Rick's house all alone? Was it Noah?

The figure disappeared from her view for a moment, and she heard the sound of someone sitting down in a chair at the kitchen table. A minute passed, and there were sounds she did not recognize. Then the figure was up, right in front of her flicking on the dim stove light. She heard something metal being placed on the stove. She watched the figure reach into his pocket and pull out some keys. Holding the keys directly under the light, he shuffled through them. Patty could now see that the man was wearing dark clothing, and a dark watch cap covered his hair. As he sorted through the keys, her eyes locked on the thin latex gloves that he was wearing. He changed his position, and then she could see what looked like a weapon of some kind on the stove. It was obvious. She was to be killed that night. She was frightened in a way that she had never been before, even more frightened than on the day when her mother had died.

The better to kill you with my dear floated into Patty's mind, and she had an absurd desire to laugh out loud.

The figure turned as he made his selection from the key ring, and for the first time, Patty was able to see the face of the intruder in the dim kitchen light. It wasn't her husband. It was her cousin.

Chapter 69

He had left Tish lying on her living room sofa snoring loudly and in a deep sleep. The sleeping pills had done their job well. He slipped the kitchen phone off the hook and left quietly by the back door. He was dressed in navy blue sweats, a dark watch cap, and thin latex gloves. The dark gym bag that he carried in his left hand contained everything that he would need. The tire iron from Noah's car. A pair of Noah's loafers. A duplicate navy sweat suit. A flashlight to help him on the road and paths through Stadler Park.

He had given himself one hour. Twenty minutes running to his house. Twenty minutes back. Twenty minutes for the unpleasant task. And it was an unpleasant task. He actually liked Patty, his little cousin, as much as he could like anyone. Except of course for Jordana. And he was doing this for Jordana. It was necessary if he wanted Jordana. Necessary for Patty to die. And then after some time had gone by, a suitable interval, Uncle Art would follow Patty to the grave. An unfortunate accident for Uncle Art, or it would not be unexpected for the old man to take his own life after his only child had been murdered by her husband. He would have to give more thought to Uncle Art's death.

But now he had to concentrate on what he was about to do tonight. He reviewed his plan as he jogged at a good pace down Iron Weed Road, keeping as close to the trees as seemed natural.

Patty's unexpected arrival at his house last evening had given him quite a start and could have caused him to abort the murder. He had planned to kill her at her own house a half hour or so before Noah was due home from work, but fortunately he had been able to improvise, convince her to stay in Hastings — and at his own house. Everything was basically the same — the sleeping pills she would take, the fears about Noah that she had expressed to Tish, the True Crime magazine that he had planted in Noah's desk, and his own multiple invitations to join them at the gourmet dinner, which he knew she would refuse.

He just would have to run a little farther, and running had long been his strength. He had been a champion runner in college, and still was one of best on the East Shore. And he would take the route he had taken hundreds of time before. Through Stadler Park, across the Post Road, and then down Flanders Road and then the street to his own house. He would break into his own back door with Noah's tire iron. Then he would change his running shoes for Noah's loafers. When he went upstairs, he would unlock the door and find Patty in a deep sleep. He would kill her quickly, striking her on the head nine or ten times with the tire iron. She would never wake up, never know what hit her. Then he would somehow make a footprint of Noah's shoes in Patty's blood. He would then change into the duplicate sweat suit. Back in the kitchen, he would change Noah's loafers for his running shoes. And then back through Stadler Park. The gym bag with its grisly contents would be hidden under a large rock he had found not far from the running path. And then to Tish's house. He would awaken Tish and convince her that she had drunk too much wine and only dozed off for a few minutes. She was so crazy about him that she would believe anything he said, especially when he finally gave in to all her romantic overtures. Then in the morning the two of them would make the tragic discovery — Patty's body.

And the clues pointing to Noah would start to appear. It wasn't even necessary for the police to have enough evidence to arrest Noah. It made no difference to him. He just wanted the police to be so focused on Noah that they would never even consider that the distraught cousin, the cousin with the perfect alibi, had anything to do with Patty's murder.

Of course he would drop Tish as soon as he could. As soon as she had solidly established his alibi. Three or four weeks at the most. But he would let her down easy. He didn't need any stalkers coming after him. He had had enough of that with Marcetta Osborne. Goodbye Tish and back to Jordana who was waiting for him in Greenwich. Jordana was now actually in love with him, but he knew how important money was to her. She had recently hinted that they should begin looking for a house in Westport or Southport. After Patty's unfortunate death and the untimely death of his Uncle Art, he would be free and clear to begin the house hunting with her.

He passed the silent technical school, went down two darkened side streets, and then was onto Parkway Drive. Using the flashlight, he ran through the road and paths of the park. Leaving the woods, he stood back from the Post Road until it was clear of passing cars, and then sprinted across the boulevard and onto Flanders Road and then Seafarer Driver. And then he was at a full run now down to his house and through to his back yard. He stood on his own back porch and took some deep breaths as he thought of Gerry Weshie, Deborah Valenshak, and Harold Trelawney. And now Patty Bass. And then there were four, he thought to himself.

He hesitated for only a moment before he took the tire iron out of his gym bag and struck out. He reached around the broken glass and unlocked his own kitchen door.

Chapter 70

Patty was so startled to see her cousin in his own kitchen that she almost spoke out to him, but as the words were forming, some template in her brain warned her that people did not enter their houses this way. They did not break their own windows. They did not wear thin gloves on their hands. They did not wear dark caps to hide their blond hair. It did not really make sense to her, but she suddenly knew that Rick had sent the Whistleblower letters. And she knew that Rick had come back to his house to kill her.

Patty was frightened in a way that she had never been before.

Her cousin left the stove, and Patty just had time to see that weapon he was carrying was a tire iron. Everything turned to slow motion as Patty cowered on the couch in the dark living room, holding her breath and tensing every muscle of her body, praying that her cousin would not look in her direction and see her silhouette, see her watching like a spectator at some grotesque play. She was barely twelve feet away from him and realized that her blond hair and white T-shirt might easily be seen against the darkness of the living room if he happened to glance in her direction, but she was too petrified to duck down on the sofa, fearing that she might make a noise of some kind which would catch his attention.

She watched her cousin stealthily leave the kitchen, tiptoe to the stairs and then start slowly ascending to the second floor. She could hear the jingle of the keys, which he carried his hand. Why does he have the keys? she asked herself. And the answer was suddenly crystal clear to her. He was going to the guestroom on the second floor and would be opening the door with the key if it were locked. He would be standing over the bed of a sleeping woman who had taken some of the sleeping pills that he had given her.

At that moment, Patty realized what small incongruity had been biting at her consciousness earlier when she was trying to fall asleep. The sleeping pills. Rick had put the bottle on the night table, but had dropped some of the pills in his pocket. He had taken them with him to Tish's house. What lover takes sleeping pills to a night of romance? The answer was obvious. He was planning to give them to Tish so that she would be sound asleep when he left to commit murder. Patty knew without question that her cousin had come back to kill her, but she had no idea in the world why.

Patty panicked as she heard rather than saw Rick reach the top of the stairs and start toward the guestroom. Within seconds he would find that she was gone and would come looking for her. She had to get away. She had to run for help. She stumbled off the couch, jerking against the table in the darkness and whacking her shins noisily. She then made her way through the darkened living room toward the front door and grabbed at the door handle. The door was locked. The lights flashed on upstairs as she struggled with the lock, and she heard Rick calling her name. Lights abruptly flooded the staircase and then the living room. More lights went on as she continued to fumble, her fingers shaking and wet with sweat, slipping on the doorknob and the lock.

"Patty, what are you doing? I came back to protect you from Noah."

She turned from the front door and looked up at him. He was standing at the top of the open staircase with a smile on his face. The watch hat on this warm summer night, the one gloved hand in front of him, the other hand behind his back were frightening, but the most frightening thing to her was that he looked the same, his face open and calm. He reached his gloved right hand out toward her in a pleading way and said, "Don't be scared. I couldn't sleep. I just came back to check on you."

His voice was familiar, so low and so gentle that Patty could almost feel herself being hypnotized. She couldn't believe this was happening. This was her cousin. Her cousin who had played such an important part in her life since her mother's death. Her cousin who was always there for her during her teenage years, helping her with homework, applauding her at high school plays, advising her about boys, driving her to college interviews. She was frozen in place, and for a moment felt as though she was just an observer, looking on as a man inched toward the stairs and put his foot on the first step while a young woman down below him recoiled in horror.

The trance was broken as she caught a glimpse of the tire iron he held at his side. She roused herself, turned and tore at the doorknob, unlocking the door and starting to pull it open. Ready to bolt, she allowed herself to look back to see him coming down the stairs. He was moving quickly now, and she knew the look on his face. She had seen it many times when he had something unpleasant to do and set about getting it over with.

"I'm sorry. I didn't want it to be this way. I thought you'd be asleep."

His face still looked the same — so familiar as he stopped on the bottom step.

She croaked out the question. "But why?"

"The farm, Patty, the farm."

There was a silence as she attempted to understand why Rick would want to kill her for the worthless farm that her father owned. Her voice was tiny, barely audible, as she repeated his words in a question. "The farm?"

"I need the farm if I want to have Jordana."

Rick's words made no sense to her, and the silence became oppressive as she tried to digest the information. She started backing up out the doorway, shaking, her legs heavy and awkward. And then Rick said the words, which made her body start to shake even more and her knees almost buckle from under her.

"Where are you going out the front door at this time of the morning, Patty?" he asked in his familiar teasing manner. "You don't think you can outrun me, do you?"

Chapter 71

Rick stood in the cemetery on that sun-bleached day, staring at the open grave, which had been made ready for her. The gravesite was crowded with grim-faced mourners — family members seen only at weddings and funerals — teachers from her school — neighbors and friends. He looked across the headstones at his mother, her face twisted in grief, as she tried to comfort his Uncle Art. And there was his own father, the sadist who had abused him, still trying to get back into the family although his mother had thrown him out and divorced him years ago.

They were all waiting for the minister to arrive, talking in low, subdued voices about the tragedy at the farm, the senseless accident, and the death of Celeste Nelson. And then he saw his pretty twelve-year old cousin Patty, curly hair a jumble, her face still and white appear from behind his mother. If he could feel pity for anyone, it would be for Patty, but he barely knew his cousin and could not spare any emotion for her. It was a bad time for him, and his mind really wasn't with any of them that day because his thoughts were on Debbie Valenshak and the Boston police.

He was twenty-two years old, had just graduated from college the week before, and was about to begin a white-collar position at Sikorsky Aircraft, but he was worried that those two detectives might show up with some new evidence against him. He could picture Gill and Silverstone coming to Hastings and asking around about him, talking to people in town, or even worse at his new job in Stratford, trying to find out what kind of reputation he had. He knew he had to make some preparations. Take some defensive steps. It came to him right then and there as he stood among the mourners. He would have to make a conscious effort to change his image. Become a kinder, gentler person. A person who cared about others. A person who could never be guilty of murder. His eyes again studied his blood relatives without any feeling for their grief as he made his plan. He would adjust his persona once more. He would become a friend, a big brother to Patty. People would talk about how good he was to his young cousin. And his Uncle Art. He would be there for the man dissolved in grief.

Yes, he definitely had to take action. Put on a big act. His little cousin Patty and his Uncle Art would be — his first project.

Chapter 72

And of course the farm. After his Aunt Celeste's death, he had heard the farm mentioned many times at family gatherings, but always in a negative way. Whenever his uncle referred to it, it was "that millstone around my neck," and Patty described the area as "Pollution. Smelly like gasoline. Ugly factories with dirty smoke," and the farm as "ugly, ugly, no trees," so in his mind it was a worthless piece of land somewhere in the boondocks upstate. Then on one of the most satisfying days of his life, on a Friday in January, when he was about to celebrate the one-year anniversary of his successful business in his own shopping center, the day of his Open House, his Uncle Art had insisted that he come over and help him with his will, insurance policies and property. Used to catering to him, used to playing the role of the compassionate nephew, he had gone.

"I want to put my affairs in order," his uncle had shouted and then made him privy to all his personal business including the terms of his will. Everything that Uncle Art had went to Patty on his death, but if she should predecease him, Rick was the heir.

And Uncle Art was now adamant. The farm had to be sold. "The taxes are sky high there. Those people upstate must be lunatics," was his uncle's comment. The blank real estate contract had been signed, and his uncle had handed him a thick pile of unopened letters tied with a red rubber band.

"These are from Peter Ginter, the real estate agent in Oldfield. He's tried to sell the place two or three times. No luck. I know you can do better. Here's his card."

Rick thought he was doing his uncle a big favor by taking on the commission and had delayed contacting Peter Ginter until one Tuesday in May when two prospects had canceled out on him. He sat in his office and looked out the window. It was a pleasant spring day, a day just made for a ride in the country. He poured over a map of Connecticut. Oldfield was almost exactly opposite Hastings on the map. Way up in northwestern Litchfield County, almost at the border of New York State. He called the number on the card that his uncle had given him.

"Ginter Real Estate. Peter Ginter here."

"Mr. Ginter, this is Rick Miller calling from Vera Miller Realty down in Hastings on the East Shore. My Uncle Art, Art Nelson, owns a small farm up your way, and he'd like me to put it on the market again. I thought you could give me some directions. I'd like to take a look at the property."

A pause. A long pause. And then, "Come by my agency. It's right in Oldfield Center. I'd be happy to drive you out to your uncle's farm and take a look at it with you." The voice on the phone was obsequious.

Probably doesn't get much business out there in the sticks and looking to co-broker, Rick thought.

"Do you have something to write with? You'll need directions to my office," the voice had continued. Rick had scribbled the long, complicated directions on an East Shore notepad and then Ginter had said, "Allow two hours. You probably won't need that much time, but you can never tell with the traffic."

Two hours, he thought. Where was this hopeless place?

Rick left his office just before eleven. Getting on Interstate 95 in Hastings, he drove south to Milford where he took the connector to the Merritt Parkway, and finally was whizzing north on Route 8, a concrete stretch of road, which he had occasionally used to get somewhere else. He gave little thought to the scenes passing by his windows, a panorama of industrialized towns with factory chimneys in the air, churches with tall spires, ribbons of three-family houses, strip malls, signs for fast food restaurants, and wooded areas. He made good time following the directions provided by Ginter. He took a turn onto Route 67 West, and he soon found himself passing through a string of pleasant small towns and hilly, tree-lined roads. He hadn't pictured it this way. Although he considered himself an authority in real estate, he had always worked on the East Shore in southeastern Connecticut, and was not really familiar with the northwestern part of the state. He was surprised when he entered the prosperous towns of Roxbury and then Washington. This can't be right, he thought, and pulled his car over again to consult his map and look more carefully at the directions, which he had placed beside him on the passenger seat.

Turn left at the gunnery. He had written what Ginter had dictated as his mind had pictured a ramshackle gun factory or gun storage area in some poor, boarded-up, half-deserted factory town. But now, he saw that it was a capital G — the Gunnery, a posh private school, which prepared almost exclusively for the Ivy League.

He continued driving and within twenty minutes was in the center of Oldfield, a quaint New England town, which he was surprised to see, looked as wealthy as the preceding towns. A steepled Protestant church stood at the main crossroads, and clapboard houses with black shutters and broad porches lined the streets. A Civil War monument had the place of honor on a smooth green commons. It looked like a very nice place to live, thought Rick. Actually like a movie set for a posh Connecticut town. He easily found Peter Ginter at a small brick house laced with ivy not far from the center of town. No sooner had he parked and gotten out of his car than the man was hurrying right out the door of his agency.

Ginter was a leathered man, wizened and old. His blue suit, starched white shirt and porkpie hat made him look like some kind of caricature from the 1950's.

A real hick, Rick thought as he shook the ropey-looking hand.

"We'll take my car," Ginter offered. They walked over and got into a roomy Lincoln Continental that had seen a lot of years but was well kept up. Soon they were on a two-lane country road lined with prosperous looking farms with cutesy names, pre-adolescent girls with ribbons in their hair riding horses in paddocks, and picturesque sloping fields and hills where brown and white cows and cloudlike sheep grazed. Here and there he spotted some stands selling plants and flowers set discretely back from the road. Ginter kept talking a blue streak, and Rick wondered if the man ever shut up.

"People from New York City love this part of Connecticut. They really think they're in the country when they come up here. Second homes. Summer homes. You name it. They come up here to relax. To get away from their faxes and their cell phones, but they always bring them with them."

Rick just nodded to be polite.

"We get some real celebrities in the area. What's the name of that singer?" Ginter asked. "That folk singer that everybody likes? He used to live near here in Washington."

Rick shrugged. He couldn't fathom what Ginter was talking about, and turned to stare out the window, enjoying the pleasant views, almost mesmerized by the fertile, green countryside — waiting for the scenery to change and the industrialized slums and the farm to appear.

Ginter went on, "Yes, those show business people especially have settled down here. A real colony. Artists, actors, directors, playwrights. They all pay top dollar for the land around here."

Ginter drove for a while, and Rick was surprised when he pulled over before a barn-like house set right next to the road. "See this house," he said. "Used to be a barn. Some woman came up from New York City and saw the potential in it and with an architect and a million dollars, she was able to turn it into a fine home." His face creased into a smile, and he drove on. Rick was still looking around, admiring the view, not saying a word, waiting for the scenery to change.

The car hummed along a road that wound up and down green pastured hills. Ginter braked again. "See this house. Used to be part of a stable. People from New York saw the potential and with the help of two architects and two million dollars, they turned it into a home."

Rick chuckled, now in on the joke, realizing that Ginter was mocking the rich New Yorkers who spent fortunes converting barns and stables into houses.

Ginter pulled over for the third time in front of a large mailbox with the number 476 on it.

"See this mailbox?"

Rick nodded as Ginter prattled on.

"Pretty soon some money bags from New York will come along and see the potential in this, and with only three million dollars and the help of three architects, she'll turn it into a magnificent home." Ginter laughed loudly at his own joke, apparently one he had made up and used before. Rick politely laughed along with him. But the man was right. It was funny. But Rick was confused and kept waiting for the landscape to change from country gentry to rural trash.

Abruptly, Ginter turned off the country road onto another one, then up a short hill, and within a few minutes, he swung onto a narrow dirt lane bordered by trees and wild flowers. He drove on — and then orchards, row after row of apple trees, in full blossom appeared, a carpet of petals on the ground. Ginter pulled over the car and said, "Here it is. This is your uncle's farm. Quite a beautiful piece of land."

Rick was astounded as he looked through the windshield. The farm was located on a plateau of pasture and rolling meadows beside the orchards, and in the distance, he could see green hills stretching out before him. Ginter followed his gaze. "Those are the Litchfield Hills. We have quite a view from here. We can see for miles and miles." He lowered his voice to a confidential tone. "Your uncle was smart to hold onto this land. With all this acreage, I could easily get him two million dollars, maybe a little more for it now."

Rick did not react. He just sat in the car and stared.

"James Taylor. James Taylor, he's the one who used to live in Washington," Ginter shouted in his left ear.

"Well, Sweet Baby James," said Rick as he slid out of the car and scanned the land around him. Who would ever have thought? So this was the farm. He had been aware that there were some beautiful areas in Litchfield County, but had no idea that Oldfield was one of them.

"But how is kept up?" he finally asked.

Ginter looked kind of shamefaced. "Well, it's not my job to patrol it, mind you, but I do believe an enterprising young man on the next farm has been pruning the apple trees and keeping up the road. Every fall he sells the apples at his stand. I think it's a fair trade off for your uncle. I wrote your uncle about it but I never heard back, so I didn't think it was my place to stop him." The two of them walked the acreage and Rick was practically struck dumb. Finally, he said, "And I understand the farmhouse burned down the winter after my aunt died."

"It did. It burned right to the ground. Some hobo had broken in, and he died in the fire. The fire chief figures the guy might have fallen asleep while he was smoking and drinking. In any case, that made three deaths within only about a year. The original farmer who committed suicide, your aunt who fell down the stairs, and the hobo. That gave the place a bad name. Some people said it was bad luck or haunted. That's why I couldn't sell it. Twice on the market and twice not sold. I started sending your uncle letters a few years ago, telling him I'd have no problem moving it now that time had passed, and memories had faded. But, I never heard from him. He never answered my letters."

"He's been ill," was Rick's only comment as he thought of the thick stack of unopened letters that Uncle Art had given him.

They had come back to Ginter's car.

"Wasn't there a barn?"

Again, Ginter looked embarrassed. "The barn kind of fell down, and I think somebody took the planks away. Folks around here like to use them for their family rooms."

"Lots of enterprising young men around," said Rick dryly.

On the way back to Ginter's real estate office, Rick said, "I'll call you soon."

"Do that," Ginter responded. "I've had a few feelers on the property, and I'd be happy to co-broker. No need for you to drive all the way up here to the opposite end of the state every time there's a phone call. I'll handle everything. You can tell your uncle that a culinary institute is interested, and a land developer is ready to make an offer."

When Rick got on Route 8 going south, he tried to reconcile the image of the farm he had heard about with the reality of the valuable real estate. He asked himself, how had Patty and Uncle Art been so wrong? Of course, they hadn't come back since Aunt Celeste's death seventeen years ago, and their memories of the place were most likely affected by the grief they felt. For Uncle Art, it was probably guilt. For Patty who had lost her mother in a freak accident, the area would seem polluted and smelly of gasoline, and the farm would forever seem ugly, without trees. But now that he thought of it, whenever Patty told the story of her mother's death, didn't she always say, "Then my father said we would take a walk in the orchards."

Of course. Patty remembered the orchards although she denied the beauty of the place where her mother had died.

And the farm was certainly worth a lot. Two million dollars, Ginter had said. He thought of the fat commission that a sale would bring to him, and then he immediately questioned himself, why shouldn't he have it all? His uncle and cousin had no idea of the farm's value. And he definitely could use the money. He hadn't told anyone but some of his business deals hadn't been quite as successful recently, and the shopping center was doing well, but not bringing in the money he had expected. And now that he was seeing Jordana again, he really wanted her. Really had to have her. But if she knew he had any his financial problems, he was afraid that he would lose her again. She was definitely an expensive proposition. Yes, he had to have money. A lot of money. Had to have something that spoke of big bucks.

As he drove south, he considered various schemes, but discarded them. No way. There was nothing, no way that he could cheat his uncle out of the farm. He would have to settle for the commission.

And then it came to him. He could have it all. He could have everything. He was only two persons away from owning the farm. He was the contingency heir in Uncle Art's will. If something happened to Patty, and then to Uncle Art, in that order, he would have a property worth over two million dollars. And of course Uncle Art's insurance and even his little house in Hastings. Again, he was the contingency heir.

So it would take two murders. Two murders for two million dollars. He had no qualms about killing the two of them, but how could he get away with it? He had been so frightened when the police questioned him after Debbie Valenshak's death. He knew that he could not take that kind of interrogation again.

And the police always followed the money after a murder. He would be the chief suspect or at least one of the chief suspects if he killed his cousin and his uncle. He would have to come up with a plan. Something to take the heat off. Something to make the police look in another direction. By the time he was pulling into his shopping center on Main Street in Hastings, he had various scenarios jumping in and out of his head, but nothing seemed foolproof. He did take the precaution of making a immediate phone call from his office.

"Peter, this is Rick Miller down here in Hastings. I've just been talking to my Uncle Art. I'm calling to tell you that he has decided not to put the farm on the market just yet. He'd like to wait another year. Till next summer."

"Oh." Ginter was obviously disappointed.

"But I told him how you've kind of been keeping an eye on it for him, and he thinks we should co-broker the deal."

"Oh, that's fine." A different tone.

"There's just one thing, and this is very, very important. My uncle isn't well and doesn't want to be disturbed so I'm asking you to make sure that any inquiries about the property are addressed to me here at my agency. If my uncle is bothered by anyone, anyone at all, then our whole co-brokering deal is off."

"Of course, Rick. There's no problem with that." Obsequious again.

And then Rick just waited. Something would happen. Some scam would come to him. The farm wasn't going anywhere. It was like money in the bank.

Chapter 73

Patty streaked down the front steps of Rick's house onto the Belgian block driveway and out into the night. Screaming at the top of her lungs, she immediately turned to the right in the direction of the Post Road where even at this hour, she hoped there would be cars and people. With a speed born of terror, she raced down Seafarer Drive. Patty was very conscious that Rick could outrun her and should easily be able to catch her, but she was hoping that one of his neighbors in the houses on the street would hear her screams and come to her aid. As she sprinted down the road, she immediately realized that this hope was futile. At this time of morning most people were asleep, and since the large homes that she had so admired were set way back from the road, no one was able to hear her cries in time to come and help. She stopped screaming at that moment, saving all her energy for running, hoping that Rick would not follow her.

With a terrified awareness, she heard sounds behind her and realized that it was the pounding of Rick's feet. He was running after her. She accelerated up the road ahead of him not daring to turn into a driveway where she could easily be cornered. She hoped for a car to turn down the street, some night owl coming home in the wee hours of the morning, since her only other chance seemed a futile one. To somehow outrun Rick and reach the Post Road before he caught her.

There were no streetlights on Seafarer Drive, only a few lampposts turned on in front of darkened houses and weak lights over garage doors. The wash of the full moon on the blacktop provided the only real illumination. As she pounded down the ribbon of road, she felt that she was caught on some alien landscape in a nightmare. But this nightmare was all too real. Her sense of powerlessness increased as she heard his steps behind her. And then Rick's familiar voice calling out, "Patty, stop. Don't run. You know you don't have a chance to get away from me."

She somehow increased her speed at the sound of his voice, and almost slipped to her left. As she lost her footing for a moment, she heard something whoosh by her ear and then the clang of the tire iron on the road. With a surge of terror, she realized that Rick had thrown the tire iron, hoping to knock her off balance and make her fall. She could hear the break in his steps as he stopped to retrieve his weapon. She continued running, her heart hammering in her chest, her feet flying faster over the blacktop. Patty had never run so fast, but after a minute, she could hear him behind her again.

She asked herself the question, why hasn't he caught me?

She got to the corner of Flanders Road and turned left toward the Post Road. She could hear those dreadful feet behind her as she raced for the only island of safety she could see. Suddenly there was another break in his footsteps, and she intuited that he was throwing the tire iron again. More by instinct than reason, she zigzagged to her right, and felt the rush of air as the tire iron flew by and missed her a second time. Again, she could hear Rick stopping to retrieve it, and she knew she was making some gains on him. She ran as she had never run before, calling on all her resources of energy, sheer adrenaline pushing her.

She could hear traffic and see occasional headlights and bright red taillights on the Post Road ahead of her, and for an instant she had hope that she would make it. Then she heard the clang of the tire iron hitting the road just behind her, but this time Rick kept running and did not stop to pick it up. Patty knew at that moment that Rick had decided to abandon the weapon and make an all-out effort to catch her. She could hear his breathing and curses. He was angry that he hadn't caught her.

But why hasn't he caught me? she again asked herself.

Patty at that moment realized how tired she was. She wasn't used to speeds like this. Her lungs were burning and her legs seemed about to give out. She tried to redouble her efforts with the awful thought of being pounced on just before she reached the Post Road. She tried to keep up her speed, but she could feel her body failing. She knew in a few moments she would fall to the ground and Rick would be upon her. She would be all alone and helpless before the man who planned to kill her. And then she heard him cursing behind her, cursing because he hadn't caught her, and she felt a fierce urge to outrun him.

In that instant, Patty saw herself sitting at her kitchen table the week before reading her monthly running magazine. She then saw herself turning to an article about a long-distance runner who got tired, and she read how the runner was able to keep going even though her body was about to give out. And suddenly the words on that page were there, not an idea, but there right in front of her with the answer. She read from the page. *The runner turned herself into a machine.* Patty took the counsel and did just that. As the page faded away, she put aside her fatigue and became a machine, a machine that could not be caught. Her breath was steam, and her legs were pistons. She could do it. She was a machine. She sprinted ahead. She was coming up to the Post Road. She was a machine that could not be stopped.

But she heard Rick's footsteps right behind her, directly behind her, and she unclasped her chunky gold bracelet and held it in her hand.

And she was there, or almost there. Just a few yards separated her from the Post Road when suddenly his hand was hard on her left shoulder and he was spinning her around. Using the momentum of the spin and a newfound strength born of desperation, she lashed out with the chunky gold bracelet in her right hand and raked Rick across his eyes with it while giving him a violent push toward the intersection with her left hand. She took no time to watch him fall back, but righted herself and stumbled onto the road.

Chapter 74

Kevin Parmenter was speeding north on the Post Road in his father's SUV, the car crowded with five other teenagers, his two best friends, and the three girls they had picked up. He was going twenty miles above the posted limit, but there was very little traffic, and he had to take the chance that a cop wasn't around. He had sworn to his father that he would have the car home by one, and here it was almost two o'clock and he had five people to drop off. The car was noisy inside with the chatter of two conversations and loud music from the radio, and close with the smell of smoke. Kevin was trying to concoct a good story for his father as he pressed his foot down on the accelerator.

Suddenly. Could this be happening? A figure in white was running out from a side street. Right in front of him. "Watch out," the girl in the front seat screamed at the top of her lungs.

He only had time to see that the figure in the road was a woman before his adolescent reflexes kicked in. He slammed his foot on the brake as his palm hit the horn and he tried to turn the steering wheel to the right.

Chapter 75

Abruptly Patty was on the Post Road and without a break, not daring to look either left or right, she thundered across the blacktop and immediately saw a speeding vehicle looming to her left. There was no way the car could avoid her. She heard the blast of a horn and the squeal of brakes, and knew she would be hit. She let out a piercing scream and felt a powerful thud as she was lifted up for a moment of free fall, thinking of Noah. Trying to put out her hands to cushion the impact, she was slammed onto the blacktop, scraping her body, feeling bones break and hearing the awful sound of her head slamming on the road. She was alive, but she knew that she could no longer run, could no longer elude the mad man who was chasing her.

All the breath seemed to have been knocked out of her, and she felt herself drift in and out of consciousness and away from the pain, which seemed to envelop her whole body. And then there were running footsteps, and she heard a shout. "She's crazy. She's Drunk. She's crazy. She's crazy. She ran right out in front of me. I couldn't stop." A young girl's voice pealing out, "Call 911. Call 911." Then she heard someone yelling, "I've got a cell phone." People started to appear, and a man was standing over her. Tears of pain blurred her vision, and she couldn't make out his face. She squinted as she fought off the dizziness that was sweeping over her. The man in black was now kneeling at her side, reaching out for her. She tried to life up her head, and screamed, "Rick." Was it Rick? Would he suffocate her as she lay helpless in the road? Would he strangle her right in front of these other people? And then her vision cleared for a moment, and she saw that it was a teenage boy. Not Rick. Where was Rick? she asked herself.

"Where is Rick?" she called out.

"Are you all right?" A young voice. And then another young voice. "Don't let her move. You're not supposed to move them. I took First Aid. Wait for the ambulance." Patty lost consciousness for a while. When she came to, her first thought was of Rick. Was he circling around to get her?

"Where is he?" she gasped out. "Rick, my cousin Rick."

"Take it easy, You'll be all right. The police are coming." A young voice, and then she heard sirens, shrill in the night, coming closer.

"Where is he, my cousin?" She tried to twist around, but felt herself held back by somebody's hands. Was it Rick?

"Be still. Don't move."

Police cruisers were now pulled over with red and blue lights whirling and flashing on light bars. She could hear different voices and the squawk of a police radio.

"My cousin, where is he?"

"Don't worry. Don't try to move." A strong calm voice. An older voice. Not Rick she thought to herself.

Another young voice, "Are you all right? Where does it hurt?"

She saw a uniformed policeman kneeling beside, his voice soothing. "Where do you hurt?"

Then other voices coming from all directions confusing her. She could hear someone talking above all the other voices, a teenage boy, protesting in a loud voice. "I couldn't see them. She ran right out in front of me. And the guy was just there coming out from the side street. He had his hands over his eyes like he couldn't see. Crazy joggers. They must be drunk. It's not my fault. I wasn't speeding. I was going the speed limit. They were right on the road. I've got witnesses."

More sirens and then the voice of a young girl. "Look at her. She must be awfully hurt, but she was only thinking of her cousin."

She looked up. Concerned faces all around her. Wonderful teenage faces. Boys and girls. Wonderful policemen. Patty could feel herself slipping away from muddled voices, which made no sense. And then she came back as she felt something being put around her neck and her body, and then she was lifted up. From her position strapped on the plastic stretcher, she could see orange security cones on the road, and she could read the gold lettering on the police cruisers spelling out *Hastings Police Department.*

There were lots of flashing lights, almost blinding her, so she turned her head away. And saw a man's shoe on the road. A loafer, bloody and torn. She squinted at it, but couldn't make the connection. It looked like Noah's shoe. Noah's loafer. But how could it be Noah's loafer? What was Noah's loafer doing here? It should be Rick's running shoe if he had been hit. Then understanding came, and she knew why Rick had not been able to catch her. He hadn't been wearing his running shoes. He had been wearing Noah's loafers, shoes several sizes too big.

She was hefted into the ambulance. Just before doors closed, she heard a young girl's voice. "She keeps asking for him. He was her cousin. She's going to take it hard."

Another girl's voice. "I can't even look over there. This is so gross."

The teenage boy's voice again, almost sobbing now. "He was all dressed in black. I never even saw him. I couldn't help it. It wasn't my fault. It wasn't my fault. I wasn't speeding. He was just there in the intersection. He was all in black and I couldn't see him." And then, "He had his hands across his eyes. When I swerved to avoid her, I hit him head on."

Chapter 76

On June 26, 1999, this item appeared on the front page of the *Hastings Morning Star*.

Jogger killed in Hastings

by Dylan Petrillo, Staff Writer

Hastings

A local man who was jogging at the intersection of Flanders Road and the Post Road was killed early Friday morning after a sports utility vehicle struck him. He was pronounced dead at Yale New Haven Hospital. A local woman was also injured in the accident. The man, only identified by police, as a 40-year old resident of the Seaview section of Hastings, was killed instantly as the driver attempted to avoid the woman who was jogging onto the road. The 30 year-old women, a Hastings resident, suffered injuries from the accident and was taken by ambulance to Yale New Haven Hospital.

No charges have been filed against the driver whose name was not released by police. The driver and his five passengers suffered only minor injuries in the 1:58 A.M. accident. According to police, the SUV was headed north on Route 1 when the two joggers suddenly appeared on the road. Swerving to avoid the woman, the SUV struck the man head-on.

Police said they do not know at this time why the joggers were running on the Boston Post Road. They comment that traffic is usually light at that time of the morning, but caution against jogging on a major traffic artery at any time. Police also comment that the light-colored clothing of the woman probably saved her life since the driver reported that he saw the woman clearly in front of him on the road and veered to avoid her. However, he did not see the man who was dressed in dark clothing. The speed limit of that section of the Boston Post Road is 45 mph and there is no evidence that the driver was speeding. Witnesses at the scene reported that the SUV had no chance (Please see Jogger, Page 5)

Chapter 77

This item appeared on the Obituary Page of the Hastings Evening Star on June 27, 1999.

Eric S. Miller, 40

Hastings — Eric Steven Miller, 40, of 181 Seafarer Drive in the Seaview section, died early Friday morning after being struck by a vehicle on the Boston Post Road. He was born in Hastings on October 15, 1958, and lived here most of his life. His mother, Vera Nelson Miller of Satellite Beach, Florida, and his father Ralph Miller of Jacksonville, Florida, survive him. Survivors also include his cousin Patricia Bass and his uncle Arthur Nelson both of Hastings. He was the owner and manager of Vera Miller Realty for twelve years. He graduated from Boston University. He was a life member and president for three years of the Hastings Jaycees. He received the Outstanding Young Businessman of Hastings Award in 1996. He was instrumental in starting the Hastings Shore Beautification Committee. Memorial contributions may be made to the Hastings Shore Beautification Committee. Services will be private.